I0523136

Striking Blind

by

Lonna Enox

Lonna Enox

For my dad, Lon...

the first cowboy I learned to love

ACKNOWLEDGEMENTS

My Heroes...My friends...My family

Tim Renfrow, Wasteland Press, created this beautiful cover as well as those of my first two books.

My pastor, retired police detective, Troy Grant, explained the make-up of a task force, what they can or cannot do, and answered my questions without ever grinning at my ignorance.

My longtime editor and friend, Sandy Stogsdill, has the patience of Job and the wisdom of Solomon. She is patient, positive, and ever diligent to push me toward the best I can do.

Friend, Lucy Nials, retired Home Economics teacher, supplied Teri's and Reed's recipes for Green Chili Stew.

My daughters, Monica and Marissa, spirited me away to Branson for a week of wacky fun when I expressed that maybe I would never finish this book. Their sense of fun reminds me of Sorrel, and revives me when I falter. Their greatest gift is their continued love and belief that I can do this. Marissa is the photographer for my back cover photo.

My son Nathan cares for my critters and home while Ron and I travel to research or promote the books.

My grandchildren, Brooke and Drake, who read my books and happily tell people at book signings that their grandma "hears voices".

My husband, Ron, saves both me and the computer from destruction during the writing process. When he hears "Oh! No!", he magically appears, taps here or there, and the hours of work that have just vanished reappear. He cooks meals and reminds me to eat them, keeps the pets content, and reminds me on a regular basis that sleeping is a necessary evil even when my characters are in a tough spot and need me. He answers the scientific questions, takes photos, and tramps through the hills and woods while we research the locale for each book. When I hold my finished book in my hands, he wipes my tears and gives me a hug.

My younger brother, Ben, for whom I wrote my first book with crayons on a brown grocery sack when I was 4 and he was 2, and my older brother, Russ, whose gorgeous western artwork captures my love for our Southwest, are my earliest friends and my loyal fans, as well as my extended family.

Lonna Enox

"Ho! Now you strike like the blind man!"

MUCH ADO ABOUT NOTHING   William Shakespeare

Prologue

Wind raged through the canyon, stirring up clouds of sand so strong that the stinging grains buried into the skin. Three shadowy shapes followed an almost invisible trail, each carrying a flashlight, stumbling occasionally, wiping gritty eyes with gloved hands, and hunching shoulders against the powerful blasts.

A fourth, his hands tied behind his back, lurched between the last two. He had no light, and his boots occasionally caught on something that caused him to pitch forward. His captors, their faces almost covered with their neckerchiefs pulled up over their mouths, muttered ugly comments while yanking him back to his feet.

The prisoner's mind searched frantically for anything to help him escape what would only be torture and death. He stumbled again, thankful that his captors blamed his clumsy journey on the darkness instead of a stalling technique. He wasn't sure how much farther they would go or how quickly his death would come. The odds didn't look good—3 to 1. Not the poker hand he'd envisioned as he'd sat down at the table in Manuel's Tavern.

Poker had intoxicated him from his very first week of college. It beckoned, flirted, excited, and challenged like nothing else in his rotten life had ever done. He often thought of how much better his childhood would have been had he discovered poker earlier. The cards brightened everything else in his life, making the ugly pain disappear.

That is . . . until earlier tonight.

He'd been too confident—too sure of himself—too cocky. And he'd broken his own cardinal rule: He'd allowed himself to be distracted.

The toe of his boot caught on something and he stumbled again, landing this time on cactus. Thorns embedded themselves in his eyebrow, and he blinked as blood trickled over his eyelid. He hunched up his shoulder in an awkward attempt to catch it, but settled for blinking rapidly several times.

It must have been the woman who'd doctored his drink! It was only water. He'd never allowed alcohol to distract him. Nor a woman either. Again and again he tried to recall when she'd done it. And as before, he remembered instead the scent of jasmine and the softness of her black hair as she bent toward him and whispered—

"There!" The first man's triumphant cry caused the others to stop suddenly. The prisoner caught himself from falling forward as the group momentarily halted. He squinted with his left eye, in spite of the gritty sand, but he couldn't see in the blackness. Blood had crusted over his right eye, obscuring most of his sight. From the grunts among the men, he sensed they'd reached—or sighted—the destination. With renewed purpose, they surged forward, picking up the pace in spite of the powerful gusts and the darkness.

After what he judged to be another half an hour, the group halted again. While his captors busied themselves with one of the packs they'd carried, he again hunched up his right shoulder and bent his head over in a desperate attempt to wipe the crusty blood from his eye. This time, he successfully cleared part of it—enough to get a glimpse of light from their flashlights.

Arms circled around his waist and knotted a rope. Another was looped around his shoulders, knotted, and connected with the one at his waist, constructing a crude harness. Were they going to drag him to death? Maybe hang him? He hadn't seen a tree tall enough for that. Two of the men moved off out of his sight, and he could hear them relieve themselves. He had to concentrate on other noises so as not to do the same. He didn't need soaked denim to add to his current misery. Funny how tricks you learned as a child returned when you called them. He remembered the hours tied in a bed, waiting until daylight, and knowing that a wet bed meant beating and hunger.

Daylight should come—even in this godforsaken country—but he didn't hold out hope that he'd be seeing it. He'd suspected as long as he could remember that he wouldn't live to be old. Maybe that was better anyway. Visions of the old grandpa who'd lived with them haunted him—his frail body wasting away in a small room that stunk of human waste. They fed him at least once a day and made him sign his check when it arrived each month. Death now—in the prime of his life—would be much better. He wouldn't be leaving much behind— especially children to live in misery as he'd done. So if the hollering preacher was right and everyone had to stand in judgement at the end of his life, he figured that would be one point in his favor.

His three captors had gathered in a group close by while he'd been daydreaming. They talked, leaning close to each other's ears, and he prayed they were near the destination. Abruptly, they broke apart. Two walked over to him, one on each side. Each grabbed an arm and tugged him behind the group's leader. Then they continued their journey.

Time had lost its meaning, but the wind had died down and the sky had lightened a bit when the four of them stopped again at the foot of a rocky hill. His companions grabbed the harness and pulled him up with them as they climbed. It was slow and by the time the party reached a small cave opening, the sky behind and around them had lightened to a pale murky pink–lavender. The leader stood in the mouth of the cave and turned his light toward them as his tormentors pulled and pushed him forward.

He squinted. The mouth of the cave was larger than it had looked. He couldn't be sure how far it went, but he doubted he'd need to know. No one spoke. Finally, he said, "Well, I won't say it was nice knowing you guys." He laughed but it sounded weak even to his ears.

No one laughed. He sensed the blow before it came and leaned away. It didn't knock him out, but he staggered and fell anyway. Maybe they wouldn't know it hadn't worked. One stood beside him after he fell, and the other two hurried about, dragging brush and boxes farther into the cave across the opening. Were they going to hang him from the cave's ceiling? He squinted up toward it; but even in the faint light, he couldn't see it. That wouldn't be very practical, he decided. What would they attach the rope to?

His captors had stilled. His eyes were becoming accustomed to the faint light; and even without seeing much, he could sense their unease.

Finally, the leader spoke loudly in accented English. "It will go easier if you don't try to fight it," he said. "We know you're awake! Answer me!"

They hadn't bought his pretense. He squinted and spoke groggily. "Why? Fight who?"

The one beside him snickered. "Not who—what."

"Why?" the leader asked. *"Dinero."*

"I don't have any money," the prisoner said. "You must have mistaken me for someone else. I lost all my money tonight at the table."

"Not your money, hombre. You have friends—or enemies—with money."

The others laughed as if he'd told a funny joke. The prisoner swallowed the panic rising up in his throat. "Wrong guy," he managed as calmly as he could.

The leader motioned toward the other two. They caught him from behind by the rope harness and held him tight. The leader knelt down and removed his shoes and socks then tied the prisoner's ankles together.

"Can we negotiate?" he asked then. "I might be able to get a loan—"

The two behind him snickered again and pulled so painfully on the harness that he gasped. One pulled off his bandana and reached toward him to tie it around his neck.

"No!" The leader paused dramatically. "We want him to see . . . and we want to hear him." Again all three laughed. The sky had lightened considerably; and even with the barricade across the mouth of the cave, the prisoner could see his surroundings. Maybe those hours locked in closets hadn't been a total waste.

Then the three men started toward the cave's opening. Their captive thought they were leaving him and started working the ropes on his hands. But they'd stopped in front of the crates, picked up a hammer, pried off the lids, and arranged them on top with a narrow opening along the edges facing him. He paused, afraid they'd notice his movement. But they hadn't.

Instead, they stared at the crates—almost hypnotically. Suddenly, they jumped back and scrambled out of the cave's opening.

He listened to their oaths and laughs until they faded in the distance. Time to start on getting out of here!

But a sound from the crates first grabbed his attention . . . and then his horror. Anyone who'd lived in the southwest as long as he had done recognized that sound. Rattlesnakes.

Somewhere far back in his childhood, he remembered hearing stories about rattlesnakes—especially in the spring, when they were shedding their skins. "The skin covers their eyes," he remembered the tales, "causing them to strike out at sound and motion. They're striking blind."

He didn't know if the stories were true or just legend. But they'd given him nightmares as a youngster.

He shivered uncontrollably as his ears registered them bumping into the boards as they found and slithered over the tops of the crates. For the first time in so many years that he couldn't even remember the last time, he felt tears running down his face. "Fellas," he called. "Can we negotiate?"

Chapter 1

"Ssh! Don't cry, baby!" I whisper in the darkness. I reach out, anxious to touch the baby, to pull it close into my arms and comfort it. But the sobbing continues and my fingers do not reach the baby. Is it moving away?

"Babies don't need to cry," I whisper, my throat aching at the sobs. "Your mama will take care of you."

The crying takes on an even more mournful tone at my words and the volume increases.

"Where are you? I'll rock you. Everything will be okay. I'll protect you, little one. You have nothing to fear." I repeat the other mantras that I've heard mamas croon through the years as they soothe their children.

I reach for the lamp switch, but it only clicks. I remain in darkness. I sit up in bed and turn toward the window. Not even a sliver of light peeks around the blinds. It must be a very dark night. Wait! The security light outside? Is it out? Maybe I should—

The baby screams louder. I turn back toward the screams. "Are you hurt?" More screams. I draw a breath and sing the familiar lines from my childhood: "Hush, little baby, don't say a word. Mama's gonna buy you a mockingbird."

"She won't, you know."

"Who's that?" I shrink down and frantically search the darkness. The voice is deep as it comes from across the room. It isn't a baby! It's either an older child—or a man?

"What good's a mockingbird anyway? What could it do?" the voice sneers.

It appears to have moved to the corner and has taken on a mean, whispery quality. I shiver again and then feel indignation rising deep inside. "Who are you?" I demand, inserting authority and my rising indignation into my voice. "What are you doing in my bedroom?"

I am almost screaming now, having raised my voice to be heard over the baby's screams.

"You didn't answer my question. What could a mockingbird do?" The voice reveals no indication of anger. It also seems to have moved again, over near the dresser. My anger melts and I fight the terror creeping up my spine. Who is this? And how did he get into my bedroom? I have a better than adequate security system, and I'm diligent in changing the code often.

What has happened to the lamp? My hand eases over and feels along the nightstand for my cellphone. Gone! I need to keep this voice—person?—occupied while I make a plan.

"Ever heard a mockingbird?" I ask.

"No."

"It repeats what it hears."

"So then you'd have it crying as well?" The voice is growing louder and sounds harsher against the wailing baby. "And this would improve things how? Lies never help anyone."

It is moving closer to me. I once again fight the urge to shrink back into the blankets. My instinct is to pull them over my head and pretend—what? My bedroom is small. Surely I can dart to the door and . . . I can . . . can—

"Lies," the voice repeats. "Mamas only tell you lies." It has taken on a singsong quality.

The baby's cries are softer, a little hoarse now, and fading into whimpers. Where is it? Is this baby all right? Who is this intruder? Outrage gives my voice almost a shrieking quality.

"What are you doing in my house? Get out before I call—"

"The baby can't hear you," the voice continues. "And I'm only here to ask you a question."

"I'm talking to you, not the baby! How did you get in my house? You're an intruder—an interloper! Why should I answer—"

"Because you must." The voice has changed. It sounds feminine . . . familiar.

I tense and look around. "Mama?"

Silence.

"Mama, what do you mean?"

"Answer his question, Sorrel," she prods.

The male voice hardens into an ugly, snarling tone. "Why? That's the question. Why do mamas lie? You act like you know everything! So just answer that for me. Why do mamas lie?"

My heart is pounding so loudly—and the baby continues to wail even though its voice is growing hoarse. I hardly hear Mama's whisper, "I'm sorry to have left this task to you, honey."

"What task, Mama?" I reach toward her, but she has moved away.

"Find the weeping child, Sorrel," she calls. "Answer the question."

As the voice faded, I clawed my way out of the dream. It was almost impossible to open my eyes—my lids felt glued—and when I did, I was disoriented. Slowly, my eyes moved over the walls of my bedroom until they focused on the painting hanging just above the small rocker. I'd found it among the paintings in John's shop—and known it could never be sold. Twice I'd considered adding it to the university collection. Finally, I'd hung it here, where I could see it when I woke.

In the painting, two children huddle in the corner of a small, bare room. The boy's arm rests protectively across the girl's shoulders. Both are painfully thin, barefoot, and dressed in oversized men's shirts. Their faces, while not especially striking, are turned toward a tiny window. Therein lies the painting's magnetic pull. Faintly, in the window, one can see a rainbow. The hunger in the eyes and faces of the children as they stare at it is heart wrenching.

I wiped my eyes. Even in the pale light of dawn, I couldn't look at it without tears. Knowing the two children—and being the child of one— broke my heart. I shook my head and climbed out of bed. The cats grumbled as I jostled the bed, glared at me, and rearranged themselves in furry circles.

When the alarm I'd forgotten to shut off sounded over an hour later, I heard their paws hitting the floor from my spot at the kitchen table. A hot shower, strong coffee, and homemade cinnamon rolls had almost restored my equilibrium. They came by for a pat and led the way to the cupboard where I stored their cat food cans, meowing as if they were starving. I almost missed the doorbell amid their racket. "Coming!" I called.

Chris Reed's finger hovered over the doorbell when I opened the door. "I'd about decided you must be sleeping in," he said, following me into my tiny living room/kitchen combo. He sniffed. "Coffee. Cinnamon rolls? Did you save me any?"

"Sit. I'll pour you a cup." I pointed to my small table and pulled a mug out of the cabinet.

By the time I swung back to set his coffee in front of him, he had already stuffed half a cinnamon roll in his mouth.

"I don't know how you do it," I said, looking pointedly at the whole plate he'd moved over in front of him. "I thought men started getting a belly after thirty something."

Chris swallowed the roll before gulping black coffee. "Hard work and clean living," he drawled, his blue eyes dancing. "I don't have the leisure of lounging around waiting for the perfect photo to appear."

I punched the air above his head. "Photography is much more than just eating bonbons and lounging around! This gift shop doesn't run itself either, especially since Teri's hours are cut with the baby coming." I refilled my own cup and sat down across from him. "Are you working today?"

"Finishing the roof on the feed barn," he said, reaching for another roll.

Chris had bought a fixer-upper ranch several months back, but at the time he was working undercover. I'd also interfered with his plans to start the barn when my bird photography trip to Bosque de Apache in November took a devastating turn toward danger. He'd somehow convinced his bosses that his case and the bodies piling up around me were connected. Frankly, I still wasn't completely clear on how they connected, but since he'd saved my life . . . well, I wasn't complaining.

"Not a good sign."

I glanced at him. "What isn't?"

"You're not stuffing your face. What's with the blue under the eyes?" He wiped his fingers on his napkin and reached down to Van. "I'll need an update, old feller," he said. Van butted his head and his squeezed huge yellow eyes shut. I could hear his purr across the table.

"Disgusting," I muttered. "I'm the one slaving in the kitchen and—"

This time Chris threw back his head and laughed. My lips twitched. Dad always said you could depend on a man with a healthy laugh. "You? Cooking?" he asked.

"I can when I need to. I just don't need to cook with Teri's family always dropping off food."

"They have the mistaken idea that you don't eat." His eyes roved over my face. "Now, I repeat, what's with the blue smudges around your eyes?"

"Nightmare." I got up and reached for the plate.

"No need to pack one lone roll away," he said, nabbing the last bun and stuffing it in his mouth. He chewed, swallowed, and drained his cup. "What nightmare? Must have been a bad one. You've not mentioned having nightmares."

I hadn't. "You've only been here a few minutes and the whole time you've either been talking about food or stuffing your own mouth!" I reached for his cup and took it over to refill.

Chris Reed had this protective streak about a yard wide where I was concerned. He knew that I'd been a television crime reporter in Houston. For most of those years, I'd been single—both parents dead—and even after I'd married Kevin I'd not changed my habits. Danger hadn't exactly been a stranger to me—and sometimes I did get afraid, but I was no coward. My curiosity and drive were always pushing me.

"You're trying to distract me. The dream?"

I let out a more dramatic sigh than I felt. "I suspect it's a by-product of our latest adventure. Remember? Dead body? Someone trying to kill us? Nightmares are understandable. What isn't is the fact that we still hang out together."

"That's easy. I'm a demented peace officer who punishes myself by hanging out with contrary redheads." He grinned, picked up his cup, and walked over to the overstuffed chair. "I think I'll make myself comfortable over here," he grumbled as he sat down. "From the look in your eyes, I expect I'll need to duck."

I followed him, scooped up Flash, and settled on the sofa with her on my lap. I didn't immediately answer. Finally, I said, "It was troublesome. So I didn't sleep well. Not a huge worry, Reed."

He didn't immediately answer, just sat there sipping on his coffee with his eyes roving over me.

"What have you been up to?" I finally asked.

Chris Reed and I had an unusual relationship. When we first met, he considered me a suspect in a murder. After he changed his mind, we started a romance of sorts. But that only continued a short while until he left his job as a police detective to work in the sheriff's department. Then we became entangled in the disappearance of my old friend, John, and returned to romance afterward.

The silence pulled my mind back to Reed. Why wasn't he talking? I stared into his eyes.

"So when do we set the date?" he asked.

"Uh, what date?"

He laughed. "Gotcha! I knew you weren't listening!"

"Guilty."

"I've been finishing up paperwork on the last assignment," he said. "But I've also been trying to get some fencing and building repairs finished. I've already told you this, but you weren't listening!"

Reed's ranch—just a couple of sections of land with a rundown house—had been owned by an elderly woman until she sold it to him and moved to Phoenix. I'd been given a tour of the property but not the house. He'd teased that he needed to finish other things before I started bossing him around about decorating the house.

"Bought any paint?"

He grinned. "There's too much to do. Paint can wait. I may never get to it. But you can paint!"

"Too busy!"

"I guess I'll have to keep the apartment then—at least until things settle down a bit."

"But you won't." I stroked Flash a moment, refusing to rise to his bait. "When do you report for duty?" I asked instead. "And where?"

"That's actually what I wanted to tell you. I've had an offer from Border Patrol and, of course, the sheriff's department is wanting me to come back there. I haven't quite decided, but they won't wait forever. My leave of absence is almost up."

"Popular guy."

"How about you?"

"You know I've had the flurry of Christmas here at the shop. I'm not complaining, but we're low on products. I'm glad I shut it down for inventory, etc."

"When will you re-open?"

"Right before Valentine's Day."

Reed emptied his cup and took it to the sink. When he returned, he walked over and stood beside me. "Sorrel?"

He waited. Finally, I looked up. I knew what he wasn't asking, so I answered him. "I've talked to the university about John's will. They are starting the process."

He sat down on the couch beside me and reached for my hand. "And the memorial service?"

"I'd like to keep it very small and personal. I'm still working on it. But there's so much to do. Personally, I'm thinking this summer might be a good time?"

Reed leaned back onto the couch, still holding my hand. "Summer might be good. The crazy thing is, Sorrel . . . I only met John for a few days, but I knew right away that he was special. What I hope you'll do, once you've worked through your grieving, is really show that person to all of us. You knew him in a way that I doubt anyone else—besides . . . well . . ."

"I will, Reed."

He sighed. "It's so hard to believe he's gone. And even harder when we both know we were so close to saving him."

"Maybe we were close. I feel sort of numb, you know? But he trusted me to set up the legacy he wanted. And I can certainly do that. Keeping busy is good."

"Just don't pull away and bury yourself, Sorrel. And before you blow up at me, both of us tend to do that. We hide emotions in work. Remember our New Year's resolution?"

"I do." I fingered the delicate gold necklace he'd given me at Christmas. When I looked up, he was staring intently at me. "Whether we head into life as friends or lovers, we will keep in touch."

He stood then, reached to pull me up, and walked me to the door. His hand on the doorknob, Reed wrapped his other arm around me and gave me a side hug. "Our business—the friends or lovers thing—can wait. But not forever."

I nodded. Just as he turned and walked down the steps, I whispered, "The nightmare. It was about the weeping child."

I knew he hadn't heard me, but it felt better to know that I had told him.

Chapter 2

The day ahead gave me no time to reflect on my silly dream or the complicated relationship Reed and I shared.

After he left, I stepped into the shop—actually the front part of my house—and surveyed the post-inventory site. Without Teri's elaborate Christmas decorations, it looked a little bare. But that wouldn't last long.

Teri and I had met shortly after I moved to Saddle Gap. She'd worked part time at the newspaper where I worked as a freelance photographer. When I left the photos from my first assignment, a crime scene, with this small, vivacious chatterbox, we became instant buddies.

Her encouragement had helped fuel me in using local craftsmen to open the shop. She'd developed a line of lotions and candles, using ideas from both her grandmother and her mother; and later she designed attractive displays for my store. I'd also found wonderful craft and artistic creations at the senior center and nursing home. Rose's Oasis had blossomed into an appealing gift shop in just a few months—and Saddle Gap became home.

Saddle Gap, although only a city of 30,000 or so, was the largest city for miles. Hunkered down in southwestern New Mexico, it attracted a fair share of tourists; and my shop was located right on a popular route. Aunt Rose, whom I'd always been told raised my mom after her parents had been killed in an automobile accident, left the shop to me. I'd originally thought to sell it until my own life had taken a turn that put me in danger. Rose's Oasis had become my own oasis.

I roamed through the light, airy room, wondering how you can live your whole life believing you know who you are only to discover at the age of thirty-one that it was all just a story. Actually, Aunt Rose hadn't been just a story. I'd only recently discovered that my own mother had been part of the downside of foster care. Aunt Rose had been the upside of it as my mother's foster mom, as well as the most stable influence in her life at that point. Still, most of what I knew about my mother's life before my birth had been stories—and I had a compulsion to kick the stories aside and find the truth.

When I came to Saddle Gap seeking refuge and a new life, I'd had no idea that the life I'd left behind—television news anchor, widow, prey of drug cartels—would not only follow me but also continue to turn over stones that I'd not known were even there. I felt like the star of one of those awful television shows. My father and mother were both dead, I had little interaction with Shane, my half-brother on my dad's side, and I had never known until a traumatic incident a few months ago that I even had another half-brother. He had apparently been adopted when my mother was a teenager, so I had no clue where—or who—he was.

"Sorrel! Are you making like a statue or something?"

I whirled around to Teri's delighted laughter. "I didn't hear you!"

"I said 'Good morning!' when I opened the door, you goose. Are you going to turn into one of those lovelorn—"

"You shouldn't be carrying so much!." I hurried over and pulled the bags out of her arms.

"Romance novel heroines? And don't you start too! Everybody is treating me like I'm an invalid!"

"You'd never be that, but chasing after first-grade twins and keeping up with your big family are more than enough. Do you want some coffee?"

"I'm off caffeine. But I will have some of those caffeine-free teas I put in your pantry last week." She followed me through the door at the back of the shop into my kitchen, chattering about the latest school conference for the twins.

"Honestly, I think it would only be fair for Jose to have to attend these conferences," she complained, petting Flash before lifting her out of the comfy chair and sitting down. "I was a good little girl. Never would I have given some little girl a pack of gummy worms with a couple of live ones among the candy ones!" She shuddered while I laughed.

"They're so creative."

"Mrs. Macias didn't appreciate their creativity," she grumbled, but her lips twitched. "But enough about my monsters. I've got news!" She waited dramatically; but when I didn't respond, she continued. "I've found a new consignee!"

I set her cup of tea on the small table beside her. She eyed the cookies I'd added and popped one in her mouth. I settled by Van at the other end of the couch and sipped my coffee. "We could use another consignee," I said, "but we really have enough of the same items. I hope this one is different."

"No more crochet or birdhouses," she said, "although both are still selling very well."

"So are my photos, but you can only hang so many in your house or office before the walls are covered. That's why I've been printing and stocking notecards. People tend to buy things they'll use up."

"Your Bosque collection is going to be a huge hit, Sorrel. Some of those snow geese and ducks are irresistible. But the sand hill cranes—spectacular."

"I can't decide whether I should put the collection out now or wait until the fall. After all, that's when they arrive in our area."

She sipped at her tea and took another cookie. "Let me tell you my ideas."

The morning passed quickly. I insisted on helping Teri decorate—it was the only way I could keep her off stepladders. Soon the shop took on a festive, loving air with hearts, cupids, and flowers. It was only when we sadly packed up the booth of an elderly consignee that she continued our earlier conversation. "I'll drop these embroidered tea towels by the senior center on my way home," she said. "Mrs. Soto's family will collect them when they stop by to get her other belongings." She sighed. "I know she was in her eighties, but I'll miss her giggle."

"And the customers will miss her tea towels," I added. "She was such a popular little lady."

"Oh, I forgot! The new consignee!" She hurried over to the box she'd carried in and lifted out a tiny box. "These are totally unique."

"Well, don't keep me holding my breath."

She opened it and pulled out a pair of earrings on a card, jiggling them as she did so. "These are completely New Mexican! They're going to be a huge draw for the tourists! And they're not priced too expensively! What do you think?"

They were earrings made from only the rattles of rattlesnakes. I shuddered at the sound. "I'm sure someone will buy those things for the novelty," I said.

"There's more." She pulled out business card holders and billfolds covered in rattlesnake skin. "And this is exquisite!" She opened a cellophane package and pulled out a clutch purse. "Isn't this unusual?"

"Very."

She looked at me curiously. "I thought you'd be pleased."

"Oh, I am. Who is this contributor, by the way?"

"I'll have to look," she said. "I thought we could make the table display look rocky or desert like," she went on. "Rattlesnakes fit in the desert."

"I know." I fought the shudder. "Uncle Jim was always warning me about them when I was here on spring break. He said they'd usually not be out until the cool or mornings or evenings. One day one of their outdoor cats came in with a huge paw. He'd been bitten, obviously trying to swat one of them. Uncle Jim and I took him to the vet, and he was fine eventually."

Something in my tone must have caught her attention. "Are you okay with these?"

"Oh, sure. As you said, I think they'll be a big hit with the tourists. I'll just keep my distance from the critters. Especially when they're shedding."

"Why then?"

"Uncle Jim always warned that you needed to be careful because they couldn't see. So they struck at sounds instead of objects. He called it striking blind."

This time she shuddered. "Well, these are safe enough!"

"I'll set up the paper work," I said. "Do you have information? Is this a local?"

"The information's in the box," she said. "I didn't really look at it—got so caught up in admiring the samples." She studied the booth. "I think I'll enlist Jose to help with the design—"

I slipped away. Talking with Teri when she was in a creative mode was next to impossible. I had a couple of hours' work in the office anyway. Tax time would be on us before we knew it, and my accountant had already sent me several sheets of instructions for the information she would need.

Teri peeked into my office later. "On my way to lunch and then the doctor's office," she said.

"Do we know yet if there's one or two? Pink or blue?"

She grinned. "Better not be two or blue!"

"And if it is?"

"No way!" she called over her shoulder. "I may donate them to you!'

I decided lunch had a nice sound, so I went back into the office, closed down my computer, and returned through the connecting door to my kitchen.

A look in the refrigerator offered very little: a shriveled salad that I would dump outside for the wild rabbits and a slab of cheese that was turning dark gold. Cooking had never been something I'd ever enjoyed; and because my days in television news demanded that I stay slim, I'd relied on quick low-calorie meals. When Kevin and I married, he'd liked grilling steaks or eating out, so I hadn't cooked. Living here on my own in Saddle Gap, my eating habits had stayed plain—mostly frozen—except when Teri hauled in delightfully fattening food.

Both Flash and Van looked up when I closed the refrigerator door then settled back to their naps. "Soup?" I asked. The small pantry produced a small can of vegetable soup. I dumped the soup into a bowl and set it in the microwave. Another peek in the pantry produced a pack of crackers. On the way to my small table, I snatched an apple from the counter. "Grocery store this afternoon," I promised the sleeping felines.

While I ate, I read through the information from the newest consignee. His address was a post office box in a nearby small town along the Mexican border. He'd printed my application offline and filled it in with a dark felt pen. He'd listed the items that he'd sent for my inspection and a list of prices. They looked reasonable to me, both for the customers and for the percentages he and I would share. Everything seemed in order, so I had no reason to shiver again. Was I turning into one of those hysterical types that I'd always hated?

I'd just bitten into an apple when I was interrupted by the *William Tell* Overture on my phone. "Hello, Detective," I said.

"Hi. Did I interrupt anything?"

"Sure did, Reed. I'm out in the pasture snapping photos of rattlesnakes."

"Liar. I can hear you crunching. Apple?"

"They don't call you detective for nothing!"

He chuckled. "I thought you might like to have dinner with me tonight. Maybe dance? And we could invite Teri and Jose. She may be bigger than a house, but she loves to dance."

"Don't you dare say that to her, Chris Reed!"

"Oops! Chris Reed. What did I say wrong?"

"That bigger-than-a-house phrase!"

"So you'll come?"

I heard voices in the background. "Just a minute," Reed said to someone. "Six? I'll pick you up. Later."

I held the phone for a minute longer before pushing the button. I hadn't even agreed to go. "Van," I said, stroking the big gray fur ball beside me. "I don't want to hear of you getting as arrogant, conceited, uh—you know!"

If he did, it didn't bother him. He continued to snore, curled up in a tight ball.

As I continued routine chores that afternoon, I wrestled with calling Reed back to decline. But that would only do a couple of things: disappoint Teri and make me try to eat my own cooking. Neither appealed. An evening with Chris Reed appealed more than I wanted to admit.

Chapter 3

Saddle Gap had several decent places to have dinner and dance afterward, but Bart's was most popular. The front door opened into a regular family steakhouse, but a side exit led into a bar and dance floor. A group of professional performers came at various times, and local groups filled in on other occasions; but the rest of the time, people danced to the music from an ancient jukebox in the corner. Whichever way, Bart's was a popular place, particularly on Friday and Saturday nights. Tonight was no different.

Reed finally found a parking spot near the alley, turning to me with an apologetic smile and shrug. "Guess no one wanted to eat at home tonight. This is the best we can do for parking, I'm afraid."

"As long as we don't take a shortcut through the alley afterward," I said.

"No way," he agreed. Both of us had grisly memories of a murder in that alley shortly after I'd moved to Saddle Gap. We picked our way through the sparsely lit parking lot and stepped into the crowded restaurant.

"We're over here!" Teri's voice easily carried over the noise.

"Is she actually hopping?" Reed asked. "That girl!"

Teri and Jose had chosen a table close to the bar exit and had already ordered iced tea. I hugged around Teri's tummy. "No more hopping," I said. "We don't want to end up at the hospital tonight."

"A little early," Jose agreed.

Teri pouted. "Are you two going to join in?" she asked us. "Tell me now, while I'm already standing and can waddle out. I refuse to spend a whole evening with three nursemaids. So tell me now."

Reed grinned, held up his hands, and motioned for me to sit in a chair across the table from Teri. Then he pulled up a chair beside me.

"We've already ordered for all of us," Teri continued.

"Hey—" Reed interrupted.

"We know what you always order, Reed. You order steak running around the plate and cheese fries. Sorrel orders steak turned into shoe leather, veggies, and salad. Since they'll be done pretty soon—you're late you know—if you want to change the order, I'll eat them."

"She would too," Jose chimed in. "My money is on two more babies this time! I'm hoping they come soon so I can avoid bankruptcy!"

The evening flew by amid the usual joking and laughter. Teri even insisted on getting on the dance floor between trips to the bathroom. I trotted along on the second trip on the pretense of checking my make-up.

"You're not fooling me, Sorrel," she hollered once she'd settled in the stall. "You're a worry wart just like Jose."

"Guilty. But I'm having fun anyway."

"Me too. I told Jose that I need to get out while I still can. And I really feel terrific."

"You told me you felt like a house."

"A terrific house."

We shared more giggles.

"On a serious note," I said, "I'm interviewing for someone to help out in the store. I'm thinking of six months—or maybe even a permanent part-time person."

"What?"

"Teri, you have the twins in first grade and then this little one . . . or ones—"

"One!"

"One, we think. But you do so much more than just manage your booth in the shop. You can look after your booth, but I'm thinking I need someone to help part time. The other booth owners come in once a week each, but we're getting some who want to pay more not to help out. For a while at least, we need someone extra."

By the end of the evening, Teri had presented my idea to the guys as hers, embracing it completely. Jose looked relieved. Reed pulled me up for the last dance—a waltz—and whispered as he drew me into his arms, "Good job!"

"And men always complain about us going to the bathroom in herds! You should think of it as a business meeting."

He grinned but I wouldn't have heard an answer if he'd given one. Some men know how to waltz, but Reed was an artist. Whirling around the dance floor in his arms was magical, and I'm a firm believer in magic.

We walked together to the parking lot. Teri and Jose had nabbed a parking spot close to the door. "That's a good thing," I told Reed. "She looks tired."

"I think she looks hungry."

We laughed and crossed the lot to Reed's truck. "Either way," I said, "I plan to find someone to help out. I know it won't make her stop, but I'm hoping that maybe she'll slow down. And speaking of slowing down . . ."

Reed unlocked my door, opened it, and waited for me to settle in before he got in on his side. "I've been trying to catch up at the ranch," he agreed. "There's just so much to do it's hard to even figure out what to do first."

"I've told you I can slap paint on walls—"

"I haven't even looked at the walls. The bathroom works, the kitchen stove works—sort of—and I can sleep—"

"In a sleeping bag on the floor, I'll bet!"

Reed grinned. "It works for right now."

We lapsed into a companionable silence. When Reed headed out of town toward my shop, I yawned and settled back against the seat. He reached over and put his hand over mine. "I loved tonight."

"Me too. I've missed the four of us—the joking, laughter, dancing."

"Still having the spooky dreams?" He squeezed my hand softly.

"I only had one."

"Well, with your sleep disorder—"

"I don't have a sleep disorder!" I tried to pull my hand, but he held fast. "Since when did having one dream turn into a disorder, Chris Reed? You've been watching too many of those television doctor shows!"

He laughed. "You just chewed on me about working too much. When would I have time to watch television?"

It had almost always been like this between us. Well, except for the very beginning when he was ranting and raving, accusing me of murder. Or when he was really mad and was extra polite with me.

"Penny for 'em," he said, turning on the blinker.

"Not worth a penny. I was just thinking about our rocky relationship."

"Rocky?" He parked in front of my living quarters at the back of the shop and turned off the engine. "I thought we were getting along great . . . aside from almost being killed by a hired killer . . . or you getting all jealous—"

"Jealous? You're dreaming!"

"Like I said, you and your nightmares and that sleep disorder."

He was impossible. I told him so and he burst out in a belly laugh. "You're too easy to rile, Sorrel. But rocky? Are you trying to break up with me?"

"Break up? Are we dating?"

He didn't answer. I pulled the door handle and stepped out. He was there instantly, trying to stifle his laughter. "Are you planning to send a poor lawman away without even a cup of coffee?"

"Maybe." My keys had been right in their spot a minute ago and now they'd taken off. "When I find my keys, I'll think about it."

Reed pushed my hand aside and pulled the keys out of the zippered compartment of my purse, unlocked my door, and held it open for me. "I'd tell my daddy he was right. Sad he's no longer with us."

I brushed past him, dropped my purse on the couch, and headed into the kitchen. "How was he right?" I asked, reaching for the coffee canister.

Reed put his hat and jacket on the hall table and settled into the overstuffed chair. Immediately, the cats jumped on the arms of the chair and began purring and butting their heads against him. I glared at them. "Traitors," I muttered, then filled the coffee carafe with water.

"He always said," Reed finally answered, "that a sorrel horse was feisty and unpredictable."

"I know you're not comparing me to a horse!"

I clicked the start switch on the coffeemaker. It was hard to ignore his chuckle. I wasn't mad really. Reed enjoyed teasing me. Sometimes he irritated me. Usually I pretended to be irritated. This was one of those times.

"I know I haven't been around with flowers, candy, and violins, Sorrel. But between work and trying to get the ranch repairs done, time is scarce. I have called at least."

"Florists' flowers don't smell and violins shriek and politicians call and we're not even in a relationship."

His lips twitched. "And the candy?"

"Makes me fat."

The coffeemaker buzzed. I reached for two mugs, filled them, and carried one over to Reed, my lips twitching as the room echoed with his laughter. I curled up on the couch and sipped, almost scalding my tongue.

Reed blew on his and took a sip. "Now, about those dreams?"

"I thought you were talking about horses."

"What did you mean by 'the weeping child'?"

I blew into my cup. "I don't remember."

Reed laughed that robust laugh that I loved to hear. "You are all woman, Sorrel. You can remember the very first conversation we ever had, word for word, and you'll be reciting it to me when we're eighty."

We sipped our coffee and Reed stroked both of the traitors now curled into balls against him.

"One of my college literature professors often used an expression when discussing characters in books. It was catchy. And I don't know if it was a genuine expression of his or if he'd borrowed if from somewhere." I took another sip and stared into my cup.

"What was the expression?"

"He said, 'In the heart of the man, a child is weeping.' He assigned us characters from Faulkner's novels and had the class analyze the weeping child for the class final paper. I had a hard time with it and ended up calling Mama. She explained that it referred to a hurt or series of hurts suffered during childhood that influenced the actions of the adult."

"And in the dream you were told to . . ."

"Find the weeping child."

Reed leaned toward me, dislodging the cats. "I can understand why you would be sad, Sorrel. Your main support system has been murdered, and you survived a harrowing experience."

"No, that's not what it's about. The weeping child is my brother."

"I didn't think you were close to—"

"Not that brother, Reed. I have almost never heard from him—even after my dad died. Even though he came for his court-ordered visitations in the summers until he was twelve, we were never close. I think he was jealous that I lived there with our dad fulltime."

Reed still looked perplexed. "Then . . . "

"I think it's my other brother. Remember? The one that Mama apparently gave up for adoption when she was a teenager? I've begun thinking of him as 'junior', because I don't know his name."

"Oh. Right." I'd read John's letter to him about the child and that he was the child's father. "So, the dream shows that it's on your mind. But how can you know the other brother even knows about his mother or you or even has had a struggle. For all we know, he may be a millionaire living on a yacht."

"I don't think so. Mama's foster family apparently wasn't an honorable bunch, and the adoptive family was their relations."

Reed didn't argue any more. "What have you done so far?"

"Nothing."

Reed raised his brows but then asked, "How can I help?"

"I don't have a plan right now. There's so much going on here at the shop, inventory and such, and I've gotten orders for my Bosque photos from a couple of shops in Flagstaff."

"And . . . "

I looked at him. "What?"

"And the something you're not telling me is . . .?"

How did he do it? "I've been offered a job with a healthy salary and some other juicy perks. I could teach some photography classes at a college in Tucson. It would mean I could pay for some big changes here in the shop. I would put more staff here and commute during the semesters."

"When did this happen?" Reed's blue eyes turned into molten steel. "I know I've not always been immediately available, but messages or texts . . . or even the drive into town or back out here . . . were suitable ways to tell me."

"I—well . . . it was quick. And I haven't had time to really think about it." I got up and put my empty cup in the sink.

I turned to Reed and gestured toward the pot.

"No thanks," he said. "I think I need to give you some time."

He stood up, put his hat on, and smiled at the protesting cats. "See you guys later." He turned toward the door.

"And? "

He stopped and looked back. "We talked about a relationship tonight, but I'm not sure we're in agreement about what that entails."

"I'm not sure what has just happened! My idea of a relationship certainly means being able to tell each other about our lives without the other one storming off in a snit!"

"You're right, Sorrel. You've told me, and I'm leaving—not storming—before I wring your pretty neck. This isn't a casual thing here. Tucson is fairly distant, and I can't even imagine why you didn't just refuse the offer immediately. Since you didn't, then you must be seriously considering it!"

"And if I am?"

"Then there's not much talking to do about our relationship, is there? But we can talk when I feel calmer and you're not so stressed from lack of sleep and bad dreams."

Before taking another step, he reached me in two long strides. "Since you're still trying to figure out what our relationship is, I'll give you something else to think about."

His kisses always wiped out any of my thoughts. It was over before I wanted, and he strode to the door without looking back. But he couldn't resist a parting shot over his shoulder when he reached the door. "Sorrel, what's a snit? I've always wondered."

Chapter 4

"Men are so frustrating!" I grumbled. Flash purred her agreement.

I figured I'd not be able to settle down for a while, but I changed into an oversized t-shirt and sleep pants and prepared for bed anyway. Reed hadn't given me the chance to explain that I wasn't interested in returning to Houston. Didn't he know me better by now? And what about him? He'd tossed out the offer from the Border Patrol. Why was he able to choose his career path and then go off the charts when I mentioned ones sent my way?

"Chris Reed, I thought better of you!" I muttered as I climbed into bed. "Now I'll have a sleepless night, thanks to you."

I drifted off to sleep before the answers to any of my questions could arrive.

My phone blasted "Wake up! Wake up! You Sleepyhead" before seven. I grimaced. That ringtone had been assigned to Randall Byrd, editor of the newspaper, because he invariably woke me up with photo requests—even when it wasn't an emergency.

I pulled hair out of my eyes, squinted at protesting cats curled at my feet, and felt for the cellphone on the nightstand. "Hello."

"Sorrel?" A short pause. "I hope you don't have anything planned."

"Of course I do. But what do you need?"

Mr. Byrd paused. "I'm not sure."

This reply—and his whole tone of voice—was uncharacteristic. "I'm not sure if we have a story or not," he continued. "But I thought you might be able to . . . could you drop by the paper this morning? I need to talk with you."

Weird! "This morning? Could I come in around ten? The shop is closed this week to prepare for the big Valentine's Day sale, but I have several things to clear up."

"That will work for me. I'm still at home, but I'll be in the office after eight."

Randall Byrd usually had immediate projects for me, so I needed to clear up things at the shop in case this one became more complicated than I might first expect. I'd recently expanded the shop by offering some of the items, especially my photography, online. Although we were in the early stages, the website had already produced several orders. My first business of the morning had to be packing and shipping those orders. I just hoped Mr. Byrd's current project would not require too much attention before I could hire a reliable temp worker.

It was closer to ten thirty by the time I parked in the newspaper lot. As always, the person at the front desk had a tranquil appearance, which made me smile. In the background, a myriad of noisy machines and bustling workers presented quite a contrast to the image she created.

"Mr. Byrd is expecting me," I told her. "I'm Sorrel Janes."

I repeated myself twice as she excused herself to answer the telephone and switch the calls to various departments. The third time she turned and asked, "And who are you?" just as a voice boomed behind her, startling us both.

"Sorrel, I've been waiting on you!" Then Mr. Byrd turned to her, "Hold my calls. Just take messages."

Once he'd seated me in his office and I'd refused a cup of coffee, he sat at his desk and opened a folder. "I've got a new story lead—which may or may not develop into something—that I thought you'd like to follow."

When he paused and seemed to be expecting an answer, I said, "You might want to give it to one of the full-time reporters, Mr. Byrd. As I told you, I'm at a busy time in the shop and—"

"You once wanted to be an investigative reporter, Sorrel," he interrupted. "Oh, I know you think of yourself as a photographer—and you're a good one—but your years as a reporter on the campus newspaper while you were in the university make you uniquely valuable to me for this assignment."

Again he paused. This time I kept quiet and he continued. "It would require a trip over to Arizona. Not too far . . . near Portal. Apparently, some guy who likes to snoop into caves has found something."

"What?" I couldn't resist and I didn't miss the twitch at the corner of his mouth.

"Chatter has it that there may be human remains. Maybe just chatter. And law enforcement is less than forthcoming with their involvement. So I thought you could go—with a reporter if you want—and check it out."

"I don't want to be rude, Mr. Byrd, but this sounds like a wild goose chase and I really have a tight schedule here." I paused. "I haven't told you that I've also been offered a job teaching photography in Tucson. It would give me a steady income and allow me to come home part of the week as well. So I've been trying to get this sale over, then set up some steady help at the store. This story—it tempts me, but I don't know if I should take the time."

"I truly need you, Sorrel. My sources say that a task force is already being organized, and they're pulling Chris Reed for it. I sent a reporter to talk to him, but he's keeping quiet. It may be nothing, but a task force isn't."

I silently agreed with what he wasn't saying—that Chris Reed may talk to me before he'd talk to anyone else. I also knew he hadn't mentioned it, but I owed Mr. Byrd for help he'd given me during my first time here in Saddle Gap.

"How about you just go over and get some photos of the outside of the caves and the general area?" he suggested. "The reporter can snoop around and you two can at least get a human interest story about the area. It's a popular tourist draw at different times—in spite of its isolation. It would make a good human interest article, if nothing else."

Cagey. He knew it was likely more than human interest. He also knew I'd love the opportunity for some photos of the area to add to my shop.

As if reading my mind, he added, "You might find some photo ops for your store."

"Who are you sending?"

"Well, you know we've been a bit short-handed. But I've made an agreement with New Mexico State University in Las Cruces. They have designed a practical journalism course where the students go out in the field—advanced students, of course. They have a young man, Will Hudson, who sent me a resume and request. I've interviewed him and I think he'd be a good candidate for this story. He's athletic and bright and seems to have a sense of adventure."

"And my role is just snapping pictures?" I asked dryly.

"Well—"

I stood up. "I appreciate the offer, Mr. Byrd, but this is really—"

"A couple of days—to see if there's even a story. If he comes up with nothing, I'll still pay you and your expenses—and you'll have some photos."

It was tempting, even though I needed to be home. He leaped into my hesitation. "I even have someone who might help out in your shop."

"Who?"

He laughed. "Only if we have a deal."

I sat back down and reached for the folder he held.

"When would you want us to go?"

"Will is coming here this afternoon. I'll brief him and have him ready to leave in the morning."

"And you truly have someone who might want to work at the shop part time?"

"Yes, I do. You could interview her this afternoon and show her around. Then you could be ready to drive up with Will in the morning."

"How long a drive is this?"

"Not too long. Portal is in eastern Arizona, a tiny community. They have cabins there—lots of birders come during the season—so I'd reserve a couple for a night or two. We could play it by ear on that."

"I'll look at this information and talk to your temp person. If I think I can do this—and if it truly isn't a long-term assignment—then I'll call you."

"By noon?"

"By noon. But I'd like to talk to this cub reporter first."

We both stood and he reached out to shake my hand. "I appreciate your even considering it, Sorrel," he said. "I realize that you've had more than your share of upheaval in the past few months. And my wife raves about your shop all the time, so I know you have plenty to keep you hopping there. But I just have this . . . this . . . "

"Gut feeling?" I finished for him.

He grimaced. "Yes, I do. My first news editor called it the curse—and it is in a way. I think we have a story here—and it may not be a pleasant one. On the other hand, it may be nothing."

"But you don't believe that."

"No, I don't. And even though you've not been with me as long as most here, I want you on this story. You have that sense . . . that touch, if you will. If I'm off track, I think you'll tell me. Better than that, I trust you to tell me."

He handed me the folder. "You'll want to review this one." Then he walked me out to the front desk and pulled another folder. "This is an ad we have coming out today from someone you might want to interview for your shop. And I have Will's info in here also."

I glared at him. "You had this ready."

He almost smiled. "I try to be prepared. You'd understand if you knew Mrs. Byrd."

"I haven't agreed to all of this."

"I know but I'm hoping you will. As I said, you're a great photographer, Sorrel, but your heart will always be with investigative reporting."

I didn't agree with him; but the morning was gone, and I had a full afternoon ahead. First on the list involved checking out this person who wanted a job.

Correction! First on the list involved the shopping I hadn't done yesterday. Cat food and litter and a list of cleaning supplies would keep all of my little family happy! I also needed to stop by the senior center—in case I lost my sanity and accepted this assignment—to check on the progress of a couple of new crafters. Then I'd check with Teri about her cousin. He probably would already be too busy to stay at the house, but I steadfastly refused to board the cats when on an open-ended assignment like this one. And Reed—

Right on cue, his ringtone blasted as I pulled up to the senior center.

"I was thinking I needed to call you!" I greeted him.

He chuckled, that sexy sound that almost made me forget we'd parted in a grumpy fashion last night. "At least you're still speaking and not giving me the silent treatment. Wait. Maybe the silent treatment would be better than chewing my ear."

"Better stop while you're ahead!"

Another chuckle. "We need to talk. Dinner?"

"Depends. Are you cooking?"

"Yes, if I can do it at your place. Mine is still in that fixer-upper mode, as you know . . . and remind me quite often."

"I have the grocery store on my list if you—"

"Nope. I have everything already. Between five and six?

I trotted into the center, his chuckle still warm in my ears.

Chapter 5

"Your buddy will be here any minute," I told the meowing cats. "I'm making coffee. He's the one who will feed you tidbits of—"

A loud crash exploded from the steps. I would have dropped the can of coffee had I not heard Reed's irritated voice. I set it on the counter, rushed to the door, and pulled it open.

Reed bit off the tirade and glared up from his spot on my stone path. Around him lay two or three split plastic bags and various food items. "Are you okay?" I asked as seriously as I could. Reed isn't one you often see in such a precarious position. "Do you need me to—"

"I can get up myself, thank you!"

I chased after the plastic bags, but only one could be used. "I'll just go get something to hold the food," I said and hurried inside before the giggles erupted.

"I hear you, Sorrel!" he bellowed.

By the time I returned, Reed had gathered the food. I held the bags while he stuffed them. "Steak," I said. My stomach growled on cue. Sometimes I forget to eat or just grab whatever is handy. Breakfast had been a banana and lunch . . . lunch?

"Are you okay? We can do this some other—"

Reed reached for the bags. "I'm fine, Sorrel. Caught my boot on the step."

He limped a little, but I carefully looked away. Once inside, Reed dumped the bags on my table and washed his hands at the sink. While he checked out the spice rack for seasonings, I rummaged through the first aid supplies.

"I'm fine," he repeated when I approached.

"I'm sure you are, but I'm putting this antibiotic cream on that abrasion on your wrist anyway!"

He sighed dramatically as I cleaned and smeared his wrist before covering it with a wide adhesive patch. "Now, what can I do to help with dinner?" I asked.

"Don't you have to kiss it better?" he asked and then snickered at my mock glare. "Never mind. And, no, you can't help. These are good groceries and I don't want you near them!"

I raised my hands in surrender. "I'll just finish making this pot of coffee then."

Within half an hour, Reed had efficiently broiled steak in the oven and cooked two potatoes in the microwave while I put a salad together and set the table. During dinner, we chatted comfortably about inconsequential things and mutual acquaintances, skirting past work. Reed is a natural storyteller, and he soon had me giggling.

"I hate to admit that I forgot dessert," he said, looking at my empty plate.

"Good thing. I can't imagine another bite!" I stood and reached for his plate. "Why don't you go relax with the other guys and I'll clear the table."

"I made the mess. I'll help you wash the dishes. And before you say anything, just remember that I will only fall asleep in the recliner and snore until the window blinds shudder if I get too comfortable."

I tossed him a tea towel. "I wash. You dry."

"Nope. I wash and you dry. I don't have a clue where everything goes . . . and we don't want your manicure ruined."

I giggled. "What manicure?" I held out my hand with my short clipped nails. "Personally, I'm happy to not be worrying about nails and make-up and—"

"Weight?"

I swatted him with the tea towel. "Get to work while you still can!"

Half an hour later, I snuggled up in the shabby overstuffed chair with Flash. Van curled upon Reed's knee on the couch. "I don't see how you can still be drinking coffee and expect to sleep tonight."

"Remember that painter? Rockwell? This is one of his type of moments. It's a moment to capture and save until you need to pull it out and relive it."

I studied him a moment. He looked tired but content as he stroked the huge, one-eared tomcat. "What's up?"

He didn't pretend to misunderstand me this time. "I'm part of a task force that's been organized in conjunction with the Border Patrol. That's what I meant to tell you earlier and ended up arguing before I could finish."

"The sheriff's office?"

"The sheriff is coming back off family leave now that his wife has finished chemotherapy and her prognosis is good. I could stay on, and he offered, but—"

"You need the rest, Reed. You don't have your ranch fixed up like you want and now you'll be off—"

"Not off all the time. And I can use the money to help pay for the renovations and other changes I need to make."

"When do you go?"

"In the morning. At least, that's the briefing. As you well know, I can't go into things much, and I'm not real clear on when I'll be around—"

"And telling you to be careful is a waste of words."

I got up, pointed to his cup, and at his nod, took it to the kitchen to refill it. When I set it on the coaster beside him, he caught my hand, pulled me down on the couch beside him, and pulled me into his arms. "Words are your gift, Sorrel. Actions are mine." The kiss that followed wiped all worries away for a time.

Later, when I was snuggled up in bed with the cats, I realized I'd not told him about my own assignment for Randall Byrd.

Chapter 6

I'd decided to tell Reed about Mr. Byrd's assignment. Actually, I'd told him that I would be photographing some scenic views in Arizona and that my partner was a male hiker/journalist. I'd left the trip schedule out of my phone message and breezed past the other details. After all, I reasoned as my current partner and I started down the highway, at this stage of our trip no one knew exactly what we might encounter—so I had complied with our agreement to be as "open as we could." With his job, Chris often encountered danger and sensitive material. Sometimes with mine, I did too.

I had persuaded Mr. Byrd to allow me to use my Jeep instead of the wildly colored SUV the newspaper owned. "Of course, if you want to advertise our presence . . . ," I'd said. He'd quickly approved my choice and given me Will's address.

Will didn't quite fit the image Mr. Byrd's description had created. Instead of the preppy, conceited guy in my imagination who planned to be the next television news anchor, Will was a wiry, hyper, kick back to the days of black-and-white movies. His rumpled plaid shirt refused to stay tucked into his jeans, which must have belonged to a much larger older brother, in spite of the wide belt cinched around his small waist. His hiking boots seemed huge for his slight frame; and his dark hair perched onto dark, framed glasses that dwarfed his thin face. When I told him he absolutely couldn't smoke in my car, he popped a round lollipop in his mouth, which he pushed in and pulled out while he talked incessantly.

I sped along the highway, his chatter drifting in my direction. Early on, he said, his parents—both scientists—were hoping he'd get over his interest in news reporting. But he felt driven—fascinated—with news. He hoped to become an international journalist for one of the major networks.

"Randall told me all about you," he confided around the lollipop. "So I doubt you embrace my perspective. No offense but college newspapers are lightweight. International journalists need tight reporting to actually build the trust of the vast television audience. That's my goal. I've never been a pretty boy, which would have been an advantage, but I'm bright and smart with words." He gave me a sidelong glance. "You're really pretty, you know, in an ordinary way. Pity you didn't aspire to bigger heights."

I swallowed a giggle. That's the first time I'd been given sympathy for my looks. It was refreshing. Ordinary was comfortable. I'd never enjoyed the time or patience required to be beautiful. It took much less time to trim my nails short, brush my hair up into a ponytail, and smooth moisturizer onto my face.

"If you want music, I have a variety in the storage box there," I said.

"I get all the country music I can stand at home," he replied. "My parents and you are—"

"Aren't peers," I interrupted smoothly, "as I was in elementary school when you were born."

He laughed. "At least you're not thin-skinned."

Will and I weren't peers either. Earplugs would have been an asset, I thought, as I sped down the interstate to Will's racket. He'd found a heavy metal station on the radio, settled back against the seat, closed his eyes, and—unbelievably— began snoring.

I missed Reed. I hoped he wasn't in harm's way on his current assignment. Although much of our relationship consisted of sparring, he was a fun companion—most of the time.

When I turned onto NM 80, Will roused, squinted out the window, and fell asleep again in spite of his body and head rocking side to side.

I loved the open spaces, with only a few vehicles sharing the road. Houston was another world, and I didn't miss it at all.

A tiny kangaroo mouse raced across the road and I braked slightly. Will stirred and checked his watch.

"They must have followed a snake to make some of these roads." Will turned off the music and squinted out at the distant mountains. "I'm relieved Byrd advised me to take meds for nausea."

I made sympathetic noises, privately relieved that I'd never had that malady. "We unfortunately will only travel on these two-lane paved roads to Portal," I said. "But we don't have a long way to go."

He groaned, pulled his cap back over his eyes, and snored happily as I turned off the road at Rodeo toward Portal. I wondered if this tiny town had risen up around a rodeo. Someday I'd like to research names of towns. I made a mental note to add that to my huge want-to-do list.

Portal had been named correctly, I decided later, pulling off into a tree-shaded parking area. It wasn't a town by most standards. Instead, it consisted of a few houses and a general store/café with rental cabins clustered behind it. But it was also the "door" opening onto the road to Chiricahua National

Monument, high in the Coronado National Forest. My fingers itched for a camera.

I gently shook Will's shoulder. "We're here. Better wipe off the drool and switch to your reporter cap." I climbed out of the Jeep and stretched as I walked up to the store. It truly was a general store. The shelves contained a wide variety of food, household items, and even personal products. As I walked to the counter, a slim, older man who had been restocking a nearby shelf walked over.

"Can I help ya?"

Before I could answer, Will spoke over my shoulder. "Restroom?"

The man waved toward the back of the store. "Go through the café area. It's in a hall between there and the larger dining room on the side."

Will grunted and headed off.

"My working partner has been sleeping to avoid carsickness," I felt obliged to explain. "He's—"

"We get all kinds," he assured me. "How can I help you?"

I stuck my hand over the counter as I spoke. "I'm Sorrel Janes with the *Saddle Gap News*. We're booked in to Cave Creek Ranch."

"I'm Everett Turner," the man said. "You've chosen a nice place. The cabins at Cave Creek are small and simply furnished, but they're located in a beautiful area and you'll find photo opportunities galore," he said. "We cater to birders who spend most of their time taking pictures out in this area. The kitchen should be equipped, but you might want to pick up food here."

Will, who had already returned, opened his mouth to answer, but I spoke first. "That should work perfectly for us. I know we're off for bird photos, but Will and I are spelunkers. Our paper is hoping to get a how-to article to provide some human interest."

"Then you'll be out most days. We do have a nice little eating place here. Lots of the birders and such eat here. Do you need directions?"

I left Everett and Will talking while I went to the ladies' room. The walls of the hall were filled with photos of birds, prices in the frames. Whoever they were, the photographers had captured the unique beauty of the birds.

When I returned, Will had already found a seat at one of the primitive tables in the small eating area. "I ordered a hamburger," he said.

"Good idea. We need to pick up some food here as our cabin has a kitchen, but I'm starved. I'll get one too."

Within a few minutes, both of us were biting into juicy hamburgers and fries. Will struck up conversations with people at the other tables, pausing to jot down notes. "Great human interest," he said through his food. I resisted the urge to tell him not to eat and talk, but his earlier references about my age made me close my mouth.

Instead, I jotted down a list of my own items we would likely need from the store. When I finished my meal, I left Will talking and walked back into the store area. Mr. Byrd had given me a credit card as well as some cash. I gathered the items on my list into a basket and headed to the counter. "I'm going to need a receipt that lists the items," I told Everett apologetically.

"No problem," he said. "My register tape will have that on it. Looks like you have chosen well. But I'd encourage you to add candles and matches if you don't have a good flashlight. Our phone service is sporadic and the weather is generally good, but you never know what it will decide to do. Beef jerky would be smart for spelunking, as well as dried fruit. Do you have a good container for water? We have bottled water in various sizes."

Will appeared just as I began loading the jeep with what I'd bought and what Mr. Turner had suggested. He enjoyed joking about my strength. "Since we seem to have reversed roles," I said casually, "I hope I bought things you can cook for dinner tonight."

"Wait a minute—"

I interrupted by starting the engine, hiding a grin as I did so, and thrusting a sheet at him. "You can read the directions to Cave Creek Ranch. Our cabin sleeps two, so we can toss a coin for the twin in the tiny bedroom or the one in the family area. I bought paper plates, but we share doing the pots and pans, along with other chores like cooking and cleaning."

If Will clearly had different ideas, he kept them to himself for the moment. "We should be able to unload quickly and still get out for a look around," he said instead.

I agreed. "But no spelunking today."

Mr. Byrd had only told Will about an adventure-type story. "He's green, excited," he'd explained. "I'm not sure what is going on, so keep your eyes and ears open. You'll have to remind Will about keeping his mouth shut, so be careful about what he says. Something big is happening. My tip came with warnings and cautions."

He'd not shared those warnings and cautions with me, but I felt the responsibility to keep an eye on Will when I could.

"I've gotten enough to write up a good human interest story for the start of the series," Will said as I pulled out of the store parking lot.

"Good. I'll enjoy snapping photos. If all goes well, we can send them to Mr. Byrd from Portal. But Everett warned me that service is sporadic at times."

The directions were accurate, but some of the road required my attention. Our cabin was located on a creek and, though small, was bright and clean. This time Will insisted on carrying in the supplies while I carried my own bags. "I'll take the twin in the main room," he said, looking around. "I stay up late at night, and you said you get up early. I'll be writing on that human interest article later tonight. Besides, you're a girl."

"Ah. I hadn't noticed."

Finally, he grinned. "I'm not really sexist."

"I never said you were. By the way, I'm a terrible cook; so my comment about your cooking was a warning."

Neither of us were hungry after the huge hamburgers, so we quickly unpacked and returned to the Jeep. "I'm hoping we can reach the Ranger station before they close," I told Will. "It's a perfect place to start. Remember, though: don't drop too much information about yourself. Our job is to learn as much as we can about the area. We don't need anyone passing information about us on to other journalists."

Will nodded wisely. I hid a grin. Thankfully, Mr. Byrd hadn't shared his suspicions about what we might encounter. Will would most likely be a helpful ally, but he did like to talk.

"Just let me take a photo of the cabin," I said. I snapped several, including the creek. I also needed to remember my own role. Since our cover included human interest stories about our adventures, this was a start.

When we got in the Jeep, I handed Will an empty soda can. "If you must smoke," I told him, "use this. Personally, I'd advise you take up chewing gum. Cigarettes leave an odor and a trail. And they turn your teeth yellow if you're not careful."

I pulled back out on the road, hiding a smile as Will pulled down the sun visor and studied his teeth in the mirror.

Chapter 7

"Sorrel, we have a new exhibitor for the Valentine's Day Event! She works at my gynecologist's office, and she brought stuff in to show me when I had my appointment this morning!"

Will sighed and wiggled impatiently. I motioned for him to go on into the ranger station without me. "I'll be along shortly," I whispered.

"What did you say?"

"No problem, Teri. I'm out on a story and was just telling my partner I'd be along. What sort of things does she make?"

"Wreaths and all sorts of things. She forms the flowers for the wreaths from a variety of unusual materials—beads, berries, porcelain. We don't have anything like them in our shop. She—"

"Do we have a spot for her? Wreaths will take up a bit of room."

"I know just the spot! And she has a good inventory because she has only been selling them to family and friends. When are you going to be back?"

"I'm not sure, but this job shouldn't take more than a couple of days." I saw Will talking to a couple who had just driven into the parking lot to our right. "But why don't you give her the proper paperwork and let her set up?"

"Are you sure?"

"Teri, I trust your judgement! But if you want, we can put her on one of those one-time sale agreements we've done with a couple of others."

"Okay. I gotta run. Cub Scouts tonight!"

"Don't run! Walk!" I cautioned.

I got out of the car and started toward Will, with Teri still chattering. "Pet the cats," I interrupted finally. "I'm in a shoot."

I wasn't, but Teri could run on for a bit.

So, it seemed, could Will! The couple had gone inside with Will following, still talking, but they came out alone shortly.

The ranger station looked more like a camp nestled in a narrow strip between the road and a creek. I took a couple of quick shots before joining Will inside. He'd snagged a man in a ranger uniform.

"This is my photographer," I heard him explaining as I neared. "She works for the newspaper."

"Sorrel Janes," I said, reaching out to shake his hand. "I'm actually a freelance photographer whom the newspaper contracts from time to time. My special interest is wildlife photography."

"Ray," he said, returning my handshake with a polite smile. "I've been warning your partner here about hiking—and most especially visiting caves in the area. The rocks in this park are old and can be fragile, and some of the trails are treacherous. We advise only guided tours for your safety."

"Do the tours include the caves?" I asked.

"Not at this time," he replied.

"Can a person even climb to them?"

"Sure. I've even spent the night in a couple. But just now, with the winter cold, I doubt if you'd want to."

"It might be safer just now to hike," I observed. "But I wonder, are rattlesnakes inclined to winter in the caves?"

Will interrupted, clearly not pleased to find the conversation drifting away from him. "They hibernate in their holes in the winter, Sorrel."

"Well," Ray said, "they may hibernate in the caves as well and may not be very active—unless you disturb them. Rattlesnakes can be quite irritable if disturbed."

"Are you from these parts, Ray?" I asked.

"Actually, I'm from Vermont." He grinned at Will's obvious surprise. "But I've been here for seven years. It's a gorgeous area, and I love the weather. Aside from the wind, that is. I'm not fond of the breezes as the old timers call them, especially in the winter. They slice right through you and leave icicles along your spine." He shuddered. "And I grew up in New England!"

"So if we want to do a bit of climbing, instead of hiking," Will said, "where can we do that?" He looked up at a couple of holes in the high rocks around us. "What about those?"

"Follow me," Ray said as we walked toward a rack of brochures. "I can give you trail information as well as information about guided tours. They won't have as many as they do in the fall, but I've seen a few groups a couple of times a week."

Will opened his mouth, but I nudged his arm with my elbow and gave him a warning glare. At first, he seemed inclined to ignore me but then fell in behind Ray.

"In fact," Ray continued, having missed our small disagreement, "one time in college we froze some rattlesnakes. They thaw out with a really awful disposition."

That diverted Will. "Froze them? Why?"

"We wanted to dissect them for parasites, so we collected them from different areas until we had several to compare."

"But freezing them alive?"

Ray chuckled. "Parasites might leave them had we killed them. At least, we weren't sure if they would, so we froze them alive." He gave us a wide smile. "A bunch of mad rattlesnakes—newly thawed—can sure clear out a lab."

Will laughed with him. I battled with sympathy for the critters and chills up my spine from the mental pictures they created.

As we walked toward the rack, I looked around the small room. Maps were on the wall ahead of us and bookshelves filled with leaflets and books about Arizona were on another. Big windows gave an airy feel. Waist-high glassed display cases contained labeled rocks and other artifacts from the area. I adjusted my light and snapped shots. We were, after all, supposedly doing a feature on the area.

Will scribbled on his notepad, following Ray around like a devoted puppy. I had to admire Ray's knowledge and enthusiasm. He shared various historical facts as well as interesting stories. How many times a day did he do that?

"How long did you say you'd been out here, Ray?" Will asked.

"Seven years." Ray grabbed a couple of brochures. "Here are some you might like to look through."

"What's that bumping noise?" I'd noticed it for some time, and it grew louder as we moved around the room.

"Here." Ray pointed toward a couple of display cases across the room. I followed him and leaned down. Several snakes lay among various rocks and dips. One rose to eye me and bumped against the glass. I jumped back before I remembered the glass.

"How do they live in there?" I asked.

Ray gestured toward tiny air vents. "Oh, of course." I leaned close again and snapped a couple of photos. "What marvelous designs they have on their skins!"

Will didn't hide his astonishment—and then dismay— that I hadn't squealed or jumped. Ray, however, pointed out the ways they could be distinguished by sex and breed and even age.

"Could I get a photo of you," I asked, "before someone else arrives and you're too busy?"

Ray smiled. "Sure. I don't get many photo requests unless someone is with me. Do you want a shot of the both of us?" Will stepped forward.

"No, I've already taken a couple of those as you two had your heads together."

As I positioned Ray against the colorful regional map, the door behind me whooshed open. "Coffee is on the desk,"

Ray called. "I can help you with questions or information after I pose."

"I'd certainly appreciate the coffee," a too familiar voice drawled.

It took all of my will power to keep my attention focused on the shot, asking Ray to lower his chin and turn slightly.

Will, on the other hand, stepped over and immediately introduced himself. "My photographer and I are here on an assignment for our local paper," I heard him say.

"Interesting. What exciting events are happening around here?"

Will, however, used what little good judgment he'd accumulated and answered evasively. "Just a human interest story on the history and beauty of the area. And you, sir? Could I interview you?"

"No need. I'm also just a traveler, enjoying the natural beauty and history of the area—and bumming a cup of coffee from the ranger here."

I managed to focus on the photo session until I heard him say, "Thanks, again!" and listened to the door click shut.

"Strange fellow," Will muttered.

Ray smiled. "Not really. We get all sorts of folks."

As if on cue, the door reopened and a group of six entered. "Hello," the leader called. "We're the Golden Age Eagles from Tucson just dropping in with lots of questions."

Will and I quickly retreated, stopping to take a photo of the group and get their names.

"Thanks again," I told Ray on the way out.

"Come back any time," he said. "I'll be here until April, when I take a month's break."

Will excused himself to visit the men's room, so I busied myself stowing my camera in the Jeep. When I opened the driver's door, a piece of paper that must have been wedged in it fell out. I bent over, picked it up, and read the familiar scrawl: "Will call your cell later tonight. Don't try mine."

Chapter 8

Will volunteered to cook dinner when we returned to our cabin and I happily agreed. I hoped he wasn't exaggerating his culinary skills, but he wouldn't have to do much to beat mine. I told him I'd like to take some evening shots. The skies are so beautiful at dusk, and I didn't want to get involved tomorrow and miss getting some photos of them. I'd shot only a couple when my cell played Reed's tune.

"Hi!"

"Surprise, surprise! If it isn't the wandering photographer!"

He sounded snippy, so I decided the best course was to ignore his answer. Otherwise, we would likely argue—something we didn't do well—and I didn't want to stay on the phone too long. I truly wanted to shoot some of the scenery in this light.

"I'm out shooting some late evening scenery. This is such a gorgeous setting!"

"And the Boy Wonder?"

"Will is cooking dinner."

"First smart thing I've heard! He can't be too dumb if he's avoiding your cooking!" I felt a smile pulling my lips but felt it best to keep things businesslike just now. We were both working, and our paths pointed to similar yet different destinations.

So I let my voice become a bit snappish. "As I don't have unlimited time to exchange pleasantries with you, why don't you tell me—"

"Tell you what? Funny how things keep working out that when I go out on police business, suddenly you appear taking pictures! What are you really doing up here?"

"Exactly what Will told you. Randy called and asked me to come here with a reporter to investigate a human interest story about the area and maybe climb to the caves."

Reed interrupted with an almost intelligible string of words.

I pretended horror. "Wow! Bet your mama would make you eat a whole bar of soap—"

"Ha! Ha! Sorrel, I don't have a lot of time, so just listen without the smart mouth. You need to round up the Boy Wonder and get out of here as early in the morning as you can! This is one thing you don't need or want to touch." He lowered his voice even further. "I don't know how Randy heard about it, but he should have known it wouldn't be safe for you."

I felt my temper simmering. "How many times—"

"And that kid is so green! Randy has better sense! He'll get you both killed at worst. At best, he'll foul up an operation that—"

"That you didn't tell me about?"

"This is a need-to-know operation because lives are at stake! I'm in law enforcement, Sorrel, as you well know, and a couple of busybodies masquerading as reporters could not only endanger lives, including yours, but also ruin an expensive and sensitive operation!"

I waited to let him catch his breath. "We really are doing human interest articles," I said calmly.

"And snooping whenever possible! I know you, Sorrel! Worse yet, I trusted Randy to at least exhibit some good sense!"

"He's a newsman, Reed, and he smells a good story. But he isn't endangering us. We are interviewing people and taking photos of the area. Should something else happen while we're here, we'll report it as well." I paused. "That's what our country—and freedom—is about."

I heard a sigh through the phone. "Why did I tie up with a stubborn redhead carrying around a divining rod that spots trouble?" He attempted a bugle call and failed miserably.

I giggled. "First time I've been accused of using props. But you're right—Will feels sort of like a divining rod. He's enthusiastic and more practical than I expected he would be." Silence. "Reed, I can't promise to just cancel my life and sit on a shelf waiting until you get home. This is what I do."

"Funny, I thought what you 'do' is photograph critters, but you are making a habit of appearing when danger beckons!" Reed sighed and then spoke in a calmer voice, deepened a bit by an obvious attempt to restore patience. "I need to go. Promise me you'll be careful and won't go snooping in places—"

"I don't even know where you're staying, Reed. How could I snoop?"

He grunted. "I'll step around that one." I heard voices nearing in the background, and he lowered his voice to just above a whisper. "Take care, Sorrel! This is nasty stuff! I don't want to think about—"

The connection broke abruptly. Images of past scrapes we'd had pushed forward, but I squashed them immediately.

Reed, like me, had a job he loved—and he was good at it. I'd worry about him later, but just now the light was fading fast. I needed to shoot before it left.

Photography absorbs me, and the challenge of finding the perfect shot and lighting is all-consuming. By the time Will hollered from the cabin door, shooting any more images would have been useless. I returned to the cabin, my conversation with Reed nestled in the "later" compartment of my mind.

"Get some good ones?" Will asked. I opened my mouth to answer and then gazed at the tiny cooking area, formerly pristine and now cluttered with every pot in the cupboard on the counter, sink, or stove. Will followed my gaze and shrugged. "I'm not too neat, but the food's good. And since the cook doesn't clear up . . ."

I shuddered. "You're the master of understatement!"

"I filled our plates." He handed one to me and carried his to the tiny table. I followed and settled opposite him. "I poured water for you," he said, "unless you'd like something else?"

"I'm good." I took a long drink. The water tasted so good, naturally cold from the faucet. Then I looked at my plate. How would I ever eat all of this? Will had cooked a ground meat mixture with onions, diced tomatoes, green chilies, and canned corn and then poured it onto a huge hamburger bun.

"Corn chips and salsa on the counter," he mumbled around a bite.

"I'm fine with this," I assured him.

And I was—not only fine but stuffed. Neither of us could eat and talk. When I took the last bite, I couldn't believe I'd cleaned my plate. Will grinned. "I am surprised that you did not eat the plate too," he said.

"Brat!"

He laughed. "I don't bake, so no dessert."

I pushed back and started clearing the table. "Good thing. I doubt there are any dishes left in the cupboards."

While I cleaned the kitchen, Will set his laptop on the cleared tabletop. "I think I'll take a shower now," I told him. "Unless you'd like to—"

He waved a hand at me and continued typing. I gathered my camera case and closed the door to the bedroom after myself. It was small but cozy. I made short work of unpacking my bag into the small bureau and hanging clothes in the tiny closet. A door opened into the bathroom both from the bedroom and the front room. I locked that door, resisted the urge to fill the tub and soak, and started the shower instead.

When I'd finished, cleaned up the area, and dressed in an oversized t-shirt and fuzzy sleep pants, I peeked around the door. "Will, I'm out."

He grunted, then got up. "I'm going out to smoke," he said. "I'll try to be quiet, but I'm a night owl, so—"

"Not to worry. Short of wild parties or heavy metal ramped up, I can sleep through most everything."

When I heard the door shut, I called Randall Byrd. He picked up right away. "I was beginning to think you two had already gotten into something," he said.

I laughed. "No more than dinner," I said. "We did go visit the ranger station. The ranger was most helpful, but he made no mention of any police or border patrol involvement in the area, although I did meet up with a friend of ours."

I heard a sigh. "Reed?"

"Uh huh." I told him about our meeting at the ranger's station, as well as the phone call I'd received from him before dinner this evening. "I didn't want to blow his cover if he needed it."

"He was undercover, I'm sure," Randall said. "You did exactly right."

"How do you want us to proceed in the morning? Or are you contacting Will—"

"I'll be in contact with Will," he said. "But, Sorrel, you're the lead on this in my mind. Will is an intern at the paper and so I didn't think he needed to know the scope of things. Still, I'll try to contact you both equally so he doesn't feel slighted."

"What did you tell him about this assignment?"

"What you told Reed. That you're there on a human interest story. He's sharp and bright but he's green and ambitious. That can be a dangerous combination. I don't know, for instance, if he'd talk too much and blow your cover."

"Mr. Byrd? You told me the same thing about the human interest story."

He gave a short laugh. "But you guessed it was more, didn't you? I asked you to use caution and hold your cards to your chest, and you did it with Reed at the ranger station. I don't know what exactly this undercover job involves yet, but my source has promised to give me more details."

"When?"

He sighed. "Soon. Later tonight, I think. Meanwhile, until I tell you otherwise, continue as you are, taking photos and interviewing people about the area. And I don't need to tell you to keep your eyes and ears open. If something seems covert, sniff around a bit. But don't endanger either you or Will. No news article is worth that."

We talked a bit longer before I heard the door open. "Will's back from his smoke," I said.

"Then I'll make a short call to him now," he said. "Do you have a plan for the morning?"

"Thought we'd check out the caves. The ranger gave me pamphlets."

"Good girl. Talk to you soon."

I gave a light reply, hung up, and heard Will's phone sound off. In spite of the confident answer I'd given Mr. Byrd, I didn't feel prepared for this assignment. I'd learned through my years as a reporter and later as a news anchor that plans needed to be a bit more settled. Did we even have a plan? Obviously something had alerted law enforcement. And just as obviously, they didn't want to alert the public just yet. I had a tricky situation ahead—complicated even more by Chris Reed and my young wild card Will.

I rummaged around until I found the pamphlets on the caves that I'd collected and started reading. I needed to find out all I could about the area tomorrow and hoped I'd remember it. But most of all, I needed to keep my wits sharp to protect not only Will and myself but Reed as well. It didn't promise a good night's sleep ahead.

Chapter 9

"I'm not a morning person," Will grumbled as he climbed into the Jeep. "What difference does it make whether we start the day before daylight or at a normal hour? You can't see anything when it's this dark." His voice took on a whining tone.

I'd learned early on to ignore grumpy partners. When I didn't comment, he squinted out the window of his door one last time before pulling his cap down over his eyes and settling down for a quick nap.

Since he'd declined breakfast, I'd made a peanut butter and jelly sandwich and stuffed the zip-lock bag into his pocket as he'd shuffled by. In both of our backpacks, I'd packed granola bars, small boxes of raisins, bottled water, and jerky, as well as flashlights and additional batteries. I hadn't seen Will make any preparations, in spite of his earlier boasts about his experience. I turned over the ignition and hoped his mood would lift when we started the climb.

We didn't have a long drive ahead of us, but I drove carefully and slowly. Not only was the road narrow and curvy, but critters could dart across without warning. Our ranger friend had predicted that the climb would only take about an hour. Of course, I hadn't been completely forthcoming about our exact plans or route. Randall Byrd had cautioned that the Border Patrol and the task force would likely have the area under surveillance, so Will and I needed to approach the area from a less direct path in case they had the cave and the trail leading up to it cordoned off.

Of course they would, I silently chided myself. Law enforcement never welcomes the press uninvited. The biggest obstacle, of course, was Reed. I could play the role of an ingenuous nature photographer with the others, but Reed could blow my cover right away. Therein lay another challenge I hadn't quite resolved. The upside would be the reaction of his team. If he acknowledged our connection, they might jump to the conclusion that he had leaked information. Because of his actions when I'd seen him at the ranger station, I hoped he'd wait to yell at me after the fact and act like a stranger if we met.

Something moved along the left side of the road. I braked just in time to miss a gorgeous deer stepping across.

"No horns. A doe." Will squinted and yawned. He stretched and looked around at the shadowy landscape. "Are we—"

"There yet?" I grinned. "Not too long."

Will grunted and stared out his window a few moments before reaching in his pocket and pulling out the slightly smashed peanut butter and jelly sandwich. He unwrapped it, took a big bite, and asked around his full mouth, "What are we going to do with the Jeep?"

"I'll find a wide spot to park it either near the trees or beside the road."

"But—"

"Didn't you see the cars parked like that yesterday?"

"Oh, yeah." He gestured toward my Styrofoam coffee cup. "You mind if I—"

"Take it," I said. "I doubt my typhoid is contagious."

He managed a weak chuckle. "I've had the shot," he said. Then he drained the cup and stuffed the last of his sandwich in his mouth. Again he spoke around it. "I looked up background info on this area last night. We should be able to reach that cave we spotted yesterday in an hour or so." At least, that's what I thought he said.

"Didn't your mother—"

"Tell me to eat first, talk later?" He grinned. "Must be part of the female genetic make-up. Never had a guy tell me that."

It was too early to entertain a conversation about gender roles. I opened my mouth to respond just as a Border Patrol truck came up fast behind us. I moved off onto the gravel alongside my lane to let it pass.

"Looks like something exciting happening," Will said, sitting up straight for the first time that morning. "Speed up! Let's see where he's heading!"

I slowed down a bit. "First off, he wouldn't be happy to see us. We'd never get close to whatever they're doing. They wouldn't welcome civilians if they have a crime scene, which they may or may not have. And second, we have an assignment for Mr. Byrd."

Will scowled, then tried a different approach. "But if we brought in a scoop, Mr. Byrd would love it. I've got enough with my research and what we've seen so far that I could fluff . . . "

He quieted as I slowed even more. "The first thing you need to learn about journalism is to forget the word 'fluff.' A good editor—and Randall Byrd is a very good one—can spot it in an instant. The second thing you need to learn is that law enforcement doesn't appreciate interference."

"I thought you were a hotshot reporter during your college days. At least, that's what Mr. Byrd mentioned when he told me we were working together. But you must have been just a piece of fluff yourself—or the college paper wasn't as tough as mine is! Can we pull over? I need a cigarette!"

Will's smile had disappeared quickly. Maybe his nicotine would calm him. Until then, I chose to ignore his comments even though I knew I'd need to address them before we started the climb.

A few minutes later, I spotted a wider spot to the right and pulled in. Will jumped out before I'd even set the brake and turned off the motor.

The sky was glowing a pinkish orange in anticipation of the sun that would soon be peeking over the mountains. Such beauty always inspired me on hiking trips. I took a deep breath and hoped my immature partner would shed his grumpiness before I lost my patience with him.

I sighed as I watched Will pacing along the narrow creek that ran parallel to the road, a cigarette in one hand and his cellphone in the other. Whoever was on the other end of the line wasn't getting a chance to say much.

What was Mr. Byrd thinking? This cub reporter had turned out to be my worst nightmare. The only good point I could see right now was that Mr. Byrd hadn't shared my whole story with him, including the recent death of my oldest friend. In fact, Mr. Byrd's advice had been for us to wander into the other story. But Will was impulsive and short-tempered—and could easily become more of a liability than we needed.

When Will climbed back into the Jeep, I handed him a small, rectangular metal box. "What's this?" he asked.

"For your cigarette butts once we get on the trail."

He grunted and slid it into his jacket pocket as I pulled back out onto the road. "It shouldn't be too much farther according to my GPS," I told him.

He grunted again and resumed staring out his window. I mentally added 'moody' to my list of complaints about my new partner. Reed was looking better by the moment.

I moved to the right to allow another official vehicle access to pass. Will sighed dramatically. I ignored him and hummed a happy tune.

A few moments later, I saw another wider spot to the right. I slowed and pulled in as closely to the trees as I could without scratching up the side of the Jeep. Will opened the door almost before I'd set the brake. I reached across the seat and touched his arm. "Before we go further, I think we need to talk," I said.

Grudgingly, he closed the door but sat stiffly and stared ahead out the windshield.

"First, I wasn't some hotshot crime reporter. I worked my internship at a nearby city during college, and my job consisted more of bringing coffee cups and checking boring details than writing news. And working crime scenes? I was lucky to write the report about a stolen dog or graffiti on the new overpasses. My college journalism professor had warned me that I'd likely be more of a gofer than a reporter. But he'd also convinced me that my job during those months was to keep my eyes and ears open and my mouth closed until opportunities for real reporting opened for me."

I waited a moment. When he neither spoke nor looked at me, I continued brusquely. "We still have time to turn around and go back to Saddle Gap."

That caught his attention. "We can't do that! Mr. Byrd expects this story— travel blurb though it is—and he wouldn't be happy if we reneged."

"He wouldn't be happy if we report we can't work together either. We don't have to love—or even like—each other. However, we do have to respect each other and treat each other professionally. Randall Byrd gave me lead on this assignment, whether you agree with him or not. If you do not honor his choice, his reaction could hurt your future prospects."

Will stared ahead, a muscle in his jaw working. Finally, he muttered, "I'm a grouch in the morning."

I figured that was the only apology I'd get. I stuck out my hand. "Deal?"

He finally looked over and shook my hand. "Deal." He still looked unhappy, but I suspected that this was the best I could expect at the moment.

"Good." I pulled out the keys and gathered up my backpack. "We'd best get started. Some of the best photo opportunities come just after dawn."

Within a few minutes, we had the Jeep locked up. I took a couple of shots of the mountains across the road, the cave high up on the side.

"Looks rugged," Will commented as we crossed the road. He puffed another cigarette. At my look, he said, "I know, I know. I have some candies to suck on the trail."

"Good! Those things are dangerous for you, but they also warn the critters we're coming and we'll likely not get any good shots. Do you want to take lead?"

I could tell I had chosen the right thing to say. Will happily surveyed the area, his whole demeanor brighter. "Do you have a compass?" he asked. "I doubt our cellphones will have any coverage, so the GPS is out."

"Oh, I have a GPS." I pushed back the cuff of my sleeve and revealed the watch-like instrument. "Battery operated. And I have extra batteries in the backpack."

Will looked impressed. We consulted it and decided where to start. I pulled my hair into a ponytail and pulled a stocking cap low over my ears. When Will pulled his on, I stepped back and snapped a photo. "Onward and upward, partner," I said.

"I'll try to keep a slower pace," he said. "Let me know when you're short of breath."

"Will do."

"Lots of rocks standing straight up—"

"Hoodoos."

"What?" he asked.

"Hoodoos. They actually will make good cover if we ever need it."

He laughed and gave me that drama-queen look. I privately hoped we wouldn't need them—ever.

"I guess it's time for us to see who do and who don't," he proclaimed, striking a final dramatic pose.

I could work with this Will, I decided. The trick would be when he realized our assignment wasn't quite what he had thought.

Chapter 10

Will hadn't exaggerated about his climbing expertise, but he needed to stop smoking. Given the age difference between us, I expected him to challenge me. Instead, although wiry and strong, he seemed winded faster than he should have been—or maybe it was just the older sister tendency I'd developed toward him.

When we paused after about half an hour, Will walked over and leaned against a hoodoo while I focused on taking some scenic shots. "These things are bigger than they seem," he said after a bit.

I focused upward toward the cave where we were headed, snapped, and then pointed my camera his direction and snapped again. Now that we were standing still, a chill on my neck making me shiver. "Yes, they are," I agreed. "You could wander around for quite a bit if you became disoriented and no one would see you."

"You say something?"

I glanced at Will, just then noticing the small recorder in his right hand. In his left dangled an ear bud. "Oops. Thought you were talking to me. I was just making idle conversation."

He shrugged, reinserted the tiny ear bud, and began speaking into his recorder again, describing his impressions of our journey so far.

With him preoccupied, I pulled out my small binoculars and surveyed the area around and below us. When the lens moved to the area across the hillside from us, I froze. So this is where those Border Patrol vehicles had been heading! They had been joined by several other law enforcement vehicles and I could see several officers busily setting up barricades and unrolling crime scene tape. I traded my binoculars for my camera and surreptitiously moved about snapping photos of the area, including the ribbon of road beneath and the vehicles parked amid the trees. We needed to keep just far enough away to strengthen our "surprise" if we wandered into their investigation.

From the activity and numbers below, I suspected a crime scene, likely in the cave or on the hillside leading up to it. I squinted through the lens again, but couldn't distinguish the faces of any of the officers below. One particularly tall figure could have been Chris Reed . . . or not. Two or three had their heads together studying something, but I couldn't make out whether it was paperwork or a handheld device of some kind. Several were scattered around, scouring the ground. Some carried toolbox-looking things, most likely lab equipment of some sort. I counted ten people, which presented our next dilemma: the nearer we were to the mouth of the cave, the more difficult keeping out of their sight would be.

The next part of our climb would require a bit of caution. Since we were approaching the cave from the opposite side of the official activity, we could use the dozens of hoodoos as cover. Most stood taller and wider than I, providing natural shields. Still, remaining unnoticed would be tricky. Should we be stopped, we had a good cover story that most of them would believe—except Chris Reed, that is.

I also wasn't sure how much I could comfortably share with Will, but I suspected his natural curiosity was piqued already. He had stopped speaking into his recorder and had moved into my line of sight as I stood gazing below. I lowered my camera and began packing it into my backpack. "Are you ready to move on?" I asked casually. "The sun is moving on up, so I've taken most of the shots I want just now."

"Did those shots include the activity below?"

I didn't answer right away, concentrating on rearranging my backpack while I searched for the story I'd been mentally preparing. I hoped it would sound more believable to Will than it sounded to me.

"You can't have missed all of those law enforcement vehicles gathering down there, as well as the people who have converged on the same cave you chose for us to investigate," he continued, lighting up yet another cigarette.

I decided to stall and play dumb for a bit longer. "There are a number of caves around here, Will. It just happens to be bigger than most and is more accessible. The morning light is perfect."

"So half of the lawmen in the area are out here for the scenic view? Snapping pictures to put in their scrapbooks? Give me a break!"

When I didn't answer immediately, Will continued. "When do you plan to tell me what our assignment out here really is?" His voice had risen even though he'd moved close enough to me that I was holding my breath to avoid inhaling his smoke. "You may be lead, Sorrel, but we're partners here! Either you tell me or I'm heading back to the Jeep. Better yet, I'll go over there and ask them myself!"

"They won't tell you," I answered, as he started to step away. "Instead, they'll load you up and take you back to the cottage . . . or put you in custody until they have time to transport you." I buckled the pack and set it down before I turned toward him. "You're upset and I can see why. But you have to understand that I've been following orders."

"Whose orders?"

"Mr. Byrd's. He's been given a tip that something big is in the wind, but he doesn't know the details. Since he knows I've dealt with law enforcement more than you, he asked me to take the lead on our assignment and say nothing to you until I felt I needed to share. And before you ask, I'll fill you in on my first few months at Saddle Gap and why the 'dealt with law enforcement' comment. But later. When we're not here on a hillside on a job."

I'd spoken in a conciliatory tone; but Will's pride had been bruised, and he obviously wasn't happy in spite of my apology. Instead, he stood with his back to me, staring in the direction of the activity below like a stubborn beagle after a rabbit's scent.

"We're the press," he finally said, "and we have the right to know what is happening and to report it to the public!"

"At this stage, they'll give us some vague story about them just following up on a tip and send us on our way so as not to jeopardize the situation."

"They can't do that!"

I half expected Will to stomp his foot, and bit my lip to hide the smile that image created before speaking. "They can and they will. You're going to have to trust me, Will!"

He remained standing, his arms crossed and his back to me. Finally, I walked around to face him and stared calmly at his mulish demeanor. Again, I kept my voice as steady and as placating as I could manage. "You're experienced enough—and have enough journalistic savvy—to agree with me. The only way we're going to get that story is to keep close and wait until they don't have another choice except to include us. But if we go storming in right now, demanding they share with the press, they will just stonewall us with all sorts of excuses and red herrings."

I could see when the truth of what I'd said filtered into him. He uncrossed his arms and nodded, and my own shoulders relaxed. His pride had taken a hit, but Will wasn't really unreasonable.

"Did I ever tell you my own story?" I asked. "I was just a college reporter, trying to get a story picked up by a larger paper, when I slipped into a biker protest rally in the city. I thought my biker outfit had fooled everyone, but when the rally heated up and became violent, an older guy near me caught my eye and made a big deal of throwing me out. I fought him hard until I stopped yelling about the freedom of the press long enough to hear what he was saying under his breath. It saved my life."

"What did he say?"

I grinned. "Most of it can't be repeated in polite conversation. But the gist of it was that I could leave while I still had my life and let him give me the rest of the story later or he could break his cover and arrest me."

"He was a cop?"

"Yeah. And he knew he'd have to break his cover if I put myself in danger, so I told him how to reach me."

"Did he?"

"Yes, as a matter of fact, he did. It was the beginning of a worthwhile relationship for both of us."

Will sighed. "So the moral of the story is that I have to trust . . ." He threw his hand up in frustration.

"That I know what I'm doing. That I'm lead. That we will work together better if neither of us chooses ego over compromise."

He nodded, albeit unhappily.

"Okay," I said. "I figure we need to continue as we were. They seem to be heading toward this same cave—which Randall's informant had described—from the side opposite us. So I thought we'd approach from this direction. However, your suggestion of the hoodoos being great for hiding is the same as mine. I'd prefer we not be seen just yet."

"Okay."

"And your cigarettes . . . "

"Got the candy in my pocket. Do you want to take the lead climbing too?"

"I think one lead at a time is all I want to manage." I leered and smiled naughtily. "Besides, your—"

Will held up his hand as his face flushed. "Don't say it!"

I struggled to keep a straight face and nodded.

He gathered up his backpack quickly and started climbing back up toward the cave. His self-consciousness didn't last long as the climb grew steeper. I smiled inwardly. He couldn't know that I'd gambled on his reaction. Had he reacted flirtatiously, I would have had a more awkward situation to handle than the one I'd been attempting to diffuse.

My first genuine smile of the day arrived with the thought of Chris Reed's reaction to my suggestive innuendo. Will glanced back just in time to see my own face flush.

"Am I going too fast? Your face is really red."

"No, I'm not out of breath," I reassured him. "Maybe I'm getting a sunburn."

I reached in my pocket and spread lotion on my face while he reached in his pocket for candy. Meanwhile, I heard echoes from my childhood: *Liar, liar, pants on fire!*

Over the next half an hour, the climb not only became more rugged, but also made our presence more difficult to hide. I hung my camera around my neck and used the lens to check the official progress on the other side.

At one point, I spotted the tall figure again. "Morning, Detective . . . Sheriff . . . etc. Looking good!" I whispered. He lifted his head suddenly and looked our way. I knew he couldn't see us—or hoped at least—but I lowered my camera instinctively and concentrated on catching up to Will. "Hey!"

"Huh?" I gestured to him to join me by a big hoodoo. "Everything okay?" he asked, dropping his equipment beside me.

"Yep! Just thought we might—"

"Duck!" Will pulled me down on the hillside beside him. From the distance, we spotted the glare of binoculars as the sun glanced off them. Something wasn't right. The glare came farther up toward the cave than the police activity. Had they sent another party ahead? No, that wouldn't be right. Chris would have gone with the advance party.

We must have someone here besides law enforcement. It could be hikers in the area as this was a popular site for that activity. But it could also be someone returning to the scene of their crime and watching the investigation.

We squatted there breathlessly for a few moments. Then Will turned to me and grinned. "I always did like hide and seek, but I'm not sure the other guys are playing!" He wiggled his eyebrows in a bad Groucho Marx imitation.

A giggle caught in my throat as another thought crossed my mind and lodged there. How could I have overlooked it? Without my having seen the crime scene being processed, past experience should have warned me. The number of officers suggested murder—and more than one. Didn't murderers often return to admire the havoc they had wrought? If so, then Will and I had wandered into more than just a crime scene.

I glanced past the area where we had seen the glare and on up to the cave. Then I turned slowly and looked behind and below us before moving back up. I felt sure I saw the glint again just before it disappeared.

My face must have paled at the thought that now filled my brain as I stared at the spot.

Will's grin faded when he looked at me. "What's wrong?"

I continued to watch that spot on the mountain, not wanting to meet Will's eyes. "What if there are three teams playing out here?" I whispered.

Will glanced over his shoulder, eyeing the same spot I was watching. When he turned back around, he seemed relatively unconcerned. "Okay, Chief," he said. "So what's Plan B?"

Chapter 11

Will bit down on the end of a piece of beef jerky and twisted until it broke off. Then he offered the remainder to me and leaned against the hoodoo with a sigh. "I'm out of shape," he grunted.

I pantomimed smoking, my mouth full of the tough wad I'd finally managed to bite off. Will chuckled.

Finally, I was able to take a long drink of water. "I've just ingested more salt in that mouthful than I've eaten in a month!" I dropped the bottle in my backpack and peeked around the huge rock, then up at the sky. Thin clouds hovered above us, providing light shade from the overhead sun. I felt sweaty from the morning climb.

We had moved diagonally from our original path up on the northeast side. I lifted my camera and adjusted the lens until I could see the official activity, but I didn't recognize anyone. Reed must have moved on to a different area. I panned my camera north, slowly snapping shots. I could see no movement. Maybe everyone had settled, like we had, to eat. *Wishful thinking, Sorrel,* I thought.

Will had finished his jerky and was quietly waiting until I had finished. He held an unlit cigarette in his fingers but, when he saw my eyes on it, grinned and returned it to his pocket.

"The information Mr. Byrd shared was sketchy at best," I told him. "We might truly be chasing a wild goose."

He crawled around to peek over my shoulder before settling beside me and popping a peppermint in his mouth. He wasn't buying my vague comments. I decided it was time to tell him all—or most—of what I knew. "Okay. Mr. Byrd heard, as I said, that something was going down at a cave here. He naturally didn't share who passed this information, but he intimated that it might have something to do with illegal immigration."

"Why send us here then? This is a good distance from Saddle Gap, and I can't see the relevance for our readers. True, we have illegals traveling through and Byrd has printed countless stories, especially about the ranchers and their battle with cut fences and the trash left behind. That's important to people in Saddle Gap. And he only covers local news except for stories he publishes from the wire. No, with his limited staff—and budget—he can't justify sending us out for a feature story that may or may not show a different aspect of illegal immigration. That's already on television and everywhere else."

When I didn't immediately reply, Will continued. "No more wild goose chase, partner!"

I couldn't ignore the sarcasm in the way he said "partner" and searched for the right words without giving away too much. "Mr. Byrd sent you because he knew I'd be coming to take some photos for my shop, and he didn't want me on my own."

Something in my tone alerted him. "You argued with him, didn't you? And he knew you'd come on your own anyway, so he blackmailed you until you agreed for me to come."

"It had nothing to do with you, Will—"

"Of course it didn't. That tall cop you 'didn't know' at the ranger station, he the one Byrd used to bribe you?"

This kid was not only sharp, he also didn't miss much—and he grinned when I said so.

I sighed. "Okay. Something happened to me last fall. Reed—that tall cop—helped me through it. It was a sticky situation—which I'm not going into!" I glared at Will. "And I was left with unanswered questions that I'd just about decided would stay unanswered."

"What did his informant pass on to Mr. Byrd?"

I hadn't noticed that I'd hunched down. "They apparently found a body in this cave."

"What does that have to do with Mr. Byrd?"

"Nothing."

"Border Patrol? I noticed several of their vehicles. And the sheriff's department from Saddle Gap?"

He deserved answers, and I searched for what information I could pass and still keep the rest hidden. "They suspect one of the Mexican cartels is involved. And I don't know which one, so don't ask. They've formed a task force. Reed is part of it."

"And? That story still doesn't need an apprentice reporter and a nature photographer from a small town paper."

"And a photo on the body may be of me." My voice had lowered to a whisper, and Will had to bend close to me to hear it. "They suspect the cave is being checked periodically, but they haven't found anything yet. Mr. Byrd—and I—don't have an ID for the body. I doubt they do either."

I didn't hear the word he whispered while reaching inside his jacket, but I doubted I wanted to. I touched his hand and shook my head. He didn't look at me as he pulled his hand out of his pocket and stared at the cave. Finally, he crawled over to another hoodoo and lit up a cigarette.

I took the opportunity to look through the shots I'd taken earlier. I hadn't noticed the rope ladder that had been connected to the outside of the cave. Somehow it didn't look official. It must have been left there. But that didn't make sense. If they'd left the ladder there, why hadn't the—I avoided the word 'body'—person just climbed down? And if the person was already dead, why leave it there? Maybe they'd shackled the person and returned periodically to torture or check on him—or her.

I flipped to the photos I'd taken earlier of the police activity. Besides Reed, I saw only a couple of officers wearing the Stetson associated with a sheriff's uniform. A dozen or so wore Border Patrol or Highway Patrol uniforms. I didn't see anything unique in them as I clicked past—except one in which Reed was glancing toward my camera as if he knew I was photographing him—until near the last. In the upper corner, I noticed a glint. I kept enlarging it until I spotted what appeared to be binoculars—pointed straight at my camera. I inhaled audibly, catching my breath, and stared at the photo.

"Let me see."

I jumped at the sound of Will's voice right behind me. "Don't sneak up on me!" I snapped.

"I didn't. You were just so focused on that photo you didn't hear me. Let me see." Will leaned close enough that I held my breath against the blend of tobacco and peppermint. He studied the photo and stepped back. "You were right. I should have caught it! We do have a third—maybe even a fourth—partner in this dance."

I checked the time stamp on the camera. "This was just a little over half an hour ago."

Will reached for the binoculars. "The sun should still be high enough that we can sneak a peek," he said, but he only looked through them briefly before lowering them and turning to me. "Plan B?"

"We're not going to get near that place right now."

Will nodded. "Retreat?"

"They need to think we have."

"It would be easier to get in that cave at night."

I shook my head. "They'll have a guard on it."

"Law enforcement will typically figure no one will come." Will stared up at the cave. "The most vulnerable time would be climbing up there—especially if we have moonlight. The most difficult part would be climbing without moonlight."

"It would be impossibly stupid to do that."

"You're not fooling me, Sorrel. You're already scheming, hatching plans to get up there to that cave." He flashed a wicked grin at me. "And wishing I'd been drowned at birth is useless. My sisters have wished that all my life!"

He excelled at reading minds. "If we're planning to take a moonlight trek, we'll need different gear. And rest wouldn't be bad either. So let's go."

I returned the camera to my backpack. We needed to regroup, and this certainly wasn't the ideal setting for that. "We should pretend to be covert so they'll think we've given up." But even as I said it, I knew that one of them wouldn't buy it.

Will repositioned his earpiece, shouldered his backpack, and grinned. "We can hope they'll think we're just hikers when we take a more roundabout descent."

I nodded. "After you, Sherlock!"

"Watson, my dear," he corrected me. "And while we're concentrating on this tricky descent, I'll wait for your story about why your 'maybe photo' would be in that cave? I wondered why the Border Patrol and state police—and whoever else—would solicit a small town deputy sheriff for a Mexican cartel task force. You can think on your explanation." He saluted cockily and started down the mountain.

"Can he swim?" I muttered to the world at large.

"Competitively!" he threw back over his shoulder and laughed wickedly. "I have four sisters!"

Chapter 12

The Jeep was a welcome sight, although our descent down the mountainside hadn't been nearly as difficult as the climb had been. But even before we'd loaded our gear, a truck bearing the sheriff's department logo pulled onto the area across the road, just a few feet ahead of the Jeep.

"Yikes!" Will muttered under his breath.

"Let me handle it. Just get us cold bottles of water, take a drink, and don't look like you're nervous about anything. We've done nothing wrong. He's probably calling in our license plates."

The deputy took a few moments to speak into something before he opened his door and stepped out.

I turned to face the deputy as he crossed and waited until he stopped in front of me. "Hello. I'm Sorrel Janes. How can I help you?"

He didn't return my smile. I couldn't see his eyes, which were almost hidden under the brim of the black felt cowboy hat, but his voice was brisk and short. "May I see your driver's license, please?"

I motioned to my backpack. "It's in there. In the front flap. Do you want me to—"

"Yes, ma'am. "

I opened the flap, pulled it out, and handed it to him. He looked at it and, still holding it, turned to Will. "I'll need yours as well."

Will reached in his back jeans pocket, pulled out his wallet, then handed his license over. Again, the officer read through it. Then he looked up. "Would you two wait right here for a moment?" Without waiting for an answer, he walked back to his truck, reached inside for a handheld mike, and spoke into it, eyeing us continually.

I opened my bottle of water and took a long, slow drink. It had been a tiring climb down, made more difficult because of the evasive maneuvers we'd taken to avoid being spotted.

The deputy hung up, walked back to us, and handed over the licenses. "Your purpose for parking the vehicle here?"

"Oh, I wondered what we'd done wrong!" I told him. "Is this a no parking area?" He didn't answer. Nor did he act congenial. "I'm a wildlife photographer. I own a gift shop in Saddle Gap where I sell prints."

He grunted and turned to Will. "And you?"

"NMSU student."

The deputy stared at him for a long moment. "Photographer?"

"Journalism."

"What story would you be chasing out here among these rocks and caves?" The deputy's tone held a derisive note that I hoped my young partner would ignore. But by the flush on his neck, I feared he wouldn't.

"I'm doing an internship this spring with the newspaper in Saddle Gap," he offered. "We're doing a story—"

"On this area as a weekend getaway spot. I'm taking the photos and Will is recording his reactions to use in the copy."

The deputy didn't warm up. "Why now? Long time to summer."

"Spring break is coming up late next month," I improvised. "The ranger said it would be a popular place for hikers then."

He grunted and turned once again to Will. "Did he mention rattlesnakes? They're coming out in the spring, shedding their skin and feeling cantankerous."

"He mentioned them. Said they were a consideration for spelunking just now as they often hibernate in the caves. I'll, of course, include that information in my feature."

"Where have you climbed?" Although he addressed us both, he seemed to focus on Will.

Will pointed in the direction of the cave. "Up there. But we decided to turn back. The rugged terrain seems a bit difficult for a family with school children. So we're going to explore some others we've noticed."

"Do we need a permit or something officer?" I asked ingenuously. "The ranger didn't mention that we'd needed a permit or anything."

"No permit needed, Ms. . . ."

"Janes. Sorrel Janes."

He nodded. "The thing is—this area isn't safe just now. Besides the snakes, vehicles left by the side of the road like this are being vandalized. You're lucky all of your tires are still here."

I turned to Will. "Did you get that? The ranger omitted that information. We'd better include it as a warning—"

"Wait—you don't need to put that in the newspaper. We don't want to scare people. I'll just relay the information to the ranger." The deputy smiled. "He'll appreciate it more if it comes from law enforcement."

Will pulled out a notepad. "We need to be as honest as possible, sir, so our readers—"

The officer held up his hand. His face had flushed and he spoke urgently. "Okay, I didn't want to share this, but the state police are closing down this area this week." He looked over his shoulder as if someone might be listening.

"Oh! Well, we'll leave right away." I smiled engagingly. "We'd planned to visit some other places anyway." I put out my hand and Will followed suit. The deputy shook our hands and then followed us as we stepped into the Jeep and closed the doors.

He remained standing there as I backed up, pulled out, turned around, and headed back toward our rental.

"So did you buy that story of his? He was lying through his teeth!" Will took a drink of his water.

"Cool your jets. What do you think he would have done had I argued with him?"

Will stared sullenly out his window. Clearly, he'd decided he'd been teamed with a coward.

I concentrated on the narrow, curving road for a bit and then observed, "Most likely, he would have invented some excuse to take us into the station—which would be miles away—and let us waste the rest of the day and half the night before releasing us, after either we were too tired to go on or the police had finished their investigation."

Will sputtered. "That could take days!"

"True. But they would have removed any evidence—and the body if they have one—and secured the cave. Had we seemed too determined, they would begin guarding that cave even more carefully . . . and likely be looking out for us."

Will didn't answer. I looked over and saw that he'd leaned back into his seat and closed his eyes. Within minutes, he was snoring. That was a good thing, I thought. In spite of his youth and his insistence on his physical stamina, Will looked exhausted.

When my phone buzzed, he didn't stir. "Hi, Reed," I said softly.

He sighed. "Sorrel, what were you—"

"My job."

The silence that followed almost made me think he had disconnected. Finally, he continued. "Trouble follows you—and then me since I'm stupid enough to—"

"Find me amazing? Cute? Talented?"

"Stubborn, nosy, interfering—"

"Thank you."

When next he spoke, his voice softened. "I should have known. A sorrel horse is always a challenge to train."

"My dad said you don't train a sorrel. You just love it and respect it enough to guide it."

Reed gave a laugh that sounded like a bark. "I'm sure your dad was smart, but he'd been charmed. The words 'train' and 'guide' do not fit in the same sentence with 'sorrel.'" He paused. "Where are you heading?"

"Back to the cabin."

"Why?"

"Not to make mad, passionate—"

"Sorrel! I don't have—"

"Okay. Rest. Eat. Regroup."

I heard a sigh on the other end. "I guess I'd be—"

"Welcome to join us." I told him where we were staying, in case he'd forgotten. "Can you get away?"

"Tempting. Wait . . . are you cooking?"

"No. Julia Child is sharing our cabin, and she—"

Reed burst out laughing. My lips twitched. A person could listen to Reed's laugh the rest of her life. Where had that thought—

"I don't know if I can. I'll let you know."

I drove along, thinking of scenarios for our trip back up the mountain, when Will asked, "So, are we eating with the enemy?"

Chapter 13

Will dozed while I maneuvered my Jeep down the narrow road. It gave me the opportunity to collect my thoughts, which weren't very clear. Usually, when I set off on a story, I either had an emotional pull for someone involved or for something which intrigued me. But this story, though promising intrigue, hadn't yet provided that emotional stimulus.

Unanswered questions floated through my brain: Who was the body found in the cave? Why had Reed been called for the task force to investigate? How had my photo appeared? Or had it? Was Randall Byrd simply manipulating me to get a story by suggesting that I'd been mentioned? And how much could I depend on my new partner, especially since I felt more motherly toward him than equal? Maternal wasn't a feeling I'd experienced before and—

"Penny for them . . . although with inflation maybe I should offer a quarter."

"You'd not be getting a bargain. Seems my mind is hopping all over the place with little direction or substance."

Will yawned and squinted down the road. "Are we still up for a midnight trek?"

"I haven't changed my mind."

"Well, with our dinner guest . . ." Will wiggled his eyebrows suggestively.

"I'm hoping your nap refreshed you. I doubt I need to say that the less you say around Reed about our adventures, the better."

I pulled into our narrow drive, stopped, and made eye contact with Will. He sighed. "You're no fun. I need some interviews—"

"An interview you can try," I interrupted. "Reed may or may not give you one. But the more you talk, the more he'll try to learn about our plans. So listen and keep mum or talk about school or something. And remember this: He's a master interrogator. It's why he's so successful in law enforcement."

I glanced at Will's red face. It was hard for me to remember that Will was still struggling with his ego, and so I quickly added as I got out of the car, "I know I'm saying what you already know. Sorry. I'm saying some of it to remind myself as well."

The flush left his face as he opened his door and gathered his belongings. When we unlocked our cottage door, he drawled, "Does he know how to whistle?" He ducked, grinning, as I swung my bag his direction. "My parents have the whole collection of Bogart and Bacall movies," he added, as he headed inside.

Once inside, Will immediately plopped onto the sofa, his backpack at his feet. "Speaking of whistles, I think I'll wet mine . . . when I can stand up." He unlaced his boots and pulled them off. His socks quickly followed.

"I think I'll hit the shower," I said. "Seems silly in a way since we're heading back out later, but I need to feel better if I'm doing battle with the stove." I headed toward the bedroom.

"Sure." Then Will called after my back, "Are you sure you don't want to go up to that little store place to eat?"

I ignored him while gathering clean clothes and walked into the bathroom. Standing under the hot shower and lathering shampoo into my hair, I felt revived. Different strategies for our next excursion up the mountainside began running through my mind. Our stop by the local sheriff's deputy might present a few obstacles. Had he been tipped off and been waiting for us? For sure, when the information hit the network, Reed had seen it. Even if the deputy bought our story, Reed would have been alerted. *Oh, well!* I thought. I'd told him our cover story, but he knew me too well by now to just accept it at face value.

"Leave some of that hot water for me," Will called.

"If I have to!" I hollered back. But I finished rinsing my hair quickly and turned off the shower.

When I emerged a few moments later, feeling human again in clean jeans and flannel shirt, the whole place was filled with wonderful smells. I followed my nose to the kitchen. Will stood at the stove stirring a skillet. "Hey, I thought—"

He looked around and grinned. "I was in Boy Scouts growing up. I learned a few emergency recipes for when there were no fast food places close . . . or I was rooming with a cook like you."

I pretended outrage. "A cook like me? You don't know what you're missing!"

"Well, I do!"

I whirled around. "Reed? When did you get here?"

"Just walked in the door," Will cut in. "I'm hitting the shower. By the time I get out, this stuff will be ready to dish up." He made a hasty retreat. "I'll be quick," he called over his shoulder. "I'm starved."

I walked into the bedroom, dumped my dirty hiking clothes in my basket, and reached for a brush. Reed followed me and closed the door after himself. "Sorrel?"

I hadn't realized how much I needed a hug just now, but Reed must have because he gathered me up into one and held me close. He finally released me reluctantly, then stepped away. "You'd better get that hair brushed and dried or you'll catch a cold."

I stepped back and started working through the tangles. Chris sat on the edge of the bed, watching me. His eyes darkened when I smiled at him.

"I guess you heard from the deputy?" I asked.

"Yep. I was relieved that you'd left the mountain."

"Is it something nasty?"

"Very."

I began working my hair into one long braid down my back while my mind searched for the right way to approach the subject. "I might as well tell you that Randall Byrd mentioned that my photo—"

"He had no business saying anything! Where does he get his info?" He got up, walked over to the tiny window, and stared out. I could almost feel the anger—or frustration—or both.

"He doesn't reveal his source, as I'm sure you know. I have no idea either . . . but by your reaction, it must be true."

"You know I can't . . ."

I tied off my braid and walked over to Reed. When he didn't turn around, I reached up and began gently massaging his tight shoulders. "I know you can't and I won't ask. What can you tell me?"

He didn't answer, but I could feel the tension easing. I continued. "Can you tell me, at least, if you have a homicide here?"

"Maybe." I knew that meant yes.

"And with the task force involved, I would guess the cartel is involved?" He didn't answer. "So the first thing that comes to mind is drugs, of course, as that's so common. The second is illegal immigration, another common factor. But I'm the wild card, so to speak."

His shoulders began to tense again, so Byrd must have had accurate information. "I think the major point of concern is not so much that my photo has come up, but whether my name is attached to it?."

He turned and hugged me close again. "Sorrel," he whispered, "I don't know whether to send you home or keep you close so I can hopefully keep an eye on you. But I can't answer your questions."

I pushed away to look him in the eye. "What are you calling me just now, Reed? Sorrel Janes? Or Staci Lee Jamison?"

I felt his muscles tense with the second name, and I knew. As a television crime reporter in Houston—in what I now referred to as my former life—that had been my name. When I left that life and came to Saddle Gap, I'd abandoned my public name, seeking privacy and a new life. Very few people would know that name.

"They've found me," I whispered. "About time, I guess."

"We're not sure. The name hasn't come up, but the photo was on the victim, so his captors may have seen it. Or he may have just been the victim of a drug deal gone wrong. We're still in the early stages of the investigation."

I felt a numbness spreading through me. "Does the task force connect the photo with me?"

"I'm not sure yet. But they will—and it won't take them long. You're a blonde in the photo, and the hairstyle is really different. But they'll connect it, I think."

"Do you think—?"

"Witness protection, I imagine."

He said it matter-of-factly. I pulled out of his arms, so angry I could hardly keep my voice to a rough whisper. "I won't start over again! This is my home! My shop! My friends! I ran once but I won't do it again!"

"What about your friends, Sorrel? Teri?"

"You?"

His voice dropped to a whisper. "I could start over, Sorrel, with you."

I couldn't breathe. When had I ever thought his blue eyes cold? "I don't know how to run anymore," I told him. "But I can give up my friends . . . and you . . . to keep you safe." And, for the first time ever, I pulled him into a kiss.

Somewhere in the background, a light tapping on the door pulled us back to the present. "Uh, guys, I hate to interrupt, but dinner is ready."

Chapter 14

"I'm dishing up your plates from the stove," Will said as we followed him into the small kitchen area.

"What is it?" I asked.

Will had picked up a piece of toasted bread and spooned meat and white sauce over it from a frying pan on the stove. "I'm not sure what it really is," he said. "Some names I've heard aren't very polite, so my mom called it beef on toast."

"It smells delicious." I carried mine over to the table where Will had set eating utensils and three small bowls of lettuce. "Didn't we buy salad dressing?"

"Beats me. You bought the stuff. If you bought lettuce . . ."

I was already rummaging in the tiny cupboard. "Here it is. It's ranch. I figured we'd both like that." I carried it to the table where the other two had already sat down. "Anyone want a bottle of water?" Both nodded, their mouths already filled with our mystery dish.

Mystery or not, we emptied our plates twice and didn't leave a bite to store in the refrigerator.

"This is the quietest meal I've had in a long time," I said as I watched the guys finish their last bites. "We were all ravenous."

"I need the recipe," Reed told Will. "Then the next time I invite a chatterbox to dinner," he said as he looked over at me, "I can eat in peace."

Will laughed.

"Guess this chatterbox will wash up." I gathered up the empty plates and carried them to the sink. Will excused himself to smoke, and Reed joined me once the door shut behind him. As he washed and I dried, he leaned close and whispered, "There will be a couple of guys guarding the cave. One of them is young and may be trigger happy."

"And I need to know this because?"

"Because I know you! But I can't know too much, so I can answer truthfully if I'm asked."

"Then I'm telling you now that I am going to bed when you leave."

"Good. A full moon is forecast, and a person would have a hard time not being seen, especially as the leaders of the team expect someone to try to snoop from the western side."

I paused then and asked innocently as I wiped the plate he'd just rinsed, "And we're discussing this because?"

He didn't answer right away. Instead, he concentrated a few moments on washing salad bowls and utensils. Then he glanced over his shoulder toward the door and leaned toward me as he set the frying pan into the soapy water. "In case you have some crazy idea," he murmured, "that I don't want to hear. There's no reason for anyone to be outdoors tonight. But I'm sure you wouldn't interfere in a police—"

"Am I interrupting anything?"

How long had Will been standing across the room?

"Yes!" I said, pretending irritation. "Come help put the last of these dishes away while I wipe the cooking utensils and the table. I know you slaved cooking, but this kitchen maid is ready to sit and put her feet up amid some civilized conversation. This cowboy has weird ideas about post dinner pleasantries." I shivered dramatically.

"We've been discussing rattlesnakes," Reed added smoothly. He ran water over the frying pan, handed it to me, and unplugged the drain. "Nasty critters sometimes. This time of year, they're like cranky hermits. Don't like to be disturbed."

Will snorted. "Women! They still tend to add drama to—"

I grabbed the still soapy dishcloth and threw it across the small room. It landed with a satisfying plop on Will's head. He gasped, grabbed it, and glared at me.

"You must be associating with the wrong kind of women," I said amid my giggles, "if you thought you could get away with those comments."

He raised his arm, but Reed intervened quickly. "Now, children, do you really want to mop up soapsuds tonight as well?"

Both of us shook our heads.

"Then let's play nicely." Reed took the dishcloth and draped it on the sink edge.

"Yes, Dad," I said.

"Well, this dad needs his sleep." Reed stretched out his hand to Will. "It was a pleasure eating your cooking. If you haven't eaten Sorrel's yet—"

"Careful, Dad!"

"You're in for a real experience," he finished quickly and ducked as I pretended to swing at him. Will was still laughing as we walked to the door.

I walked Reed to the truck amid the chuckles. He reached for my hand and whispered, "We may be better off to act like this is just a romantic visit. The less the kid knows, the better." He opened the truck door and, in the light of the open door, pulled me close and kissed me. "That should dispel some of his curiosity," he whispered, still holding tightly. "Everything in that cave will have been removed, Sorrel. I know you. You're determined to go look for yourself, and I suspect you've planned it for tonight. If you do something that crazy, be careful in that cave. Better still, be careful about being seen at all. I don't think law enforcement will be the only ones watching it."

"I will."

He sighed. "Sorrel Janes, how am I ever going to get a night's sleep with you—"

"Reed, I'm a big girl."

"I know. That's part of the problem here." He hugged me close before he released me. I stepped back so he could get inside the truck. He started the engine and whispered, "Be careful, Sorrel." And then, "I could get used to these pretend romantic visits, you know."

I watched the taillights disappear before I headed back inside. Will had finished wiping down the sink and counter and put the dishes in the cupboards. "Thanks, Will," I said. Before he could speak, I headed into the bathroom.

One look in the mirror confirmed it. I had rosy cheeks and a sparkle in my eyes. Reed always did this—whether from anger, laughter, or frustration. John had said that we created sparks. I could hear his voice even now:

That's why, in the generations past, they referred to it as sparking, Sorrel.

Sparking? I'd laughed.

Yep. Sparking was when a young man and young woman tried to pretend they weren't falling in love and fought so hard they caused sparks to fly. I did some of that myself.

I hadn't noticed the tears running down my cheeks until some dripped onto my hand. In my thirty-three years, I'd lost so many people in my life—Mom, Dad, Kevin. But John still brought tears. He'd been my mentor, my friend, my soulmate. "What should I do just now?" I whispered to him. "I don't want to put this young guy in harm's way. I hope you're watching over somewhere, and if I make one of my crazy—just pinch me!"

"Sorrel? Are you okay?"

I wiped my face again. "Just washing my face," I answered, opening the door. "Sorry. I forgot we only have one bathroom. I'm being a girl, I guess."

"No problem. I just thought I heard someone talking, and I thought Reed had left. Anyway, I figured we needed to talk about our strategy and plans for tonight."

I walked over to the armchair and sat down. Will sat on edge of the small sofa. "Did Reed tell you anything about—"

"No," I said quickly. "He's law enforcement through and through. He's sworn not to share that sort of information with us press people."

Will bought my lie. "Okay," he said, "did you glean anything from him during the necking out there?"

I pretended shock. "Necking?"

His laugh was contagious. When I sobered up, I said, "Well, he did mention he wasn't on tonight. So that means they have people who are. He added that he was glad he was no longer a grunt, so that means—"

"We're not dealing with a lot of experience."

"True. Still, when I asked why they'd leave anyone up there, he said they weren't finished with the scene. But more, they weren't sure if the criminals were either."

"Caution necessary in both directions."

"So we need to make our plans."

Will reached beside the sofa and picked up a plastic bag. "Glad I packed this," he said as he pulled out a small spray can. "Dad and I use this when we're deer hunting. You smear it on your face and hands and it disguises your smell as well as your face." He sprayed some on his hands and began rubbing it on the backs.

"Whew! That stinks! And just after my bath!"

He continued to cover his face then passed it on to me. "Added incentive not to get caught," he said. "Imagine your lawman seeing his glamorous photographer now!"

I shook my fist at him, then sighed. "Okay, let's get our strategy straight. We need to travel light so we can move quickly. I'll smear while you talk."

"Right. And we also need to be careful about what we have on us—in case we're detained."

It wasn't a thought I welcomed, but one I knew was important. My partner wasn't as green as I'd feared.

Chapter 15

I drove slower now to avoid the animals that darted across the narrow road while Will checked phone messages and emails. A full moon had been forecast; but at the moment, a thin blanket of clouds hovered just above us, partially obscuring all but the nearby landscape. The opening lines from my dad's favorite ghost stories echoed in my memory: *It was a cold winter night! Low, scraggly clouds hugged the treetops, and night critters peeked out from the shadows.*

"What did you say?" Will asked.

"Nothing . . . did I?"

"Something about shadows."

I repeated the lines. "My dad always started scary stories with those lines. We'd be sitting around the campfire, full of hot dogs and burnt marshmallows—just us kids. The moms were already in their tents or campers by then. Dad's voice would be just above a whisper, and we'd lean close enough to hear every word—and to scorch ourselves if we weren't careful. Every story started that same way."

"He must have been quite the storyteller. My dad wouldn't be sitting around a campfire—too far from the television. His idea of camping out is a tent for the kids in the back yard."

"We didn't go often—late fall, which was colder than winter is here, and early spring when we checked on newborn calves. Neighboring ranchers helped each other out. Ours was the only one where Dad insisted on bringing the families. Those years he spent in the military made him appreciate family more, I guess."

"Were you the only child?"

"Sort of." I slowed just in time for a deer to run across the road in front of us. "He had been married just out of high school and had a son very soon afterward. The marriage didn't last long, and the relationship wasn't good. His ex-wife never followed the visitation set by the court. I think Dad just got tired of arguing and stopped. But he paid the child support."

"So you never saw your brother?"

"Oh, he came occasionally. But it was at odd times when his mom had a new husband or boyfriend and didn't want him around. That's what he told me, anyway. But we never bonded. He was angry and probably jealous of me. He certainly resented me."

"Where is he now?"

"I don't know for sure. He and I weren't close. He was four or five years older, so I was a bratty kid to him. And he resented the fact, I think, that I had Dad all the time. Dad tried—and so did Mom. But he really sassed her when Dad wasn't around." I slowed and squinted to the left. "Isn't that where we turn?"

Will leaned forward and peered out the windshield. "No. Remember? We thought it was—"

"And had to turn around."

We laughed together. Most of the few cabins and trailer houses looked like they'd been closed for the winter. Some looked abandoned completely. But at this moment—near eleven o'clock at night—they all looked alike.

"Hey!" Will said, pointing to the left. "There's the sign! We're past where we parked this morning. But you wanted to go west, so we could just drive down another couple of miles—"

"That's the road!" I slowed and turned. "I meant to bring this up earlier, but I don't know if it's wise to leave the Jeep alongside the road like we did earlier. Since the deputy has already called the plates and description in, we'd just be asking for trouble."

"What about the ranger station?"

"That's not too wise either. They might drive by there and wonder where we were parked there—thinking maybe something had happened—or wake the ranger—"

"Trouble," Will sighed.

The road twisted around another old trailer and I slowed. "I think I know what we should do!"

Will jumped. "About?"'

I pulled into the driveway—if you could call the collection of rocks, gravel, and mud a driveway. "We can leave it here!" I pulled up next to the mobile home and stopped. "See those boarded windows? They've winterized it to keep people out."

"Nah! This is an abandoned mobile home, Sorrel. No one would be interested in breaking in."

I let the tires roll forward a few feet. "See that old shack back there?"

Will squinted. "Yeah. Another abandoned shack."

"A garage." I crept forward a bit. When the lights hit the building, it didn't look like a shack—just a boarded-up, locked building. "There's a four-wheeler in there. Betcha!" I put the gear in park and turned off the lights and motor.

"What are you doing? Are you crazy?"

"No, just curious." I grabbed a flashlight and opened the door. "You coming?"

Will didn't answer, so I shut my door and started walking. I'd only taken a few steps when I heard his door open and saw the beam of another light switched on behind me. He caught up with me just as I reached the building.

The door had a combination lock. I gave my flashlight to Will to hold, aiming it so that the beam centered on the lock.

"If you break it, someone will notice right away," he said.

I started spinning the lock, stopping at various numbers.

Will laughed. "Do you know what the chances are of figuring out a combination lock? Not to mention that we'll still be here at daylight—"

Click! The lock fell open and I slid it out of the hasp. "Let's just look inside," I said, pulling on the handle of the heavy door.

Will stepped aside as it began to open, shining the light inside. "I can't believe it!" he said, as the light sliced across a four-wheeler. Will walked up to the vehicle, his light moving inside, outside, and all over it. "This beauty is even painted in camouflage."

I gazed at the mud-smeared, dented, dirty vehicle. "Beauty truly must be in the eye of the . . . " I stopped just in time to avoid hurting Will's feelings. When he didn't reply, I turned so I could see his face. He wasn't even listening to me. Instead, Will was "in love"—with a nasty, old four-wheeler!

"I always wanted one of these," he whispered, moving close enough to run his hand over the dirty fender nearest him.

"Well, then, let's look for the key and take a ride. We can park this thing almost anywhere and it won't look as obvious as the Jeep."

Something scurried past Will and he jumped a little, startled. "I said I always wanted one," he said. "I didn't say I always wanted to be a felon."

"Where's your sense of adventure, Will?" I moved toward the vehicle. "I bet they hide it under the bumper . . . or maybe under a seat." I ran my hand along the bumper then moved to open the driver's door. "Shine the light this way."

"Let's get out of here, Sorrel."

"Found it!" I held up a key on an old chain. "Do you want to start it up and drive it outside?" I let the key dangle in the light of his flashlight. I could see the indecision in his eyes and—almost—allowed myself to feel a touch of guilt. But just before I was about to give in and relieve that guilt, Will snatched the key from my hand.

"If they catch us," he said, climbing into the driver's seat, "I'm telling them you threatened me to do this." When the motor started up, he asked, "Is there anything in the way?"

"Besides the Jeep? Give me a second and I'll move it." I hoped Will heard me, because at this moment his face looked like a kid's on Christmas morning.

As I started toward the door, I heard it. "Lights off, Will! Truck!"

I ran to the heavy door and started pulling it shut, but I could only move it about twelve inches.

"Hurry!" Will called.

"Help me! It's stuck!"

The truck had either stopped or slowed. I couldn't hear the whir of the tires. Will's hand brushed me as he caught the door casing and gave it a mighty shove. "Duck!"

We both ducked, but the truck was already backing out. A moment later, it headed down the road—or maybe back the way it had come. I couldn't see. Will let out a big sigh, and I felt myself do the same.

"Ready to try again?" I asked.

"I guess. We're already guilty of breaking and entering."

After Will drove the four-wheeler out, I pulled the Jeep inside, removed our gear, and closed the outside doors. I quickly refitted the combination lock into the hasp and—

"Don't—" Will yelled.

"Don't what?" I snapped the lock shut, walked to the passenger side, put our gear in the basketlike trunk, climbed in, and glanced over to Will. "Ready?"

"Don't you realize what you've done?" Will's voice rose and he started making choking noises.

"Are you all right?"

Will stared at me. "You locked the door! We can't get back in!"

"Oh, my . . . I guess I'll have to work on it like I did before." I fastened the seat belt. "I assume you're driving this buggy and I'm navigating?"

Will slammed his hand on the wheel, ground the gear into place, and pulled out. "Where to?" he muttered.

I was glad I hadn't given in to my earlier guilty conscience. Had I told Will who had given me the combination to this machine—and the directions—well, it was a good thing I hadn't told him. Will was in that odd stage of man/boy. At times, he was wiser and smarter than I thought. But if he was interrogated, he would tell all. And that would have horrible consequences. His current outrage about my actions and his concern about them might work to our advantage.

"Have you ever driven one of these before?" I asked as we sped down the road, my eyes scouring the sides for critters I hoped we'd miss.

Will didn't answer right away. I hadn't figured him for a pouter. "Once when I was young, we stopped at a dealer. Unfortunately, my mom was on the test ride with Dad and me." He glared at me. "You know how moms—females—are."

I did. In fact, I knew—in that moment—that being a mom might just not be a wise choice for me to make in the future. I held my breath as we narrowly missed some critter. "You'll have to slow down now," I said. "We need to look for a place to hide this thing while we continue our journey."

I missed most of what Will muttered, but what I heard, well, it wasn't pretty.

He swerved into a spot between a pair of large trees and stopped. I stepped out and walked a few feet away, looking back. "This might work," I told him. "Come have a look."

Will turned off the engine and joined me. "We probably shouldn't leave it right here," he finally said, "but it looks like we could put it in that brushy area over there." He walked in the direction he'd pointed and called back. "Hey, there's a creek here! Just a trickle, but still a creek."

When I joined him, his good nature had returned. "Looks like a small grouping of trees over there." I pointed my flashlight in that direction and squinted. "Wonder if this wasn't some camp or home place that someone abandoned."

"Could be. I could drive it back there and it should be protected from the road." Will had fallen in with my plan.

"Sounds good. I'll help guide you with my flashlight."

A half hour later, we stepped away and looked back at our handiwork. Will pulled out his GPS. "I'll just drop a pin," he said, "in case we get disoriented and forget our way back."

I was relieved that his good nature had returned, along with his growing excitement and sense of adventure. I shivered. "I'm ready to start climbing and warm up!"

Will chuckled. "That cold wind isn't my idea of warming up."

"Mine either. You leading?" Then I added quickly, "Just don't charge off and leave me straggling behind."

Will's laugh sent a chill up my spine. It was eerily reminiscent of the laugh in that recent dream I'd had that still plagued me. *Find the weeping child*, the voice had whispered, *and change the tears to laughter.*

Chapter 16

"I think I could be the poster girl for an ice maiden!" I muttered. I'd dressed warmly, but the wind on this hillside felt like it had blown in straight from the North Pole. But Will never faltered, climbing steadily through the trees along the ridgeline toward the large cave that had been the focus of law enforcement earlier in the day.

There were actually three caves along the peaks, a smaller one on each side of a large one. Each was separated from the other by a wooded ridgeline. We'd driven the four-wheeler past the first ridgeline where we'd climbed earlier. Coming in from the west—we hoped—would give us a better view of the activity below.

But so far, we hadn't seen or heard the deputies Reed had mentioned might be guarding the caves, and it looked like most of the activity above us had ceased. We had noticed a couple of official vehicles and two or three people standing around along the road when we'd driven past earlier.

"If they stop us," Will had whispered, "I'll show my press pass. Then we'll have to give a different story." His different story involved our being a couple. Personally, I wasn't too happy about my role as a cougar with a young lover, so I was relieved that they waved us on when Will started to slow the four-wheeler.

I judged a half hour had passed when Will looked back and motioned toward a tree. He dropped his backpack by the trunk and walked on past and out of sight. I walked over, dropped my own pack, and looked back down at the path we'd just climbed. Whew! It was steeper than I'd thought!

I blew into my gloves and wiggled my fingers. If I sat down for a moment, I knew it would be harder for me to get up and move again—but I was tempted. Instead, I did some stretching exercises to relax my tight thigh muscles.

"Aside from the cold, our climb hasn't been nearly as bad as it was this morning." Will laughed when I jumped. "What's the matter? Did I spook you?"

"Not spooked. Startled. I just didn't hear you approach."

He grunted but chose not to argue. "I don't think they will see us up here with all of these trees."

"True. Today they could see a spot of color or the sun glancing off something. But even with the moon, it's dark tonight in these trees."

"So that's good." Will took a long drink of water. "Piece of cake."

"Of course, we can't see anyone else either."

"Who would be up here?"

"Maybe the ones who did whatever was done in that cave?" I found my own bottle of water and drank, stamping my feet to keep them from getting colder. "From the activity earlier, I imagine it was a murder, but we don't know anything else. And with the number and variety of law enforcement here today, I suspect it was either someone important or there were indications of other illegal activities."

"That's why I thought we should have interviewed people today," Will complained.

"Then we would have been on their radar. I wanted to see the layout first. There were other press people here, and we would have been given the same canned story—still probably will be. But with our cover story and waiting to talk to unofficial types, like these guys who are just guarding the scene, we may get something more. You remember that our cover story is a family travel piece—at least it will be tomorrow. If we run into someone tonight, we'll have to use your alternate cover." I inwardly shuddered.

Will laughed. "I saw that shudder." He pulled a strip of beef jerky out of his pocket and bit a piece off. "Do you need to . . . you know . . ."

This time I laughed. "Not now. I'm ready to go when you are."

By the time we arrived at the edge of the cave, both of us were ready to stop again. "The good news is—," Will wheezed.

"It will be easier going down."

"Are all cougars this irritating?" he wondered aloud.

I ignored him and stared up at the cave. From this angle, it looked more like a wash out or a dome. "It's just been scooped out of the rock," I murmured. "I doubt it's very deep."

"I like that term," Will said, moving over beside me and staring up. "Scooped. What do you think happened up there?"

"Most likely someone was murdered, but the story must be why it happened or who was murdered or how it happened."

"You keep mentioning murder. Someone could have hidden a stash of drugs or guns or something like that."

"True." I looked down toward the road. I thought I saw a light beside the road, like someone walking. "Do you see that?"

"Yeah. It must be the guard."

"Wouldn't he be up here?" I squinted toward the dark hole, visible in the moonlight. Had the person—persons—walked up like we had? I doubted it. They would have probably come from above, climbed around to the top of the cave's mouth and dropped a rope over.

"Maybe," Will said when I told him my theory. "Getting into it from this side would take a ladder—a big ladder—that they'd have to haul. It certainly would have taken a gang of people. "

I felt a shiver crawl up my spine. "Someone step on your mama's grave?" I looked around then at Will. Didn't he hear? No. Will continued to stare up at the cave. Great! Now I was hearing voices!

"Don't you remember?" I asked. "We saw a rope ladder earlier today. Maybe they used that. But I guess that could have been put there by law enforcement just as easily."

I reached out and squeezed Will's elbow through his thick jacket and adopted my best drawl. "So now that we've gotten our closer look . . . and experienced the nuances . . . and frozen our assets . . . ready to get out of here?"

He didn't answer right away. When he spoke, he leaned toward me as if making sure no one could overhear. "Something bad happened here. I can feel it."

Suddenly, I grabbed his arm. "I see movement . . . up by the mouth of the cave," I whispered.

We froze, listening and watching. There it was again—just a faint rustle. Then a faint gleam of light bounced off the rocky surface. "Maybe a guard," Will whispered in my ear.

"I don't think so. Why so furtive?" I whispered. We watched the light move away from us, disappearing around the opposite side. "Whoever it is must have come from above." Then I knew. "They've been inside."

"How? This place has been crawling with law enforcement. Surely nothing is left."

"They know their way around, Will. Whatever they came back to retrieve was important to them. But it would have to be something small."

We listened and watched for another ten minutes or so but detected no further movement near the cave.

Finally, I touched Will's shoulder. "I'll lead us back down."

The hardest part about descending was trying not to slide. When we reached our four-wheeler, my calf muscles, already sore from the same exercise yesterday, reminded me that I'd not been running as much lately. Getting the store ready for Valentine's Day had overridden my routine. Now I was paying for slacking on my exercise.

Will obviously felt the same. He'd wheezed more than usual tonight. I told him so as we moved on. "Those cigarettes," I told him at one point when I had to wait for him. He immediately reached for a cigarette then stuffed some tobacco substitute gum into his mouth instead.

"Cougars!" he complained around the wad of gum.

Before we started down, we'd discussed whether or not we should just spread sleeping bags and wait until morning to leave. If law enforcement were guarding the area, they would surely hear the motor.

"I don't know about you," I told Will, "but this wind is cold and we have warm beds waiting!"

So we formed another plan. "Follow my lead," I told Will, and we climbed onto the machine. I wondered if I'd forever be bowlegged after tonight. I might never get off this thing.

The four-wheeler sounded louder than ever in the dark night. When we pulled onto the narrow paved road, we stayed on the dirt edge and headed back, headlights gleaming. "Looks like the guards for the site have arrived. Were they on unofficial dinner break before? Lazy suckers sitting in the car instead of patrolling," Will muttered when we neared a couple of vehicles. "Guess they are patrolling from the road."

We slowed as a security guard stepped forward. Will slowed and stopped.

The guard made a show of shining his light into our faces and over the four-wheeler. "What are you folks up to? It's kinda late to be four-wheelin'. Hard to miss critters on the road."

Will gave an exaggerated sigh and shrugged his shoulder in my direction. "She's changed her mind about camping."

"Camping? This time of year?" The guard looked skeptical at best. "You two aren't poaching are you?" He stepped back and spoke into his shoulder mike. "Would you please shut off the engine and step off?" he asked.

I climbed off first and walked over to the guard. Will turned off the motor and followed. He began complaining before he reached us. "She insisted on coming along, so my buddies backed out!" he complained. "But right away she began complaining about everything! When we started to put down the sleeping bag, she had to make sure nothing was under it. Then she thought she heard animals." He leaned toward the deputy and lowered his voice conspiratorially, "Wolves! And bears!"

He'd captured his audience, from the chuckles. Another guard, thinner and younger, arrived. "Excuse me a moment," our first guard told us. "Wait here." He strolled over to his partner and, from the snickers that followed, was relating Will's story.

I pulled my stocking cap further down and whispered to Will, "Don't let them get too close a look at you. And get ready to fly when they let us go."

When the two came back, our first guard introduced both of them and told us we could go. "But be careful in that thing. Critters are out. Do you have far to go?"

"Nah," Will assured them. He leaned forward and whispered something.

We could hear their laughter as we drove off. "Don't tell me," I muttered to Will. "I'm too cold to kill you right now, and you might wreck this thing."

I could feel his back shaking. I shook too but not from laughter. Something ugly had happened up in that cave. The aura had drifted toward us, and I prayed it wouldn't affect us.

Chapter 17

"You were so caught up in the role you created that you forgot to pump the guards," I complained.

We were once more at our ramshackle barn. In spite of the moon high above, the trees overhanging obscured most of the light. Will ignored me, climbed off, and flashed his light off to the left of the barn. "I thought I'd seen it!"

"What?"

"An outhouse. Do you want to go first? Oh, wait! You'll have hysterics about critters or something." He waited expectantly.

I climbed off the four-wheeler and stretched my legs before answering. "Gosh! Darn! I hope there aren't any spiders!" I squealed, exaggerating my squeamishness as much as possible.

"Okay. Maybe I was a little caught up in the role."

"You think? Yes, I'll go first. And then I'll work on that combination lock."

Will groaned. "I forgot about that! If we can't find a bolt cutter, we might as well find a place to sleep!"

I turned on my flashlight and marched off toward the outhouse without answering him. He deserved to worry a little after that chauvinistic attitude he'd enjoyed with the watchmen back at the site.

I wasn't a novice to outhouses, but I'd never admit they were my favorite place. This one emitted a foul smell even before I opened the door. The hinges groaned but the door opened easily enough. I moved my light up, down, and in the corners before stepping inside and was pleasantly surprised. True, it smelled; but I didn't see spider webs or signs of other critters. And a plastic container held hand sanitizer and paper.

While Will visited the facility, I quickly opened the lock and began stowing our backpacks into the back of the Jeep. He reappeared as I was backing it out. I almost felt guilty at his relieved grin. He made short work of returning the four-wheeler to the barn and locking up.

I turned onto the road seconds before we met an official vehicle. "We cut it a bit close," I murmured. "Would you check to see if the thermos I filled with hot coffee—and forgot to take with us last night—is still warm?"

It was. I preferred hot but warm would do for now. Will rummaged around and found a couple of granola bars as well. "A feast!" he crowed, happily unwrapping both and munching after I'd waved mine away.

"Now, did you learn anything while I was lounging on that uncomfortable four-wheeler pretending to be a cougar?" I slowed for another sharp turn and pulled right a bit as another vehicle zoomed by.

Will's mouth was stuffed with granola bar. He finally swallowed, followed up with coffee, and answered. "I asked the dumber one why they were guarding the cave when the body had already been removed."

"Good job," I murmured. "So they had a body."

"I went on about how dumb hikers weren't prepared to survive the elements, etc. And I threw in a complaint about the expense to taxpayers for stupidity but that it seemed ridiculous to guard the cave. Were they thinking more hikers were there . . . or coming?" Will was proud of himself, and no matter how impatient I might be, he was going to tell the story his own way.

"Did he buy it?"

"I think so. He started to say that it wasn't dumb hikers; but when the other guy came up and interrupted, he clammed up."

"Did he mention his boss's name or anything about a press conference?"

"Nope. In fact, I doubt either of them knows much more than what he shared. These guys aren't eating from the top of the tree."

I hid a giggle at Will's characterization of the two officers. "Well, we can check on the web when we get back to the cabin and see if anything has hit the news."

"I can't wait to hit the bed."

"When does Mr. Byrd expect the travel article?" I asked.

"I figured I'd get that out to him this evening."

"Okay. That will give me time to look through the photos."

Neither of us wanted food when we got back to our cabin. Will smoked a cigarette, then staggered inside and fell on his bed fully clothed. I took a very brief shower and checked phone messages before climbing in bed a half hour later.

I jerked awake a few hours later to the low murmur of voices. I easily recognized the deeper one. I rolled out, pulled on jeans and a tee shirt, bunched my hair into a ponytail, and stepped out.

"Oh, hi!" Reed looked a bit more rested than I felt, but it hadn't improved his disposition, judging from the icy blue eyes.

"Would you be interested in coffee?" I asked.

"Not me," Will mumbled.

"Actually, I wondered if you'd like to go with me up to the store and eat lunch," Reed answered.

"Uh—"

"You look fine."

Right. "Well, let me put on some shoes at least. I doubt they let barefoot customers in an eating establishment." I didn't even see a trace of a smile from either man. It didn't promise to be an entertaining meal.

I walked into the bedroom and put on socks and sneakers. Then I excused myself to the bathroom, brushed my teeth, and smoothed face cream onto the scratches I'd hardly noticed last night. With a final touch of defiance, I added lip gloss and deodorant.

When I opened the door, Reed was sitting at the small table. Will had fallen back into his bed, his snores filling the otherwise quiet room. I slipped into a jacket, grabbed my camera bag/purse, and crooked my finger for Reed to follow.

"Mine or yours?" I asked when we got outside.

He quirked an eyebrow at me. I walked over to his truck and reached for the handle, but his big hand pulled it open before I could. Once I'd settled in, Reed walked around to his side and hopped in. He started to reach toward the keys but then turned to me and pulled me into a hug. "Glad you're all in one piece," he whispered before he released me.

I told him about our evening adventures as he drove up to the small restaurant behind the store. He was still chuckling about the cougar story when we parked and stepped out into the cold air. Too late I warned him, "And that is classified information!"

He ushered me through the store to the back. "It smells great in here!" he said.

As grumpy as I felt, I couldn't argue about that. The few tables were full, so we gave our order and prepared to wait. "Here, you two sit right here," a man in work clothes said, standing up.

"Oh, don't—"

"My lunch break is up. I'm just sitting here gossiping anyway," he insisted, and stepped back for me to sit at the small table. Reed thanked him, but he waved good-naturedly and said something in Reed's ear.

"What did he say?" I asked after the waitress had set two glasses of iced tea in front of us.

"Nothing," Reed said.

I gave him my I-don't-believe-you look, took a long drink from the big glass of tea, and glanced around at the other diners. It was an interesting mix of locals and birders. "I would think it would be a little late for birds," I told Reed.

"Water birds maybe," someone from the next table answered me. "But we're not on the water here. The best season is just ahead."

The voice belonged to a retired school teacher who launched into an interesting discussion of the local birds. His food arrived and he apologized before biting into his sandwich. After swallowing, he continued. "But I see you're a photographer. I'm sure you've researched it. Is this your first trip?"

I nodded.

"It's my fifth," he said. "I'm not sorry to miss the Vermont winter, especially since my sons and grandkids have moved to California. And I must admit, this area is addictive after a while."

He continued to eat and we chatted until our cheeseburgers arrived. Then he finished his last swallow of tea, stood, shook hands with Reed, and left.

Neither of us talked much after that for several minutes. I finally pushed the last part of the huge cheeseburger away reluctantly. "My dad would say I'm eating like a field hand," I joked.

Reed smiled. "You could ask for a carry-out box."

I dipped a homemade French fry into a puddle of ketch-up and popped it into my mouth. "I think I'll propose to the cook," I said.

I heard a hearty laugh behind me. "She's already taken," a skinny, bald-headed man told me. "I found her first."

I met Reed's eyes. We rose, nodded to our fellow diners, and walked out the side door onto a tiny patio. The trees let very little sunlight through and I shivered.

"Let's talk in the car," he said.

"I won't argue with that."

Reed made an imaginary mark in the air.

"Or with you—right now!"

Once settled, Reed pulled out and drove down the small road that ran through Portal, what there was of it. "I presume your excursion was without incident?" he asked.

"Unremarkable."

"The guards reported a couple of campers. Nothing more."

He passed the last residence, pulled off into a birder's scenic viewing area, and turned off the truck. "The crime scene is still being watched, but the focus has moved on," he said.

"I figured as much."

"Did you see anyone out there?"

"Not besides the guards." I focused on the horizon. "But we weren't in the caves. Will thought we were just researching the area with a travel article in view. I doubt he'll recommend night hiking for his readers!"

"Did you fill him in on the four-wheeler?"

I laughed. "The combination lock blew his mind. I decided not to share any more information."

He laughed. "He may decide he needs a fulltime cougar!" Then he sobered. "Sorrel—"

"I know . . . but I've been thinking about things. The fact that my stage photo—my news anchor photo—was found and not one of Sorrel Janes . . . it could be insignificant. I left that life behind nearly two years year ago. Maybe it was just a photo that looked like me. Besides, I doubt anyone even remembers me!"

"It was a newspaper clipping with a photo."

I turned and grabbed his elbow. He stared ahead without looking at me. Finally, he said, "It was an old one. The station had just hired you, and this was the first interview."

"That's years old!"

"Creased and worn. Like it had been carried in a wallet or pocket."

"Any writing?"

"Just a faded ink underlining beneath your name."

"Where did they find it?"

He stared off in the distance. "In a pocket," he finally whispered.

I waited but he didn't continue. "Of the victim?" I probed.

He nodded.

"This is weird! Maybe he was one of those, you know, celebrity stalkers." I stared intently at him. "I've stayed out of the public eye and moved and changed my name. There's no need to think this murder has anything to do with me." My voice was questioning more than stating my conclusion.

"You're probably right. So what are your plans?"

I slipped my hand into his. "I expect we'll head on back to Saddle Gap. I have enough photos for Will's travel story. He plans to check with law enforcement about the crime as well, but I won't be in on that. I've cautioned him to take a casual 'Hey! What's going on?' kind of approach."

Reed raised our clasped hands to his mouth and kissed mine. "I'll be relieved to have you home," he said.

"Which raises the question—when are you coming home?"

"I have a bit to finish up here first." He slowly pulled his hand loose and started up the truck. "Time to get back to work."

We kept our conversation to personal things on the way back to my cabin: his plans for the ranch house renovation, Teri and Jose's new baby, my February store event.

It wasn't until we pulled up to the cottage and I reached for the door handle that it struck me. I turned toward Reed. "You never said how this guy died."

He leaned over, pecked me on the cheek, got out, and walked around to open my door. I stepped out but held onto his hand. "Reed?"

He pulled his hand from mine, closed the door, and turned to walk around the front of the truck.

"Christopher Reed!" I didn't stamp my foot but I felt like it.

Without looking back at me, he said, "Rattlesnakes."

I raced after him and caught his arm as he stepped into the driver's seat. "What?"

"Rattlesnakes," he said, his back turned away from me.

"That's weird. Do you think he accidentally stepped into—"

"His hands were tied. There were several crates. I couldn't count the number of bites." He climbed into the truck and closed the door. "Go home, Sorrel," he said, staring hard at me. He started the truck and drove off without a backward look.

Chapter 18

The image Chris's words had created settled into my brain as I stood at the door watching his truck pull away. The terror the man in the cave must have felt with the snakes—as well as the pain as each set of fangs sank into him—chilled my very soul.

"What did you do to make such enemies?" I whispered. My experience with cruel crime scenes made me want to agree with Reed. It could have been the cartel or a deal gone bad, but something about it felt more personal.

The door behind me opened and I jumped. "Aren't you coming inside?" Will asked.

I whirled around, a short remark on my lips, and then stopped. Instead, a smile curled as I took in Will's appearance: his hair sticking up in the air and a ratty sweatshirt hanging low over superhero boxers. "Is it safe?"

He grimaced. "Well, I'm not leaping tall buildings, but I will get cleaned up. Then I'll fix breakfast." He backed out of the doorway so I could enter.

"Not for me. I've eaten. Why don't you clean up and I'll fix you some breakfast?" Will nodded and gathered up clean clothes.

I put coffee on to perk, four sausages into the microwave, and toast in the toaster. I'd just set a plate and eating utensils on the small table when my phone rang.

"Sorrel?"

"Jose? Is Teri okay?"

"Great! In fact, over the moon. We should have a baby soon—starting to drop. But the doctor put her on bedrest."

"Oh, I see."

"She wanted me to tell you that the lady who has been helping finish the store for the sale has offered to fill in for her when you return—whenever that is. How's it going?"

I spent a few minutes filling him in on the tourism article we were completing, asked about the boys, and dodged the subject of Chris Reed.

"How are my kitties?" I asked before we hung up. Jose laughed and muttered something about spoiled beasts.

I'd forgotten about the toast. It was too cold to melt butter, so I spread peanut butter on it instead and put two more slices in. Will emerged in a cloud of steam just as it popped up. I poured two cups of coffee, set one down beside the peanut butter toast and sipped from the other. "Sausages in the microwave," I told him. I added the fresh toast to his plate.

Will devoured everything and washed it down with coffee in record time. Finally, he looked across at me and asked, "So, what's our plan today?"

"What did you have in mind?"

"I'd like to make another trip to our cave and see if we can sniff out any details of what happened there," he said. "But we also need to look at these other two camping areas. What do you think?"

"How about an interview with some of the birders?" I suggested. "They would likely have a different slant to add to the article. Did you send it in?"

"Nope. I called the paper and said I'd bring it in when we return." He glanced at his watch. "How about we go to the cave area and sniff around first?"

I nodded. "Then visit the other two areas and end up at the store? They seem to gather there. But we may be too late to catch anyone if we don't hurry."

We could still see the crime tape as we neared the cave a half hour later, but everyone seemed to have left except for a couple of guys sitting in a car with a sheriff's department logo. Both were typing into their cellphones until we pulled in behind them, stopped, and opened our doors.

The older guy on the passenger side immediately opened his door and stepped out. "May I help you?"

Will showed him his press card. "I'm here for the newspaper in Saddle Gap, New Mexico," he said.

"Sorry, the press releases can be picked up in Portal . . . at the store."

"Oh," I interrupted, "we're here to do a travel article about the area. We came by a couple of days ago, but my photos weren't very good. I thought I'd just climb up there a bit—"

"Sorry again." He didn't sound sorry, and I didn't like his smirk as he took a few seconds to let his eyes rove over me suggestively. "This area is closed to civilian traffic just now."

"What happened?" Will sounded genuinely surprised.

"Someone—", the younger guy began, but his partner coughed loudly and he stopped.

"Our orders are to keep people out for now until the extermination crew arrives," the partner explained. "There's a report of snakes in the area."

"Snakes?" Will looked from one to the other. "Well, I thought that was a known fact. I mean, this is, after all, wilderness. Surely an extermination crew doesn't expect to kill all of the snakes—"

The older guy moved closer to Will. "Our orders are to keep people out. So you need to take your cameras and . . . her . . . and check in at the store. They'll tell you when the area will be open again."

"No problem," I told him. "Come on, Will." I touched his arm and turned toward the Jeep.

"Hey, wait!"

I looked back. The younger guy seemed mesmerized by my face. "Sir?" I asked.

He stared at me. "I've seen you somewhere. Who are you?"

His partner took a closer look at my face then. "You're right," he said. "She looks familiar, but I can't . . ."

"They say everyone has a twin," I smiled and headed on to the car. "I'm just a photographer, and I don't know a soul in the area."

Will and I waved as we drove away. "Sorrel, what was that all about?" he asked.

"Beats me," I said. "A couple of weird guys."

Will grunted. I could feel his eyes on me occasionally during our drive to the two campgrounds, but he didn't say anything more. I took more photos while Will interviewed a couple staying in one of the rustic cabins.

By the time we arrived at the store, he'd written several of his illegible notes onto his small tablet and hopped out with his usual enthusiasm. "Looks like a good crowd," he said, "and smells as good as ever!"

We didn't stay much longer than an hour in Portal. Will collected the news release and then spoke to a couple of people while I snapped some evening photos outside. I never tired of the sunsets and huge expanses of sky, but I welcomed Will's announcement that he'd finished his interview and was ready to return to our camp.

"Did you find new information for our article?" I asked as we backed out of the parking area.

"I got some great personal interviews with campers," he said.

I waited, thinking he would continue. Finally, I glanced over. He was reading. "The news release?"

"Yeah."

"Read it. I'm curious."

When Will didn't answer, I glanced over. He stared at the paper, a strange mixture of interest, fascination, and horror. "Will?"

"Weird," he finally breathed. "They found an unidentified male, approximately forty to forty-five years of age, trussed with rope around his ankles and on his wrists behind his back. He was gagged. No set time of death yet—waiting on the medical examiner. No clues about his background." I could hear Will suck in a deep breath. "Oh, man . . ."

"What's wrong?"

"Death was by snakebite."

"That's unusual," I murmured. Of course, I knew this because Reed had already told me; but I couldn't help shivering at revisiting the idea. "I know that people die from snakebites still, but it isn't common. I wonder if his captors—whoever they were—planned to return."

"I doubt it. He must have done something vile to merit that sort of treatment. I wonder if it was the cartel . . . some sort of drug deal gone bad."

"Possibly."

We didn't say much more until I pulled into our unit and reached for my door. Will sat staring out the windshield, uncharacteristically quiet.

"You coming?"

"The snakes bother me."

"Well, I'm not in love with the idea of them either. Maybe they wanted to send out a warning or something."

Will didn't acknowledge my comment at first, just stared straight ahead. Finally, he said, "If they wanted to send a statement to someone, why leave him in such an isolated place? Would this 'someone' be in the area? I mean, it could be months before anyone stumbled upon this guy!"

"Maybe law enforcement was given a tip? Does it mention how they came upon him?"

He looked back to the paper. "A ranger who likes to hike decided to explore the cave." He looked over at me. "Is it just me or is that explanation too—"

"I agree."

I climbed out of the Jeep and Will followed. "If it was the cartel, they'd want the statement—or threat—out there right away to warn others who thought they could do whatever they weren't supposed to do," he muttered.

"Death by snakebite is unusual," I mused as I unlocked the door.

"I wonder if they meant to let him starve?" Will asked.

I looked over my shoulder. "What do you think?"

He walked over to the refrigerator and pulled out a bottle of water. "I think this is complicated, and we don't have enough of the pieces," he said. "And I think I need to get on this uncomplicated travel story."

"Good idea. I need to put my stuff together if we're heading out in the morning. Do you want to look through the photos I've taken?"

"Maybe later. Right now, I'd like to just throw my thoughts on paper . . . after I have a cigarette and gather them a bit."

Will had scarcely closed the outside door when my phone rang.

"Sorrel?"

I walked into the bedroom and closed the door. "You're the only person I know who can put a whole paragraph into my name."

"Are you leaving soon?"

"Tomorrow."

"Good."

"Something you don't want to tell me?"

"This doesn't feel right. No one is saying much, so I don't have the conflict of what to say or not say. But I can't think your being here is a good idea."

I felt the familiar frustration building. "Reed, I can—"

"Take care of yourself."

Neither of us spoke for a moment, memories of when that statement hadn't exactly been true swirling unspoken between us.

"That news clipping likely has no significance, Sorrel," he finally said.

"I'm thinking the same thing. Not going to lose sleep over it anyway. Tomorrow is a long drive and I need to get some rest."

We hung up on those lies.

Chapter 19

"Looks like a slow day," Will observed as we parked outside the store in Portal the next morning. The Jeep was alone in the parking spaces in front of the sweeping porch.

"Birders are usually up and out early, like we should have been," I grumbled. I'd had a difficult time getting Will up and out of our rental. Even now, he looked like a hamster, his eyes squinting and his stocking cap pulled down to his eyebrows.

"Ouch!" He smirked and climbed out. "Sounds like we both—especially one of us—need food and coffee."

Will hadn't slept much through the night, his mind apparently filled with the story he'd been assigned to write and with the one he planned to submit as well. In typical college student mode, he had needed music and food to do his best work, oblivious to the noise he created. When I groused about it to him at least twice during the late hours, he'd grinned and offered me a piece of the frozen pizza he'd just overcooked. I'd finally fallen into a fitful sleep in the predawn hours, sleeping restlessly and waking often.

When I got up, I'd felt decidedly grumpy. Will, on the other hand, had still seemed focused on someone in his "storyland." We'd loaded the Jeep and cleaned up without eating breakfast—or talking much, for that matter.

Following Will, I dropped off the envelope containing our keys in the appropriate drop-box beside the front door and joined him at a small table at the back of the little café. The same lady who had waited on us before appeared, a coffee pot in her hand. "Coffee?" she asked.

"Coffee!" we chorused.

She smiled, filled the cups already sitting on the table, and handed us a menu. "Breakfast or lunch is available at this time."

"Cheeseburger and fries," Will announced before she could step away and handed her his unopened menu.

She wrote it down and looked at me. "A scrambled egg and wheat toast," I said.

Neither of us felt the need to talk. Will typed steadily on his tablet, and I read emails on my phone until our waitress returned with our food and refilled our cups. I thanked her and waited for her to walk away before speaking to Will. "Sorry to be cross."

"No problem." He grinned. "I've always been a noisy pig when I'm working. My mom says she'll be lucky if I ever find anyone to take me off their hands."

I watched as he poured at least a third of the ketchup bottle onto his heap of fries, silently commiserating with his mother. "How's the story coming?" I finally asked.

"I'm happy with the rough," he said and took a big bite of burger.

He might have continued had a commotion at the front of the store not drawn our attention. Six Homeland Security officers had entered, laughing and talking as they walked in our direction. I held a finger to my lips, sweeping my eyes toward them to warn Will. I looked down at my phone and bit into my toast, hoping no one would recognize either of us. Will concentrated on his cheeseburger.

"You guys want to sit in or out?" our waitress asked them.

"Out," several said at once, so she led the noisy group through the double doors behind us to a small shaded patio. They pulled seats into a wide circle around a picnic-style table and ordered coffee all around.

"I'll put on the gallon-sized pot!" she called as she stepped back inside. "You two okay?" she asked as she passed us.

We nodded, our mouths full. She grinned and hurried back to the kitchen.

The group outside didn't seem concerned with discretion, immediately jumping into the case that had obviously been their most recent focus. It was difficult to separate the bits of conversation with so many commenting. I leaned toward Will to suggest a strategy when I saw that he'd put his phone to his ear. Who did he plan to call? When he didn't speak, I realized he was recording the conversation behind him. Clever! We could sort through it later.

Cheers erupted when the server pushed a cart with a large coffee urn and cups past us and out the door. Will lowered his phone, finished off his cheeseburger, and waited for her to come back through. She paused at our table. "Can I get you anything else?"

I smiled. "Just a check, I guess."

She reached in her pocket and pulled it out. "Right here." She tilted her head toward the officers. "When they called ahead, I figured I'd need to be prepared. Y'all come back soon!"

I excused myself to visit the ladies' room, which was the last door in a tiny hall that opened onto another outdoor patio opposite the one currently occupied by the DHS agents. I slipped out onto it and dialed Reed. He didn't pick up, and I didn't leave voicemail. I considered calling Randall Byrd but really didn't have much to report to him either.

This whole escapade felt decidedly overrated to me. True, someone had died— murdered—in a horrible manner. And in his possession had been a picture of me in a faded newspaper story—both old. But it wasn't a picture of Sorrel Janes. It was a news photo of a blonde Staci Lyn Jamison, news anchor/crime reporter from Houston, Texas, who'd left the station after her husband had been murdered. Old news. Already forgotten. Who knew why people clipped such things and kept them? Maybe he'd had a thing for blondes. I didn't have time just now to tramp all over these mountains following vague clues.

I dialed Teri then and was rewarded with her chirpy, "About time!"

"Are you home, in the hospital, at the ice cream parlor—"

"Funny! I'm on the sofa when I should be finishing up my display and hoping my vanishing buddy—"

"Is heading home!"

"About time! The cats are considering themselves abandoned in spite of the lavish and constant attention all of us are giving them! And Jose is terrified he'll be here amid a huge sale while I'm in the hospital—"

"I know. I'm so sorry, Teri! It was crazy of me to accept that job—"

"Hush! It gives Jose something to worry about and me something to do besides eat and eat and eat!" A voice called to her. "Coming!" she called. "When—"

"We've checked out of our place and will be arriving home later this evening. We just want to double check some of the facts before we leave. You don't need to be out at the store. Leave it as it is. I'll see you tomorrow. And would you pass the message on to the cats and their caretaker?"

She laughed. "Their devoted slave, you mean? Will do! And I'm excited to see you soon!"

I smiled. Teri was a fresh breath in my life—and always made me smile.

"Everything okay?"

I jumped and whirled around at the sound of Reed's voice. "I didn't hear you—"

"And I don't want everyone else to hear us either!" Reed pulled me under a small overhang at the end of the patio. "I heard you say you've checked out?"

"Yes. We need to get back. Anything I should know?"

He glanced toward the door and spoke quickly. "I don't think you need to be here. If something comes up—and I can— I'll let you know."

"Has anyone made the connection between me and—"

"The blonde bombshell? I don't think so, but if they see you just right—"

"Bombshell? Give me a break!"

Instead, he kissed me and stepped around a bush just as Will came through the door. He looked around suspiciously. "Who were you talking to?"

"My cellphone, nosy! My assistant is about to have another baby and I have this huge sale coming up and I'm here chasing rattlesnakes!"

"Not to mention touring outhouses!" Will supplied.

"We need to pay and—"

"Already done. I thought you had skipped out—"

"Has the mob left?"

"Yep."

I pointed for him to lead the way. "Then we can talk."

I glanced behind me just in time to see a hat tipped before it vanished. High drama, I thought, but for his sake we truly needed to be cautious.

A couple of locals had taken our table, but otherwise the store was quiet. I thanked the older man at the counter and followed Will out to the Jeep.

"I could live here," Will observed.

"You must be dreaming!" I said. "You?"

He climbed in beside me, grinning. "Yeah. It appeals to my inner rough and ready—"

My giggles echoed through the car as I started up and turned.

"Hey! Aren't we heading back to Saddle Gap?" Will said. "You turned the wrong way!"

"Oh, I just thought we might have one last visit with that ranger before we leave the area," I said casually. "You might get a good quote or something from him."

"I've already interviewed him. What would he be able to add?"

"Quite a bit if you ask the right questions. Where does everyone stop when heading to the area? Who do they ask for directions? Who hears the bits of information they drop?"

Will didn't say anything for a bit. "I should have thought of that."

"While we drive, why don't we eavesdrop on Homeland?"

"Great idea! But I'm not sure how much of it is clear enough to hear. Phone recordings pick up background noise."

"Why don't you take notes? With two sets of ears, maybe we'll learn something."

By the time we pulled into the ranger station, we agreed that our eavesdropping clearly fit into the mundane category. Aside from the joking, crude comments, and complaints about various things, the men had passed little information. Will clicked the off button in midsentence when I turned off the ignition.

"See what I meant?" he said.

"Wait! What was that last bit?"

Will looked at me. "What?"

"Play the last bit back for me, please?"

He shrugged but complied. We both listened to the raucous laughter and unintelligible words. Then it came. "Striking blind!"

"Rewind it," I said. "We missed the first of the comment."

But in spite of rewinding it a half dozen times, we couldn't make out the whole sentence. Will shrugged. "Just an off-the cuff comment, likely. Doesn't even fit the conversation." He opened the door. "I want to catch a quick smoke. Meet you inside?"

"Don't be long!" I said.

Privately, I was happy to have a few moments alone with the ranger. As I entered, he was just finishing up replenishing the coffee table he kept in a corner near the door. "Hello!" he said. "Want a cup?"

"No, thanks. Just ate up at Portal. I'm stuffed."

"How can I help you?"

"I'm curious about these guys." I indicated the large rattlesnake cage near a large window. "Did you catch them?"

"No, the guy before me caught most of them. Beautiful, aren't they?"

I nodded. It wasn't totally a lie. The patterns on their skins were truly works of art. I told the ranger that and he happily launched into a lecture on western rattlesnakes.

"Are there many here?"

I hadn't heard Will's approach until the smell of cigarette smoke alerted me.

"Plenty," the ranger replied. "Of course, this time of year they're hibernating."

"Caves?" I asked.

"Among other places. You're not as likely to run into them crawling around. Too cold. Now the spring—that's when you need to watch out. Another month or two and they'll be out and shedding. In that process, they often strike at sounds when their skin is obscuring their eyes." He grinned. "It's not a safe time to be out without looking where you step."

"Interesting," I murmured and moved on to look at a rock collection. Will continued to chat, but their voices faded as I moved to the big window and stared up at the caves. But I wasn't seeing holes. I was seeing a blindfolded man lying frozen in terror, covered with rattlesnakes.

Chapter 20

Will seemed disinclined to talk on the trip home. Instead, he kept his ear buds in and typed on his tablet. I was relieved. It gave me the opportunity to reflect on our past few days, mentally gnawing on bits and pieces of information. Except for the horror surrounding the man's death, this cave murder seemed just one more senseless crime in an increasingly violent world. I'd happily left the news anchor job to escape it. Yet now, once more, its tentacles had reached out to me.

At least, that was Reed's hypothesis. But during the quiet journey home, glancing out at the wide, open countryside, I questioned Reed's ideas. My news clipping being found on the dead man seemed less sinister now. What evidence did they really have besides an old newspaper clipping of a blonde news reporter—a clipping at least four or more years old—to tie me to this crime? I didn't know him—and I doubted he knew me. Maybe he liked blondes. Maybe someone had sent it to him. Maybe it wasn't even his. After all, I'd been a minor celebrity, I supposed, but the station had replaced me with yet another blonde—younger, of course—and I'd wager not a half dozen people on the streets of Houston still remembered my name.

I glanced in the rearview mirror, searching for anything in my reflection that warranted a description of "glamourous." The blonde hair had returned to my natural red and, although still long, no longer had salon highlights and a clever cut. I opted for a casual ponytail most of the time and dropped in the local beauty college for a trim occasionally. Also gone were my manicured nails, arched brows, and skillful make-up. Except for special occasions, I only dabbed on moisturizer and lip gloss and, occasionally, eye shadow.

"Penny for 'em."

I jerked. "You startled me, Will!"

"You were so deep in thought I wanted to make sure you were awake!"

"My dad called it woolgathering. I wonder where that expression originated. It conjures up funny pictures for me. But in answer to your question, I was thinking about your articles. Did you finish them?"

"I may have to tweak something here or there, but they're basically done." He stretched and asked hopefully, "Is there any chance you might stop so a guy could grab a smoke?"

I motioned toward the center console. "There are lollipops in there. Have one. It's better for you."

"Now that's a controversial topic," Will grumbled, poking around in the console and extracting two red ones. "Tobacco versus sugar." He popped one in his mouth then pulled it out to wave in the air as he continued his thought. "Nonsmokers die of lung cancer too. And then there's my great grandpa who died with a cigarette in his hand—at ninety! And we haven't even broached the topic of diabetes from so much sugar!"

"Sounds like an editorial," I teased. But I'll agree to a truce—for our ride home!"

Will grinned at that. He crunched the lollipop off the stick, swallowed, and immediately unwrapped the other one. "The family vacation article was easier," he said. "I'm okay with it, but the other one isn't quite there yet. I mean, I could submit it as is, but it just doesn't feel right yet."

"Why don't you read them aloud?" I suggested. "Sometimes you hear things that you may have overlooked. It also gives me ideas of which photos might go with them."

Will crunched the second lollipop. "See? I can't just leave one of these in my mouth. So I end up eating a dozen. Sugar overload. And don't suggest gum! I have good teeth—so far!"

I ignored him. "I'm waiting."

"All right." Will studied his tablet. "I'll read the vacation article first."

Will's writing sounded much like himself, matter-of-fact observations peppered with bits of dry humor. He focused on the economics, the natural experiences, and family bonding. In his summary, he urged "back-to-nature without sleeping on the ground" and "a real bathroom."

"I like it," I said, when he'd finished.

"Let's hope Mr. Byrd does."

As he read the news piece, I offered bits of advice in places and he corrected himself verbally at other points. "This one needs a bit more to it," he said, "but I'll wait until I talk to Mr. Byrd."

I slowed and pulled up beside a gas pump in a tiny town. Before I could turn off the motor, Will had opened his door with one hand and reached for a cigarette with the other. I sighed. "Don't say it!" he said, offering a cheeky grin.

After I'd filled the tank, I stepped inside the store for a quick visit to the ladies' room. Three small tables were lined up against the wall on the right, two aisles holding random food and cleaning supplies filled the middle, and a man and woman worked behind a counter on the left. She stood by the cash register while he flipped hamburgers on a small grill.

Leaving the ladies' room, I pulled a bottle of water from the cooler. Will was paying for potato chips and a bottled Dr. Pepper at the register. He settled at the table by the front door while I paid my bill.

By the time I joined him, he had already stuffed his mouth with chips and was staring out the window. "Must be good," I said.

He didn't answer. I repeated myself. No answer. Then I noticed his earbuds, so I abandoned any conversation and drank my water.

"I heard it was nasty," a man at the table behind me said. "Must've made some powerful enemies to end up dead like that."

"Crazy buzzards!" his companion agreed. "Whatever happened to just shootin' somebody?"

"They was makin' a statement, that's why. Warnin' anyone else who's thinkin' about crossin' 'em."

"Don't talk so loud," a third voice warned. "He said not to say anything. They're keeping it quiet."

"They won't be able to keep it quiet for long! I heard something on the TV this morning . . . just not the details," the first voice said. "Everybody knows it's the cartel—has to be! And the cartel likes it to be out there. Keeps people afraid of them."

"I figure anybody tangles with those guys is just as bad. They git what they deserve."

Chairs scraped the floor as they stood up to leave. I glanced up quickly as they shuffled by, but they didn't look familiar.

"I wonder if they were part of the bunch we saw at Portal," Will whispered as they went outside. "Don't think so."

"How—?" Then I looked closer at Will. The earbuds hung on the outer edges of his ears.

"You were—"

"Taping them," he finished. "Thought I might get some local reaction to what was happening. People tend to be cautious about making statements to reporters. This way, I can mention what they say in a general way without identifying them. They won't even know who had overheard them."

"They sound like they've been talking to someone who knew what happened. Did you pick up anything useful?"

"They mentioned a guy in his thirties. I'm more interested in the pin-up . . . some page he'd torn out of a magazine or something. One said it was maybe a girlfriend and the others laughed. That was new information, maybe worth mentioning." Will stood and gathered up his trash. "I'm grabbing another quick smoke. I doubt you'll stop again." He waited a second for me to scold him, shrugged, and left.

A pin-up. For all of my rationalization, I knew that photo of me couldn't just be ignored. Time for me to reach out to my buddies at the television station. I also needed to get to my computer to search back copies of the *Houston Chronicle*.

I tossed the trash and smiled at the woman cleaning tables. She looked at me a little curiously but then walked toward the back. I walked as casually as anyone can after having been discussed as a pin-up in connection with a ghastly murder.

For the last part of the trip, Will abandoned his ear buds and chattered nonstop about our adventures. "I just wish we could get the name of the guy in the cave!"

"The authorities probably don't know it yet," I told him. "I doubt the killers left his ID there."

"Wonder why they left the news clipping with the girl's photo then? Are they trying to send some kind of message?"

"Who knows? Killers aren't always geniuses, you know. Maybe they wanted to throw the investigation off-track. Maybe the victim didn't even know her."

"Maybe." Will pulled out another lollipop. "Wasn't it difficult to make the switch from news to taking photos of critters?" he asked. "I don't want to be rude, but don't you miss the excitement of trying to scoop the other reporters, competing for that first interview, chasing down leads, capturing the sheer energy of the news?"

"Well, you don't get a lot of that in a college newspaper. I did my internship at a city television station and, while it was fun, it was highly competitive. I just didn't seem to have what it took."

Will seemed to be swallowing my lies. I truly didn't fit his personal picture of a news anchor, which worked in my favor.

"Sometimes I wonder how it might have been to try television news fulltime. But I've fallen in love with the sheer energy and beauty of the critters and the raw beauty of the outdoors. I'm competing against myself with my photography. Besides, do I want to spend half my life worrying about weight, hair, make-up, and dodging really mean, ambitious women?"

"Doesn't sound like you," Will admitted. "When Mr. Byrd said you'd been a journalism major in college, he was vague about the details of your experience . . . and I guess I imagined it was more than it was."

I injected an even more casual tone in my voice. "The thing about news—and most things we do in the public eye—is that we're just a moment. Then someone just as good or better fills our spot. Fans of anything are usually fickle." I laughed. "And as I said, fans don't follow college newspapers."

Will crunched on the candy. I thought he'd abandoned the subject until he said, "I'm going to be a household name someday." He grinned. "Wait and see!"

"Then you'd better get off those weeds you're smoking," I scolded. "You'll want to live to enjoy the fame!"

Chapter 21

Will and I drove to the newspaper office and spent the next hour discussing the article with Mr. Byrd. We also selected a number of my photos for him to consider. I finally left the two of them, promising to email any more shots he might need in the morning.

When I pulled into my parking lot, an overwhelming sense of happiness, home, and peace settled in my chest. And, as with every other time I'd returned from a trip, I had the urge to never leave again.

"Come out, come out, wherever you are!" I called, as I stepped into my house.

"Meow?" Flash peeked around the end of the sofa, blinked, raced over to me, and started weaving around my ankles.

I dropped my case with a thump and bent down to pet her. "Where's your brother?" I asked.

A raspy grumble erupted behind the sofa. I continued to pet and talk to Flash until a cranky gray face peeked out at us. "Van? Who ruffled your fur?"

Van flattened his only ear against his head and hissed. He clearly wasn't happy. "I haven't been away that long," I crooned and reached toward him. He hissed, then growled, and backed away. "Weird. You don't usually hold a grudge. I just have to leave sometimes." He scooted behind the sofa.

I picked up my suitcase, carried it into the bedroom, and laid it on the bed, Flash at my heels. Teri had left a note on the bedside table. "Sorrel, I'm leaving a little early to go to the Cub Scout Pinewood Derby. Both boys are sure they'll win. We may have war in our house if only one does. There's an odd-shaped box in the office from an Adam Gimbol. I don't recognize him from any of our consignees. Did you order something? See you tomorrow."

Adam Gimbol? Odd name. It didn't sound familiar. "I'll take care of it later," I told Flash. She jumped up on the bed and climbed onto my suitcase. I picked her up and cuddled her for a minute. "I'll wait to unpack this. Let's check your food dish and I'll see what I can scrounge up for a light meal."

Teri had left a plate of enchiladas and beans in the refrigerator. I popped the plate into the microwave and refilled the cats' water and food dishes. Flash sniffed them before walking to the sofa and perching on an arm.

I ate only a couple of bites of the delicious food before covering it up again and putting it back in the refrigerator. After these few hectic days and a long day of travel, I felt overcome with weariness. So I took a hot shower, letting the water relax my tense neck and shoulder muscles. The mail and other messages could wait until tomorrow.

As I snuggled into my bed, Van finally decided I was staying the night, abandoned his spot under the sofa, and curled up at the end of my bed. Flash braced herself against my thigh and began an elaborate bath. Relaxed from my own shower, I reached toward the lamp when Reed's ring tone sounded.

"Caught you in bed, snuggled up with the felines?" he asked.

"Yes. You're lucky I even answered the phone."

"That I am." I could hear voices behind him. "I don't have a long time to talk. I just wanted to know you were home and all is well."

"What aren't you saying, Reed?"

"In a minute," he said to someone. Then he lowered his voice almost to a whisper. "You may have ties to this victim. If so, expect company."

"As in your crew?"

"Maybe."

"Am I in trouble?"

"Not to worry, sweetheart," he said louder than usual. "Sorry I won't be home tonight." There were laughs and comments behind him. Then he whispered again, "Just a heads up." Then, louder again, "Bye, Toots." He hung up amid more laughter. He was going to pay for that "Toots!"

People always tell you not to worry; but when they say that, you invariably will. As comfy as my own bed felt and as sleepy as I'd been earlier, I couldn't manage to fall asleep. The hidden warning in Reed's voice alerted me. My common sense argued that I couldn't know this guy or what had caused him to end up dead in that cave. Besides, even if I did have visitors who questioned me, I wasn't inexperienced in being interrogated. I knew how to conduct myself.

I expected to fall asleep right away.

But I couldn't stop tossing and turning and so I climbed out of bed. Maybe a cup of hot peppermint tea would relax me.

While I waited for the kettle to boil, I called my buddy at the station. His phone went straight to voicemail, so he was probably working on production. "Hey! It's your pesky former crime reporter/news anchor. I've got a crazy coincidence here. Thought you might be able to point me in the right direction. Call me when you have a free moment!" After ending the call, I realized he might not still have my number. So I redialed and left both my business and cell numbers.

I poured a cup of tea and headed to the connecting door to the office. Someone hadn't locked it, I realized. Maybe I needed to install one of those doors that lock automatically and can only be opened with a key. Maybe I was overreacting.

The mail had been stacked in a wicker basket on my desk. Teri had logged each letter in the notebook, along with the date it had arrived, and had bound them together with a rubber band.   The advertisements were loose in the bottom of the basket. I sat down and glanced through them first, tossing most of them in the trash and setting a couple back in the basket. Then I arranged the letters by date and opened them in order.

Some were bills, so I wrote checks and prepared them for tomorrow's post. Others were invitations to local charity events, people who wanted information about consignments, or requests from local organizations for sponsorships or donations. I put those off. With Teri's baby due soon, I would likely keep the new worker. But I wanted to get a better sense of how much she either could or would work before we committed ourselves to events.

A yawn erupted and I glanced at the clock. I'd been there almost an hour. "Time flies!" I murmured and straightened up the paperwork. As I rose, a strange noise alerted me.

"Are you mangy cats into something?" I asked. Then I remembered I'd closed the door to keep them out of the office so I wouldn't have to chase them down when I left. I glanced around, turning slowly in a circle. Nothing looked like it was disturbed. The strange noise had stopped—if it had even been there in the first place and wasn't just a figment of my imagination.

"What's that old adage about letting your imagination go crazy?" I asked. Then I laughed. "Or the one about talking to yourself?"

It was time to get some sleep. I'd only taken a couple of steps before I heard it again. Something about it was vaguely familiar. I looked around the office again, searching for anything new or different that could be the culprit. But it was neat as a pin, everything in its own place, just like Teri liked to keep it.

I reached for the light switch. Maybe living alone was making me—wait! I heard it again. It niggled at my brain, vaguely familiar. Where had I . . .? It seemed to come from the file cabinet. How could it have? We only kept tax files and consignment files and—even as the thought arrived, I felt chills.

I walked slowly over to the file cabinet and inched open the bottom drawer. The movement—even as careful as I'd been—brought the sound again. I stepped back, reached for the long-handled dust pan we kept beside the cabinet, and pushed the drawer as fast and hard as I could. The noise continued for a moment and I thought I saw a slight movement—but surely this was all my crazy imagination. Or was it?

I backed out of the office, clicked off the light switch, and locked the door. I continued backing up until I felt the doorknob to my living quarters, opened it, and quickly backed inside. I locked it and stood for a moment, my eyes sweeping my kitchen and living room combination. The cats had settled into their beds near the sofa and padded over when they saw me. Flash rubbed against my leg, but Van stopped short and hissed as he'd done earlier. How strange!

I wasn't sure what I should do next. You don't call the police and have them come all the way out on the report of a strange sound in a file cabinet. At least I didn't. I could call Jose, but with Teri hugely pregnant and the twins, he had enough on his hands. I needed something more to suggest probable cause, didn't I? I could hear it now. *Officer? There's a strange noise in my filing cabinet, and my tomcat is growling and hissing at me.*

I rinsed the teacup, turned out the light, and returned to my bed. In the dark, I noticed a flashing light from the bedside table. Was that my cell? I hadn't heard it. Then I noticed the text. I picked it up and opened it. It was from Reed. "R U ok? Text if no."

"Good grief, Sorrel!" I murmured. "When did you turn into—"

A noise in the kitchen shut me up. I climbed out of bed again and walked to the bedroom door. It was a combination growl/hiss. I flipped on the light switch again. Van was hunkered down in front of the connecting door, his fur standing up, his tail twitching, and his throat emitting a low, whining growl interspersed with intermittent hisses. I looked down at my phone.

I'm ok, but something weird, I typed back. Then I looked at the clock. It was 11 p.m. I should have waited until the morning. *Check in am*, I added.

I coaxed Van away from the door with a treat; and once both cats were inside the bedroom munching on treats, I closed the door and locked it. Then I climbed back into bed, telling the cats and myself that tomorrow would be a busy day for me and I needed to get some sleep.

An hour or so later, I finally gave up the pretense. Sitting up, I clicked on the lamp and squinted at the phone. Reed hadn't answered. Maybe someone was sleeping.

Funny how lines from songs appear at times like this. My dad had been a huge country music fan, and I had spent much time riding with him in his pick-up truck with it blaring on the radio. I hadn't thought of that in a long time, but a line came back to me now. "But sleep won't come," the singer had crooned. I couldn't remember why he couldn't sleep, and I seriously doubted he and I suffered from the same—

A noise, different from before, cut into my memories. This night continued to be stranger and stranger.

I switched off the small lamp, climbed out of bed, dropped to my knees, and crept to the window. Even through the thin slat of my bedroom blind, I could see the faint light and hear the crunching of tires. A vehicle—by its size it was a pick-up—had turned off the highway, switching from headlights to parking lights only as it rolled slowly toward my shop/home. Then another followed it closely, lights also off except for parking lights. I dropped the slat and listened to doors softly opened and quietly eased shut.

I had a handgun in my chest, but reason told me I wouldn't stand a chance against three or four guys. Instead, I crawled back toward my bed and my cell phone. Flashlight beams glanced against my wall through the tiny opening between window slats. Frantically, I typed, *Help! Peeps here!*

Immediately, a response shot back: *R U alone?*

Think so.

Open 4 me.

I rose, unlocked the bedroom door, and crept to the front door. As I reached for the lock, I stopped. *Sign?* I typed.

Toots.

Chapter 22

"Gentlemen, may I ask why you're here at this hour of the night?" I stepped through the storm door but held onto the handle and remained on the step.

When no one answered right away, I turned to Reed. "Deputy Reed, may I help you?" I inserted an iciness in my voice and eyes. Then letting my eyes sweep over the officers behind him, I continued, "Had I known you were coming I'd have dressed for the occasion."

A burly, red-haired man behind Reed pushed around him. "Ms. Janes?" he barked.

"For my whole life," I replied. "And you are--?"

He flashed a badge. "Border Patrol. Could you step outside?"

I looked down at my fuzzy pajama bottoms—pink with big grey dots—and my oversized t-shirt. "This couldn't wait until morning? I was in bed, sir. I'm not dressed for the outdoors, as you can see. And it is cold. If you'd like to speak to me, please step inside." He didn't answer. "Otherwise, you may wait while I get something warmer—and my shoes—on."

Reed said something to his companion then turned to me once again. "Could we step inside and talk with you, Ms. Janes? We have a police matter to discuss that may involve your personal safety."

"It couldn't have waited until the morning?"

When no one answered, I stepped aside and swept my hand in an invitation. Then I turned and stepped back inside. The officer remained on the step, speaking to the others behind him while Reed followed me into the house.

"They know we are friends, Sorrel," he whispered, barely moving his lips. "Follow my lead."

We stood just inside the door without speaking further. The officer strode up to the door only a few moments later and stepped inside. "I'm sorry to intrude at this time of night, ma'am," he said. "We wouldn't have arrived this late and interrupted your night, but Officer Reed indicated you were acquainted. We're working on a case and hope you might add some helpful information." He glanced toward Reed and added, "I'm Sgt. Pearce."

I motioned to the sofa. "Would you like to sit, Sergeant?"

He didn't answer but instead scanned the small room as if mentally tallying details. Reed asked, "Where are the kitties?"

"Probably hiding under the bed," I grumbled, but one look at the wicked gleam in his eyes made me add, "discussing the weird noises they have heard all night."

"Brave cats," Reed murmured.

"Do you have a security system Ms. Janes?" Sgt. Pearce asked.

"Yes. Why would you ask?"

"You're out here on the highway, on your own, and in the direct path of illegal alien traffic . . . to name a reason or two." He regarded me with a mixture of exasperation and caution.

"So is that why you are here? Are you expecting trouble? I wouldn't think that my little shop and I would demand a half dozen Border Patrol agents and a sheriff's deputy."

In the silence that followed, I hoped I'd not pushed him too far.

Finally, he shrugged and gestured toward Reed. "According to Deputy Reed, you're no stranger to personal danger—both before and after moving out here."

"Please sit down," I said. "I can make coffee."

"No coffee," Pearce said.

I walked over to the easy chair and sat down. Reed sat on the couch, and Sgt. Pearce perched on the other end.

"How may I help you?" I asked.

Sgt. Pearce glanced at Reed but saw no help there. "We are investigating a homicide," he finally said. "In Arizona."

He waited for me to say something but I didn't.

"You know something of it," he almost growled, "since you've only just returned from the same place. So let's not play games. I've looked into your background, and I've worked in law enforcement long enough to recognize some unusual gaps. I'm not saying witness protection here—"

A loud cough from Reed interrupted him. He glanced toward Reed's icy glare, and the two exchanged a silent conversation for several seconds. Neither seemed inclined to compromise, so the tap at the front door might have been a good intervention.

Pearce rose, strode to the door, and barked, "What?" He listened a moment then muttered over his shoulder before stepping outside. "You might want to hear this, Deputy."

Chris rose and turned. When he heard me rise, he called over his shoulder, "Wait here a minute, Sorrel."

They were all huddled, listening to one of the Border Patrol officers when I joined them, my feet hastily stuffed into sneakers and a jacket thrown over my tee-shirt.

"Don't you ever—?" Pearce began.

"Wait by the fire until I'm told what else to do?" I asked. "You were just saying you'd researched me, Sergeant. Surely nothing you read suggested I would be a 'fireside female'; but if it did, rest assured it is false. This is my home, my life. I have every right to know what is going on."

I let my eyes drift over the officers. They avoided my glance, keeping their eyes on Pearce. "I'd like to know what you found," I addressed them. "Evidence of a problem with the security system? Another dead body? Ghosts?"

Pearce growled, "Cute! This is official—"

"Business," I finished for him. "But it's also my life."

"We're not talking photography here!"

"A crime?" I waited. Then I smiled innocently and said, "Then I'll just go back to bed. If you want to talk further, we'll all be better rested in the morning." I glanced at Chris. "Bye."

I turned but had only taken a couple of steps when Sgt. Pearce spoke up. "Wait! Let's talk inside." He turned to the other officers. "We won't be long. Continue."

"I thought we were going to talk earlier," I said. "I don't know what game you're playing, but it's late, cold, and I'm tired. And what do they need to finish?"

Pearce sighed. "You left out the stubborn mule part in your description," he said to Reed. "After you," he said, gesturing to the house.

I figured I'd pushed him about as far as I should, so I headed back inside, the two men following closely. We sat once more, but before Sgt. Pearce could speak I asked, "You mentioned that you had researched me. What did you learn and what motivated you to do so?"

He didn't answer my question but asked one of his own. "Why were you in Arizona recently?"

"I'm a wildlife photographer, but I sometimes freelance for the local paper," I said. "I was asked to accompany a reporter and take photos to accompany his news article."

"What article?"

"A feature on local family vacation spots—hiking and spelunking the caves."

"And if I contact this reporter, he'll back you up?"

"Of course he will. So will the publisher/editor, Randall Byrd."

"And, of course, you had no knowledge—"

Chris rose. "I'm making a pot of coffee," he said. "Even if you don't want it, Dan, the guys outside will appreciate it."

Pearce nodded briefly and continued to question me about where Will and I had gone and what we had seen. A few minutes later, Chris carried a tray full of Styrofoam-filled cups out the door. When he returned, he motioned for the sergeant. "They need to see you," he said.

When we were alone, he leaned over and whispered, "You've done well. But hard-lining time is over. Time for feminine charm."

"What's up?"

"Later." Footsteps on the porch made him hop up, fill a cup with water, and stick it in the microwave. "Peppermint? Sleepy-time?" he asked as Sgt. Pearce reentered.

"Just coffee," he said.

"Tea. Plain tea," I said.

When we were once more settled and sipping on our drinks, Sgt. Pearce turned to me. "Ms. Janes," he began, "I don't want to alarm you further, but we need to search your store and office area."

"Why?"

"We've found some evidence of tampering." He sipped his coffee.

When he didn't continue, I asked, "Someone trying to steal? That wouldn't be cause for federal concern."

He stared at me. "Ms. Janes . . . or whoever you are . . . and I don't want or need to know . . . we have cause to believe someone else may know." When I didn't speak, he continued, "For that reason, what I am going to tell you must remain classified. Do you understand? Do I have your guarantee that it will not leave this room?"

I nodded.

"A photo of a well-known crime reporter in Texas was found in the pocket of a murdered man."

"The one in that cave? He was murdered?"

"So you did know that."

"Well, yes," I said. "When we arrived there to climb, we were stopped by guards and official vehicles were everywhere. The crime tape over the entrance of the cave we'd planned to explore didn't hide the fact that a crime had occurred there. So we climbed around a bit then left."

He stared hard into my eyes. "And you didn't wonder about it?"

"I'm a wildlife photographer. Of course I was curious, but I wasn't as interested in it as Will. He's the reporter."

"I would like to speak to him," he said.

"Sure," I said. "I've got his address in my bedroom. And I'll give you Mr. Byrd's number as well."

I got up and walked into the room, seemingly oblivious to the silent communication he and Reed were exchanging. When I returned with a piece of paper containing the information, Reed was rinsing out coffee cups at the sink.

"We suspected someone had died," I continued conversationally, handing Sgt. Pearce the paper. "But we were there to get photos and information about the area, and the officers told us any information would be given in press releases when available. I don't know whether or not Will knew, but I doubt it."

He stood. "Could we look in your store?" he asked.

"Sure. May I ask why?"

Instead of answering, he started toward the door.

"We can go this way," I said and pointed to the connecting door. "My office is tiny. It's on the right."

"Have you been there since returning?"

"Well, sure," I said, unlocking the door and flipping on the shop lights. "I spent some time with mail, etc." I stepped inside then stopped. "What's going on?"

The front door to my shop stood open, and the other officers were roaming about the store. Stacks of cloth handwork littered floor, Teri's artistic towers of creams and oils had toppled, wall paintings had fallen or hung askew, and several Valentine decorations had been trampled on the floor. "Who did this? Did your men—"

"No, ma'am."

I hadn't noticed the youngest of the officers standing nearby.

"We found it this way," he said.

I turned back to Reed and Pearce. "But I was in my office working! I would have seen this! Surely I would have heard it if it happened once I locked up!"

"How long since you left here?" Chris asked.

"A couple of hours . . . maybe three."

"Do you leave lights on?" Pearce asked.

"Yes. Not full lights but security lighting. And now that you mention it, why didn't the security system alert me?"

The young officer answered. "Sabotage."

"This doesn't make sense! We have homemade crafts in this store. Why would someone go to the trouble to sabotage the security system and do this? The mess here looks like kids, but they wouldn't—" I broke off and stared at Pearce. "It was a professional job. And now I think you need to tell me why you are here."

He motioned toward the office. "Let's look in here. And then we'll talk."

My office was just as I had left it.

"That's weird," I said. "Why would the front of my store be destroyed and my office untouched? If someone was looking to rob me, wouldn"t they have looked there?"

Both men followed my gaze. "Do you see anything out of place?" Chris asked.

"No." I started to explain when he shushed me.

In the silence, we heard a noise coming from inside the file cabinet.

"Don't open it!" Sgt. Pearce said.

"Rex!" he called over his shoulder. "This is your baby."

The young officer stepped forward and the room grew quiet. As he approached, he pulled on an unusual pair of thick gloves. He eased the chair back a couple of inches then stopped. He opened the file cabinet and stared at the package. The box moved slightly—on its own. Everyone froze, holding their breaths. A faint rattle sounded.

Chapter 23

Rex looked at Pearce. "There's something in that box!"

"That sounds like a snake . . . a rattler, maybe." Rex approached the box cautiously while the other officers crowded outside the door.

I scooped up Flash and carried her back into my apartment.

As I re-entered the office, Rex reached inside and lifted out a small mailing box. He placed it gently on the floor. Once out of the cabinet, we could hear noises and something hitting against the inside of the box.

Rex looked up at Pierce. "It's a rattler. I need to get something out of the truck to set this box in." He stepped through the crowd at the door. Pierce looked at the others, and they left to begin working on the disaster in the store.

"How can it be alive?" I asked. "With transport and the heat—"

"This box wasn't officially transported," Reed interrupted. "Look at the postage. It hasn't been stamped or cancelled. This box was likely hand carried here and left in your office. Do you have any idea when it arrived?"

"Not long ago . . . maybe a couple of days. Let me check Teri's log-in sheet." I walked over to my desk, making sure to keep a distance from the box, and retrieved her log-in. "Here it is. The box was logged in this morning. I don't see a time. Wait! It has just a.m. Teri's baby is due soon and she's been on bed rest for a bit, so it probably came while the new girl was here. She doesn't say how it was delivered. But I expect it looked like someone official and she would have directed whoever delivered it to leave it here."

"Were you expecting an order or something?" Reed persisted.

"No . . . but Teri did mention she had signed up a new consignee." When no one spoke, I repeated my argument, in part to convince myself. "Surely you don't think this is a snake. Someone would have heard it during the time it was carried into the store and while it was being moved around . . . and what would be the motivation? This is some prank—"

Rex had returned and Pierce motioned for me to leave.

"No way. I've already spent quite a bit of time with this guy and it's time we were introduced."

Pierce looked at Reed who just shrugged.

Pearce muttered almost to himself. "Who would pull such a prank? And a rattlesnake? That's certainly not a common choice for a joke."

He didn't wait for an answer before barking orders to a couple of officers. "Rex. You have your gear, so open this thing! Everyone else step back into the shop."

"You carry snake gear?" I asked as we stepped into the shop and peered into the window.

"In New Mexico and Arizona? Of course," Pierce said. Then, he turned to two officers. "Check around the building and grounds again for any sign of tampering or disturbance. The rest of you continue processing this crime scene out here."

They shuffled off, leaving Pearce, Reed, and me. We watched Rex work in silence.

Rex had carried in a thick plastic crate with a lid. Wearing the strange gloves, he picked up the shipping box and placed it gently into the crate. Holding it away from his body, he carefully walked out of the office.

"Why didn't I hear the noise earlier when I was here in the office?" I asked.

Rex called back over his shoulder. "I think it was packed in dry ice and has just thawed. I'll know better when I get it out where I can examine it."

I looked at Reed. "Have you ever known anyone to die of snake bite?" I asked.

"No. Chickens . . . a cat . . . dogs. But mostly cats and dogs just swell up unless they're bitten in the face . . . or several times. Of course, I expect that if it hit your eye, you'd lose it and any facial bite would cause considerable discomfort . . . even permanent scarring."

I couldn't hide the shudder the visual picture he'd created left with me. "What does this mean then?"

Pearce had pulled on plastic gloves and was inspecting the inside of the cabinet. "Scare tactic," he said. "A warning maybe. Have you had a verbal disagreement with anyone? Maybe refused to carry their products in the store here? You said it was consignment," he added, "so maybe the person didn't like your terms."

"I've not turned anyone down. A couple have decided they didn't want to wait for their money, but they didn't seem upset—just didn't consign."

"Any enemies? Threatening letters? Hang-up calls? Pranksters?"

I shook my head. "The only pranksters I've heard about in this town are school kids . . . and only around April Fools' Day . . . and, frankly, I don't see them choosing a rattlesnake. Most people are frightened of them and believe the stories of what they do, even though they're more fiction than fact."

Pearce rose and looked up as an officer returned from outside. "See anything?" he asked the officer.

The officer shrugged. "No more snakes," he said. "Tampering will take a while to check."

"Won't know much tonight so we'll be on our way," Pearce said. "No reason to keep you up for the few hours left in the night. We'll seal the shop up and I'll have the officers process it in the morning." He glanced at Reed. "Anything to add?"

"I think you need to tell me what you're not telling," I said. "What's going on here?"

The officer who'd returned from outside spoke up. "You might want to call your security person, ma'am," he said. "There's been a breach."

"A need to know," I observed. No one commented.

Reed spoke up. "Do you want us to wait while you pack and move to a motel or somewhere?"

"And why would I do that?"

"Safety? A good night's sleep?" Reed answered.

"Are you telling me I should feel threatened or afraid?" I asked, looking at both of them.

When neither answered, I walked out of the office. The men followed me through the adjoining door into my residence. "I assume you've checked everything on this side?" I said, catching Reed's eye.

He grinned. "Redhead," he said to Pearce.

"Sorrel," I corrected. "We find coddling restrictive. Give us the open range and the wind in our mane."

The two stepped toward the front door.

"I can leave a couple of officers here," Pierce said.

"Why?"

"We need to make sure no one disturbs the evidence until we can process it. They'll remain outside."

"I'm staying inside," Reed said. He looked at me. "Van and I will need a pillow and a quilt. I'll walk the officers out. Back in a minute."

I couldn't hear their remarks as they left, but I suddenly felt tired enough to sleep. "Come on, Flash," I said. "The guys will watch over us tonight."

Chapter 24

Disjointed orange fingers of light spread across a deep blue morning sky. I could make out the shape of a critter through my kitchen window but couldn't differentiate between an antelope and a cow. It could be a small cow—possibly a yearling—but an antelope or a young deer would get my vote. My fingers itched for my camera.

I spooned the last bite of raspberry yogurt into my mouth and stared at my to-do list on the refrigerator magnetic pad. Restoring my shop had been added to the list, but this morning would be too soon for that. I needed to wait for the security company. Besides, I had a deputy sheriff snoring on the couch. And in spite of two officers dozing out front, I didn't want to leave the shop unattended until I felt comfortable with the security. My shop was full of things people had entrusted to me, and I hoped the break-in hadn't broken their things. Sure, I had insurance; but some things just are difficult to replace—especially when I had just advertised a huge sale coming up.

The shop was closed and so I didn't have helpers here to worry about whether they'd be safe.

"Maybe I should get a dog," I mused, glancing at my felines bathing in their cat beds. Both cats glared at me. "Or maybe not."

I should call Teri next, I thought. I didn't think she planned to come in, but she needed to know not to come...as well as anyone else she had scheduled.

As if on cue, my cell phone rang. "Hi, Teri! How are you?"

"Besides waddling around on swollen feet which I can't see over the watermelon in my stomach?"

"Need help?"

She giggled. "No. Mom was here at dawn, I think. Dinner is in the refrigerator, every thread in the house has been washed, and the twins are off to school. Then Mom will take them to the library afterschool craft class."

"And you will be resting."

"If I have to stay here, I'll go crazy! Sorrel, I am surrounded by family—crazy family—who watch me like a ticking bomb!"

I couldn't swallow the giggle fast enough.

"Do you think it's funny? I thought you were my friend! I promise—if I don't escape before they descend, I'll—"

"Okay. I'm coming to town to pick up groceries. I could swing by there on my way home, collect you, and let you put your feet up while you catch me up on all of the progress here since I've been away. Besides, I've a turn of events that I need to discuss with you. We may have to change some plans."

"Thank you, Sorrel! You're my best friend—"

"Skip the honey talk, Teri. You promise me that you'll stay home until I stop by."

"I guess I don't have a choice!"

"Is the part-timer scheduled to come in today?"

"No, I was waiting to hear if you were back before talking to her."

"Then cancel her. And then, just rest. I'll be there in an hour or so."

"Sorrel?" Teri asked. "I'm going to enjoy finding out what happened to you the past few days. You're sounding like something out of some old Western movie."

A knock at the door signaled the security company representative. "Gotta go," I interrupted then drawled, "Just call me Miss Kitty!" Teri's giggles were a welcome sound.

Reed had abandoned the couch when I turned to open the door. I explained to the security technician about what had happened. "Just give me a call when the scene has been processed and I can return," he said.

Chris stuck his head out of the bedroom when he heard the door close. "Can I take a shower now?" he asked.

"Sure can. I'm heading to the grocery store and stopping by Teri's."

I made quick work of shopping, gathering fresh milk, fruit, and vegetables. At the last moment, I remembered bread and then headed to the check-out line.

"Nice photos in the paper," I overheard someone say. I snatched one just before unloading my basket onto the counter.

I didn't even have time to turn off the engine when I turned onto her driveway. She waddled over to my car from her porch and plopped into the passenger seat. "All clear!" she said and promptly started on details of everything that had happened while I'd been gone.

I was happy to see that no law enforcement were guarding my house when I arrived. They must have finished processing things while I'd been gone.

Once inside, Teri blithely ignored me, opened the refrigerator door, and began unloading a bag.

"You haven't told me anything about your trip," she said. "I thought the photos that Mr. Byrd added to the article are some of the best you've done!"

"Thanks. I haven't had time to read the article yet. How did Will do?" I took her arm and led to a chair. "Let me put my things in the fridge."

"He's not bad. Age and experience will add some depth, but he's bright and ambitious."

I stacked the bag onto a shelf and turned. "What aren't you saying? And do you want something to drink?"

"Not if you want me to rest. I drink then I visit the bathroom. I can't remember why I thought this would be a good idea!" She made a face.

I smiled. "Maybe the hope of a little girl that you could cover in ribbons and lace?" I filled two glasses with water and handed one to her. "Let's sit and catch up on what I've missed."

"No big secrets here, Sorrel, unless—did you find that weird package?"

"Yes, I found it in the file cabinet when I went in the office last night. When did you say it arrived?"

"The other gal was here. She called and I told her to just put it on your desk . . . or near it. You say it was in the file cabinet? Was that okay?"

"Sure." I moved the conversation away from the package and asked about the sale.

As I'd suspected, Teri had organized our sale right down to a timetable for volunteer shifts and food wagons in the parking lot.

"Teri, you can't know how much I appreciate what you've done! But no more sales after this one."

"But—"

"Let's try to capture some of the tourist trade when we plan the next one," I continued. "Maybe July 4th."

I'd spoken the magical words, "sale" and "plans," and Teri leaped into her favorite world. I sipped my water, enjoying the animated expressions on her face as she tossed out ideas. Hopefully, I'd sidestepped the new consignee for a moment.

In the middle of her brainstorming, someone knocked at the door. "Oh, no! They've found me!" she sighed. I walked over and opened the door.

"Not you. Me." I held the door open wider and Chris Reed stepped inside.

He grinned at Teri. "I told Jose you'd be here," he said. He turned back and re-opened the door. "Your wife's hiding out in here," he called. "Do you want me to cuff her?"

Teri started a long list of threats to Reed, stopping only when Jose stepped inside, a big grin on his face. "Can't I go anywhere without my keepers checking up on me?" she complained.

"Keepers!" Jose grumbled. "Can't a man surprise his wife with lunch at her favorite place?"

"Barts?"

"Uh . . . her second favorite place? You've been talking about waffles!"

A huge smile spread across Teri's face. Jose helped her up, stopping only long enough to kiss her and ask, "You okay?"

"Sorrel and I have only just started." She glanced over at me apologetically. "We were having shop talk. I can't just take off—"

"Yes, you can," I told her. "If you don't, you'll be thinking about waffles the rest of the day."

"Why don't you two come with us?" Jose offered.

"I've got too much catch-up work," I told him. "And I need to to get these groceries home." I glanced at Reed.

"I just stopped by to check on a couple of things," he said. "Then I'm heading out to my place to crash."

Looking closer, I could see the exhaustion around Reed's eyes. "So you two didn't ride together?"

"No," Jose said. "He dropped by the house to ask about this gad-a-bout wife of mine just as I pulled into the driveway myself." He mock-glared at Teri. "I've had all sorts of calls from the family asking where you went."

"Anything to drink or eat?" I intervened.

"We have enough at home for an army," Jose answered. "Why don't you two—"

"Too tired!" we chorused.

Teri and Jose looked knowingly at each other then grinned. "Sure you are," Teri said.

"They don't need food," Jose teased. "They're living on—"

They skipped out as Reed glared.

Chapter 25

"Anything else surface?" Reed asked as soon as the door closed.

"No. Let me get you something to eat."

He leaned forward. "Something weird is going on, Sorrel. Somehow it doesn't feel like a cartel thing." He sighed. "Well, the murder is gory and does make a statement, but something's off. And your photo—"

"They know it's mine?"

"Not all. It's on a 'need to know'. I watched their faces as they looked at you. None of them seemed to put the two together except—"

"The . . ." I made quotes with my fingers in the air.

"Yeah. Our illustrious task force leader." He closed his eyes, settled back into the chair, and sighed.

I stood. "Sandwich or something hot?"

He didn't answer and his breathing deepened. I watched quietly. Mama always said you learn more from watching someone sleep. She wasn't wrong. In his sleep, Reed looked almost boyish—softer and unguarded. An errant lock of hair dropped onto his forehead. Before I succumbed to the urge to brush it back, I tiptoed to the kitchen and started a pot of coffee. A half hour nap should refresh him enough to eat something and drive home.

Reed slept closer to forty-five minutes before the smell of fresh coffee and fried bacon roused him. "I wanted something hot and you didn't say anything so I made it," I said when he grinned at me.

He stood and stretched. "I won't argue with that," he said and walked toward the bathroom. I cracked four eggs into a bowl, added salt and pepper, and dumped them into a skillet. With bread slices in the toaster and butter and jelly on the table, I started to stir the eggs.

I didn't even hear Reed's return until he took the spoon from me. "I'll stir the eggs."

"Thanks."

I thought of the term "companionable silence" as we completed our tasks and sat across from each other at my small table. "Coffee!" I said and jumped back up to fill mugs for each of us. Chris dished food onto the plates, which we emptied quickly.

"We're acting like an old married couple," I said, looking down at my empty plate.

Reed smiled. "How's that?"

"Everything's already been said. Of course, since we're really just friends . . ."

His eyebrow lifted. "I don't know if that's entirely true, Sorrel. After all, we have slept together."

"Chris Reed! What a liar!"

His laughter was contagious, and I found myself fighting giggles. "As I recall, we did," he said when he caught his breath. "Of course, we were dressed and that mangy, one-eared gray cat slept between us."

It felt good to giggle. I started to stand but he beat me. "I'll clear the table. You cooked, after all, and we even managed to eat it." He whistled. "Better circle today's date on the calendar."

The banter continued until we had cleaned up the kitchen and settled in the living room with the last of the coffee. "Tell me what feels off to you, Reed."

"The photo, for one. Why would they plant it? For the police? For some hiker who found the body?"

"I thought of that too. He must have had it in his pocket, but I'm not sure it ties in with his murder either. It's an old photo, so he's had it a long time. Maybe he forgot it was even there. Don't you have things shoved into your wallet that you don't even notice any more?"

"I guess I do. Do you have any idea when it was taken?"

"Well, as I said, it was one of the promotional photos announcing my joining the station. That would have been about ten years ago."

Reed drained his cup. "He may have had some personal attachment to you—or even an obsession—to carry it around so long. But the killers? Especially the cartel? Why would they even care? I wonder if they even knew it was there. Well, they'd likely go through his pockets, I guess; but I'm not sure they'd—I hope they'd ignore it. They'd have no reason to care about photos he had in his wallet unless they wanted to continue a vendetta." He started to lift his empty cup.

"Want more coffee? I can make another pot."

"No, thanks." He carried his cup to the sink. "But the snake box showing up in your shop gives me pause."

"Could be a coincidence. As I said, I do have a new consignee who makes items from rattlesnake skins and rattles."

"Anything about him/her seem odd?"

"Him. I've never seen him. Transactions have been made either when I've been gone or through the mail."

"He'd have no reason to send a live snake," Chris mused. "It could have been someone else."

"And therein lies the coincidence," I said. "But someone would have had to watch and set the box there without being noticed. Unless you were paying close attention, it would look like it came from a legitimate parcel service."

"Do they carry parcels inside or do they just leave a note for you?"

I thought. "Yes to both, because I wouldn't want merchandise sitting on the steps. They have instructions to call before they deliver a box unless the truck has other packages to deliver out in this area."

"Anyone mention it?"

I thought. "I remember finding a note from Teri about a box that she'd had put in my office. I don't know if she received it or if one of the volunteers took the delivery. But there were other boxes left which had been opened. I remember her talking about carrying trash from deliveries."

"With the confusion of getting the place ready for a sale and Teri's preoccupation with the upcoming delivery of her own, someone could have slipped around the counter and left the box."

I still wasn't convinced. "A lot of ifs there," I said. "Besides, that returns us to the original quandary. How does any of this connect my photo to a poor guy murdered and left in a cave?"

"I can't figure it yet. But coincidences bother me, especially when there's murder—and someone special—involved." He pulled me into a hug. "Your living out here alone bothers me."

I snuggled into the hug. "I'm not alone. My two roommates—"

"Are just mangy critters whose greatest concern in life is when and how they're getting the next meal!"

I pulled back a little and grinned up into his face. "I suspect you can relate with them!"

I watched his truck pull away shortly afterward, his loud laughter still filling the air.

Chapter 26

"Sorrel, I need your help."

Will's phone message sounded more like the kid he seemed to me than an almost university graduate. I didn't have time for his histrionics today. My new part-time employee, Lily, and I had spent a grueling couple of days readying the shop for the Valentine's Day sale. Our job had been made more difficult due to Teri's official lighter schedule, although I wasn't complaining about that. Her doctor agreed with our concerns and ordered her to light activities and rest.

I reluctantly dialed the number Will had attached to his message. He picked up immediately and, before I could speak, asked, "Sorrel?"

"Hi, Will. Before you ask, I'm really swamped right now. Mr. Byrd has other photographers—"

"Sorrel, are you home?"

"I'm working short-handed here, Will. Just call Mr. Byrd."

I hung up the phone, twinges of guilt flitting by. I hated to turn him down, but this was the only time I could frame some of the shots I'd taken at Portal. After those were finished, I wanted to print notecards as well. Tourists had consistently bought the ones I'd made from Bosque. And on top of it all, I'd lost a couple of days with the trashing of my store.

Both cats joined me, lying in the sun on window sills, as I measured, cut, and matted a sunset shot I'd taken one evening near our cottage. Neither flinched when my CD player switched and Backstreet Boys increased the musical volume in our tiny room. I danced toward them, holding the ruler like a microphone and singing. Van opened a big yellow eye then closed it. He clearly wasn't impressed. Flash made a circle and snored.

By the time the song ended, I'd almost finished the mat for the cave shot. It wasn't The One, naturally, but an interesting—

Some sort of loud noise filtered through the music—a hammering. I sighed and followed it to my front door. A peek confirmed my suspicion. Will.

"What part of no don't you understand?" I snapped, holding the door only partly open. "I'm only part-time for the paper, and I only accept assignments from Mr. Byrd. And now till the Valentine Sale, I'm—"

"I'm in trouble," he mumbled.

I looked—really looked—at Will. He had dark smudges under his eyes, his hair stuck out like a badly cut Mohawk, and he'd thrown a faded jersey on with pajama bottoms and flip-flops. "I doubt the fashion police throw people in jail," I murmured, opening the door for him to enter.

"This isn't funny," he muttered. Any moment, he was going to cry.

"I knew comedy wasn't my talent," I said. I pushed the door, but it wouldn't close.

"Is this a private party?"

"Reed? What are you doing here?"

"Happy to see you too. Hello, Will." Reed stepped by me into the room, and I shut the door after him. "Any coffee?"

"Iced tea. Dr. Pepper." I looked at my intruders and sighed audibly. When I received no reaction, I motioned toward the couch. "Have a seat. I'll make coffee."

While the coffeemaker brewed, I made several peanut butter-and-jelly sandwiches and piled them onto a plate. After a glance at the silent pair, I also pulled out a divided plate and filled it with baby dill pickles, cherry tomatoes, crackers, and black olives. Finally, I opened a bag of cookies.

"Okay, guys, I've made coffee and I've put out some food. But I'm not going to serve it to you. You need to come to the table."

I stacked paper plates beside the food. Reed poured coffee for himself and Will. "Sorrel?"

"I guess." Unfortunately, the way things were playing out, I'd likely be working late on my framing job. But I had to be honest with myself as well. Will's demeanor was strange. And Reed? Well, I wasn't totally unhappy to see him.

Will's scare hadn't disturbed his appetite, I soon decided. I watched him devour at least half of the items I'd set out as I nibbled on the veggies and crackers. Reed swallowed the last of a sandwich and reached for the cookies. "Am I interrupting something?" he finally asked.

I looked at Will. "Are you comfortable talking with Reed here?" I asked. "He's law enforcement."

Reed looked from me to Will, who stared down at his plate. "He's also a friend who is out of uniform," Reed said. "Do you need help, Will?"

Will reached inside the waistband of the pajama pants and pulled out the front page of yesterday's newspaper, *Gap News*. He handed it over to Reed. I leaned close enough to read the words printed across the newsprint in a black marker: WORDS + PITCHERS = DETH. A skull grinned eerily beneath.

"When did you get this?" I asked.

"Found it when I got in last night—about eight," he said. "It was stuffed in my mailbox with the rest of the mail."

"Do you have a post office box?" Reed asked.

Will shook his head. "I live in those apartments on Third Street," he said. "Our mailboxes are small black ones attached to the brick beside the door."

"Did you ask around to see if anyone saw anything?" I asked.

"No one is around during the day. Everyone works except for the old woman two apartments down. I didn't ask her. You never see her out."

"Anything else unusual? Hang-ups, that feeling of being watched, someone seeming to be everywhere you go?" Reed glanced over the paper again as he spoke, not touching it but noting details.

"Nah. But I wouldn't notice anyway. I'm tired. I've been putting in long hours at the paper, trying to make sure this internship is successful." Will slumped back in his chair. "That article was a good piece, I thought. I need this job here to work out so I can graduate. And now this!"

Reed swallowed a cookie and washed it down with coffee. I stood up and brought the pot, refilling his and mine. I motioned toward Will's cup, but he didn't seem to notice. I refilled it anyway.

"You can't give it too much attention just yet," I told him when I'd sat back down. "It could be a prank, someone who is jealous, or—"

"Or someone who is warning me away!"

I couldn't totally argue with that. I looked at Reed but he just shrugged. "My name is on the photos," I continued. "I haven't gotten anything. So—"

Reed cleared his throat. Will remained slumped; but when I looked, Reed caught my eye and made a slight movement with the brim of his hat. It took only a second or two before I followed his thought. My office! The box with the snake! I started to open my mouth but stopped at the slight negative shake of his hat.

"What's your schedule like for today?" he asked Will.

"Nothing set. I got in late because I was covering a City Parks and Recreation Board meeting. They gave me a packet, so I stayed up and wrote the article. Emailed it in. Then looked at my mail."

"When are they expecting you at the paper?"

"Mr. Byrd gave me today off. Said I'd been putting in a lot of overtime hours."

"Then how about you hang out with me today?" I asked. "I can use the extra hands."

Will didn't jump at the offer. "Doing what?" he asked finally.

"Watching the shop while I kidnap Sorrel," Reed answered. "She needs a break, and I need her advice on a project at the ranch."

I opened my mouth, but I felt his knee nudge mine under the table. "It's quiet here," I told Will. "You look like you could use some sleep. The shop's closed; but with my being gone so much lately, I like to give the appearance of someone on the grounds. Your car parked out there would signal someone is here."

He swallowed another gulp of coffee. "I don't want to put anyone out. We need to—"

"Let me make some inquiries," Reed interrupted. "I doubt it's more than malicious mischief, but let me follow some checkpoints and get back to you. We won't be gone too long, and you'll think clearer with some sleep." He turned to me. "Do you have a large Ziploc bag I could use to protect this? Fingerprints will be useless as half of Saddle Gap has probably touched it by now, but the bag will keep it in one piece." He looked at Will. "Do you mind if I take it?"

Will shrugged, caught in the middle of a yawn, and made a trip to the bathroom while Reed and I cleared the kitchen.

When he returned, Will made a few more token arguments. When Reed and I drove away less than a half hour later, he was already snoring on my sofa. I'd offered my guest bed, but he waved me away saying it was probably too frilly. I didn't argue. From the looks of him, Will could probably use a good shower and a change of clothes. I didn't mention that though because he needed sleep more, so I found a pillow and covered him with a light blanket.

Reed waited until we were out on the highway before he asked, "What's your take on the newspaper?"

"I'm not sure. It feels almost juvenile to me. Intentionally misspelled words. Marker on newspaper. And if I were the intended target—as the photo would suggest—why threaten Will?"

"Good point. The cartel doesn't usually operate that way, so who does?"

"Speaking of the cartel, why aren't you with the task force?"

"They don't need so many of us to do this stage of the investigation. I've contributed about all they need from me."

"Did they send anyone else home?"

He smiled. "Yes."

We rode in silence for a few minutes before he asked, "Have you heard anything from Teri?"

"Nothing happening so far."

"She was just like this with the twins. Impatient."

"Most women I've known are. It's like knowing you're getting exactly what you've dreamed about for Christmas but aren't allowed to open the package. At least, that's what I think it would be like."

Reed flipped on his blinker. "You ever plan to have any?"

"I wouldn't mind. You?"

He never answered. Instead, he stepped on the brake. "What the—"

Straight ahead, sitting on the tailgate of his truck, was Sgt. Pearce.

Chapter 27

Pearce stood still after Reed drove past him and parked on the driveway. He didn't approach and, upon closer inspection, I saw he was speaking into a small cellphone. When we stepped out of the truck and walked toward him, Pearce ended his conversation, slid the phone into his shirt pocket, and smiled.

"Finding you two together saves me some steps," he said.

Reed grinned. "You're a lucky guy to catch us both. What can we do for you?"

Pearce addressed me first. "We checked your box routing, ma'am, and we didn't find a record of a box—with or without a snake-- shipped to your address. My officers are working their way through private delivery companies that service your area, but it may be a week or two. I'm sorry I don't have anything for you yet. These companies are so meticulous and have all these computers and such. Makes me wonder if someone—a kid or someone-- may just be pulling a joke on you."

"A complicated, elaborate joke," Reed commented drily.

"I'm not laughing," I said. "And sending someone a reptile that could cause harm isn't my idea of a joke. I suppose my sense of humor and that of the Border Patrol are incompatible." I stared at him.

Pearce's face flushed but he didn't answer. He turned toward Reed instead and hurried into a coded commentary about "certain evidence" that hadn't been yet "explained."

"Is this evidence you collected from my shop," I finally interrupted, "or is it evidence you collected from the cave murder?"

"Not to be rude," he said, "but police business—"

"Is my business if it involves photos of someone who looks like me."

Pearce shot a look at Reed.

"No," I continued, "he didn't tell me. The editor of the newspaper where I do freelance photography told me. He'd learned about it from a confidential source—and it wasn't Chris Reed, because I asked."

"When?"

"Before I was asked to accompany a reporter on a travel article to Portal. And, before you ask, I didn't share the information with him."

From his face, Pearce didn't believe much of what I'd said. "Why would this editor tell you?"

"I'd think you'd know. If my photo—and an article about me—were on the body of a dead man, one who was likely murdered, wouldn't he be curious, as I suspect you are, about the reason?"

Pearce looked like he'd like to either add me to the murdered list or tear into Reed.

"I don't have a comfortable home here yet," Reed drawled, "but before this conversation gets any more heated, I suggest we move to my bachelor pad makeover and have something cold to drink while we air differences."

Once we were seated around Reed's kitchen table, he offered sodas and bottled water from an ancient refrigerator. Pearce chose a Coke and Reed handed me a bottled water before I answered. I saw Pearce's eyebrow lift, but he chose to ignore it. Instead, he looked around the kitchen and said, "Your idea of a bachelor pad and mine are worlds apart."

Reed laughed. "If I weren't working so much, it would look different."

"Ever think about hiring it done?"

"What? And miss the thrill of aching back and knees, power tools, paint flecked clothes—"

"On my friendly neighbor as I watch?" I interrupted.

Pearce glanced at me, then Reed. Everyone laughed. "You've got to teach me your persuasive techniques," he told Reed.

"Read Tom Sawyer," Reed said.

His strategy had worked. Mama always said it was hard to stay mad around a kitchen table. I watched Pearce relax and felt my own hostility softening a bit. He was just doing his job, after all, and it wasn't an easy one. But he wasn't a beginner in law enforcement either, and he wouldn't be easily pacified with vague answers.

I sipped the water quietly while Reed and Pearce made small talk about home repair. Finally, I stood and turned to Reed. "Mind if I take a look at your barn and corrals? You were asking for my advice on the way over here, and I'm not familiar with them."

Both men made as if to stand, but I continued, "No need to come along." Then I caught Pearce's eye. "I suspect you have things to discuss without an audience." I stuck out my hand and he reluctantly shook it. "Thanks for following up on the box. As you say, I doubt we'll find much more than a practical joker behind it."

I left through the back door. My light jacket wasn't quite heavy enough for an early February day, but the sunshine soon warmed me up a bit. I hadn't been completely untruthful. Reed had asked my advice several weeks ago, but it had been about the house, not the corrals and barn. Still, I enjoyed exploring them more closely than I'd done before. Although the ranch had run down as its older owner had fallen ill, it wasn't past help. I unbolted the barn door and pulled it open.

Immediately, I heard a stealthy rustling. The door protested—needed some oil on the hinges—and I gripped it with both hands and pulled. As my eyes adjusted to the dim interior, I stepped just inside the door and looked up at the hay storage area high toward the ceiling. I saw a light bulb and searched along the inside wall for a switch. But once I flicked it with my finger, I realized the bulb had burned out. So I turned back and opened the doors wide and blocked them from closing with a couple of small logs that probably had been placed there for that reason.

Several stalls along the opposite wall had probably housed horses or cows. Reed had already begun the clean-up process there. He'd have to repair some of them as well. The floor creaked as I stepped further inside and rotated slowly. I turned to look behind me and saw a ladder. I followed it up to another storage area and—a growl, low at first, then growing in volume—came too closely behind me for comfort.

Coyote? Surely not. They were shy critters and certainly wouldn't have sheltered in a building. Unless . . . could it have rabies? I couldn't remember hearing about a case of coyotes with rabies. Wolves didn't live around here, did they?

During my mental rambling, the growl changed tone slightly. Yelps? A slight movement followed. I squinted in the direction of the sound. Tiny whines and yelps had replaced the growl. "It's a friend, not foe," I crooned softly, hardly daring to breathe. A brown and white head lifted from behind a pile of old straw, the brown eyes glaring with a mixture of fear, warning, and . . . hunger? The pile of straw wiggled. Wiggled? "Are you hurt?" I crooned. Crooning almost always works with critters, Mama always said. I hoped she was right.

After what seemed like an hour, the creature sat up. I could barely make out the outline of a dog. I crept forward a half step, crooning nonsense phrases softly, until I could see it better in the dim light. Suddenly, the rustling began again and the straw moved. "Babies!" I murmured. I knelt down and slowly crawled as close as I dared.

She was a medium-sized dog, likely of several breeds mixed together. But despite her size, she was prepared to defend her babies, starving though she appeared to be. I felt in my jacket pocket and pulled out a packet of crackers. I opened them while she eyed them suspiciously—and hungrily—and placed them on the floor in front of me. Then I got up slowly and backed carefully away toward the open doors, speaking soft crooning nonsense until I felt a body behind—a body?

I glanced around and would have yelled, but Reed planted a kiss on my round mouth. When he finished, he whispered, "I couldn't think of any other way to shut you up, Sorrel Janes!" Before I could reply, he continued, "Can't I leave you alone in my barn for fifteen minutes without you finding a stray wild dog with a litter of pups?"

I turned back just in time to see the dog disappearing into the darkened stall, leaving behind no sign of the crackers. "Let's go," I whispered, "so I can kill you out there. She's already scared enough!"

After we backed out into the light, I turned to Reed. "You can turn me loose now."

Although he lifted his hands with no resistance, he didn't try to hide the wide grin. We moved the logs, closed the barn door, and started back toward the house. I noticed Pearce's vehicle was gone. "He finds you nearly as frustrating as I do," Reed observed.

"Good! Maybe it gives Mrs. Pearce a break!"

"He didn't say it, but I think he suspects you may have moved here through witness protection," Reed continued, ignoring my smart mouth as best he could. "And he's frustrated with this case. Everything about it leads off into a new direction but veers into a dead end. You know as well as I do that most cases like this one don't come to a quick conclusion in an hour like they do on television."

"Really!"

"Sarcasm will get you nowhere, Sorrel."

I could hear the laughter behind his words, so I changed the subject.

"We need to go to town before you take me home," I said.

"Why?"

"Dog food! That little lady is starving."

We had reached the house and he'd pulled open the screen door. "She'll likely have those pups moved by the time we get back," he said.

"Do you have anything?"

"Moldy bread? Remember, I've been gone for a while!"

I walked over to his cupboard, opened it up, and looked over the meager canned goods. "You need a serious nutritionist, Chris Reed," I murmured. I pulled a can of beef stew, wrinkled my nose, and handed it to him. "Hopefully, this won't kill her." Then I crouched down to rummage through the cabinet beside the stove, pulled out a battered tin pie pan, and handed it over my shoulder. "This won't be a huge loss. You need a housewarming party when you get this thing redone, Chris!"

When he didn't answer, I looked over my shoulder. He was holding the pan in his hands carefully, a strange expression on his face. "Everything okay?" I asked, standing up.

"Fine," he whispered. He blinked and I could almost see his eyes welling up a bit. "This was Mama's pan. I remember telling her that she'd better get rid of it and the others because I was buying her a whole new set." He grinned awkwardly. "She was a lot like you—sassy. She told me old pans or new, it was the cook who mattered."

Then he carried it to the counter, rummaged around for a can opener, and opened the stew. When he'd dumped it, he grinned at me with his usual smirk. "Come along! I figure you need to be the one to set this inside as she seems to trust you. Weird, trusting a cat lady! Anyway, I'll catch you up on Pearce's news on the way into town."

Sometimes Chris Reed reminded me that life before him might have been a little dull—but the feeling usually passed quickly. Still, I wanted to hear about Pearce's reason for a visit, so I followed, as meekly as I could muster, to the barn.

Chapter 28

"She was gobbling it as fast as she could, even with me standing nearby. Poor little thing is about starved, and she has all those pups to feed. We need to make sure the dog food has the proper nutrients for a nursing mother." I took a breath and glanced at Reed. "How can you laugh?"

"You're so funny, that's how! Except for the pups you inserted in the sentence, anyone would think you were speaking about a human!"

"And that's so funny? Critters need our care too. If—"

"This one looks like a good one." Reed pointed toward a popular brand at the beginning of the aisle. "I'll—"

"Let me check the ingredients." I shook my head as I read them. "No, this won't work." I moved on down the aisle until I found something with the ingredients the veterinarian I had talked with here in the pet store had suggested. "This is what she needs."

By the time we exited the pet store, both our arms were filled. Reed put everything in the back of the truck, started the engine, and looked over at me. "What plans do you have for the nursery?" His eyes gleamed with mischief.

"It will have to wait until after the sale this weekend!" I gave him a sassy grin.

"Speaking of," Reed snapped his fingers, "I got a text to call Jose. Almost forgot. Let me check it."

He glanced at his phone, handed it to me, and backed out of the parking spot quickly. His whole demeanor changed. I read the text: *SOS. Hospital.*

Minutes later we were parked in the hospital emergency zone. Reed put a permit on his mirror and joined me on the curb. Seeing my raised eyebrows, he drawled, "It's an emergency. Jose sounds like a cardiac patient!"

We didn't need to ask for directions. It looked like half of Saddle Gap's population had gathered in the small waiting area. But the scary part was the silence.

Glancing quickly, we saw Teri's mother sitting stone-faced, her eyes puffy with tears. When she noticed us, she closed the distance and grabbed Reed in a hug, weeping softly. At some point, she began speaking into his wet shirt. One of her sisters moved to pull her away, but Reed gave a small headshake and murmured to her softly. Whatever he said must have soothed her. Her shoulders relaxed a bit, and she started to pull away. Reed reached over, picked a tissue out of the box on the table, and offered it to her casually as he stepped over to shake hands with other family members.

One of Teri's sisters-in-law, Ramona, asked if I wanted a cup of coffee. "No, I'm fine," I said. "What's up?"

"Teri fell."

"Oh, no! The baby—"

"They're checking. She was spotting when she came in. And they're not sure whether her ankle was sprained or broken."

"Whatever was she doing?"

Ramona made a face. "You know Teri. She decided to hang the curtains in the nursery. Jose has been busy and she grew tired of waiting for him to do it."

"I thought she was going to wait until the baby was born."

"Seems she has known the sex but wanted to do this big surprise reveal for all of us."

Reed had come over in time to hear the last part. "What about when the baby just appears?" he asked. "That's how I'd like it."

I looked at him in mock horror. "You are the most curious person I know! I see no way that you'd wait."

"Isn't it a little like opening your Christmas gift way early and then acting all surprised when the day arrives?"

"But it's so much more practical," Ramona jumped in. "That way you have everything ready." She gave Reed a mock punch in the arm. "Men!"

A stir at the doorway caught our attention. Jose and the doctor had walked in and, as if on cue, everyone stopped talking and waited. The doctor, who looked like a young girl herself, spoke to the group but addressed herself toward Teri's mother. "Mother and baby are fine," she began. "Falls happen sometimes during pregnancy because mothers are often a little off balance due to size. But this fall, from a step ladder, is a bit more complicated. The sprain—"

"Sprain!" someone gasped.

"Requires her to be off her feet. She has also had a bit of bleeding and some contractions, so we are keeping her with us for a day or so just to watch how things go." She smiled encouragingly to Jose. "Jose has assured us that she has enough family and friends to help, so we won't need to keep her here until the baby's birth."

The crowd grew restless and I could hear numerous comments, most in Spanish. Someone asked about the baby. "We detect no problems there," she reassured the room, making sure again to catch the eye of the older crew who were seated in the middle. "Right now," she continued, "I'm restricting visitors so that she can rest. Jose has said he can stay with her, and she will want to see the boys for a few minutes. She's resting just now and that's the best thing for her." She smiled as she swept the room with her eyes and left.

Immediately, the crowd converged on Jose, questions and comments flying. Reed caught Jose's eye, nodded, then gestured for me to follow him out of the door. "They'll keep him busy for a while," he whispered, "so we can get out before they realize it. They'll all have opinions about her working at your place, and you'll be kept here forever otherwise."

"Well, of course, she won't be able to work at the shop! I've already made some provisions, and now I'll just need to make a few more. I wasn't really comfortable with her there anyway, you know."

"Yes, I do know. Teri is hard to contain."

"Nice turn of phrase."

"Well, how about this one? I'm starving! How about you?"

"A burger sounds good," I admitted.

It tasted good too. We'd taken the dog food to Reed's barn and put some out, as well as water, for the hungry dog. We'd then headed over to my place to eat the burgers and fries we'd bought. Reed plowed into his while I poured glasses of iced tea.

"Did you notice that the doctor referred to one baby?" I asked.

Reed grinned. "Bet that's a relief to both of them."

We lapsed into silence for a bit, enjoying the food. I pushed most of my fries over to Chris, and he happily ate them. "Had you noticed the dog before now?" I asked.

"No. I imagine someone dropped her off, though . . . probably while I was gone. She doesn't seem like a wild dog."

"How sad to be struggling to feed a litter of puppies when you don't have enough to eat yourself."

He smiled and drained his tea glass. "There goes that heart of yours."

"I know . . . collecting strays."

"Loving strays. It's one of your most attractive traits. Probably why I keep getting caught up in helping you. I'm surprised you didn't become a vet." He refilled his glass and motioned toward mine. I shook my head.

"Who knows? That may be off somewhere in the future. My parents were both dead, and I wasn't sure I could afford that much schooling—but I did consider it. I suppose I followed a similar career in a way . . . because the people whose stories I shared needed a voice also, and I gave it to them. And now I share photos of wild critters."

"Can I help you with anything here? No decorating, I hope."

I couldn't resist teasing. "You could cut out some hearts—"

Chris groaned but his phone interrupted any further teasing. "Reed," he said. "I'm not home but I can talk." He motioned to me and stepped outside.

I cleared the table then stepped out to the office to check phone messages there. I didn't have many: the usual sales calls advertising products I neither wanted nor needed, hang-ups, a call from Randall Byrd asking me to come by the paper in the morning if possible, and a couple of locals asking if I shipped items. I jotted down notes on the ones that needed answers and pushed the erase button.

By the time I returned to my living area, Chris had returned and seated himself in the overstuffed chair, Flash on his knee. "Everything okay?" he asked.

"Just clearing the message machine. Nothing pressing." I sat on the sofa and Van immediately settled on my lap. "Now that we're comfortable, can you tell me why Pearce finds me difficult?"

"Besides the fact that you're smart, sassy, opinionated—and not too hard on the eyes?" He pantomimed dodging a bullet then continued. "Oh, and worse yet, you're a newswoman."

I glared at him.

"I'll be leaving again tomorrow. He doesn't expect I'll be more than a couple of days. Maybe three. Just to wrap up loose ends."

"The body?"

"They haven't identified him yet. They do know that he died, as they suspected, from multiple snake bites, which probably led to a heart attack. He didn't go into details with me . . . just gave general facts."

"Horrible."

"Yes, I imagine it was. He was dehydrated and looked like he'd walked a long distance—and he'd been beaten." He paused. "Please don't share this information, Sorrel."

"I won't."

"Even with—"

"I won't. Besides, I wasn't the reporter on that trip . . . just the photographer."

"Right."

I ignored the skepticism in his voice. "Will you let me know, at least, when—if—they identify him? I know its police business, but it's personal for me, you know! The questions swirl in my brain: Why my photo? Why keep it but nothing else? Why did they leave the photo on him?"

Reed decided to change the subject. "I have a guy to keep an eye on my place. He's also doing some of the repairs that I don't have time to do. I've told him about the dog, but I'd appreciate if you'd peek in on her if/when you have the chance." He grinned. "I know you don't have anything else to do." He dodged another pretend bullet.

"You're racking up a big bill. Hope you can afford it."

After Reed left, I returned Mr. Byrd's call. I doubted he would still be there, but he picked up on the second ring.

"Hi! Sorrel here. Sorry I missed your call."

"Hi, Sorrel. Are you about ready for your big sale?"

"Actually, we are. At least, the store is almost ready; but Teri is in the hospital."

"She is? The baby?"

I explained about her fall. "The doctor is putting her on bedrest and limited activity, so I'll need to check on adequate help here at the store."

"Is there any way you can come in to visit with me at the paper in the morning? I have something to discuss with you."

"And Will?"

He paused. "Could you meet me at—"

"Could we meet here?"

"In fact, that might be better."

"I don't have anyone scheduled because the shop is closed."

"Good. About seven okay?

"Sure."

Later that night, after I'd finished the novel I'd started a couple of weeks ago—and had to reread parts because of the time lapse—and clicked off the lamp, I snuggled under my warm quilt amid the two cats. Unanswered questions swirled in my brain. I'd spent much of my life alone, so loneliness hadn't been anything I'd noticed . . . until lately. I wished I could call John.

Instead, I let my mind roam over happy things like the store, Teri's new baby, plans for my photography, and Reed's puppies. As sleep descended and I started to drift off, I heard Mama's voice: *The child weeps, Sorrel. Keep looking.*

I sat up, looked around, then curled back up, and covered my ears. This time, I slept.

Chapter 29

After waking from a sound sleep to the 6:00 a.m. alarm, I showered, fed the cats, and started coffee. My refrigerator revealed a can of biscuits, which I popped in the oven. While they cooked, I set out butter, strawberry jam, and two cups and saucers.

Randall Byrd arrived exactly at seven, his customary suit creased and his tie already askew. He carried an electronic tablet, which he set at the table where I'd indicated a chair. "I've already eaten," he said, "but don't let me interrupt you." He sniffed. "I wouldn't say no to a cup of coffee. Smells fresh brewed."

I hid a smile, thinking of the tar he referred to as coffee at the news office. I poured us each a cup and sat across from him at the small table. While he opened the tablet and searched for the notes he'd entered, I reached for a biscuit and smeared it with butter and jam.

"Your photos of the caves and other landscapes in Arizona were first rate," he said. He reached inside his jacket and pulled out an envelope, which he handed across the table to me. "I thought I'd just deliver your check since I was coming out."

I left it unopened by my plate and thanked him. "I appreciate the business. My little shop provides me with a sporadic income, as does my photography, but we're still in the very early stages of business."

He took a drink of his coffee and smiled. "My wife loves it, especially your bird photographs."

I thanked him and bit into my biscuit.

He looked down at his tablet, his mind moving to the real purpose of his visit. "I assume you have read Will's article?"

I swallowed. "Yes, I did. I think he's a promising newsman once he finishes—"

"Growing up?" Mr. Byrd took another drink of his coffee. "Did you two work together well? I mean, any real problems?"

"No." I wasn't quite feeling what he wasn't saying or where this conversation was leading.

"I'm not sure he bought the whole story of a family piece," Byrd continued. "He's been nosing around a bit . . . about you. Apparently he's been reading up on articles about your Socorro adventures."

When I didn't comment, he continued. "We received a news release about the body found in a cave there. Will began ferreting information about you shortly after."

"He has a natural reporter's curiosity."

"Does he know about—"

"About Reed and my time in Socorro? Almost nothing. Reed did drop by one evening, and I think that Will decided we are a couple. So we didn't disabuse him of the idea."

"Lots of people are thinking the same way." Randall took another gulp of coffee. When I didn't comment, he continued. "I'm not sure it makes any difference, and sometimes their speculation keeps attention diverted from other things."

"Like who was this young—dead—man and why was my photo in his pocket?"

"Right." Randall Byrd cleared his throat. "I wish I had more information for you, but law enforcement are playing their hand close to their chests."

"What do they know?"

Randall Byrd drained his coffee cup and stood. "They're still searching for his identity. His prints haven't come up in their databases, and they haven't had a missing person report matching him."

I stood as well. "And the look-alike photo?"

"They know who it is—or was—but Sorrel Janes isn't connected to it." He added, "But my source isn't necessarily law enforcement. It could surface."

I knew it was possible but pretended a calm I didn't feel and followed him to the door. He stepped out on the porch and turned, offering a comforting smile. "I know you're busy, especially with Teri out. Didn't want to burden you but thought you'd be interested in an update. I may have some other small jobs for you if you think you can manage the time."

"I appreciate it. I'll manage the time."

"Well, hold your appreciation until you look over the list of activities my secretary will email you later this morning. Spring is busy times with the kids, you know, and everyone— including their grandmas—want to see photos in the paper. Doesn't hurt our circulation either." He took a step toward his car then turned back. "I'll keep you posted when—if—I hear anything."

I watched him drive away a few minutes later. In spite of his gruff exterior, Randall Byrd had a fatherly bent toward me. The photos he needed helped both of us: circulation for him and advertisement for me. I appreciated the small income as well.

But he was a newspaperman at heart, and so I continued to keep my own counsel around him except on need-to-know situations. When I'd first come here, he hadn't known my background completely. What parts he knew, he'd kept to himself. I trusted his discretion, but I still didn't share all I knew.

The plan forming in my mind hadn't gotten to that point, but I wouldn't be sharing it with him either. I needed to organize things here first. With Teri's condition, I needed to schedule additional help at the store for the sale. I also needed to finish some of the photo projects with the shots I'd taken of the caves. Ideas for those—and a dozen others—floated through my mind as I stuffed clothes in the washing machine before pulling out the vacuum.

After I'd dispensed with chores at home, I drove over to Reed's place to check on the little dog. She didn't come out to meet me or anything, but I could feel her eyes on me. When she rose, I heard the puppies yipping. I didn't look her direction. "Hello, little mama. Sounds like your babies are a rambunctious bunch. You must be hungry." I kept my voice soft. When I'd filled both food and water dishes, I turned and walked softly toward the door. Before leaving, I stood a moment and glanced over my shoulder. She'd slunk close to the food, her eyes mostly on me, although they were flicking toward the food. When her eyes locked with mine, she froze, ready to vanish into the darkness. Even as starved and scraggly as she was, she was willing to take on any predator.

I stepped out and closed up the barn then waited until I heard the sounds of her eating.

"We all have our secrets," I murmured as I drove away. "Sometimes they haunt us. Sometimes we hide them by burying them deep enough that we hope no one will find them." And I knew—more personally than most—what could happen when someone did find them.

By early afternoon, I'd framed a number of prints from the recent trip to Portal and added them to the display area in the shop. I'd spoken with Teri, who didn't offer much argument with her enforced home stay but instead offered a cousin who could fill in at the shop during our sale and beforehand should I need help organizing. I accepted her offer and took the cousin's phone number.

I strolled through the shop, straightening the various displays, visually examining the hanging items to make sure they were straight and not too low or high. Several still needed to be redone after the break-in. Then I walked to the door in the front, stepped out, and stepped back in.

Wow! Aunt Rose would have been so proud! This, in part, had been her dream. We were truly prepared for our Valentine's Day sale—well, almost. Anything I changed or touched wouldn't make it any better.

Yet again, I scanned the displays as I walked to the back of the store. I passed by my desk, trying not to glance at the cabinet where the snake box had been hidden, and stepped through the door into my kitchen. Something niggled at the back of my mind. What was I missing? Everything looked exactly as I'd left it. Then I mentally scolded myself. "Are you getting paranoid?" I whispered.

I walked into my bedroom, sweeping it with my eyes. Nothing. What did I expect? What was I looking for?

The doorbell pealed, followed by a heavy knock. I jumped. Another knock. I rose, and stepped into the kitchen, pulling my bedroom door closed. When I peeked through the peephole Jose had installed, I sighed. Not now! Not again!

I swung open the door, only to swallow the words. He wasn't alone. I opened the door. "I'm in the middle of something," I said, stepping out.

"That's why we're wanting to talk to you," Sgt. Pearce said. He looked over his shoulder at Reed then back to me. "We can talk at the sheriff's office if you'd like."

Chapter 30

I walked with Pearce and Reed to the sheriff's office in the courthouse. A number of scenarios had raced through my mind on the drive there, but the most likely one was what I might have discovered when Will and I searched the hillside near the cave. But hadn't Mr. Byrd told me they didn't connect the photo to Sorrel Janes? So it must be something else. What?

Pearce strode into the office first. Reed stood back for me to enter, touching me lightly at the waist as I walked past. It was a simple thing, but I found the touch reassuring. I wasn't worried or afraid, but I knew I needed to exhibit caution with anything I said.

My mind shifted into investigative reporter mode. I'd learned years earlier that asking the questions before they asked them might control the direction of the interview. However, Pearce was both intelligent and experienced. I reminded myself to say as little as possible.

He walked over to the sheriff's desk and motioned us to draw up chairs. When we had done this, he said, "I need to clarify some points here," and looked down at a notepad he'd pulled out of his pocket. I suspected he wanted to use a recorder but didn't, maybe to disarm us. Recorders usually signaled "official."

I pulled out my small recorder and started it.

"This isn't an official conversation," he assured me.

"I just like to record things so I remember them correctly," I answered, my voice innocent and naïve. Reed nudged my knee with his, but I ignored it. "I never know where I'll find quotes for photo captions," I added.

Pearce looked at me, obviously trying to follow my logic—or lack of it. Watching the thoughts chasing across his face then being quickly shuttered, I felt an inner flow of satisfaction. I'd accomplished my goal. He obviously had decided I was the lightweight he'd hope I'd be.

"My photos of the rattlesnakes in the ranger station turned out better than I thought they would," I continued enthusiastically. "I regret I didn't take any of the one in my office—nor of you, Sgt. Pearce. I really need to correct that omission."

Reed nudged my knee again. I scooted my chair away from Reed a bit and leaned toward Pearce. "Would you like to make a comment I could use in the photo's caption?" I asked him. "Randall Byrd, our newspaper's editor, buys my freelance photos and I—"

"This isn't in regards to the snake in your office."

I feigned surprise. "Oh."

"Ms. Janes, why did you travel to Portal, Arizona, recently?"

"Mr. Byrd asked me to accompany a reporter and shoot photos to illustrate his travel article."

"Would you describe where you accompanied this . . . reporter?"

"Will. First, we checked in at the store there in Portal."

"That would be . . . ?"

"I don't remember. It's the only store there. We picked up the keys for the cabin that Mr. Byrd had reserved for us and bought supplies."

"Was the store busy?"

"Then? No. I spoke with the man at the counter, Mr. Turner, and took some photos. I took a few photos back in the little restaurant area also. Will was hungry and ordered hamburgers for us."

"Then?"

"Then we found our cabin at Cave Creek and unpacked. I made a phone call to check on my store. My next-in-charge is pregnant, so I checked in fairly often."

I could sense his patience stretching. "Have you ever been to Cave Creek?" I asked.

"Just answer the questions please, Ms. Janes." Did I hear a sigh? I felt the familiar knee nudge. Reed must have scooted over closer.

"What did you do next?"

"Will wanted to visit the ranger station. We met the ranger there, and he shared information about the area."

"Were any other people present during your time at the ranger station?"

"No." Then I pretended to search my memory. "Yes, a senior group from Arizona—Tucson?—came before we left."

"And?"

I waited for him to continue, a confused look on my face.

"Did you not see your friend Chris Reed there as well?"

"Oh . . . I do think he came in shortly before we left."

Sgt. Pearce stared into my eyes. I probably had drug this out long enough. "Oddly, the ranger isn't aware that you knew him at all. His recollection—and Will's—is that you didn't acknowledge Chris Reed at all. That's curious."

He hadn't really asked a question, but he seemed to expect me to speak. "Well, I wasn't sure if he was there on official business . . . "

"Wouldn't that be out of his jurisdiction?" Pearce's patience stretched with each syllable of the last word.

"I know. So if he didn't want to be noticed . . . "

Pearce sighed. "Ms. Janes, let's pretend you ignored Chris Reed for personal reasons." His voice underlined the last two words. "Is it your answer that you did not speak to him at all during your time in Arizona?"

Again, I felt the knee nudge. "I saw him a couple of times."

"At the station?"

"Yes. And later he ate dinner with us."

"Did you ask why he was there?"

"I suspected he was there on business, as I said. He looked tired and I asked if he'd like to eat dinner with us. And he agreed . . . especially when he heard I wasn't cooking."

"You didn't ask him why he was in Arizona," Pearce said, his voice filled with disbelief. Again, I felt the knee pressure.

I looked him squarely in the eye and said, "I don't know why you are asking me about my relationship with Chris Reed, Sgt. Pearce. Obviously—or at least I thought it was obvious—he is single and I like the way he looks." I held his gaze, defiance in my face.

"Did you share with him that you planned to climb up to a cave, coincidentally the same cave where my team was investigating a crime?" His voice had grown steely, serious.

"No."

"He ate dinner with you and never asked why you were there?"

"Sure and we told him we were there to get photos of the area. But we never discussed where we were climbing. At that time, we hadn't decided." It was partially true, so maybe my voice rang true. "We only realized that when we saw the officers there the next morning. And we didn't go near where they were working. Neither did we climb up to the cave."

He stared at me for a long moment. Then he shoved a photo across the desk. "Do you recognize this person?"

I looked down at the photograph the television station had taken to advertise my addition to their news team. I stared at the long, golden hair and the artistically made-up face. I looked so young there. "She is so young," I mused.

Sgt. Pearce snorted. I looked up at him, only then realizing I'd spoken aloud.

"She looks a bit like me, doesn't she?" I continued. "Of course, my hair is red, and I don't wear make-up or that expensive clothing. She could almost be my sister. Who is she?"

He stared at me for a long time. "I think we're finished for today," he said. "I may need to visit with you again."

"I hope so," I answered. "I'd like to know who sent that snake to my shop!"

Chapter 31

Reed stayed to confer with Sgt. Pearce, but I climbed into my Jeep, which I'd insisted on driving from home when Pearce had "requested" a meeting. I headed over to the small grocery market nearby in the older part of town. I found parking in a small lot in the back. Once inside, I grabbed a woven shopping bag from a hook near the door and started filling it with bananas, freshly cooked tortillas, brown eggs, natural butter, and orange juice. At the register, I grabbed a newspaper and dropped it on my small stack. My next destination was the post office.

On the drive home, only minutes later, I tried to ignore the ominous feeling creeping across my neck. I hadn't lied about the photo. It didn't look much like me now. It could, in fact, be a sister to me. The weird part was that I felt that way . . . the woman in that photo and I might look alike—might even be related—but it wasn't me. It had never really been me. As a crime reporter and news journalist, I'd loved the chase for stories at first, but the job had quickly grown old. Getting into people's faces, demanding to know details about someone whom they had just been told had died, often violently, not reacting to the ravages of grief and anger spilling out of their mouths had been almost daily events for a city the size of Houston. In the beginning, I defended it with the belief that we had a right to know, a mantra often parroted by my bosses, who chased higher ratings instead of compassion and justice.

So I hadn't lied to Sgt. Pearce, I reassured myself. That wasn't my photo. Not any longer. And I didn't want it to be me again. I supposed if he pushed it long enough and hard enough, he could push until I admitted it was me. He probably already knew anyway. Hadn't I heard that most good interrogators already know the answers before they ask the questions? After all, it wasn't exactly a secret any more, I supposed. But besides John, Reed was the only one here in Saddle Gap who knew; and he'd only stumbled on it when I'd accidentally gotten involved in a murder case shortly after moving here. It seemed like trouble followed me around. I just hoped Pearce wouldn't broadcast my background to the whole town.

I'd gone into federal witness protection when I'd been urged to do so after my husband, Kevin, was murdered and the authorities suspected one of the Mexican cartels of killing him in retaliation for my job as a crime reporter. I'd taken my own name back, which I hadn't used in Houston at all, and relocated here where an aunt had left me property. I'd come here as a child and loved the area. And I'd hoped—unrealistically, it seemed—to keep that part of my past what it was, my past, and start again with a clean slate.

The incident at Bosque had threatened my new life last fall. Because of what happened there, the feds had insisted I relocate again and start over once more. Instead, I'd left the program.

I didn't share the information about my former life in Houston with anyone after leaving witness protection except Reed, who'd known by then, and Mr. Byrd, who'd figured something was missing from my life's experiences, but didn't publicize it. John had known also, of course, but he wasn't in a position to argue with me. I made the choice myself. After a while, a person has to evaluate the life she is living and decide whether or not it is worth fighting to keep. That first one in Houston wasn't. This one in Saddle Gap was.

I could see a note stuck to my door as I pulled into my usual parking spot. I walked up to inspect it and recognized the name of a parcel service. As a precaution, I'd asked the parcel service to leave packages inside a small building behind my store if I wasn't home and the store was closed. I'd put a metal trash can, with a lid, behind my aunt's ancient car, so the parcels would be out of sight and safe from the weather should I be gone for a few days. I stepped up to read the note on the door. One parcel, it said. I unlocked the door and returned to the Jeep to carry in groceries first.

The cats met me at the door, probably because of the food bags I carried. I put the perishables away and left the others until later. Then I went out to collect the box.

Before I lifted the lid of the trash can, I moved the can a bit. No sounds came from the box, so I lifted the can lid and cautiously peered inside. Turning on the tiny penlight on my keychain, I checked the label. I hadn't realized I'd been holding my breath until I recognized the sender. There were no surprises here. It was the toner I'd ordered for my store computer. I scooped it up and carried it inside and back to my office.

The rest of the morning sped by with the usual chores, messages to answer, and the final tasks for the sale. We only had five days remaining, so I called Teri's cousin to schedule a training session for this afternoon. In case something unexpected came up, I wanted everything in place. Next, I called Jose to check on Teri.

"She's home," he said. "But we're not letting everyone know. The doctor wants rest and quiet."

"I can understand that," I told him. "If she asks, everything is set for the sale. I don't want her worrying about a thing this direction."

"Stopping her from worrying will be about like telling a dog to stop chasing a cat," he laughed. "But we can only try."

His reference to a dog reminded me. Reed hadn't said anything about the little dog, so I didn't know if he'd taken care of her . . . or had even stopped by his place. So I closed up the shop and house and drove over.

When I opened the barn door, I sang a lullaby softly to warn the little mama that I was coming. I stood at the open door for a moment, letting my eyes adjust to the darkness. A tiny sound pulled my eyes to my right, maybe a couple of yards away. She stood motionless, as if prepared to fight for her babies if necessary. My heart broke at the bony frame beneath the rough fur.

I continued to hum and I moved forward but walked a wide path to the left until I reached her food dish. It was empty. I scooped the water dish up as well. It was almost empty. I could hear the soft, sweet sound of puppies. She sensed that I'd heard them and crept toward the back of the barn far from the babies in a ploy to distract me. I pretended to be distracted and carried the dishes to the door and outside to clean them out and refill them.

Mama stood guard while I placed the dishes back. I now crooned a string of nonsense comments. Then I set a dog biscuit beside the dish and backed away to the door. Reed and I had discovered earlier that a small door in the back had been her entry/exit to the barn.

"I think I'll call you Madonna," I whispered as I backed out of the barn. As I quietly closed the door, I could hear the crunch of the biscuit.

I backed away a few feet until I bumped into a broad body. I opened my mouth to squeal, but a hand clamped over my mouth. I twisted and fought against the arms that gripped me into a tight hold.

"Hush! She's just beginning to trust you!" Reed muttered into my ear.

He shuffled us a few yards back and then loosed his hold. I rounded on him with my fists raised. "Chris Reed, I'm going to kill you one of these days! Sneaking up on a person—"

"I didn't know you could sing . . . a little off key." He continued to lead me away from the barn.

"I . . . off key? That's a lie! Are you some sort of musical critic?" I sputtered. "What are you doing?"

"Distracting you so you don't have screaming hysterics and scare my dog."

I yanked my arm away from him at the gate to the house. "You are the most despicable—"

"I know you think so," he muttered, gathering me close into a full body hug. "I'm also crazy to be doing this," he whispered before his head bent for a kiss.

It couldn't have lasted more than a few seconds, not long for a kiss. He'd caught me off guard, I thought, resisting the urge to wipe my mouth. I wouldn't give him the satisfaction, but I saw a gleam in his eyes that told me he expected me to do it. Instead, I casually backed away when he loosened his hold and said, "On a scale of one to ten, I'd rate this one—"

"A sweet nine," he said. "I didn't mean to scare you, but I won't apologize for the kiss."

I turned and took a couple of steps toward the Jeep. "I'll bet you say that to all the women."

"No. Just irritatingly beautiful redheads who are too stubborn to admit that they—"

"Don't want a role in a love story."

His chuckle turned into a full roar. I waited until he caught his breath and grumbled, "I'm glad I have enlivened your day with entertainment!"

His full-throated laugh, always—in spite of myself—pulled giggles from me.

When we both sobered, Reed said, "I think we both could use some entertainment after our earlier season at the courthouse. Would you like to join me for coffee?"

"Tea. I put a jug in the sun before I left. Even though it's the end of winter, this sun should be warm enough to have brewed it by now. I need to get home anyway. I have an appointment there in a couple of hours."

"Sounds good to me." His arm snaked around me and opened the Jeep door before me. I stepped inside, inserted the ignition key, and started it up.

He held the door when I tried to close it. The lightness gone from his voice, he began, "Sorrel," and waited until I looked up into his eyes. "I hope you won't be offended by what I am about to say."

"That's hard to promise." He continued to stare into my eyes. "Oh, all right," I said and again reached for the door handle.

"I just wanted to say," Chris said, his voice softening a bit, "that you're a star, whether you want it or not—"

"Chris Reed! You—"

"In a murder mystery novel. No, make that a whole series."

He stood up and creased an imaginary handlebar mustache. "And I, your faithful cohort, am—"

"The bumbling side-kick! One that I would happily . . . ." I searched for an appropriate word, then just started the Jeep and reached for the gear shift. Reed jumped back as I stepped on the gas, leaving a cloud of dirt.

Caution made me slow and glance in the mirror to make sure he was okay. He'd swept off his hat and bowed. I couldn't tell for sure, but I thought I saw his shoulders shaking.

On the ride home, I mentally scolded myself for allowing him to kiss me, to rile me, to . . . make me laugh.

Sorrel, my Aunt Rose told me that summer long ago when Mama and I had come here for a visit, *you need to find a man like your uncle someday.*

I'd smiled politely. *Oh, I know what you're thinking,* she continued. *Those heroes of your romance books sound wonderful. But for sharing a lifetime, you need one that stirs up your deepest emotions. You'll love him and want to hold him close, never let him go, and then you'll get so irritated with him that you'll want to murder him. Hearts and flowers are boring unless you have a reason to make up. And you need one who'll make you laugh. It's laughter that makes life worth living.*

"You must be jinxing me, Aunt Rose," I grumbled, speeding down the two-lane road.

Chris Reed was a friend—sometimes. He'd distracted me from this man who'd been murdered in that cave. But I didn't need to have a romance with him, no matter how well he kissed. I needed to get this sale finished and—

A bell sounded on my phone. I glanced at the screen. A text. Probably Teri.

After I pulled up to the house, I checked the text. It was from the one buddy from Houston I'd reconnected with. His message was not reassuring: "Flies buzzing again."

Chapter 32

Irma didn't resemble her cousin Teri at all. First, she was taller, slimmer, and almost as well sculpted as a body builder. Second, she only spoke when necessary. Last, I'm doubtful she had ever giggled. But she was a hard worker and quick. Like Teri, she had an imagination, listened carefully, and offered good suggestions—tentatively at first—when a display offered problems. Best of all, she quickly figured out the tally system we had devised and offered a suggestion on how to streamline it even more.

At the end of our two-hour session, I walked her to her car. "I want you to stop by Teri's and collect her key," I said.

Irma grinned. "That may keep her away . . . for a short time."

"We think alike," I agreed. "If she protests after a bit, then we'll have to devise another plan."

I watched her drive away with relief. I felt certain that I could leave the store in her hands. She'd agreed to look after the cats in my absence as well. As if they recognized a new ally, both cats had taken to her right away.

Once inside my office again, I called Reed to ask if I needed to feed the dog. "Actually, I've just put it out," he said. "When I checked, the dishes you had filled this morning were empty. But I'd appreciate your keeping an eye on her as I'm heading out to the investigation in Arizona shortly."

"Oh. Will you be gone long? If so, how about I buy some of those feeders?" I suggested. "That way she'll have ample water and some dry dog food there in case I'm late with the canned food."

"Good idea. I'll—Sorrel, I have a call coming in."

"Catch you later."

My mind skipped to what I needed to accomplish before following my latest idea. I dialed a familiar number and waited to leave a message. A familiar voice prompted, "Dig-a-me." I simply responded, "Pronto!" Within moments, my phone rang.

"Sorrel! *Que pasa?*"

"Hi, Vicente! How are things going?"

"I keep waiting for NBC to snap me up. Are you still slinking around taking photos of birds and other creatures?"

"Mostly. Just returned from a photo shoot for the local news."

"You need to come back to us! The new girl—she doesn't even know I'm here! No little gifts from Starbucks when I have to work late, no flirty notes—dullsville."

Vicente and I had started at the television station in Houston within weeks of each other—me in front of the camera and him in production. Our partnership had been the hardest part of my former life to leave. I'd only contacted him once a few months ago when I needed help.

"So what's up?" he asked when I didn't comment. "Another family member to research? Need some help with that cowboy cop?"

"Something unusual has turned up." I explained about the photo of me that had been discovered in the young man's pocket.

He heard me out then commented. "Newsprint or photograph?"

"Newsprint . . . with intro story."

"And you're certain it's legit? You know people can do all sorts of things with computers."

"It's been copied from a paper, folded to fit in his pocket, and creased."

"He show it to you?"

"He's dead. Murdered." I explained about how he'd been found and where.

Vicente whistled. "What a way to go! I may have nightmares!"

"I know!"

"What do you want from me?"

"Is there any way to trace those photos?"

"Those were just promo photos, Sorrel. We send them out with each new anchor."

"Mail? Hand out?"

"Probably both. Email also. And someone could print them out. As old as this one is—how old?"

"Almost ten years."

Vicente whistled. "I'm surprised there are any left out there!"

He was only expressing what I'd known, but hearing it spoken aloud made it more final. "I knew it was crazy, but I guess I just hoped—"

"I'll nose around and see if I can find anything. Won't hurt to check if someone has asked about you or submitted a follow-up for a job interview—something like that. More than that . . . unless you can send the photo . . . "

"No chance. Law enforcement has it."

"Give me a few days, *chica*. I'm just sorry you weren't calling to invite me to a wedding!"

"Already did that . . . once. Next time, I'll send you a card from Maui!"

He laughed and started to say something else, but I heard someone in the background calling for him. "Soon as I can," he called. Then, "Stay safe, little one."

Safe was a relative term, I thought after I'd hung up. I'd never thought much about it, even out on the streets reporting horrible crimes—usually in the middle of the night. Now, not only did it sound heavenly, but it also sounded elusive. My earlier scrapes with danger had been the result of the job. But the last one . . . it had been more personal.

Did the man's death even have anything to do with the photo in his pocket? Couldn't he have just tried to cheat the wrong guys . . . or gotten too far into gambling to pay his debts? That certainly made more sense. If so, my photo in his pocket was just a coincidence. In fact, the evidence pointed heavily toward that conclusion.

Then why the snake? an inner voice whispered.

Another coincidence, I thought.

As I dozed off to sleep later that night, a thought struck that made me sit up in bed. I'd called Vicente because he'd sent a message to me! I must be getting soft, I thought, as I once again rang Vicente's number. Maybe he'd forgotten too!

On the third ring, Vicente's machine caught the call and told me to leave a message. "We didn't talk about how to exterminate the flies!" I said. He didn't pick up so I hung up, but I couldn't go back to sleep. Something just felt weird.

After tossing for a while, I got up and put a cup of water in the microwave to heat. Green tea with honey—just a tiny bit—sometimes made me calm. Once it brewed, I returned to bed, added an extra pillow against the headboard, settled the tea on the nightstand, and climbed in, jostling the sleepy cats. I started a new crossword puzzle but tossed it aside when I could only find two answers. I reached for a notepad inside the drawer of the nightstand and started a list: Weeping Child. The first ones to come to mind were my mom and John. Both were gone. Who else could it be? What adult did I know who had a sad child hiding inside? Reed? Maybe my half-brothers? I continued with the list, scratching out names almost as quickly as I wrote them down. Finally, I tore the sheet of paper off and wadded it up.

"Sorrel Janes," I scolded, "since when did you start believing stuff you dream? This isn't the movies here!"

The green tea had begun to work its magic. I turned out the light and snuggled under the covers. A few minutes later and I would have missed the soft buzz of a message coming through my cellphone.

"I'll get it later," I mumbled.

Then I roused, switched the light on again, and punched play. "*Chica*, I don't think we're playing the same game. Flies?

Exterminator? Whatever you're drinking, think I'll pass. I'm turning off. Talk tomorrow?" I sat straight up in bed, causing my feline bedmates to complain. Then I replayed the message several times, listening for signs of teasing or hidden innuendoes. There were none. He sounded genuinely puzzled. The only conclusion I could now draw was that Vicente hadn't sent the original 'flies' message. But if he didn't, who did?

Closely following that question were several others. How did they get the number and know it was mine? Vicente and I had devised a code system between us to disguise it. Now someone had broken it. Even worse came the most obvious deduction. The person sending that warning to me had hoped I'd do just what I had done—call Vicente. Now that person not only knew how to contact me but also knew about the photo. Could it be someone who worked at the station? I searched my tired brain for possibilities, but none surfaced. That wasn't a surprise as I'd been gone for a while. People in the news business often left the way I had: Here one day; gone and never spoken about the next. I'd been a local celebrity, but I doubted very few there today remembered me.

I settled back under the quilts and mentally repeated the mantra I'd used often in the past couple of years. "Breathe, inhale, think of music, think of happy sounds, think of poetry—"

Abruptly, I tensed. Wasn't it Emily Dickinson who had written: "I heard a fly buzz—when I died!"?

Chapter 33

In spite of my interrupted sleep the night before, I ate an early breakfast, vacuumed my small living area, completed other household chores, and arrived at the pet store just as it opened.

The store manager steered me toward the gravity-style feeders and waterers for dogs and cats. I selected one of each for the dogs. On second thought, I added one of each for the cats as well. With Teri unavailable, I didn't have a person I could call on to care for them at the last minute if my plans changed quickly. Then, I added a couple of puppy toys, even though I knew they were still a bit young, and—at the last moment—selected a pink fuzzy dog bed.

"You get a new dog?" he asked as he rang up the purchases.

"I think the new dog chose my friend and I'm the dog sitter," I said.

He grinned. "Looks like she's a smart dog," he remarked before telling me the amount.

I loaded everything into the Jeep and drove over to Reed's place. Shortly before I arrived, I heard the familiar ping of a message on my phone. I checked it after I'd parked and saw it was the paper's number. "You'll have to wait, Mr. Byrd," I said.

Madonna peeked out when I hummed the lullaby, but she eyed the new feeders suspiciously until I'd filled one with water and the other with dry food. I refilled the bowl with wet food as well and then stepped out to retrieve the new, furry bed. When I returned, she continued to watch me suspiciously but gulped the wet food without hesitation. I could hear the grunts and whines of little ones, and she glanced over her shoulder but continued to eat. When she had emptied the bowl and licked it clean, she slunk back into the hiding place. I placed the bed as close to her hideout as I dared and sang, "I'll be back, Madonna," as I backed out.

I called Mr. Byrd from my store office space. His secretary put me on hold, so I sorted mail—all junk except for a couple of small bills and a note addressed to—

"Sorrel?"

"Hello, Mr. Byrd."

"I have a quick assignment to offer you. I know you're only days from your store opening—"

"That I am. I'm not sure I can—"

"The story comes out on the mysterious murder/photo today."

"Is the photo—"

"No. Just a mention of an unnamed female. Got the story over the wire and it's on the press. But I'd like to send you and Will back over there—maybe give it a less canned feel."

"I—"

"Hear me out first. I think you could do it in one day—a long day. At most, spend one night and come back tomorrow. I'd like some local reaction, maybe an interview from the ranger and people living in the area. Use your imagination."

"I thought you'd want me to do the photos—"

"I do. But Will's still green. I thought you two could share the credits."

"And you've spoken to Will already?"

"Not yet. He's finishing up a piece on the school board meeting. He can send that to me later this morning if he hasn't finished it already."

"So you want me to leave—"

"An hour ago. They're planning to issue formal statements in a press conference later this morning. I can handle that. What I want from you and Will—" he paused.

"Is to nose around behind the scenes?"

"Can you do it?"

"I can. But a couple of days only."

"Okay. I'll send Will out there in half an hour—tops." Then he paused. "Be careful."

I set up the cat feeders, called and left a message for Irma, packed a few necessities in my overnight bag, and stuck the bills into my camera bag. Will arrived just as I'd finished stuffing granola bars, nuts, peanut butter crackers, and several small apples in my backpack. As I started to close it, I reached for a package of cookies. Will had a sweet tooth.

"I have a cooler with water and drinks," he announced when I opened the door, handing him the backpack.

I unlocked the Jeep doors remotely with my keys. "You can start loading," I said. "These are snacks."

I glanced around, gave the cats a pat, grabbed my camera and overnight bag, and closed the door. Then I set the security system which had thankfully been repaired yesterday.

"I'll take those." I handed them over to Will and locked up the house. He finished the cigarette stuck in his lips, ground it out, and jumped in the passenger side. "The cig—"

"Oops!" He picked it up and stuck it in his pocket.

"Nasty habit," I said. "You need to—"

"I know."

I climbed into the driver's seat and buckled the seatbelt. Scolding Will about smoking would only add tension to the trip—and make me feel maternal. He wasn't that much younger than I! Besides, I needed a partner on this assignment.

I noticed he'd placed two Starbucks coffees in the holder. Maybe I did have a partner. I took a sip from the cup closest to me. It was exactly right.

I started the Jeep, backed out, and drove to the end of the driveway. "Do you want to brief me on what you know?" I asked, turning on the signal. Two fast-moving trucks passed before he said anything.

"Will?"

I glanced over. He had ear buds in. Odd. I touched his arm. He pulled out one. "What?"

"Mr. Byrd said you'd be filling me in—"

"I'm on a call. Will do it in a few."

I nodded. Was he blushing? Had our Will found a new lady friend? A quick side glance showed a less shaggy look, a button-up shirt, and—were those new jeans? And a call? With ear buds?

Traffic cleared a few miles out. I mentally reviewed what I knew about this case, which didn't take long. If they had sent out formal news announcements, maybe that was why Reed had been recalled. Or had they found some new evidence? If they had, they would likely keep quiet about it. I hadn't seen anything about the case in our paper after the first, small, front-page article. It had stated that the body of a hiker had been found in a cave near Portal, authorities were working on an identification, and anyone who had information needed to call the authorities. A couple of other sentences had implied that the hiker had likely died as a result of the climb or an accident.

"Uh, sorry." Will had pulled out the ear buds and reached for his coffee cup.

"Thanks for the coffee."

Will drank from his and replaced it in the holder. "Sorry—"

I waved my hand dismissively. "This is a surprise trip."

"Luckily, I recorded the school board meeting and was just listening . . . "

I nodded. "Mr. Byrd said you were finishing up a story."

"Oh, well, yes . . . "

I felt my mouth twitch, and the urge to tease him surfaced. Obviously, it had been something besides the board meeting. But we had work to do, and I didn't want him clamming up if my questions or teasing irritated him. Instead, I asked, "What do you know about our assignment here?"

Over the next several miles, Will talked about what he knew, which wasn't much more than I did. In fact, he had no clue who the woman in the photo might be . . . or even that it was a woman in the photo. The body had still not been identified. The cause of death had not yet been given in the article. He finished up with a frustrated complaint about "old news."

"I would have thought they would have put this in the news sooner," I agreed. "Did they give any indication of how long this guy had been there?"

"We were there last week. They're giving a couple of weeks as the estimated time, but that seems a little long to me."

"Was it only a week since we were here? Times flies . . ."

"Well, so it was a little less than a week. From what I understand, it takes a while for a medical examiner to check out everything . . . not like they do on those television shows and it's all solved in an hour or so."

"Really? Now I'm really surprised!" I loved teasing him.

But instead of responding, Will just took another long drink from his coffee, swallowed, and stared out his window.

"Everything okay, Will?"

"Sure." He didn't look back at me.

"Have I offended you? What's up?"

He stared out his window for a bit longer but finally said, "When were you going to tell me about your being pulled in by the task force?"

"What? I—"

"I mean . . . I understand that I'm just an intern, but you're just the paper photographer. If they had questions about our investigation, why was I left out?"

Ah. Now I understood the aloof attitude this morning. "It wasn't even connected to our story there," I fibbed. "I had a suspicious package delivered to the shop. I called Chris Reed, and he came by to look at it. The task force stopped by to see him while he was at my place. Later, they had me meet with them at the sheriff's office in the courthouse. They told me they hadn't discovered who had sent the package and even insinuated that it might just be a prank!"

I hoped I sounded convincing enough, so I inserted outrage in my voice—which wasn't totally play-acting.

Will asked warily, still looking out his window, "What was suspicious about the package?"

"A live rattlesnake."

That grabbed his attention. "What do you mean? A live snake? In a postal package?"

"Special messenger."

"What did you do?"

"Let them open the box and then take the creature away." My shiver wasn't totally just for show.

"Cool!" Will laughed. "Wish I could have seen it!"

"Sure you do," I joked. "You'd be sitting on the file cabinet!"

I was happy to see that the story had broken the heavy atmosphere. Will had visibly relaxed and once more chatted and joked in his usual way until we neared our destination.

"Are we staying at the same place?" he asked as we pulled into the store.

"Yes. At least for a night. Mr. Byrd didn't think we'd be here long."

"That's what he told me too. Let's grab something to eat. Then we can pick up the key."

"Sounds good! Maybe they've picked up some frozen dinners or something to sell here."

"Frozen dinners! How about you get the key while I buy the food!" He headed toward the food aisles right away, commenting just loudly enough for me to hear, "I never thought I'd be thanking my mom for teaching me how to cook the basic things!"

I only remembered later, when we unpacked the car, that Will hadn't told me much at all about the news conference. Who was our contact? I'd asked once, but he'd gone to the bathroom. After we unloaded, we needed to talk about that.

But the question that had haunted my recent sleepless nights hadn't been about our victim. Who had warned me about the flies buzzing? Just when I had almost convinced myself that it was all a practical joke, I remembered coming upon a dead cow in the pasture once. It had looked black from a distance. Only when I rode nearer did I realize that its black hide was actually flies covering the dead body. I was getting paranoid because of a crazy dream!

Exhaustion had finally pulled me from that scene—and the sound—of the buzzing flies. But it had left me tired and jumpy today. I grabbed a soda, hoping it would give me the energy boost I needed.

Chapter 34

Will and I had agreed that our plan of action should include a visit with our friendly park ranger as well as with any locals who might have information to share, specifically the Portal store owner and residents we'd met in the store. We'd also agreed that climbing to the cave would give us a better perspective on a follow-up article. With a little luck, we might even get some statements from law enforcement.

We'd also chosen to eat from our snack bag instead of taking time at the café. We hadn't seen anyone there much, so the next morning might be better to interview people. So we simply had collected the key to the cabin. We could unload later as we wanted to get to the ranger station before it closed.

At the last moment, Will noticed my soda and ran back inside to get one for himself.

My cell phone buzzed. I saw an unfamiliar number displayed on the screen. I answered carefully. "Hello?"

"Clear?" It was Vicente.

"Yeah. I'm alone. What's up?"

"My cell was hacked. It's a huge mess. So I got this burner phone and wanted to give you the number, as well as a warning. I've no way of knowing at this point how much the hacker may have discovered—or even who it may be!"

I felt a chill travel up my spine but strove to keep a calm voice. "Probably just a teenager. They get a thrill out of breaking into all sorts of sites. Maybe they found yours too boring to snoop much."

Vicente didn't laugh and the silence that followed wasn't encouraging. Finally, he muttered, "I wouldn't be so fortunate."

"Is this a Code Red?"

We'd devised the code when I broke my witness protection secret to enlist his help shortly after moving to Saddle Gap. Vicente and I had developed an unusual friendship at the television station. As my producer, we'd maintained a professional relationship. As friends, we'd shared personal challenges and secrets, including his diagnosis of multiple sclerosis. Now, I'd entrusted him with my own safety.

"It could be." Vicente sighed and lowered his voice even more. "This is one of those cheap phones I bought at Walmart. Did you get the number on your screen?"

"Yes."

"You okay?"

"Yes. Away from the nest."

"Last night means—"

"A hawk in the chicken coop. Message about 'flies buzzing there.'"

Silence.

"Vicente?"

"When you can, get one of these phones too, Sorrel. Flies are buzzing around the photo, but I didn't send the notice. Lots of noise. Nothing hitting the target at this time."

Will returned with not only a huge coke, but also a bag of chips.

"I don't know how you do it!" I teased.

He inserted his ear bud while he crunched on the chips, and I mentally reviewed my latest challenge. Obviously, my photo had raised questions at the Houston television station, but Vicente would have warned me had they tied it to Sorrel Janes.

Staci Lee Jamison had disappeared shortly after the murder of her husband, an oil executive. And much about the case remained a mystery, even though his killer had been named and killed. The greater mystery lay within the motivation for the hit. Evidence still pointed heavily toward the Mexican cartel. Staci had made dangerous enemies with her investigative reporting, her husband killed shortly after a television special featuring her story aired. Staci surely wasn't important enough to stay in hiding, but Sorrel had left that profession. I hoped the memories of the television audience there had faded.

I smiled wryly. I was thinking about myself in the third person as if I were someone important.

"You awake?" Will asked.

"Yep. Sorry. Just couldn't resist daydreaming while my partner had his ears plugged and probably damaged from heavy metal music."

"You won't change my taste in music," Will said. "I had all those sisters who felt it was their duty to try to instruct me into all sorts of music, literature, equal rights and even traditional role models. They even taught me to crochet."

"Crochet? As in the needlecraft? Do you make doilies?"

"Not anymore."

I took pity and changed the subject. "So, are we heading to the ranger station or do you want to climb?"

"I vote for the station. It's late enough that maybe he won't be leading some discussion group."

"My thoughts also."

Will reinserted his ear buds.

When we pulled into the ranger station parking lot, a family van was backing out. "Perfect timing!" Will said. "Who takes lead?"

"You're the writer. I'll take some shots of the two of you."

"Have you taken any of the snakes?" Will shot me a sassy grin.

"Human or reptilian?" I winked. "Think I may have a look around out here. I didn't do that the last time."

I held the door for Will, then closed it, and turned toward the back of the ranger station. I'd only taken a step or two when I heard Will's surprised voice. "Hello. Where's the ranger?"

He blocked my view, but I heard an unfamiliar voice. "Sorry, the station is closing early today. Your ranger has had an unexpected family emergency, and I'm just finishing up feeding the reptiles."

"Will he return—"

"Three or four days at the most, I've been told."

Will backed out and I stepped aside. He looked perplexed but didn't comment as we headed back to the Jeep and got inside. "So, on to our hike, I guess," I mused and turned out of the parking lot. Will didn't answer at first, so I flipped the blinker and turned onto the winding, two-lane road once again.

Any suggestion of the recent police activity wasn't immediately discernable. This time, we parked the Jeep where their vehicles had been parked before, getting it as far off the narrow road in the widest spot. Will still hadn't spoken. I glanced at him when I set the brake and reached for the door. He sat still, staring ahead.

"Everything okay?"

He looked over at me, sort of jerked out of thought, and reached toward his pocket. "Yeah."

We opened our doors simultaneously. I walked around to the back; he walked ahead and lit a cigarette. He seemed moody. I watched him a moment, shrugged, and began unloading our gear. I hoped it wasn't long-lasting. We had a rugged climb ahead, as our previous experience had proven, and needed all our attention on the task. I told him as much when he finished his smoke and joined me.

He shrugged into his backpack without speaking. Maybe he was already mentally composing his story. I focused on my gear, checking yet another time to make sure I hadn't forgotten something.

"Ready?" I finally asked.

"Yeah."

I double checked the locks on the Jeep and started walking toward the base of the mountain. The cave we'd not been able to approach on our earlier trip looked much higher than it had before. "I figure this time we can take the curved walk path," I said over my shoulder. "No need to keep out of sight this time. Besides, the trees offer some protection until they stop near the top."

Will grunted and followed. The rugged path showed obvious signs of the earlier law enforcement traffic, but it wasn't much easier than it had been before. My nose and cheeks felt cold. I could see tiny puffs when I breathed. I glanced behind me and saw that Will's face had turned red as well. He wasn't following as closely as he'd done before, and he looked back over his shoulder as I watched.

About a half hour into our climb, I told him I wanted to get some shots and stepped a bit off the path we were traveling. He grunted and dropped his gear. I focused and started snapping. When I glanced behind at Will, he was sitting on his pack smoking. My first instinct was to remind him about fire, but I saw him flick the ash into a small box. I needed to curb my maternal attitude toward him anyway. I didn't know why it had surfaced, but he didn't like it and our working relationship suffered because of it.

I stepped a bit farther away and used my camera lens to see if we were still on our own. No cars had parked, although I'd heard at least a couple traveling along the road. I couldn't see anyone along the path, although they would be partially obscured by the trees. Tourists weren't totally uncommon in this area, but late spring was more appealing than February for climbers. The wind hadn't seemed as cold when we were moving as it did now that I'd slowed.

Stepping back, I asked, "Ready to move on?" Instead of answering, Will stubbed out his cigarette, stood up, and shrugged into his backpack.

After maybe half an hour of climbing, we stopped once more. The cave loomed above us, challenging and much larger than before. Again, Will dropped his gear and stepped off to smoke. I eased mine down and once more pulled out my camera. The view was more spectacular, if possible, than it had been before. I focused and did some initial shooting to test different angles.

"Didn't seem this high up before."

I jumped. "Will! You startled me!" My foot slid a bit and he reached out to steady me.

"Sorry." He held onto me and offered me a water bottle with his other hand.

"This view is spectacular." I stepped away after regaining my footing, capped the camera lens, and accepted the water. He stared back toward the trail we'd traveled while I took a long drink.

When he didn't speak, I looked down the trail as well. "This tastes really good. Thanks. Is something worrying you, Will?"

He didn't answer right away. Then he said, "Maybe I'm just being too sensitive."

"How?"

Again, he paused before finally answering. "Sometimes . . . you know how it feels like someone is watching you?"

Instead of answering, I scanned the area we'd traveled. "As far as I can see with my naked eye, we're up here on our own—except for the critters. But once we leave the cover of the trees, we won't be." I shouldn't have said that. My mind filled with unwelcome visions of the rattlesnakes Reed had mentioned they'd found in the cave—on the victim's body— creating a shiver that crawled up the base of my spine and crept right on up to my shoulders.

Will didn't acknowledge what I'd said. He seemed extraordinarily deep in thought.

"Will? What's up, really?"

Finally he looked at me. "It's the ranger."

"What ranger?"

"The new one. The substitute."

Again I waited.

"Sorrel, you know how sometimes something just isn't right? You can't put your finger on it, but you have this weird feeling just niggling at your brain? It's been there with me ever since we pulled out of that parking lot."

"Did he say something odd?"

"No. Well . . . maybe. I keep replaying our conversation in my brain. Something is off."

"What did he say again? Where did he say Ray had gone?"

"He didn't. He just said Ray had a family emergency and wouldn't be back for a few days."

"And that seems weird how?"

"I don't know. Ray spoke about his family back East. But I didn't get the impression he was that close to them."

"Doesn't seem weird to me." I tried to keep my impatience curbed. "You ready to continue our climb?"

He didn't seem to hear me. "Another thing. He was there to feed the snakes. But he didn't call them snakes. He called them reptiles. Ray called them snakes."

I knew my impatience was starting to surface. "Will, people call them all sorts of things. I won't mention what I'd like to call them."

No smile on his face. "He wasn't wearing a badge."

"Maybe he was just a local."

"No, he had an accent of some sort—but not local."

"Ray had an accent. And he wasn't local."

Will turned and stared at me. "Sorrel, listen to me. I don't know why, but that ranger set off warning bells. I'm not sure—"

I caught a glint over Will's shoulder, like a camera lens in the distance below. "What's that?" I asked, then grabbed his jacket and pulled him down with me. He fell onto me and we slid into a bush.

"Sorrel, are you crazy?"

"Did you hear that?"

He hadn't heard it the first time, but now that he'd stopped speaking, the ping of a rifle shell nearby was difficult to miss.

"Run in a crouch!" I hissed. "Don't step far from the trail, but get off it."

I crouched down, moved my camera from my chest to my back, and crept as quickly as I could away from the climbing path. Another ping bounced off the trees nearby. I glanced back in time to see Will duck and then follow me. We ducked behind the large trunk in quick succession.

"You okay?" I whispered.

No answer. I glanced back. Will's white face stared below.

"Will?"

"Sorrel? I think I'm having an epiphany. Maybe I'm in the wrong career." His voice shook.

I looked back in the distance as I slipped off my camera. "Why would you think that?" I whispered. "Some young hunter probably just thinks we're deer."

"It's not deer season."

"Do you have binoculars by any chance?"

I heard rustling. Then Will slipped a small pair into the hand I held behind me. I peeked around the trunk and tried to see below. "I don't see anyone," I whispered. "Just—"

I saw the glint and ducked just before another ping came nearby. I looked over at Will's white face. Then he reached for a rock and tossed it far to the right. The ping moved in that direction. He looked at me and grinned. "Maybe baseball is paying off after all." Then he picked some other rocks and put them in his pocket. "I'm going to try to crawl to the tree line over there. You work your way in a more circular pattern. Whoever it is can't follow the both of us at once."

I opened my mouth to object, but he'd already started in a sort of running crouch, downhill a bit and far right. I watched him reach a narrow tree, duck around it, and throw a rock farther right but downhill. The pings followed it. I cautiously proceeded in a crouch the opposite direction, toward the trees bordering the rocky face of the cliff. It was slow progress. My thighs and back ached, burned, and then went numb.

After what seemed like an hour but could only have been minutes, I reached them and fell back against my pack. I slowed my breath, looked up at what seemed like miles to the cave in the rock's center. Then I listened for the pings.

Had they stopped? "God," I whispered, "let Will be okay."

"We finally agree on something."

I would have squealed had Will not clamped his hand over my mouth. "I don't know if our voices will carry well enough for someone to hear them," he whispered, "but at this point, I think we need to be careful of everything."

"Whoever is hunting us is on the walking path," I whispered. "We need to get off it and circle back down. There's no way we need to try to get any closer to that cave."

"I think I've seen enough of that cave to last me the rest of my . . . hopefully not short . . . life," Will whispered. Then he grinned. "Where's a hoodoo when you need one?"

Chapter 35

We crawled to a couple of larger trees and crouched behind them. I took off my backpack, leaned it against a tree, and sank back against it.

Then I turned my head and glared at Will. "Don't ever scare me like that again!"

He leaned his backpack against a tree close by, oblivious to my emotions. "This is weird, you know," he spoke conversationally.

I glared at him. "Do you have weird on the brain?"

"Maybe." Will squinted downhill although he surely couldn't see anything due to the trees. "Why would anyone be shooting at us?"

"Obviously because they want to kill us. Or, less obviously, because they want to scare us into leaving."

"Then they ought to be better shots." He looked off to the right. "I think the smart thing right now would be to—"

"Find a way back down and leave," I finished for him. "I'm not sure what we think we may find on this hill anyway. If the murder occurred in the cave, which is halfway up to forever on the big rock, we're never going to get to it today without a huge ladder . . . or a miracle."

Will ignored me. "I was going to say we need to come back in the dark."

I thought a bit. "I think our challenge is to find out who just fired off those shots . . . and why. The sheriff is finished with this cave, or he'd have officers turning people away. Why would anyone want to scare us off? That was hypothetical. Don't answer!"

"As I said—"

"I don't know how much we'd be able to find in the dark, Will. Besides, snakes are out at night."

"Don't go all girly on me, Sorrel. Snakes?"

"I am all girly, Will, in case you haven't noticed. I'm a girl. I hate that term—girly! Anyway, I don't care to be bitten by the critters. This hill is steep and difficult enough to navigate without that."

He shrugged and grinned. "Now you're sounding like yourself. I was afraid you were going to—"

"Throttle you?" I grinned as well. "I'd say we need some sort of Plan B or C, though. I'm not ready to wave a white flag yet. You?"

"Nope." He sat forward, turned to his backpack, and opened it. "Do you want something to eat?"

"No."

He pulled out a small water, uncapped it, took a sip, and offered it to me. I shook my head, so he recapped it and put it away. I reached for my camera and looked through the shots I'd taken earlier.

"I think I have what we need to do the story," I told him. I leaned over to show him a shot of the cave. "That's all Mr. Byrd will likely want to illustrate your story. I have several, as well as shots from below. I even have shots of the ranger station. I think we're done here."

Will snorted. "So now all we have to do is walk down to the Jeep." He pulled out a cigarette and put it in his mouth. Then he pulled it out and grinned. "I'm not lighting up. I'm just hoping to satisfy the urge to have something in my mouth."

"Next time I'll pack some of those candy cigarettes," I grumbled.

Will jumped a little at a noise nearby. "We probably shouldn't sit here too long. Whoever is enjoying the target practice may decide to come closer."

I put my finger to my lips. We listened. Besides the wind, which whistled around us, I could hear distant bird calls and stirring—probably—critters. I'd mentioned snakes to Will, hoping to distract him, which it had. But the snakes we needed to fear were the human ones. The others would be hibernating until it warmed up.

"My suggestion is that we take a circuitous route back down," I said. "For whatever reason, the shooter doesn't seem to want to kill us, or I think he or she could have done so already. Maybe whoever it is just wants to discourage us from trying to get up into that cave."

"If that's so, then why didn't he just turn us away at the road?"

"He? Have we met this shooter?"

"Well, I still think—"

"I think we need to get back down to our car . . . after first checking to see if the shooter is still there. My feeling right now is that this is an attempt to scare us off. So, since we're not in a winning position—at least, not in my opinion—we can pretend to give up and leave."

I could see that Will wasn't excited by that idea, but he shrugged and reached for his backpack. "I guess our minds may work better in a warmer spot," he offered. "How do we retreat?"

I wiggled into my backpack as well. "We have the trees. I think we should abandon the trail—makes us an obvious target—and try a zigzag retreat . . . until we draw fire."

"Might work. How about I lead?"

"Fine with me." The sun had dropped, and the wind numbed my fingers. "I may have some beef jerky if you're still wanting something to nibble."

"I'm okay. Just popped some gum in—hoping to fool myself."

"You need to do that more often instead of a cigarette."

"Yes, Mom!"

I grinned. "After you then! I have my second wind—for the moment."

Will broke a branch off a fallen limb and tossed it the opposite direction. All remained quiet. Then he repeated his action. Still no shot.

I took a final couple of distance photos of the cave opening, high up in the rock cliff above us, before packing my camera. Then I nodded to him as I adjusted my backpack. Will motioned the direction we would start, parallel to the path, and began a slow descent. I followed, also crouched. My thighs protested. I chided myself for sitting down and not stretching them when we stood. Then my reasonable self, reminded me that I'd had other things—like avoiding bullets—on my mind.

During the descent, which took at least an hour instead of the forty-five minutes we'd spent in the ascent, we heard nothing from the shooter. Will used his small binoculars a couple of times but saw no sign of human movement at all. "You could almost believe we imagined the shots," he whispered over his shoulder.

"We didn't." I wasn't proud that my answer came out huffy. Coming downhill always seemed like it should be easier, but the muscles in my legs disagreed with that idea.

"I don't see any sign of anyone," he repeated when we looked out at the roadside where we'd parked the Jeep. "So—"

"Ssh! Truck!"

We ducked as a truck sped by, followed by a couple of other vehicles. One was a utility vehicle, but I spied children in the back seat. Surely, that wasn't our sniper.

After another quiet ten minutes, Will whispered, "Well, it's now or never. I'll—"

"We'll go together. Stand tall, act casual, as if we're here for a recreational climb. In fact, I think we should do this." I moved over close to Will and grabbed his hand. "Can you smile at me? Forget that you just called me mom. Act like I'm your heart's desire. If he is looking, maybe he'll think we're lovers." Then another thought surfaced. "Wait." I pulled out a yellow toboggan cap and stuffed my hair inside it. It had been a joke gift at a party—I couldn't even remember when and surely couldn't remember why I'd stuffed it in the backpack. It had black yarn braids connected to the sides, a bill that shaded my forehead and eyes, and a wild orange ribbon bow on the crown.

Will eyed me dubiously. "That thing draws attention—"

"Maybe. But it certainly hides my red hair. I'm hoping it will hide my age as well."

"Maybe . . . Grandma."

He ducked my swing, chuckling. Then he sobered. "In case—"

"When—not in case—we get back to the cabin, you're cooking!"

I hoped his chuckle wouldn't be his last . . . or the last I'd be around to hear.

Chapter 36

Neither Will nor I had been hungry last night, so I made peanut butter sandwiches for our breakfast as we started out early the next morning. Neither of us had slept soundly, if the puffiness around our eyes was any indication. But we had avoided talking about our experiences and retired early anyway.

I glanced over at him. He'd finished his sandwich and was licking his fingers.

"We're approaching the ranger station. I'm going inside to take some photos."

"I think I'll just look at the snakes then. I—"

"You're right. It's as good a time as any to nudge your theory about the substitute ranger." I parked beside an economy car. "Doesn't look too busy."

It wasn't busy at all. The only person there was an older man cleaning one of the snake tanks. He glanced up as I closed the door and smiled. "Hi, folks! I'm a bit busy just now, but I can answer any questions you need."

"Ladies'?" I figured that would give Will a moment to quiz the ranger.

"Both are back there." He pointed toward the right corner of the small room and continued with his task. I looked over at Will and gave him a questioning look. He gave a negative head shake and walked on over to the man.

"Do you mind if I watch?" he asked. He made a comment I couldn't hear and they both laughed.

Will and the caretaker were still talking when I came out, so I browsed among the leaflets and peeked in at a couple of other aquariums, snapping a photo or two. Finally, the caretaker glanced my way and smiled.

"I was telling the young man here that you two lucked out catching me here. I'm only the caretaker when the ranger's away."

I avoided Will's 'I told you so!' smirk. "Is the ranger on vacation?"

"Family illness. He's up in one of those tree states . . . Massachusetts . . . Vermont . . . whatever."

"And the substitute?"

"None so far. But I suspect they'll have one in a couple of weeks. This is slow season just now, especially with the crime up on the mountain. They'll want to have someone here by spring break if he hasn't returned. Meanwhile, I just fill in. I'm Juan. Just live back over there a ways." He gestured vaguely off to an area past the station.

I glanced at Will. "Guess we'd better head on back." I turned to the caretaker. "Thank you for letting us use the facilities. I hope we didn't delay you."

"Nah. I enjoyed the company. As I said, I just take care of the critters and check on things a couple of times a day. You folks on vacation?"

I saw Will open his mouth, so I hurriedly slid my hand into the crook of Will's arm and grinned up at him. "No, we just wanted a romantic weekend." I gave his elbow a warning squeeze.

"I see," Juan said and waved even as he turned back to his chores.

But he didn't see—at least, I hoped not.

Will kept quiet until we'd turned onto the highway. "Romantic weekend?" he sputtered.

"Just trying to improve your image—a young guy with an older chick."

He either failed to find a retort or decided to ignore me. Either way, he buried himself in his text messages. I used the drive to contemplate our situation. Whoever had used us for target practice troubled me. The site had been closed, and I knew that the cave had been cleared up by law enforcement. Why would anyone care that we were hiking in the area? Was it just some random sniper? Just as quickly, I thought about the box with the rattlesnake that had been delivered to my shop. I'd treated it as a practical joke; but with this latest sniper activity, I couldn't brush it off as easily.

I needed to talk to Reed, to let him know. But since he'd been recalled by the task force, I wouldn't try to contact him until he contacted me.

"Do you want to do any more interviews for your article?" I asked Will.

"I thought I'd speak to Mr. Byrd. Just sent him a text. I want to be sure which direction he wants me to go on this thing." Will fingered an unlit cigarette.

"Good idea. I doubt families would want to hike in this area with gunshots and murders prevalent."

Will didn't respond to my sarcastic tone. Instead, he mused, "Something about this whole assignment feels strange. Makes me wonder if Mr. Byrd has known something all along."

"Like what?"

"Like that a man was murdered in that cave." He stared out the passenger window.

"Why would you think that? We had specific directions and we followed them. The article appeared in the family section, remember?"

"Yeah. But what doesn't feel right is this follow-up. And with you and the task force—"

"Why do you keep saying that? I am not with the task force. I had a problem with a break-in at the store."

"All I'm saying is that if we're being sent into a crime scene, I'm surprised he doesn't give us more background information going in. Your journalism experience—meagre though it may be--and my background warrant more than what we're being given. So I'm asking him whether or not he wants us to concentrate on the vacation angle or do a follow-up on the scene after a gruesome murder."

Yesterday had shaken Will more than I'd thought.

"Will, I think I need to clear something up with you. You've made references a couple of times to my experience as a television crime reporter."

"Mr. Byrd mentioned it when he prepped me for this trip," he said, defensively.

"I don't want you building it up to more than it is. I filled in at a television station my last year in college when the reporter had an unexpected pregnancy and needed bed rest. I certainly wasn't some expert."

Will looked confused. "But he said—"

"I know. This is a small town and when I listed my experience on my resume, he never listened to more than the three months I filled in for her. Maybe I could have cleared it up better, but I needed a job."

"I see." Will grinned. "I wondered, you know. I mean, you're not old or anything, but most crime reporters—they almost need connections. And a small college station . . . well, you know."

I agreed with him and concentrated on the road and my own thoughts. The recent connection to the news anchor would maybe explain any comments Mr. Byrd might slip about my have television experience. Will seemed to accept my wild story as truth.

When we arrived at the general store to turn in the key, the eating area was empty except for a birder drinking a soda. "Hi!" he called. "Where are you two from?"

"Saddle Gap, New Mexico," I answered. I caught Will's eye and hoped he read my message to once again play our game. We sat down at a table next to him. "And you?"

"Virginia."

"Long way," Will said. "Is this your first trip here?"

A waitress delivered a hamburger and fries to our neighbor. "Can I get you anything else?" she asked.

"No, this is about as much not-on-my-diet food as I dare order," he said, winking mischievously.

She laughed and came over to us. "What can I get you two?"

"I want a burrito plate," Will said.

"Red or green?"

"Red."

She turned to me. "The same?"

I grinned. "No, thanks. I'm happy to keep the lining of my stomach intact. I'll have a ham and cheese sandwich and iced water with lemon."

She glanced at Will. "Anything to drink?"

"Coffee—black."

As she left, our neighbor resumed the conversation. "I've been to these parts a couple of times. But usually I come with a group. This is my first solo trip." He took a sip of his soda. "Beautiful out here but a little isolated for my taste . . . at least, for a year-round home."

"Good weekend getaway," I agreed. I felt Will nudge my foot under the table. I ignored the nudge and smiled flirtatiously at him. "It's a romantic spot, actually."

The waitress reappeared with our drinks just as a noisy trio entered from the patio. They hailed our neighbor and settled on his other side. He turned back to his food. Soon they had him engaged in a lively conversation about their local adventures.

Will rose. "I'm going outside to smoke," he hissed, "before I get stuck in this sticky romance you're creating." I half expected him to stomp out.

The first genuine grin all day tugged at my mouth, but before I could answer, I felt my phone buzz in my jeans pocket. Seeing an unfamiliar number, I paused, unsure whether or not I should answer it. "Aren't you going to answer it?" Will asked.

"No." I punched the button to hang it up. "It's probably another one of those advertising calls," I grumbled. "I don't know how they got my number, but I'm thinking about getting one of those cheap burner phones."

"That's what I got," our neighbor broke in. "It's better for trips away from home. It's cheaper and I don't have to answer calls from the kids worrying if I'm taking care of myself." He turned back to his garrulous neighbors then on the other side.

Will walked over to the patio door and stepped outside to the smoking area. He hadn't panicked yesterday, but I could see the strain from it in his face. He would make a topnotch reporter someday, and I'd be proud of my role in tutoring him. Of course, we'd both have to survive this current story first, and just now I wasn't gambling on our chances.

Chapter 37

I'd just finished my sandwich and stepped inside the ladies' room when my phone buzzed again. It was a single stall place, and so provided me with more privacy than I'd probably seen all day. Still, I answered my cell phone cautiously. "Hello?"

"I need to speak with Staci, please." The male voice had an unfamiliar accent.

"I'm sorry. You have the wrong number."

"This is the number I was given." The accent had deepened, tinged with impatience.

"By whom?" I could see that it was blocked. When he didn't answer, I said, "You have the wrong number." I clicked off the phone and put it back in my pocket.

When I stepped back into the hall a few minutes later, I forced myself to walk casually toward the front of the store, smiling and nodding to the older gentleman at the counter. I stepped off the porch, counted the steps to the Jeep, and clicked the keyring to unlock it. I felt strangely like I'd stepped out of my body and was moving in slow motion.

Several months ago—what seemed like a lifetime ago— I'd imagined this moment. All sorts of scenarios had flashed through my mind, but none had prepared me for the jolt that voice had given me when he asked for Staci. I needed to act quickly—before Will joined me.

Once inside the Jeep, I called Randall Byrd. His phone went to message. "Mr. Byrd, this is your free-lance photographer. Please return my call when you get this message."

Then I dialed Reed. His phone went to message. "Detective, this is the caregiver for your new dog. Could you give me a call when you receive this message?"

Finally, I dialed the number Vincente had given me for his burn phone. I listened to yet another recorded message. "Does anyone answer their phones? Mayday. If you hear this, call me."

A knock on my window made me jump. "Sorry," Will said when I rolled it down. "Didn't mean to startle you. Just wanted to make sure you weren't having a private conversation or—"

I held up my empty hands. "Conversation with whom?"

He laughed. I noticed a cigarette hidden in his palm. "I'll just—"

"I'll be ready to go when you finish that nasty thing." I must have sounded normal as he gave me a cheeky salute.

While he smoked, he walked around past the Jeep's tailgate. Numbly, I reached over to the back seat, grabbed my camera bag, and got out as well. For the moment, I needed to keep my hands busy, appear as normal as possible, and construct some sort of plan as quickly—and carefully—as possible.

I moved away from the Jeep, toward the road. I hadn't taken any photos of the cabins behind the store and today they beckoned. With their wooden sides and simple roofs, they snuggled comfortably against the colorful backdrop—a panorama of blue sky, thin stringy clouds, and tall hills. They were a photographer's dream.

Unfortunately, this photographer was as numb as a sleepwalker. I could almost see myself going through the process, still on autopilot. I hoped the photos would not be as soulless as I felt at this moment. My fingers moved easily, but my mind struggled to process the situation. Someone had connected my phone number with Staci, a name I'd left behind in Houston and hoped never to have anyone call me again. Worse, this person had my cellphone number. I couldn't replace it with a burn phone until we returned home.

When I'd finally taken as many photos as I thought appropriate, I looked over at Will. He wasn't at the tailgate, but I heard his voice nearby. "Don't you go crazy without cable or decent internet access? I mean, how far do you drive to go to a movie?"

"I don't. Why would I want to? I came here to connect with nature. If the connection breaks, I'll move on." The speaker's accent tickled my memory. I'd heard it before. Was it Midwestern? Maybe even farther north?

"How long have you been here?" Will asked.

"This trip? Only a couple of weeks so far."

"Don't you ever get bored?"

"Oh, yes, son, I do. I can't stand endless shopping malls, cars screeching, noisy stereos blasting awful stuff that vibrates, kids wailing to parents who have their ears plugged—and . . . oh, do you mean here? Never. Every day I find something new, a miracle."

I fought the laughter inside, imagining what Will's expression must be.

I walked back to the Jeep and started packing up my camera. While I was buckling the clasp, my phone blasted the

William Tell overture. I grabbed it but not before Will's head turned my way.

"Hi, Reed."

"Everything okay? You sound a little out of breath."

"Yes. I—"

"Pups okay?"

"Yes, Papa, they are being watched by my new helper."

"You're not home." His voice was hushed but brusque.

"Neither are you."

"It just sounded like maybe—you mentioned the new caretaker—"

"Back taking some more Byrd photos."

"I see. Boy Wonder?"

"He's enriching tobacco growers. Then wants to interview a birder. Are you nearby?"

"Doubtful."

"I got a phone call a few minutes ago. It was a wrong number."

"Wrong number?"

"Yes, a guy asked for someone named Staci. Wanted to argue when I told him I don't have a clue who she is."

"Recognize the caller?"

"No. Had a beautiful accent."

"Figure your photos are done? Talked to a bird?" He meant Randall.

"Flew before I could talk to it."

"Sounds like you've finished your session."

He thought we should head back. "Thinking so. Will gather the goods and circle the wagons."

"Better to do it in sunlight." He paused then forced a teasing note into his voice. "It's harder to circle the wagons after dark." His voice deepened. "Tell the *señora* hello. Then I guess you'd better save your battery."

I hung up without saying goodbye. Reed's last comment had been advising me to spend the night at the bed and breakfast in town instead of returning to my own place. It was good advice, I guess, but I had a home. I'd retreated from one home, and I refused to let someone take this one away as well. However, even though I did agree that turning off my cell might be the safest thing I could do, I needed to keep it on until I heard from Mr. Byrd.

When Will returned, his face glowed with excitement. "You finished?" I asked.

"Got a good human interest story," he said. "Also got some great leads for some other articles."

"Let's head on back then," I said casually. "I let them know inside that we're finished with the cabin and left the key. If we leave in the next hour, we'll make it back before nightfall. You okay with that?"

"Totally okay." His mind had already moved to the story he planned to write.

I ran back into the store to get a photo or two.

"Come back any time," an older lady behind the counter called. I didn't remember her name, so I just smiled and waved.

"What's up?" Will asked when I buckled in.

"Nothing. Just snapping one last photo." When he didn't answer, I looked over; he'd already inserted the ear buds in his ears. "I hope your future wife doesn't talk much," I muttered.

He glanced my way and smiled absently. For the first time in years, I envied his carefree existence. Of course, he worried about deadlines and stories. But when compared to tiptoeing through a mine field—my life for the past several months—it sounded heavenly.

We burned another hour or two stopping for photos or speaking to people out birdwatching, and then we headed toward Saddle Gap once more.

Staci? The voice kept echoing in my mind as I drove, the accent niggling in my memory. But no matter how I tried, I couldn't quite place it. I was also mentally creating numerous scenarios in response—but packing up, moving, and leaving the life I'd grown to love wasn't one of them.

Chapter 38

"I still don't understand the ranger thing. Who was that guy who pretended to be the substitute?"

Will had been gnawing on this topic for longer than I'd hoped. Finally, I said, "Could it have been a law enforcement officer working undercover?"

"You mean—"

"The family illness may be legitimate or not. If it is, maybe it was a great opportunity to place someone there undercover for a few days. If not, maybe the ranger took vacation and didn't even know his replacement was an officer. That would ensure he wouldn't say something that would blow the person's cover."

"Then why not now as well? The caretaker said the replacement was coming this weekend. But we saw the substitute earlier. Sorrel, it doesn't make sense unless . . . were they just watching us?"

I sighed. "Will, why would they watch us? I doubt we're even on their radar."

He chewed on the gum he'd stuffed into his mouth. "Maybe. But I still think he may be the guy who took the shots at us."

"Why? The shooter could just as easily be someone poaching. Or maybe someone thought we were poaching. I don't think any hunting seasons are open right now."

"Really, Sorrel? I doubt the authorities—and this wouldn't be them—would take shots at poachers. They'd just wait until we hauled out the illegal game and haul us off! And if he were poaching, why draw attention to himself by shooting at us?" He chewed harder. I hoped he didn't bite his tongue . . . or maybe that would be a good thing.

"And anyway," he continued, "it was more likely the criminals, not the law. I'm wondering if those shots weren't just to scare us from snooping. The body had been discovered and moved and we weren't up in that cave . . . and didn't plan to be. Of course, they wouldn't know that, but it would have taken more equipment than we had to get up there! Now, if only we could figure out why they didn't want us there."

"I read up on Arizona gun laws, and it's against the law to shoot into a cave. So maybe it was law enforcement trying to scare us so we wouldn't go into that cave."

Will's voice rose. "Why scare us off if nothing's there? None of this makes any sense to me!"

"Unless they're waiting for the bad guys to return? That's the only thing I can think of right now."

Will sighed. "Bad guys? Really, Sorrel?"

I grinned. "At least, it's a mystery that will make a great story to share with your fraternity when you return to school in the fall."

Will grunted, adjusted his I-Pod, and inserted his ear buds. Even across from him, I could hear the music but only softly, so I could tolerate it. He adjusted his seat to recline and pulled his cap over his eyes. I hoped he'd sleep the remainder of the trip home. Surely I hadn't been this pesky as a younger sibling!

Closely following that thought came the return of the phrase in the dream: weeping child. The child that first returned to my mind after the dream was my unknown half-brother who'd been adopted at birth. Second choice was Shane, who, according to the last I'd heard from him, was married, raising his own family, and happily rid of me as well as my mother.

The next moment another possibility popped up from— who knew where? What if the weeping child was not related to me? Should I be thinking outside the box here? My head ached, every muscle in my neck and shoulders felt tight. Since when did I start obsessing about a dream?

I needed to just drive and so I forced myself to focus on the terrain on either side of the two-lane highway. We'd only met a couple of pick-up trucks in the last hour.

Will roused when I slowed on our approach to a little store and diner. They had gas pumps out front. It was a one-stop shop. "Need anything?" I asked.

"Not really."

"We're okay on gas," I said, "but I want a cold bottle of water. I have a headache." I parked beside an ancient VW Beetle and walked into the store. I started to hold the door for Will until I realized he had remained in the Jeep.

A teenager standing behind the counter glanced at me as I stepped inside. "Bathrooms at the back," he said, his fingers moving quickly on the game he held. I walked in the direction he pointed, saying hello to a couple of older men drinking coffee at a table as I passed. They nodded and I could feel their eyes following my progress to the identical doors in the corner.

When I walked back a few moments later, one of them asked, "You camping near here?"

I paused. "No, just passing through on my way to Saddle Gap. I've been on a trip to shoot some photos to sell in my gift shop there."

He grunted. "Tourists will buy anything."

His companion spoke up then. "You got a young guy with you. He came in after you." His tone bordered on insulting. "He helping you shoot?" He laughed at his own choice of words.

I turned toward the counter. "Do you have Tylenol?" I asked the teenager. "And cold water?" I glanced back at the two. "Have a nice day."

When I paid the teenager, he whispered, "Don't mind those two. They hang out here but I don't think they mean to be rude."

I gathered up my purchase and turned away—then looked back at him. "Do you work here every day?"

"Most afternoons. I'm being homeschooled. My last year."

"You see a lot of campers?"

"Not this time of year."

"Oh," I said. "Seemed odd they'd ask if I were camping."

He shrugged and glanced down at his game. "Might be that bunch that came through yesterday. They said something about hunting. Weird. No hunting season open just now. They talked to those two over there a bit. Like I said, I think those two just like to talk."

Will had stopped beside them now. I thanked the teen and walked on out to the Jeep. Once settled inside, I checked my phone. The flashing light signaled a text message, so I checked. It was Reed: "Changing landscape." So he would be traveling as well. I might or might not be hearing from him any time soon.

Then I noticed the message light. I punched in the code and listened to Randall Byrd. "Sorry I missed you," he said. "Check in again when you can."

The passenger door opened. Will had a bag of chips and a large, iced Coke cup. He smelled of cigarette smoke and I wrinkled my nose.

"Interesting old guys in there," he said, fastening the seatbelt and settling his food, oblivious to my nose wrinkle.

I turned the ignition key and checked the mirror before turning back onto the highway. "They were rude," I said.

He laughed. "Dirty old guys," he agreed, his mouth full of chips. "They think we are an item."

I ignored the bait.

"But they were a good source of information."

"I didn't get anything from them."

"I did." He stuck another chip in his mouth. When he'd washed it down with Coke, he continued. "After congratulating me on 'snagging an older gal who didn't look too bad,' they asked if our buddy had caught up with us."

The Jeep swerved a little as I looked over at him. "Buddy?"

"Yeah. Came through recently. I acted like we were expecting one. Threw out a vague description of Detective Reed." He took another sip of Coke.

"And?" I could tell he was savoring this moment of having information he knew I wanted.

"It didn't fit him. But, surprisingly enough, their description did fit someone else we know."

I pulled off the highway onto the graveled side, put the gearshift into park, and turned to Will. "Enough of the fun and games! I admit I deserve the hassle with my recent teasing, but just tell me what you know."

"Sorry. Couldn't resist. Anyway, it sounded remarkably like our ranger substitute."

"Really? That's—"

Will went on as if I hadn't spoken. "I told you he had some sort of weird aura around him. Anyway, the old guys said he described you and me and made a joke about May–December. Implied that he was a private detective, hired by your husband. It was a juicy story for them. I doubt they believed my version."

"No wonder they insinuated—"

"They did compliment me on my taste, if that helps," Will offered, making no attempt to hide his grin.

"Enough already. Did they have any other information to pass on to you?"

"Nah. But he'll be checking back with them. I acted naïve."

I groaned. "I told them about Saddle Gap."

"They said you did. I told them it was our cover story. Then I made up enough juicy details to keep them diverted for the rest of the day." Will wiggled his eyebrows in his lousy

Grouchy Marx imitation. "I asked them to send him toward Lordsburg. And slipped them a twenty."

I glared at him. "And you think that will shut their mouths?"

"Not totally. But I may have promised them photos in the near future." He ducked down.

"I ought to kill you, Will!" I checked the rearview mirror and pulled back onto the highway. "You'd better start praying right now I don't do it before we get home!"

Undeterred, Will laughed. "I'll pray they get a juicier tale . . . or add enough to this one as they repeat it. But I've never been a good boy. At least, I've been kind to two old gossips."

I didn't comment. Will's lightheartedness had distracted him, but I felt a chill settling into my bones. Every new detail we uncovered only hinted at another one buried. A sense of renewed urgency to clear the lingering questions from the past surged through me, even as dread crept into my soul.

"You cold?" Will asked.

"What?"

"You just shivered."

I started to snap back at him, but my phone rang. I glanced down at the lighted screen. It was an unknown number.

"You gonna answer that?"

"No," I said, trying to sound casual. "They can leave a message." Then I refocused on the highway, gripping the steering wheel as yet another shiver coursed through me.

Chapter 39

Will spent the drive home typing up his notes and roughing out his story, his I-Pad ear bud inserted. Besides an occasional comment or question, he didn't speak.

I welcomed the silence as I mentally rehashed the days since the body had been discovered in the cave. The murder—and the unknown identity of the victim—saddened me; but the early photo of Staci (me) and the subsequent phone messages echoed back to the weeks after Kevin's murder. Because they feared he'd died due to my recent stories about a Mexican cartel, I'd relocated to Branson and my friend, John, dropping my public name in favor of my own. Unfortunately, I now had to admit that although those weeks had given me time to recover from the shock, I hadn't escaped unscathed. Would I ever be able to stop looking over my shoulder?

As we drove to my little shop, I vowed I'd do everything I could to not bring any more danger to my new friends here in Saddle Gap. For the first time since I'd left my life in Houston in the dark of night, I had allowed myself to dream of forever. I wasn't abandoning it without a fight. But more than that, I didn't want to endanger any of the people who had accepted me with kindness and faith. Will got out and moved his things into his car.

Since we both needed to speak with Mr. Byrd and Will needed to write his article, he followed me to the newspaper office. When I walked into Mr. Byrd's office, his secretary looked up from her computer and smiled over her glasses.

"Mr. Byrd is expecting you, Ms. Janes," she chirped. "Did you have fun?"

"It was a memorable experience," I said. "Thank you for making the arrangements. I got some gorgeous photos and can't wait to go through them again!"

Mr. Byrd caught my last words as he stepped out of his office. "I'll enjoy seeing those as well. Your photos are always great, Sorrel!" He looked behind me. "Where's our reporter?"

"Just finishing up his story. He said to tell you he'd be in right away."

"I'd like to visit with you," he said and turned to his secretary. "Would you tell Will when he gets here that I want to visit with him before I leave?"

"Yes, sir." She looked at me. "Would you like something to drink? Bottled water? Coffee?"

"No, thanks."

She looked toward Mr. Byrd, who shook his head. "You can lock up after Will comes in," he told her. "I appreciate your staying late."

Mr. Byrd closed the door after I'd walked through and motioned for me to sit on one of two easy chairs in the corner. "I got your call quite a while after you'd left Portal," he said, sitting in the chair opposite me, "but by that time I figured we could talk better in person. You discovered some surprises?"

"A few." I told him about our adventure with the sniper and the stories we'd been given about the ranger.

"Interesting," he said. "Like you, I can't understand why anyone would target the two of you, especially since law enforcement has removed its presence from the area."

"Maybe that made the person braver," I told him. "We didn't see a soul around when we parked, so we started climbing the established trail with no inkling of danger. In fact, when we'd spoken to the ranger earlier, he'd indicated that the trail is the one prepared for hikers and would be ideal for us. There were no other vehicles besides ours parked up or down the road when we started the hike, and the Jeep was the only one there when we came back down."

"Did you report the incident to local law enforcement? Or Deputy Reed?" he asked.

"No, but I left him a message when I sent yours." I smiled. "I think Will was scared, but by now he's rewritten the morning with his imagination, just as he embellishes a few things when he talks about our experiences."

"I would expect as much. I'll have to tone him down a bit if his article reflects that."

"It's all a learning process."

"I agree. Now, we need to address the elephant in the kitchen. Your phone call. Was that related to your photo and the dead man?"

As much as I wanted to tell him about the phone calls—which had prompted me to call him even more than our decision to return home—I'd mulled it over during the drive home and changed my mind. What could he do? Call the police? I hadn't been threatened with bodily harm. They would simply pass it off as a wrong number and regard me as just a hysterical woman. I had never enjoyed drama—and I wasn't terrified of a vague threat. So I attempted to look embarrassed and shrugged.

"No, the sniper just rattled us both a bit. We were tired, scared a little, and still caught up in an adrenalin moment. Law enforcement wasn't available to inform, and we decided our shooter must have been a poacher, but . . . who knows? So I called to let you know we would be returning unless you wanted us to remain in the area. When we didn't hear from you, we came on home. I apologize if I worried you." My chuckle wasn't totally convincing, so I added, "I think Will and I may both be prone to drama at times."

Mr. Byrd focused on my eyes during my story. I doubted he believed it all, but he didn't argue with my conclusions.

"I assume you have photos to support Will's articles," he said instead. "Since they're human interest instead of breaking news, we'll likely run them later this week. In fact, they'll make great news for the Sunday edition. We're leading with a controversial city council decision in tomorrow's paper, and that's likely to have follow-ups."

"I know that he conducted some interesting interviews with birders from others states and old-timers in the area. They should make wonderful human interest stories. I hope my shots will do the same."

"I have no doubt they will."

He rose, waited until I'd stood as well, and walked me to the door. Then he paused, his hand on the knob, turned and spoke softly but urgently, his eyes boring into mine. "Take care, Sorrel. I suspect you've abbreviated your experiences just now and I'm concerned. Putting yourself in danger is becoming a habit of yours."

"I'm going to follow your advice and buy a track phone. None were available, of course, where we were, so I'll let you know the number when I get it."

He nodded. "I'm relieved about that. Are you sure there's nothing else you'd like to tell me?"

"I—"

A knock on the door startled me and I jumped. Mr. Byrd opened it, surprising Will, his hand raised to knock again. The first thing I noticed was his heightened color and agitated movements.

Randall Byrd motioned Will to enter and closed the door. Both of us watched as Will paced around the small office, clearly somewhere between agitated and excited, with a dose of fear thrown in. Amid waving his arms in the air and striking dramatic facial expressions, he raved about an email he'd found on his desk. "It's an attempt to censor the press," he said. "Terror tactics. We've reverted back to—"

"Do you have a copy of the email?" Mr. Byrd interrupted.

Will handed him the paper he'd stuffed in his back pocket.

Mr. Byrd asked. "Sit down, Will, and calm down." He gestured toward his own chair as he stood and walked over behind his desk. "Sorrel, you listen to this. I'll read it." He waited as Will perched on the edge of the seat and then read: "*Stay Home! Pokin yur nose into other people's bizness ain't healthy. Yu and that fancy pants pitcher gal better stop messin in our place, yu here? Lead poisin ain't healthy.*"

"See?" Will started up with his rant. "Like I said—"

"Will, calm down." Mr. Byrd stared at the email a bit longer. "Someone is obviously trying to sound ignorant. He can spell 'healthy' but not 'you'? He uses complete sentences even with the atrocious spelling? And he knows how to use email and track you here?" He smiled. "What a joke! I've half a mind to publish this 'as is' on my editorial page."

"It's straight-out censorship!" Will had warmed to his topic, and Mr. Byrd's reaction to the email clearly wasn't what he expected.

"In fact, I believe I will use it," Mr. Byrd continued, ignoring Will's interruption. He picked up his desk phone and dialed. "Rick? Have you started on the Editorial page? Wonderful! Hold it! I'm making a last minute change. Hope it doesn't make you too late. Something unexpected has come up."

He hung up the phone and grinned at us. "This will be fun! I've been getting stuffy! Will, I won't need your article until tomorrow. The paper is already full of city council stuff, so why don't you go on home and write your stuff in the morning? I've already told Sorrel she doesn't need to send the photos until then. You both look like you could use a good meal."

Will clearly hadn't expected this reaction. His disappointment clung to him as he rose and started toward the door without looking at either of us. "Yes, Chief," he said, opening the door and stepping out.

"I'm afraid I've disillusioned that young man," Randall Byrd murmured when the door clicked shut. "He came prepared for a full-fledged march and no one followed his lead."

"I can't believe I didn't have my camera out," I said.

"Why?"

"I've never seen Will slink off anywhere. And his mouth was shut!"

We both laughed softly. Then I rose as well. "I don't mind having a day to go through the shots I took. An evening at home with the critters sounds more like heaven than anything right now."

He grunted. "We're just shelving our talk," he said. "Have a good rest."

Chapter 40

The ride back to my house was quiet. As I pulled into my spot at the back of the shop and parked, I'd never felt happier to be here. My little shop/house huddled down against the vast southwestern sky was home.

As I started to go into the house, I remembered Madonna and her little family. I'd left water and food in the containers I'd bought from the pet store, which the clerk had assured me would be adequate for at least four days for a dog her size. So, figuring the clerk knew his product, I decided to wait until morning to check on her when I had adequate light.

Inside, I was greeted by my two cats—sort of. Van called out a cranky meow when he saw me and Flash hissed. "So much for keeping the home fires warm and welcoming!" I muttered. I returned to the Jeep to bring in the last of my luggage and put everything away. Still, the felines weren't clamoring to be petted. I checked their food and water dishes, then put treats out.

"Suit yourselves," I told them and rummaged in the cupboard. I pulled out a small prepared meal—pasta and sauce—and popped it in the microwave. While it heated, I checked the phone for messages. Since I'd had someone here answering the phone during the day, there were only a couple of hang-ups and a message from Teri. I punched play on the machine.

"Hey, Sorrel! Am I going to keep you home long enough for the sale? I'm being held prisoner here by Jose and the relatives. Come save me!" It ended with a giggle.

When the microwave dinged, I pulled out the dish and rummaged for crackers. I missed that giggle. I blew on a spoonful of pasta, then took a bite. "Ugh. I miss more than the giggle," I told the cats gathered at my feet. "I miss the leftovers from Teri's cooking! Bet you do too!"

I managed to swallow a couple more bites with liberal doses of crackers before I dumped it and rinsed out my spoon. "Maybe I need a hot shower and an early night to brighten my perspective," I muttered.

As if on cue, my cell rang. "Hello?" I said. Since the ringtone wasn't one of those I'd assigned to the people who called me regularly, I figured it was a sales call.

"Miss Sorrel? Found your number tacked up on a board in the kitchen. You need to come!"

I didn't recognize the voice, but I could hear the agitation and fear. "Who is this please?"

"He said to call if something wasn't right." I could tell it was a male . . . maybe older . . . and heavily accented.

"Who is 'he'?"

"I've called the sheriff, but you need to come!"

"Don't hang up yet!" I said. "Come where?"

"Mister Reed's!"

Then I recognized the voice. "I'm on my way!" I told him, even as I realized trying to get any more out of the man was futile. He was Reed's older neighbor, who spoke very little. The one time I'd met him, he'd not spoken, just nodded and shook my hand. And even though his current agitation had overcome his shyness, he clearly wasn't comprehending much of what I was saying.

I threw on a coat, locked the door, and ran to the Jeep. Darkness had fallen since I'd been home and the overcast sky didn't offer much visibility. Speeding as quickly as I dared, I first prayed that Reed's house—and his little canine family—were okay. Then I prayed Reed hadn't been home and been injured. But with each passing mile, my mind conjured up scarier scenarios. "Time to block out thoughts and just drive as quickly and safely as possible," I muttered, narrowly missing a rabbit crossing the road.

Smoke billowed high in the sky as I turned into Reed's lane. An officer appeared from the entrance and raised his hand for me to stop. I rolled down my window.

"I'm Sorrel Janes," I told him when he leaned down toward my window and flashed his light in my face. "Chris Reed's older caretaker called me. I've been helping with his place as well."

I could see lights from a fire engine behind him, as well as several other cars with their lights flashing. Most appeared to be stopped outside the barn, where flames licked up out of the roof.

"We do not have things under control just now, ma'am," he said. "You'll need to leave and check in later. It isn't safe."

"I can call Chris Reed," I argued, "but the older gentleman who called me will vouch for me too. I need to check on his pets!"

"I'm sorry, ma'am, but I have my orders. No civilian traffic—"

"Sorrel?" I saw Jose running up behind the officer.

"She's okay," he told the officer when he reached us. "She's the girlfriend. I'll look after her." He opened the passenger door and slid inside.

The officer reluctantly stepped back and waved me through. I started maneuvering the Jeep through the group of official vehicles.

"Jose, what happened?" I exclaimed. "Is Chris here?"

"No. Pull over there, Sorrel. You'll be out of the way there."

Jose jumped out as soon as I parked and ran around to open my door. "Looks like the fire was set," he told me as soon as I stepped out. "The barn is gone I'm afraid."

"Did they get the dog out?"

"Dog? I haven't heard any—"

I ran toward the barn.

"Sorrel! Stop!" Jose yelled.

Tears were already interfering with my sight, but I brushed them away as I charged on. Just as the barn door loomed before me, the toe of my shoe caught on a patch of rubble. As I overcorrected trying to catch my balance, I pitched forward into the broad shoulders of . . . Reed? "I hoped you'd be able to," I gasped, "get here in time!"

"We tried, ma'am," the young firefighter said.

I squinted up into his face. "You're not Reed."

"No, ma'am, but if I were, I'd still not let you go into that barn. Look!"

Still holding me by my arms, he turned me toward the barn. Up close I could feel the heat of the raging inferno. Nothing could have survived it. I felt myself crumple; then he pulled me back toward a pick-up truck with the back gate lowered. "She's had a shock," I heard him tell someone. Hands guided me closer and someone half-lifted me into a sitting perch. I shivered, in spite of the heat rushing into the air from the blaze. A warm blanket landed on my shoulders and cocooned me with warmth. A wet cloth wiped my face, and someone held a bottle of cold water for me to drink. I swallowed twice and turned away. Voices faded beneath the roar of the blaze and the crashing of lumber.

"I didn't keep them safe!" I heard someone cry out. "She worked so hard to keep them safe and I didn't help her!"

"She's distraught!" someone murmured. "A sedative?"

"Please, God, don't let him be in that fire!" the person cried.

"They haven't found anyone in the fire," someone told me. "Are you still cold?"

I squinted to focus. It was Jose. "No," I told him through chattering teeth. "Find him!"

"I think we're taking you—"

"No! I'm not leaving!" I struggled to stand. My knees wobbled, so I settled back down. "I'll be okay. I need to wait for the dog."

I could feel Jose's breath against my face. "Sorrel, I don't know about a dog. You're exhausted and in shock. We need—"

A whine and tiny yip interrupted him. I struggled to focus. A firefighter bent close, his coat wrapped around a bundle. Inches from my face, the little mama dog peeked out and whined. I reached out, and she licked my fingers. "Babies?" I asked.

"She'd carried them all to safety," he said. "Now we need to take her to the animal hospital."

I looked in her eyes. I reached for her and cuddled her bony body to my chest. "It's okay," I told her. II turned to Jose. "Let's get her to the doctor," I said. Then darkness enveloped me.

Chapter 41

"I advise you to let us admit you to the hospital overnight. A glucose drip would hydrate you, and we could keep watch over you until morning." The emergency room doctor spoke a little louder in case I wasn't hearing her.

"I appreciate what you have done," I told her, "but apart from this leg, which you have so nicely stitched and cleaned, and some smoke inhalation, I'm fine. I have animals at home to care for, and I certainly will sleep better in my own bed."

"I advise you not to drive," she insisted. "I know the stitches are in your left leg, but you need to let them heal. Besides, you need a clearer head than you have tonight."

Jose spoke up then. "I'll drive her home and then I'll go collect her Jeep from the fire scene. She will have someone at home to help with her care."

"This is still against my better judgement," she said, looking from one of us to the other. Then she shrugged. "I'll send you something to help you sleep tonight and something to change your bandage tomorrow. I'm also sending some salve for the light burns on your face. First thing tomorrow, I want you to call and make an appointment with your primary care doctor. Do you understand what I've told you?"

I nodded dutifully, avoiding both her and Jose's eyes. I'd agree to anything to avoid staying in the hospital tonight, and I suspected they knew that.

The young doctor gave me one last parting shot before moving to her next patient. "Since you live alone, I'm sending a walker for you to use to get around. Try not to put weight on that leg."

Again I nodded. Fifteen minutes later, a nurse's aide wheeled me to the emergency exit and helped me get into Jose's truck. Once we'd started home, I broke the heavy silence. "I'm sorry to be such a bother, Jose."

"Bother is your middle name, Sorrel," he said.

"I don't want you doing any more. You have Teri to care for."

"I wouldn't be able to get back in the house tonight if I hadn't done this. Teri wanted to be at the hospital instead."

We rode the rest of the way home in an uncomfortable silence until we pulled into my driveway and parked beside a small red car. "Whose car is that?" I asked.

"One of Teri's cousins, and before you say anything, let me just say this. Teri doesn't need to be stressed right now, and she will be if you follow your stubborn route and refuse to let people help you! If you care about Teri at all, just shut your mouth, smile, and play nice." He turned off the motor and jumped out.

Jose had never spoken to me like that. Even though reason intervened to remind me that he was tired and stressed also, frustration boiled up inside me. I hated feeling helpless and having people wait on me. I'd only scraped my leg in the fall, and I had a little blistering from the fire. Why did everyone insist on turning me into an invalid? Had I not been so tired, I'd have told him that it wasn't easy playing nice, it seldom worked and much more.

I wished I didn't need his help, and briefly thought about refusing it. But that small voice of reason reminded me that I probably would just end up in a heap somewhere.

Jose held my elbow as I slid out of the truck. He continued to cup it as I hopped to the porch and up the two steps to the door. Once inside, we continued to my bedroom, where I sank wearily on the bed.

"I'll send her in to get you dressed for bed," he said and turned to go.

"Jose? Thank you."

He didn't turn or look at me. "I'm just mad right now, Sorrel. You take so many risks, just running into that fire. You weren't thinking of the people who care for you. I'm doing this for Reed and for Teri. We can talk about this—maybe—when I calm down." He didn't look back as he left.

I stared after him. He was right. I'd known not to run toward the fire, but I'd been following my heart, not my head.

"He'll cool down," a soft voice said. I looked up into warm brown eyes. "I'm Celia. He's more scared than mad. It must have been a bad sight out there. If you'll tell me where your night clothes are, I'll get you settled."

In a short time, Celia had helped me sponge my face and arms, change into soft pajamas, settle into bed, swallow the tablets the doctor had sent, and drink a cup of hot green tea. "I can manage nicely with that walker," I told Celia when she asked if I needed anything else. "You don't need to stay the night. I'm really just more shaken up than hurt."

She looked at me thoughtfully then asked me to get up and walk to the bathroom. It wasn't easy, but I used the last of my willpower to keep an expressionless face and take small steps. When she was satisfied that I could do that well enough, Celia nodded.

"Okay," she said. "I think you can do that well enough. But I'll be back in the morning to help you dress and change your bandage. I enjoy helping people, so don't start feeling like it's a bother."

"Are you a nurse?" I asked.

Celia smiled. "No, just the oldest of six kids—the rest boys who always were coming in with injuries from sports or fights or just falling out of trees." She placed a jug of water beside my bed, as well as my cell phone. "I've written my number on the pad. Please call if you need something. I'm a light sleeper and I don't live far."

I thanked her again, promising to let her know if I needed her through the night. We both knew I wouldn't, but we also knew I wasn't really in critical shape. The cats, having been given wet food and treats by Celia, cuddled up at the foot of the bed. I listened as her car pulled away then checked the house phone for messages.

I'd had several calls. I listened to the messages, mostly from people hoping I hadn't been badly hurt and offering help should I need it. I deleted most. A couple were hang-ups and there were the usual number of calls offering new credit cards, exciting vacation cruises, or a variety of other offers. I yawned, turned the lamp off, and snuggled under the covers. Before I drifted off to sleep, I whispered a prayer for the little dog and her babies.

Sorrel? Sorrel?

The familiar whisper woke me. I looked at the window. Moonlight peeked through the curtains. My eyes finally cleared.

I kept completely still, hardly daring to breathe, and moved my eyes to every corner of the room. I could see no one there. I must have been dreaming.

As sleep crept back over me, I heard the familiar whisper: *Things aren't always what they seem. The tears inside are silent.*

I wanted to ask who was whispering to me and why the riddles. "Why don't you just say what you mean?" I tried to reply. "Enough with the games already!"

But the drugs I'd been given for pain caught me, and once again, I slept.

Chapter 42

The cats had snuggled against me in the night, and I found their warm bodies a comfort when I woke up. When I moved, they sat up, stretched, and then sat with me in the pale light. We watched as the sky turned pink and spread into orange fingertips. My own fingertips itched for the camera. What gorgeous colors!

I slept better than I'd expected and woke early. So many questions, emotions, and images bombarded me and called to me.

My mind moved to the night before. Immediately, unwanted images of the little mother struggling to carry her babies, one by one, to safety brought fresh tears. I still couldn't understand why anyone set fires. I brushed the tears away and turned on my side. Pain shot through my leg, reminding me that I'd not left the fire unscathed. I turned back onto my back and blew through my mouth while I mentally counted softly. At twenty, I stopped and forced myself to relax the tense muscles.

I'd gotten up once in the night; and, although the walker had been nearby, I hadn't needed it. I realized now that the pain meds had probably helped.

I tentatively moved my leg again. It was sore and stiff, but I didn't want to coddle it. Various childhood scrapes had taught me not to coddle the injury.

"I could use a cup of coffee," I murmured to the room in general, but mostly to bolster myself. Van and Flash perked up. "No coffee for you two! But I guess a taste of canned food might be in order." They leaped to the floor, meowing in unison.

Getting up wasn't a quick process. Besides my leg, several new aches had surfaced in my shoulders and arms. If I didn't rush things, I figured I could make it. Once on my feet, I discovered that every muscle in my body ached, sometimes screaming in protest of my idiotic decision to walk. Stubbornly, I pushed on, the I-can-make-it mantra playing in my brain.

Making it and doing something well aren't quite the same thing. After almost dumping the cat dishes and spilling water on the kitchen counter, I decided against filling and starting the coffeemaker. Instead, I settled for a cup of tea, which I sipped while leaning against the counter by the microwave.

When I finished the tea, I began the painful trip back to the bedroom. My leg had stiffened during the night; and experience from my running days reminded me that I needed to take a hot shower and my meds and then walk in shorter steps. Had I not had stitches, I would have done stretching exercises.

As I walked, the phone rang; but by the time I reached it, the caller had hung up without leaving a message. I settled gingerly on the chair beside the bed and checked the number. It was unfamiliar.

I fought a battle between immediately pressing redial and getting more comfortable. Comfort won.

I hobbled to the shower, using the walker this time. Standing under hot water felt good, but I knew I couldn't stay long. Still, after wrapping up in my ancient terrycloth robe, I felt better.

It was still early, so I wrestled the walker back to my bed, deciding that the phone call was most likely a wrong number. I found the antibiotic cream on the nightstand and covered the stitches. Did it need a dressing? I couldn't remember the instructions, so I didn't reach for one. The shower had relaxed me, and the cramping had eased a bit. Maybe I could catch a short nap before—what was her name?—Teri's cousin came back.

In my dream, I kept running toward the flames. *Sorrel, come back!* Was that Reed? No. Mama? Someone caught my arm and I wrestled it free. "I can't hear you!" I yelled. "My ears are ringing!"

I opened my eyes, letting them wander around my bedroom and finally to the nightstand where my phone's light was fading.

I picked it up and checked for a message. Again, none had been left. This time I pressed redial.

The phone only rang twice before it was answered. "Hello!"

"Vicente? Sorrel here. I heard the phone but couldn't get to it quickly enough, and I didn't know it was you. Have you changed numbers? Sorry I missed you!"

"I bought a new burner phone after you sent a strange message. Was planning to leave the new number with you but wasn't sure if I should leave it on a message. What have you gotten into now, *chica*?"

I told him what had been happening, skipping over all but the barest details. "I have some stitches in my leg," I finished. "There goes my modeling career!"

Vicente didn't laugh. He remained silent a moment then scolded. "If trouble doesn't find you, you seek it yourself!"

"No trouble actually. I've had bumps and bruises before."

"But the fire—that doesn't sound like bumps and bruises. Has the handsome detective discovered what caused it?"

"Haven't a clue." I felt reticent about discussing Reed. Vicente's mocking tone made me feel a bit uncomfortable. "He's on an away assignment. I haven't seen him in a while." Then, before he could say more, I continued. "How are things there? You said you had to change your burn phone. Is this number forty-eight?"

"I've lost count!" Vicente laughed. "You know I change them out when one is compromised. I received a message from you referring to a message someone had left from this phone. I hadn't left one, so I switched it right away."

"Oh, sorry, Vicente."

"But I called to ask about the message. What did it say?"

A door slammed outside. Teri's cousin must have arrived. "I can't remember," I lied. "Nothing important. Gotta go! My helper has arrived."

"Wait, Sorrel!"

"Yes?"

"I'll be quick! Just wanted you to know someone contacted the station about an early photo of you. I didn't hear about it until recently. One of the young production assistants handled it but didn't let me know."

"Who asked?"

"She didn't remember. Didn't keep a record. Just shot off a copy of a press release that had your early photo on it to an email."

"When?"

"A couple of months ago. I'm so sorry. You know I'd never have allowed that. I hope it hasn't caused any—"

"Not a bit," I interrupted. "I wouldn't mind talking to her though."

"She's gone. She quit shortly after I chewed her out. Good riddance. You can't have a thin skin in that job." I could hear voices behind him. He lowered his voice. "I hope you are okay. I have removed the clip from the files. Who would ever have thought—"

"Thanks for letting me know. You couldn't have predicted any of this, and I've imposed on our friendship so much already. Don't give it another thought."

"Call if you need me!"

I hung up.

A deep voice behind me drawled, "I thought I said to call me if you needed me, but you didn't—call, that is."

"Reed! You scared the—"

"Ms. Sorrel?" It was Celia and she sounded like she was just outside the door.

"I'll make a pot of coffee," Reed whispered and stepped out. "She's in here, ma'am. I'm making the coffee, but she may need you to help her with other things. By the way, I'm Chris Reed, with the sheriff's department."

"Pleased to meet you, sir. I'll just see about Ms. Sorrel."

By the time she stepped into the bedroom, I'd managed to get under the bedclothes. She glanced and seemed to decide she hadn't interrupted a lover's tryst. "HI, Cella. I managed my shower and a cup of tea. I was on the verge of calling to let you know you didn't need to make this trip. Thank you. I hate to bother you."

Celia laughed. "No bother." She went into the bathroom and gathered up the supplies she needed, talking as she went. "Teri is still complaining about that baby not coming yet."

I laughed. "Then I know she's feeling better."

Celia watched as I walked into the kitchen and over to the sofa. She'd slipped me into sleep pants and a t-shirt and brushed my hair until it shone. "I'll just make the bed," she said.

"That's a good idea," Chris drawled from the easy chair. "I'll get her a cup of coffee, and I'll feed her, but my housekeeping skills aren't too terrific."

"Fibber!" I said. "You brag about everything being spotless!"

Shortly after, Celia reluctantly left me in Reed's care, smiling a little as he stuffed the last bite of a muffin in his mouth.

"She's Teri's cousin," I told him.

"I figured as much. It's a good thing she has a dozen of them. I think the rest are at her house."

We spent a couple of minutes in silence as I savored the last of my coffee. Then, I knew I couldn't wait a moment longer. "Reed, the little dog?"

"I called the vet first thing this morning. She's not in great shape."

"Will they—Reed, I can pay for it. We can't just let her— it's my fault you know."

To my embarrassment, the tears had started. In an instant, I found myself bawling into Reed's shoulder while he gingerly rocked me. Finally, he whispered, "Are you about finished? I don't mind, but I don't have a handkerchief."

He untangled himself and snatched a box of tissues. He wiped my face, commanded me to blow, and tried to wipe some of it off his shoulder. "I told him to keep the puppies with her," he said. "They need to nurse, and she needs a reason to fight. So they have them in a tiny cage adjoining hers."

"She's such a good little mama," I whispered.

"She's a little fighter. When they take the puppies back to their cage, she growls." Reed chuckled. "Reminds me of someone I know." He pulled me against him again.

"I should have—"

"Sorrel, you couldn't have known some crazy person would set fire to that barn!"

"Have they—?"

"No. They're thinking it may have been someone crossing the border who stayed the night there."

"And then someone spooked them."

"Yep. The place still looks like no one lives there. I've been away so much. Maybe they had built a fire and didn't put it out well enough." He sighed. Until then, I hadn't noticed how exhausted he looked. "I don't want to push it really. That old barn really needed to go. I'd been planning on it anyway. And from what they found inside, I think there may have been . . . well, a family. Legal or not, I don't want to throw a dad in jail who was just trying to feed his kids."

I pulled away to look into his eyes. "Neither do I. But I mean it, Reed. I want to pay—"

"Then I have a proposition for you!"

"Anything—almost."

"Sorrel, I'm going to need help with this dog family," he said. "With replacing the barn, I figure I'll also need someone to boss me around about how it should look and where that bunch of critters is going to live. So I'll just make a down payment—"

He couldn't get anything else out as both of us shared a hearty laugh. Reed handed me another tissue as he stood up and then grabbed our cups. "I could use another cup while I listen to your tales—and I'm sure you have plenty. You?"

"No, but I wouldn't mind a muffin, if you've left any."

His laugh warmed me just as it always did.

Chapter 43

"I don't have time for a nap, but I'll admit it sounds good. I need to make at least half a dozen phone calls," Reed sighed. "There's the insurance company and . . ." He trailed off and gazed out the window.

I didn't argue with him, as I knew how stubborn he could be about work. But I'd watched his tired gait when he brought me coffee and a muffin. He was exhausted.

"Let's compromise then. I need to make a quick check in my office and—"

"I'm sure there's nothing there that can't wait, Sorrel. I can—

"I know they're not crucial, but with the big sale on my doorstep, so to speak, I thought I might at least look through mail and check messages. Meanwhile, you can use my bedroom to make your phone calls—privacy in case more of Teri's relatives invade us."

He covered a yawn. "I came to take care of you. Besides, I need to interview you about—"

"Mail I can open and toss. Anything that requires brain function is more than I can swing. I won't be long, Reed. After all, my office is just through that door, not in Tucson!" I batted my eyelashes and gave him my best wilting violet imitation— ruined when we both burst out laughing.

To pacify him, I used the walker when I walked into the office to check mail, return phone calls, and generally reassure myself that the upcoming Valentine's Day event plans were proceeding as they should. He followed me anyway, snooping around a bit. "No more snakes?" I asked.

"So far," he said. "At least, no reptiles."

"I won't be long," I promised again, lowering myself into the chair. It was a bit awkward with my leg, but it wasn't hurting—just sore. "No more than half an hour."

"Sure." He turned to go then reached back to give my ponytail a tug. "I've missed you, Red—like a toothache."

I made a face. "You're brave when I'm incapacitated! Try that again when I'm one hundred percent!"

He stepped out then peeked around the door facing. "Promises, promises!"

My half hour stretched into two hours. I kept busy with consignees checking on me, my calling to check on Teri, some necessary time spent writing out checks for small bills, and a longer call with Mr. Byrd. When I'd given him an update on the fire, he passed me on to Will, who asked if I'd gotten any photos from the fire.

"That's like asking someone fleeing a shark if he got photos!" I teased him.

He didn't even laugh. "What can you tell me?" he asked, his voice uncharacteristically brusque.

I told him why I had been there and what I'd seen, avoiding any mention of my injuries. "I didn't see you there," I told him, "but the place was a madhouse."

"Pecking order here at the paper," he said, keeping his voice low. "I wasn't given a call. But now, I'm scrambling to find a human interest story or some other angle to pursue."

"I see. So someone else has it already." Now I understood the cause for his grumpiness!

"Yeah." He didn't enlighten me about who it was.

"Will, you're going to be in debt to me big time."

"What do you mean? You didn't give me anything."

"Do you have a pen?" Then I told him the story about the little dog and her pups. "She's recovering just now," I said, "but the best part is I have some photos of her from before the fire. You could use one of those. This will make a wonderful human interest story. Oh, and she belongs to Deputy Sheriff Chris Reed, so don't make a plea for people to adopt. Just write a sweet story."

Will had several questions for me. When he was finally done, he grudgingly added, "Sorrel, I owe you."

"Yes, you do, youngster. And I may collect someday!"

I hung up to the sound of his chuckles.

My leg had begun to ache. It was time to change positions. I eased out of the chair, feeling twice my years, and yawned. It was just half past noon, I noticed, as I looked at the little desk clock. Time to check on my lawman.

When I opened the door into my living quarters, I first noticed a wonderful smell. Green chili stew. I didn't know how to make green chili stew, but I certainly loved to eat it. My stomach grumbled in response, and I suddenly realized how hungry I was.

I glanced throughout the kitchen/living room area but saw no sign of Reed. Then I noticed a note on the counter. "Ms. Sorrel, I've left some stew in the crockpot and tortillas warming in the oven. I didn't have the heart to wake Mr. Reed, but I left enough for him as well. Celia."

Bless her! Both of us had been spared a peanut butter sandwich meal!

My first inclination was to eat. But, first, I tiptoed to the door of my bedroom, opened it, and peeked inside. Reed and the cats were snuggled under the warm comforter—sound asleep. I tiptoed over to Reed and whispered in his ear. "You and the cats are snoring loud enough to lift the roof off my house. I think I'll eat this terrific meal myself!"

He smiled but didn't open his eyes. The cats yawned and leapt off the bed. The three of us went to the kitchen where I put food in their bowls and filled my own.

After I'd eaten, I remembered that I'd promised Will photos. So I returned to the office to select them, crop them, and email them. By the time I returned to the kitchen, I found Reed sitting at my table with a bowl of his own.

"Good stuff," he said. "I can't believe you made it!"

"That's because I didn't. Celia left it. Did you find the tortillas?"

"No. I knew you wouldn't have those, so I've been eating it on its own."

"They're on the counter in that little flat container." I eased down on the couch and lifted my leg with both hands. "I'd get them for you—and make coffee—but . . ."

"Coffee's made. Would you like a cup?"

"Yes. I can—"

"Give your leg a rest while I get it for you."

I smiled up at him when he brought me my cup. "I could grow accustomed to this."

I sipped the coffee while he finished eating. He cleared the table and refilled his cup, then settled in the easy chair beside me. "Are you staying around this time?" I asked.

"Yes. I've finished my job with the task force," he said. "Wish I'd finished a few hours sooner. Then I would have been home."

Chris was avoiding my eyes. "Can you tell me anything?" He knew what I wanted to know: the identity of the man who'd been killed in the cave and why he'd had my photo.

"I'm back on the job here. Sheriff's department," he said.

"I'm glad to hear it. But can you tell me anything else?"

He took a drink of coffee and reached down to stroke Flash. "They've identified the body. I imagine it has made the papers, so I can let you know what I know. He had been living in Las Vegas."

"And?"

"And that's the official release."

He wasn't meeting my eyes. "You know I can keep my mouth shut when I need to. Something is weird here. You're suddenly off the task force and back on your job, but you know nothing about the incident?"

"It's on a need-to-know basis. You know how that goes, Sorrel."

"And I need to know, Chris Reed! Call your people and tell them that! Better yet, tell them I'm going to find out on my own! Or better yet, I'll trade information that I've already discovered." Reed stared in my eyes a moment. "I'm not bluffing!"

He stood up. "I'll just make the call outside," he said.

I walked into the bedroom, wishing I could stomp but my leg wouldn't handle it, and straightened the bed. The whole time, I ranted mentally at the injustice of these lawmen keeping vital information from me. Of course, my rational side reminded me, this is normal procedure. *And you know it, Sorrel. You're prepared to keep the information Vicente gave to you. What's the difference?*

Not for the first time, something niggled at me about that conversation with Vicente. I couldn't quite decide what it was. He and I had been colleagues the whole time I'd worked for the television station. We'd competed for promotions, shared frustrations and successes, and exchanged angry words on occasion. I trusted him. He kept a tight rein on his production crew. I wondered why he hadn't moved up to news anchor after I left. We'd competed for the spot when it had opened; but when I won, he'd congratulated me.

"He'd like to be here." Reed's light, teasing mood had vanished.

"Is he angry with you? Me?"

"Hard to tell."

"But you're angry with me," I muttered.

"Not really. I have little patience for posturing." Then he smiled. "Why don't you and I go in town and check on the critters?"

"What about this guy who's coming?"

"He has my phone number. Besides, it will take him awhile to get here. And our pups have waited long enough!"

"Yes! Give me two minutes to wash these few things up so the cats don't hop up and do it!"

I washed and Reed dried. Then I went to the bedroom and changed into jogging pants. My jeans would probably be painful right now.

Within a few minutes, we were headed into town. I glanced over at my quiet companion. "Truce?"

"We're not at war, Sorrel. I'm just thinking. Something just doesn't feel right. I've wanted to bring you on board all along. But sometimes rules and regulations—"

"I know, Reed. I shouldn't have been so sharp with you. We're both stressed with the situations we're living through."

I glanced over at him just in time for him to glance at me and smile. "I keep telling you, Red. We fight pretty well, but we don't hold grudges. Makes me figure we'd be really good at a lot of things."

I didn't touch that one, just grinned. "Then let's try a new thing: co-parenting this brood of pups."

He laughed a deep belly laugh. "You have to be the only female I know who thinks of critters as people."

"They're better than most people I've met lately!"

He reached over and covered my hand with his. "On that, we agree."

Chapter 44

"They're the cutest little pups!" Reed murmured, watching the little brown, black, and white critters yipping and wiggling, vying for our attention. "I can't believe she managed to get them out!"

"She almost didn't get those two," the young vet assistant said, pointing to two that hadn't moved much and seemed content to watch their siblings.

"Will they be okay?" I asked.

"We think so."

Reed squeezed a squeaker toy and smiled as the little ones waddled after it. I focused on their mama. Patches of fur had been shaved for stitches and for intravenous fluids to hydrate her. Her paws were bandaged, the nails blackened. When I bent close to talk softly to her, she wagged the tip of her tail slightly. However, she kept her eyes focused on Reed and her pups.

When Reed's cellphone rang and he stepped away to answer, I reached out to touch a puppy. "Do you want to hold one?" the assistant asked.

"May I?"

"Sure. In fact, our volunteers come in to do just that. They need human contact to restore their trust." She picked up a fluffy little girl and put her in my arms. I stroked her, murmuring nonsense phrases and instinctively swaying. Before long, she closed her eyes.

"I hate to disturb this moment," Reed said, "but we have a meeting with someone."

I returned her reluctantly to the assistant and stroked Mama's head one last time. "I'll be back, little Madonna," I whispered.

Reed seemed a little preoccupied as he helped me into the truck. After he'd climbed into the driver's seat and fastened his seatbelt, Reed turned and looked at me. "Sgt. Pearce is at the bed and breakfast. Mrs. Sanchez is putting us in the little private alcove while he eats." He started the engine and backed out. Then he added, "I thought you were just a cat person. That was bad enough. Are there any critters you don't fall in love with?"

I thought a moment. "Snakes. And scorpions. And most bugs."

He laughed aloud. We drove to the bed and breakfast without talking. Reed climbed out and hurried around to open my door and help me out. "How's the leg holding up?" he asked.

"Still here," I answered, stepping gingerly.

He held out his arm. "Hang onto this until we get inside. This rock path is charming, but I'm not sure it's ideal for your latest handicap."

I might have objected just to harass him, but he wasn't wrong. When we entered the small lobby area, Mrs. Sanchez met us and ushered us to the small room tucked into a corner near the kitchen.

"Let me get you some hot chocolate to drink," she told me. "You look too thin and pale. And now the leg!"

"You're so sweet, but I'd prefer iced water with lemon," I told her.

She smiled at Reed. "And I think coffee for you?"

"Yes, ma'am."

He watched her leave and picked up his cell. "I'll just text to let him know we're here."

Mrs. Sanchez returned with our drinks on a small tray, along with chips and salsa. Once she'd set it on the table, she turned to leave. Then she said, "I heard about the fire. Such a bad thing."

"I know," I said. "It could have been so much worse though. We just visited the little dog that was living with her puppies in the barn. They're still fragile but are all fighters."

She shook her head. "Sad." Then she asked, "Do you want to order food?"

"We'll wait until our guest arrives," Reed told her. He dipped a chip in the salsa and offered it to me, and then did the same for himself.

We didn't wait long. Sgt. Pearce arrived before either of us had drunk anything. He seated himself and told Mrs. Sanchez, "Just bring another cup of coffee, please."

The next few minutes, we talked about the fire, my leg, the critters, and everything except the questions on my mind. It was only after we'd finally given our dinner orders to Mrs. Sanchez that he cleared his throat and turned to me. "I hear you have questions. Chris has been under a gag order, as is customary with ongoing investigations. And I will still not address some details, but I can tell you that the man in the cave shows no connection to you that we can trace except the news article and photo."

"What is his name?"

He gave an apologetic shrug. "I won't share that, but I can tell you that he seems to be a small-time private investigator."

"But you don't know who hired him."

Again, he shrugged. "Not at this time. In fact, anything we try to find out turns up a dead end, including your photo—or even whether or not it is your photo. And, truthfully, I have my doubts about that. With the difference in hair color and style and even with your face a little fuller, I don't think it is your photo. Detective Reed, what do you think?"

We both looked at Reed. He didn't meet my eyes when he said noncommittally, "It resembles her, but it isn't exact enough for me to say it is her photo."

"Do you have it with you? May I see it?"

Sgt. Pearce pulled out his phone and pulled up the photo. I studied it carefully. Had I not known it was me, I wouldn't have recognized myself. I'd been a few years younger, single, and more carefree. Life had imprinted subtle changes, as had the blonde hair that had grown out and been styled differently. I looked into his eyes and handed the phone back to him. "I'm sorry to have bothered you. Like you said, it bears a small resemblance to me."

The food arrived then and the topic moved to other things, mostly the fire. Sgt. Pearce agreed with Reed's assessment of illegal travelers having camped there. He listened as I described my own injuries and those of the stray dogs.

"Sad," he said, "but it could have been so much worse had your helper not come upon the fire before it spread."

We agreed. "So are you finished with the caves?" I asked.

"Just a little paperwork. The family notification is pending until we can locate them. The park is now clear for visitors again."

"Even during hunting season?"

"Hunting season?" Pearce raised his eyebrows.

"Yes. Has it ended already?" I felt Chris nudge my foot, but I continued innocently. "My reporter friend and I were there again a few days ago, thinking we could get more photos and information for a follow-up on the original travel article. We hadn't been able to climb up to the cave the first time, so we wanted to do it, you know, so we could relay the feel of the experience." I leaned conspiratorially toward Sgt. Pearce. "We had no idea it was hunting season until the bullets started flying! Luckily, we ducked for cover fast enough to avoid harm, and we didn't waste any time getting out of there."

He finally smiled weakly. "It sounds like you're a lucky girl."

I took a bite and chewed, sending Chris an innocent look and a small shrug, before moving the conversation on. "It would have helped had that new ranger known it wasn't hunting season, though. We visited with him before we went to the cave, but he didn't say a thing about it."

I pretended not to see the exchange of glances between the two men.

We ate in silence for a bit before Sgt. Pearce said, "By the way, we didn't find out much about the package you received. We traced it back to a mail order house that sells reptiles, but they had no information about the purchaser except your name."

I stared into his eyes. "I didn't order the things. I'm terrified of them. Maybe they had a mix-up."

"That would be hard to do. They had your name and address."

"Then it must have been a cruel practical joke." I looked over at Reed. "Remember last year when we went to the party downtown and someone covered my jeep in dog . . . stuff?"

"How could I forget?" Reed made a face. "We had to hold our breath on the drive to the carwash."

"They wouldn't let us use their facility," I laughed, "so we had to go to Teri and Jose's house to use their hose."

Reed joined in the laughter. "They still remind me that we will pay that back someday," he told Pearce. "Teri claimed the stench didn't leave for weeks!"

We finished the meal soon after. Reed told Sgt. Pearce he'd be back after he took me home. I thanked him for following up on my questions.

The drive home was quiet until we pulled up to my house. Reed insisted on helping me inside the house and stood awkwardly as I fed the cats. "I'm sorry you didn't get more answers," he said.

"At least it's closed," I said. I eased down on the couch.

He continued standing, staring at me. "When were you planning to tell me about the sniper?"

"When I saw you next. Then the fire sidetracked us and I really hadn't thought of it until then."

"I don't like it. And you say the park ranger was new?"

"Only when we were on our way out to start the climb. When we came back, there was an elderly caretaker there. He said the ranger was back East on a family emergency."

He came over and perched on the edge of the easy chair, his eyes trained on my face. "I can't believe you didn't tell me, Sorrel. I know we've had this fire thing, but you've had time."

"Not really. From the moment you arrived, we've been tied up with the fire and the pups and my leg. You're exhausted. And I really didn't think of that part until I was talking to Sgt. Pearce."

"I've been grouchy, haven't I?"

"Your barn is burned, your critters are injured, you're dead tired—I wouldn't classify it as grouchy." I smiled in his eyes. "I'm glad you're here, grouchy or not."

He sighed and stood. "I need to get back to talk with Pearce."

"I imagine that will be a lengthy talk."

"Where are you staying?" I asked him.

"Probably the apartment. But I don't like the idea of you here on your own either. Any intruder wouldn't be safe and I might need to rescue him."

I giggled and pretended to swat at him. "Please come back. You can have your choice of the couch or the spare bedroom. Oh," I reached in my purse for my key, "here's my house key just in case you stay out really late. I gave the extra one to Teri's cousin . . . the one who's helping out in the store."

He took it, leaned over and kissed me, and murmured, "I'll lock up after myself. That way you won't have to be trotting to the door unless you want to do so. When I come in later, I'll check out the office and the store door. I know, you're about to argue, but I'm double checking. If I don't get back in time tonight, let's plan to talk some more in the morning. I have no idea how long-winded Pearce will be." I nodded, my mind already hopping to things I needed to do.

First, I called to check on Teri and spent half an hour listening to her frustration at being "watched like a ticking bomb." Then I went to my workroom/porch and looked through the photos I'd taken during the past several days. I wanted to look for any of the substitute ranger, the one that Will suspected wasn't really a ranger. I'd taken several shots, but none were good. Either he'd moved and blurred the photo or his face was turned away. Usually, I didn't make amateur mistakes like that.

The rest of the evening, I puttered around, petting the kitties and watching a news show. Sooner than usual, I made my way into my bedroom, with the cats following behind.

Although getting ready for bed still wasn't easy, I managed to change into my pajamas, brush my teeth, and pull the covers back on the bed. But even though I was tired, something kept niggling at me and I couldn't fall asleep. Instead, long after the cats and I had settled into bed, I kept running the evening conversation through my mind. What was I missing?

Chapter 45

I woke with a start. The clock beside my bed read twelve o'clock. Had Reed just arrived and I'd subconsciously heard him? Or was it something that had been niggling at my brain since last night?

Easing out of bed as quietly as I could, I grabbed my cell phone off the nightstand. The small light on it illuminated a narrow path in case I stumbled across something. I pulled the bedroom door open slightly. The lamp I'd left on near the couch had been turned off. I stepped out carefully and eased toward the small living room area, stopping to listen for Reed. I couldn't hear anything. Maybe he hadn't yet arrived.

In case he had, I sent a beam of light toward the kitchen area first. Maybe a drink would help me settle. I'd only taken a step before the hand grabbed my elbow. Without a sound, I jabbed it back into a trim belly and jerked lose, my hands raised to continue.

"Sorrel! Wait!"

"Reed?" I shone the light in his face. He was bent over holding his stomach.

"Remind me not to worry about you defending yourself," he gasped.

"I'm so sorry, but you startled me!" I turned on the overhead light. "I didn't hear you, so I thought you were still out. Are you all right?"

Reed straightened up and began walking toward the couch. He had left his jeans on and was now pulling a tee shirt from the back of the couch to put on as well. "You just surprised me, that's all." He gave me a wicked grin. "Here I was dreaming about this beauty queen—"

I giggled. Then I sobered, suddenly remembering what had been niggling at me since Vicente's phone call. "The file!"

"What file?"

"He said he'd have the file cleared."

"Either you're sleepwalking or I've missed the first part of this conversation."

I sank down in the easy chair. "I got a call from Vicente, you know, the guy from where I once worked. He said someone had contacted the station wanting a photo of me and a new employee had sent a copy without being given permission to do so. He'd fired her when he discovered what she had done. Then he said he'd removed information about me from the file."

"What file?"

"Exactly. All files had already been removed—I did it. Any mention of me was deleted from the computers."

"But how would he have known about the photo?" Chris picked up Flash and sat down on the couch, plopping her on his lap.

"Odd, isn't it? Do you want a cup of tea?"

"I'm not much of a tea drinker—at least, not hot tea. You wouldn't have instant cocoa, would you?"

"Sure do. In fact, it sounds better to me too." I moved into the kitchen, filled two mugs with water, and put them in the microwave to heat while I found the packets of cocoa mix. "No marshmallows, I'm afraid."

"I'll suffer through it—this time. The price is right."

I knew his trick. He was trying to make me relax a bit, maybe laugh a bit. I didn't feel much like laughing. Instead, I asked, "Have you been in long? I didn't hear you."

"No. In fact, I'd just taken off my tee shirt and was lying down, thinking." He stroked Flash's head, and I could hear her purring. He didn't elaborate on what he was thinking.

The microwave bell dinged. I removed our mugs, stirred in the mix, and carried them to the table. "Are you hungry? My pantry isn't the greatest just now, but—"

"This is fine." He set Flash on the couch then moved to the table. "My mom was big on making a cup of cocoa when she couldn't sleep." He stood by his chair and gestured for me to sit before he followed suit.

"Sgt. Pearce seemed to be a man of few words at dinner," I said. "Do you think he bought the story about that not being my photo?"

"I'm not sure. But when I saw it, I had to question it. You look much different."

I blew on my cocoa. "Since this guy's a private investigator, the only conclusion I can reach is that he was looking for me. I just wonder who his client is and why they want information on me. Do employers even hire private investigators anymore? You give references when you apply for a job, and they call to check them out. After people leave a job—unless they've embezzled money or done something illegal so that the former employer would call the police—people just forget about them. People come and go frequently and usually are quickly forgotten."

"Even small time investigators aren't cheap," Reed agreed. "He would have expenses besides his fee. Can you think of anyone who would have the money and the motivation to hire him?"

"No. I didn't have close friends and even fewer enemies. And my college friends weren't wealthy, for sure. Why would anyone be looking for me? We socialize with coworkers or friends and promise we'll keep in touch, but we seldom do."

Neither of us spoke for a bit, just sipping the cocoa in a companionable silence. Finally, Reed spoke. "I don't think it's a friend."

"Neither do I."

"Although he didn't say it, I doubt Pearce has closed the books on this guy."

"Did he grill you about me?"

"No, but I inferred that he suspects someone set fire to my barn, knowing that you'd be the one looking after it, and hoped to smoke you out. He asked if you'd been staying over there. So you are still in his spotlight, so to speak."

"That theory leaves too much to chance, Reed. I haven't been here much. And the PI—supposing that he found where I live—may or may not have reported the information to anyone before he was murdered." I yawned. "None of this makes sense. And the biggest thing that doesn't add up is that I'm not some sort of criminal or anyone important."

Reed hesitated then asked, "Any chance you could have been romantically involved with someone who holds a grudge?"

"No."

"What about someone from work? Could it be this guy Vicente? How well do you know him?"

"Vicente? No. We were casual friends. The thing that I keep returning to is the motivation for someone to be focusing on me. It can't be that at all." I didn't mention that I'd reported many stories that would have angered people. Reporters come and go, and I doubted any of those people even remembered my name. "Is there some reason Pearce is not sharing this guy's name?"

"The usual policy demands we wait until his family has been notified." Reed drained his cup and rose. "Are you finished? I think we need to try to get a little sleep tonight—and that's about all that's left. Half of Teri's relatives will be descending on us bright and early!"

I handed him my cup and watched while he carried them to the sink and rinsed them. "Reed, did you see this guy?"

"Yes. Why?"

"How old would you think he is?"

Reed made a face. "Sorrel, he'd been in that cave a while . . . and . . . there were other circumstances. It was hard to tell. He had dark hair, though. No gray."

"And he didn't have anything on him to even hint at an identity?"

"No."

"Then how did they know he's a private eye?"

Reed scowled. "I'd hoped you'd missed that." He sighed. "One had been reported missing from Las Vegas. They could be the same. Pearce is waiting for confirmation from the medical examiner. And that may take a while."

"Las Vegas. He could just as easily have lost a poker game and owed money." I covered another yawn.

Chris shook his head. "I know you're tired now. Otherwise, you wouldn't be suggesting this private eye lost at poker, sneaked off owing money, trekked across a few states during a cold winter night, and hid out in a cave that he showed no signs of having climbed into. And to keep himself company, he took a photo of someone who isn't you but might be you . . . and a dozen rattlesnakes—"

"Rattlesnakes! There were rattlesnakes!" That box in my office took new significance.

Chris said something under his breath, walked over and picked me up, and started toward my bedroom. "I'm putting you in bed before your imagination—and my tongue—gets us into more trouble than we need!" He made as if to drop me on the bed but settled me gently instead. "Let's not let our imaginations go crazy. We can look at this much more clearly in the morning. Okay?"

I nodded. He pulled the covers up, tucked them around me, and turned to go. "Chris?"

He sighed audibly and turned back around. "What now?"

"Isn't it just a bit too coincidental that a rattlesnake was mailed to me . . . and this guy . . ."

He sighed. "You're not going to settle down, are you?" He turned back to the door.

"What are you doing now?"

He paused at the door. When he spoke, I could hardly hear him. "I'll get my blanket and pillow from the couch and stay here until you go to sleep."

"Thanks."

He returned quickly, wrapped his blanket around himself, and lay down on the other side of the bed. I could hear him sigh. "Sorrel?"

"Yes."

"Remember that this business is like a big jigsaw puzzle. The pieces have to fit together just right. Sometimes it seems several of them fit, and then you find just the right one. If we get impatient and try to make one fit . . . well, it just doesn't."

"I know."

"Teri does too."

"What do you mean?"

"They went to the hospital this evening sure she was having the baby. Then they went home."

"Is she okay? I feel like a bad friend. I haven't even talked to her much or helped—"

"If she has any more help over there, with her relatives all pouring in, Jose will run them all off!"

He told some funny stories, laughing with me, until I felt my eyes closing. "Reed?" I whispered, reaching for his hand.

"Huh?"

"We forgot one thing."

"What?" His voice was little more than a murmur.

"Who was shooting at Will and me when we were trying to get up to the cave?"

He didn't answer, but he held onto my hand as he slept and I lay awake with the question—but no answers—swirling through my mind.

Chapter 46

"I think I'm paranoid now." I took a gulp of coffee, scorching the tip of my tongue. "I'm second-guessing everything I say, hear, or see. I can't trust anyone. Maybe I'm crazy!"

Neither cat commented on my diatribe. Instead, both stared solemnly ahead, sitting side by side in sphinxlike poses.

"Crazy? No. But you might be a bit more selective with your audience if you want a second opinion."

I emitted a squeak. Reed hadn't shaved and his hair stood up on the crown of his head. Then I grinned. "Looks like you need a cup of coffee. I'll pour the first one for you, but only because I doubt you can manage it."

He grunted and sat down on the couch. When I approached with his coffee, both cats had settled on his lap. "Just call me the crazy cat man," he grumbled, stroking each. Then he yawned. "The bed is more comfortable than the couch, but I didn't get to sleep right away. Must have been your idea of bedtime chat."

I sank into the chair across from him. "The vet's office called a few minutes ago. Our Madonna is still serious but is continuing to respond to treatment."

He blew on his coffee and took a drink. "I'm happy to hear that. What about the babies?"

"The pups have won the hearts of the whole staff and are being given plenty of attention."

He laughed then sniffed. "What do I smell?"

"Celia has come and gone, leaving homemade cinnamon rolls. I told her she didn't need to keep checking as I'm doing fine now."

"I hate for you to do that. Now I'll be starving . . . with your—"

"Cooking? I'm glad you just volunteered to take that chore off my hands." I laughed at the look on his face.

Reed disentangled himself from the felines and walked into the kitchen. "Do you want one?"

"Yes, I do. I waited for you—was afraid I'd not be able to stop eating until they were gone. But had you slept any later, I doubt I could have resisted."

He washed and dried his hands then set a roll on a saucer for each of us. I joined him at the table. "Could I impose even more than I already have and put some clothes in your washer," he asked. "I have more at the ranch, but they have it all roped off right now.

"Sure!" I would have teased him more, but my mouth was full of the delicious bun.

"I've been thinking about what you mentioned last night, Sorrel. About the identity of the shooter? Do you have any ideas? Did either of you see anyone?"

"No. But I've been mulling over everything this morning, trying to focus on details that I might have just glossed over during the stress of the time. Will was terrified. I doubt he's ever had anything like that happen. He mentioned that his dad likes to hunt, but I get the impression he was the video game-playing nerd type. Then again, he wasn't afraid of hiking and talked about doing some of that with college buddies."

"So you never got a glimpse of the shooter. Did he—or she—seem to be aiming at you two or just shooting to scare you?"

"That's a good question. They came close to us."

"I think he was trying to scare you off so you would leave. An experienced shooter would have had a scope on the rifle. I doubt he would have missed. Maybe he wouldn't have killed you since you were moving targets and there were two of you. He would have hit you, however, at least once. It would have slowed you down so he could catch you."

The idea sent chills up my spine. I took another drink of hot coffee. "So that plays into the motive."

"Sure does. Several of them have been bouncing around my head in the night. For instance, it could be someone who had returned to retrieve something from the cave and needed you two to leave. Were you heading to the cave?"

"We'd played with the idea, but we needed more equipment to scale that rock up to it. Neither of us had the equipment or the experience for that. And, truly, for the article and photos, we just needed a closer look and a general idea of what tourists might need."

Reed shoved the last bite of his second cinnamon bun in his mouth and washed it down with coffee. "Sgt. Pearce and the law enforcement crew had special equipment and it still was a hard climb. That's something they've been discussing—how this guy was able to get up there."

"Better yet, how was he taken up there? I doubt he made the trip on his own if he ended up murdered—unless he made it with friends who turned on him." I rose, cleared up the plates, and brought the coffeepot to refill our cups. "Do you want me to make a new pot? This one is gone."

"No, this will be plenty. Do you have a pen and paper handy?"

I found a tablet and pen in a kitchen drawer.

Reed drew a line down the middle of the page. "Okay, this side here," he indicated the left side of the tablet, "is what we know from the evidence." He pointed to the right column. "This is what we suspect because of that same evidence. I'm putting the murder first, of course."

"The shooting at Will and me goes on the left," I added.

"The photo of you with the dead guy. Let's just put photo, because we also have a question about why it was requested and how the new employee could have found it if the file had been closed."

"I'm going to add that it took several people to get that guy up in that cave. And . . ."

I waited but he didn't continue, just wrote. "He was bound, right? Hands behind his back?" I asked.

"Yes, but they haven't publicized the—"

I rose and walked to the kitchen counter. "Celia brought in the paper when she came." I handed it to Reed.

"Man Murdered by Rattlesnakes," he read aloud. He read down the article silently then looked up at me incredulously. "They suspect a gang initiation? Surely they could have come up with a better—oh, here it adds 'or Mexican cartel involvement.'"

"I wish I didn't have such a vivid imagination. I may never get the picture that article created out of my brain. And I don't see the rattlesnake craft items that my new vendor has made being popular items."

Reed sighed. "Unfortunately, you probably won't be able to keep them in stock . . . at least, at first. People are ghoulish, you know. Okay, back to our list."

"Why did they go to such trouble?" I mused. "They could have tortured him and murdered him without the hardship of getting him there."

"Maybe they didn't want him found right away. If they killed him in a motel or his house, he would have been found sooner."

"Did they speculate about how long he'd been there?" I asked.

"Not in the paper, but it wasn't recent—as in a week. I think the medical examiner is still working on that." He scanned down the page. "Here. They just say the medical examiner's office hasn't finished their evaluation."

"Did Pearce talk about this last night?"

"Sorrel, I've violated some rules because I felt you needed to know. Anything else I shouldn't say."

"All right then. We have the shooting at Will and me. We know that's a fact. What do we suspect?"

Chris wrote a couple of short phrases. I leaned over his shoulder and read: "They wanted to scare you off . . . they planned to move the body before it was discovered . . . it was fun?"

"Fun! Chris Reed, you don't really think—"

"I hope not." He reached over, covered my hand. "Haven't you heard that murder is seldom about anger? The things that motivate people to inflict pain and death are often as simple as that. One of my early cases was a man who killed his brother because he didn't want to share the inheritance when his parents finally died. A young mother killed her baby because the new boyfriend didn't want to share her attention." He sighed. "Life is filled with ugly people."

"My photo?" I whispered. "Do you think they put a hit out on me?" Then I pulled my hand from his and stood up. "How dare they?" I sputtered. "What right do they have to—"

"Since he was a private investigator, I actually think they had nothing to do with that photo. They might have left it in his pocket thinking you were his girlfriend and that he'd die looking at it. But I think someone had hired him to find you, not to kill you. They have uncovered no evidence that he would be in that line of work."

"How would they know? It's not as if they could ask him!" I began cleaning up our breakfast dishes, an unexplainable rage boiling inside me. I put the saucers in the sink with such clatter I hoped I'd not broken them.

Then I noticed that Reed was writing on the bottom of our list. I peeked over his shoulder and read: "We need to find them before they find Sorrel."

"So we need a new list," Reed said. Then he drawled, "I hope they didn't eat something you cooked and . . ." He ducked but the dishcloth landed on the back of his head anyway, splattering soapy water on him and me both. "After we get cleaned up, we'll start on that list," he gasped between shouts of laughter.

As I stood under the hot shower later, I shivered. I'd searched my memory, but I couldn't figure out why anyone would consider me important enough to murder and risk prison. I'd closed my whole life and started a new one without ever knowing whether I'd caused the death of someone. Now, some unknown predator appeared to be closing in once more on my new life. Why?

I shivered again as I imagined the horrible death the man had suffered in the cave.

I turned off the water and grabbed a towel. As I dried my body, the shivers stopped and a cold resolve set in. I smeared medication on my leg; dressed carefully in jeans, shirt, and sneakers; and brushed my hair into a ponytail.

As I stepped into the kitchen, Reed told someone goodbye and closed his phone. "You feel better?"

"Yes, I do. What have you been up to?"

"Talking to Sgt. Pearce. He's arranging for me to stay here—"

"And be my bodyguard? No way!"

He sighed. "I knew you'd react this way. But will you just calm down—"

"Why do men always tell a woman to calm down when she isn't upset?"

"And let's talk. We have a plan."

I looked around his shoulder and then back up to him. "We? Do you have a mouse in your pocket?"

Reed sighed and looked up at the ceiling. "Lord, spare me from redheads!"

"Who is we?"

"I am." Reed's boss, Sheriff Hernandez, rose from the couch. "I didn't mean to eavesdrop on your conversation, but maybe we can all collaborate and work out a plan. I apologize for not speaking up sooner," he smiled, "but it isn't often I'm able to see Reed being scolded so well. I'm sure he deserves it; but since Sgt. Pearce is arriving soon, he may want to clean up."

I gestured toward my bedroom door. "The bathroom is all yours."

After he left, I turned to Sheriff Hernandez. "Can I offer you anything? The coffee is gone, but I can make another pot. And I have—"

"Nothing just now," he interrupted. "I wouldn't mind visiting with you a bit, though. I was so sorry to hear about the little dog. And I'm amazed that you're healing so well. You ran into that fire—"

"You were there?"

"Such a shame. Is she doing okay? And the puppies?"

"I think they're all recovering," I said. "I suspect Reed will be looking for adoptive families in a few weeks. Do you and your wife have a dog?"

He laughed and winked. "I'm not sure we would pass the adoptive interviews!"

Chapter 47

I'd met Sheriff Hernandez and his wife a couple of times before, but I couldn't say I knew him. I'd certainly not witnessed his teasing nature before. Now, I wondered if he was attempting to put me at ease. Either way, I liked him.

"I haven't finished designing the puppy application form," I told him. "But when I do, I'm sure Reed will be happy to give you one. Did you say Sgt. Pearce is coming?"

"Yes."

"Then I definitely need to put on another pot of coffee." I walked over to the counter. "The beauty of my little house is you can do that and carry on a conversation with your guests at the same time."

He smiled. "I won't argue with you then. I like what you've done with the place. Rose would have been proud."

I poured water in the coffeemaker and switched it on. "You knew my great aunt?"

"Oh, sure. She was such a sweet person, and she and her husband spent their lives helping children in this community."

"I know. My mom was one of her foster children."

"Yes, I remember her."

"Could you tell me about her?"

Although he'd been a bit younger, the sheriff remembered my mom well enough and shared some funny stories about her. "She was a good basketball player," he said.

"Really? She never told me that."

By the time Reed reappeared, the coffee was finished and I was pouring cups. "Your boss has been telling me stories about my mom," I told him. "He was younger, but he remembers her."

A knock at the door interrupted us. "I'll get it," Reed said. "It will be Sgt. Pearce."

After making sure that everyone had coffee and greeting Pearce, I prepared to leave. "I'm going into town to see about the dogs," I told them, "and leave you guys to your business."

"You don't have to leave," Reed protested. "We can go—"

"I don't mind. I want to see them. And I want to stop by and see Teri."

"Then I'll call when we're done."

"I've got my other deputy on a call," the sheriff said, "but if you'll wait, I can call him to go with you."

"Why?"

All three men found meeting my eyes difficult. "Reed, what is going on?" I walked over to him and waited until he looked at me.

"We'd be happier if you had someone with you right now."

"Here? In Saddle Gap?"

Sgt. Pearce spoke up. "In looking into the background of the man in the cave, your name came up. At this time, we'd just feel more comfortable if you weren't running around on your own."

"Why would anyone be interested in me?"

No one answered. Finally, I turned. "I'll go to the animal hospital. I'll call from there when I'm ready to leave. How's that?" I looked at Reed. "You can walk me to my Jeep."

The other two men nodded.

When Reed opened the door for me, I slid inside and sighed. "Isn't this a little dramatic?"

"It's never a bad thing to be cautious, Sorrel." He leaned in and kissed me. "I haven't been briefed yet; but I know from memories of your past escapades, caution isn't a bad idea."

"All right, but when we meet for lunch, I intend for you three to fill me in on what you know! It's not like I'm some pansy or something, and I have only a couple of days until my big sale. I've got too much to do."

"Hug that little mama dog for me," he said.

Reed stood watching me until I turned onto the highway. He'd never done that before, and it felt a bit odd. I'd turn back and demand we talk right then, but we both had people waiting for us.

Knowing I had three nursemaids now, I turned my phone to silent. "They can just leave messages," I said and focused on the road ahead.

Chapter 48

The puppies were rambunctious, rolling and tumbling as they played with each other. They growled and yapped and wrestled. "How cute!" I told the vet tech. "Luckily, I brought my camera! I'm just hoping I can get them to hold still long enough to get a few shots. They're in constant motion!"

"They are," she said. "I don't think the detective will have any trouble finding homes for them."

"His trouble," I said, "will be letting them go. They're so precious!"

Their mama had improved also. She was no longer connected to the intravenous tubes and sat in the corner of the cage watching her brood. When I spoke to her, she looked toward me and waited for me to pet her. "I think she knows me," I murmured. "That will make it easier to get some photos of her as well."

"Sure she does. She's such a sweetheart."

An hour flew by before I rose to leave. "I'll be back tomorrow," I promised Madonna.

"She has warmed up to you better than anyone," the young lady gushed. "You're a dog person."

"Don't let my cats hear that!"

We both laughed and I left feeling much more lighthearted than when I'd arrived. Once inside the Jeep, I noticed my message light flashing on the cellphone.

The first voice mail was from Teri. "Sorrel, I'm sorry, but I have to go to the doctor this morning instead of tomorrow. Nothing serious—just my labs. I'll call when I'm out. Maybe we can get together tomorrow? Call me tonight."

The next was a call from Mr. Byrd. "Sorrel, I'm interested in some photos and a follow-up story on the critters saved in the fire. Will says he'll be in touch, but I wanted to let you know in case you can get some photos ahead. I know you'll be busy with your sale."

I had a couple of hang-ups—the kind where someone waits until the machine kicks in, listens to the message, then breathes into the machine for a few seconds. "High school kids," I muttered. I put the phone back in my pocket, started the car, and backed out. Since I wouldn't be going to Teri's and since the men should have left my house to go look at Reed's place, I headed home. It would be nice to have quiet time in the office. I'd promised to call after the veterinary visit, so I'd do that when I got home. They wouldn't be expecting me this soon, and maybe I'd have a few minutes without them breathing down my neck.

As I turned onto the highway toward home, my phone rang again. I glanced at the screen when I pulled it out of my pocket. "Unknown. Not another sales call!" I muttered. "Hello?"

It echoed. I glanced at it again. "Hello?"

An echo.

Then I felt something hard and cold against the back of my neck. "Don't turn around or look in your mirror," a man's voice whispered. "Put your phone down and drive to the highway. If you make any attempt to crash the car or startle me, you should remember I have a gun buried in the back of your head and a nervous trigger finger."

Something familiar niggled in my brain, but I pushed it aside. I had only a few moments before I would reach the driveway into my shop. Leaving my car wouldn't be a good idea. Once inside, whoever this man was would have the advantage—even more than now. A car accident would put him in danger as well. Should I try it?

"No, you shouldn't try to wreck your car," he whispered. "You're alive as long as you follow my instructions. Do you want to die a hero?"

"No," I said. I glanced down at the speedometer. Maybe I could ease off—

"And don't slow down until you need to do so. I can always tie you up and stuff you in the trunk. That doesn't sound bad, actually." Something about the whisper niggled at my brain. Had I heard it before? "You'll drive on past your driveway."

"But that's—"

"Don't argue. Do as I say."

I remembered a self-defense class I'd taken a few years back that talked about what you should do if you found yourself alone in your car with someone holding a gun on you. The advice had been to avoid leaving the car if at all possible. "You have a much more dangerous weapon than the intruder has," the instructor had told us. "But you need to use it wisely."

We passed my shop. All of the other cars were gone. I looked, praying it wouldn't be the last time I'd see it.

Chapter 49

I'd seen people abducted in movies and on television shows. "Why doesn't he wreck the car?" I'd ask, along with, "Surely, she'd sneak a peek at her abductor anyway" and *"How could she continue to drive?"* What I hadn't wondered was what the hostage was thinking as she was driving down the road. Now I knew the answer.

The cold nose of the gun burrowed through my hair and into the nape of my neck, and I prayed I'd not hit a bump that would discharge it. Was it a handgun? If so, I should be able to catch his scent or smell his breath or something. It would also attract attention from passing motorists, wouldn't it? Then again, a rifle might also be discernible.

Wait! With the tint I'd added to the windows for protection from the sun, the gun wouldn't be easily spotted. Still, a lone woman driving and a lone man sitting close behind her should raise suspicions. I prayed they would.

Not looking in the rearview mirror took concentrated effort. I'd never thought about it before but, if there were a rearview-looking group, I'd be president. The ridiculousness of that thought calmed me a bit—or maybe the shock of this whole situation was easing a bit. Still, I needed to keep my wits about me and think.

Because we were driving on a two-lane highway, traffic tended to pass us regularly. If I kept to the speed limit, I'd be one of the few doing so. Patrolmen were scarce and the roads stretched ahead long and straight. A slow-moving vehicle would be noticed.

My abductor seemed to be reading my mind. "Keep up with the traffic," he growled in a hoarse whisper. "Since no one else is following the speed limit, you don't want to draw attention. But you don't want attention by having an accident either."

Again, the voice niggled at me. "Where are we—"

"Shut up and drive."

Something about the tone felt familiar . . . maybe. Or maybe I was just grasping for anything in my desperation. I searched the faces of drivers meeting us but didn't recognize anyone. Maybe a patrolman would come along and notice that one person driving and another person sitting right up against her neck wasn't an ordinary situation. Or maybe people just zoned out driving down the road and noticed nothing.

I glanced at the clock on the dashboard. Reed would expect me to be with Teri right now. Would he run by or call? Even if he did, he'd realize Teri wasn't home and think I had either gone with her or gone somewhere else. But more than likely, Reed and the officers were still in a meeting of sorts and I wasn't in their minds at all.

Another thought startled me: What if this was just a carjacking? I almost laughed aloud. Just? Was I actually thinking *just a carjacking*? I had to swallow to smother a giggle. When did a carjacking become less dangerous? The urge to laugh and never stop rose inside me.

I swallowed again. I couldn't lose my control. I had to think. Every moment in this car was valuable. I had a good brain. I'd been in tight spots before and had gotten out, so I guessed that qualified as experience. What I didn't have was unlimited time.

Maybe he was a random thief who just planned to have me drive out of town and abandon me somewhere in the uninhabited areas that fill much of New Mexico and Arizona. Leaving me stranded was my best hope just now. Of course, I knew better. It was slim and I needed a reason to believe it—a reason I hadn't yet discovered.

Enough! I didn't have any more time to waste in fantasy. This was more than a carjacking. It showed planning and thought. He'd researched my habits and life carefully.

"Turn right at the sign!" he demanded.

My slim hope vanished. We were following the route to Portal. If he planned to take me to that cave and to the same grisly death the unknown investigator had suffered, he likely had someone to help him at the other end. Once his companions joined us, I'd have few chances to escape them. I figured I had a couple of hours at most to come up with a plan.

As I drove, the road narrowed even more, even though it was still two lanes. I brightened when I realized the traffic would be largely local residents. During my visits to Portal, I'd found them friendly but curious. Anyone seeing us in our current set-up, with me driving and him sitting so close behind me, would find it odd. He would have to move to the front seat to avoid their curiosity.

Or he could do what he'd threatened to do earlier and stuff me in the trunk so he could drive himself. Wait! The Jeep has no trunk! I'd been too scared to catch his mistake earlier! So, to conceal me, he had to change cars. And that would give me a chance—a small crumb of hope that I quickly snapped up.

A light clicking sound coming from behind me grabbed my attention. Was he texting someone? It was certainly more reliable than the sketchy phone service in this area and more private. But how was he managing to text and still hold the gun? Was he using only one hand or propping up the gun? If it were propped, I might be able to jar it loose.

I slowed as I approached the sign, hit the blinker, and turned right. I tried to see the side mirror without moving my eyes, but he growled, "I'll tell you when to turn."

The traffic had thinned to nothing. I couldn't see if anyone was behind us or to the left, but no one had met or passed us recently.

"Turn now. And don't try anything. My finger is getting tired . . . and touchy."

I turned. Again, I could see no houses or cars nearby.

"Why don't you just drop me off somewhere out here?" I asked, trying a new approach. But the trembling in my voice belied the strong, fearless impression I had hoped to make. Then again, maybe trembling would suit his ego.

"Right!" He smothered a laugh. "And you wouldn't tell anyone. Especially your sheriff boyfriend and all of his friends. Just imagine how he'll feel when he finds you . . . with all of your new buddies! Will he realize how lucky he was when he escaped being chained to a vain turncoat? But then he may not find you at all. Maybe he'll just think you deserted him for someone richer. How could a county sheriff's deputy compete with the nation's rich and famous bachelors?"

The second chuckle sounded familiar. I knew this person—or I'd heard this person before. Why couldn't I place him? The answer floated just out of reach in my memory—and I was losing precious time.

He quieted, almost as if he'd heard my thought. Was he trying another intimidation technique? As if answering my question, he lightly caressed the back of my neck with the barrel of the gun. I shivered. He smothered a chuckle and murmured hoarsely, "Sorry. I realize this isn't an ideal date for someone of your caliber, but it's the best I can manage just now." Then he laughed. One thing was certain: He was enjoying this game.

I focused on his voice. I doubted he lived in Saddle Gap or even in New Mexico. He didn't have that western twang most of the residents had. In fact, even though he whispered most of the time, I couldn't hear an accent of any sort. Most people have some sort of accent, however faint. He didn't. That meant he'd consciously dropped the accent and was watching every word, or he'd had formal training to remove it. A certainty settled inside me: I'd identified an important clue. Now I only needed to live long enough to use it.

"Pull over to that old building ahead."

I'd noticed this abandoned adobe structure during photography trips. In fact, I'd snapped some photos of it at sunset. Although the wooden roof had fallen inside the two-room house, the outer walls seemed to stand protectively around it.

Should I make a move? Try to escape? I could think of worse places to die—like a cave filled with snakes. But it felt cowardly to do that. Besides, I might have a better chance later.

Other thoughts flitted through my brain, but I pushed them aside. Whatever indignities he might inflict on my body or ugliness he might say, he would never touch me—that person with so many reasons to live.

I flipped on the right blinker and slowed. The Jeep jerkily swerved off the road, scattering gravel.

"Pull behind it and stop."

I followed his directions, hoping my acquiescence would lull him into giving me an opportunity to overpower him . . . or run. I wasn't half bad at running. Of course, that was different now that I'd injured my leg at the fire.

"Put it in park and turn off the motor."

I followed his instructions and again felt the gun barrel jostled against my neck during the less-than-smooth process. I doubted he had the trigger cocked and had only been using it as a threat. I filed that tiny fact away.

"Put your hands back on the steering wheel and grip it—hard."

As soon as I'd complied, he started pulling a heavy hood down over my face. Instinctively, my hands flew up. I fought to grab the hood and managed to get hold of the bottom. But as I tried to pull it away, his fist slammed into my cheek and I cried out. He then yanked it down

The last thing I remembered before everything went dark was the feel of him tightening a cord around my neck.

Chapter 50

My eyes wouldn't open! Were they weighted? Something heavy seemed to be pressing them closed. My head pounded, a steady rhythmic drumming behind my eyes. My cheek throbbed and burned. After several attempts, I raised my head a fraction only to drop it back immediately against the rough carpet beneath my check. I gritted my teeth against the surge of nausea as my body swayed.

Mind over matter. I remembered my dad telling me that when I'd been preparing for running competitions. *Don't think about the exhaustion, the competition, the pain of healing blisters. Focus on something else. Focus on the end goal.*

My end goal was surviving this situation—and living out my life!

Through the throbbing pain in my body, Dad's voice echoed in rhythm with the tires: *Focus, Sorrel. Your mind controls your actions.*

His advice had served me well then, so I must follow it now. I pulled the last of my mental strength together with my faltering hope and started my pep talk: *The only thing you can completely control right now is your mind. You must use your brain to regain control of my body. You must focus on action— not reaction. This slogan from your high school running days pushed you to victory!*

How appropriate for it to surface now when I needed strength and discipline to win. It was all I had left just now.

First, I had to assess the situation: what I knew and what I didn't. I knew I'd been knocked unconscious from at least two blows to my face and head. I didn't know how long I'd been unconscious or if I'd been given something to keep me out. So time lost was an unknown, but I could estimate. I'd been traveling toward Portal before the attack, but I didn't know how many miles I'd driven toward it. So . . . I hoped for an hour or so.

Panic threatened momentarily at the thought of the time left, but I pushed it back. "Focus," I told myself, but the word came out as a confusing grunt. My tongue brushed against cotton. I was gagged and blindfolded.

So reviewing my physical situation was the next priority. I was lying in a circle of sorts, my knees almost to my chest. Everything ached and I wasn't sure I could feel my feet and toes. I tried moving them. My feet only moved slightly, and the stinging in my toes made me catch my breath. I tried to reach down to rub them, but my hands were behind my back and tied together. I wiggled my fingers and pain shot through them. My elbows ached.

Suddenly, my body was jolted and moved to the left then back again in a constant but uneven rocking motion. I was definitely in the trunk of a car. I must have been moved from the Jeep. But when? My last memory was of pulling off the highway and parking behind the abandoned building.

Had there been a car parked somewhere behind that building? I hadn't seen one but there were several places someone could have hidden one from view. Even though I hadn't seen anyone, the blow that knocked me unconscious came so quickly that my abductor couldn't be working alone. That meant . . . this was actually an organized abduction!

Despair settled in with that thought. My chances of being rescued had dropped considerably. Did anyone even know I was missing? That thought added to the ever-growing anxiety creeping into my thoughts. It might be hours before anyone realized . . . hours.

The horror of my situation came in waves; and with each, my brain responded with increasingly terrifying images. Tears began to cascade down my cheeks, making the cloth around my eyes soggy. I'd never had a dream like this one. But this wasn't a dream. It was a nightmare—and I was living it.

As the reality of what was ahead finally overwhelmed me, my resolve to use mind over matter vanished and real terror set in. What had I done to make someone so angry? I cried out to God, begging him to tell me so I would know why I was going to die today. The muffled noises I emitted only made my throat scratchy and dry.

Sorrel, stop. Thrashing doesn't help. I'll help. Listen to me.

"Mama? Mama, are you here? No, you died. I must be losing my mind . . . or dying. I don't want to die. I haven't finished living yet!"

I'm losing my mind, I thought. *I'm making these dumb grunting noises that no one can understand and I'm hallucinating. Focus.* I told myself to stay as still as possible. *Is there enough oxygen in here for me to survive? If he's taking me to the cave, maybe dying ahead of time would be merciful.*

You're my strong girl, honey. Don't give up. Remember what they say: It isn't over until it's over.

Daddy? You're dead too. Have I died already? I thought heaven would be a happy place. If I'm dead, this isn't what I'd imagined.

That's because you're not dead, silly! You've been whacked in the face and stuffed in the back of a car after being tied up and gagged. You're a fighter. I've never seen you give up. So get your brain in gear and figure out how to get out of this mess.

John? If I'm not dead, why am I having conversations with all of you dead people? Answer that for me!

I'll answer it! It's because we're in your heart, not your brain! You have the biggest heart of anyone I ever knew. And you're smarter too! Had I not been so selfish and not listened to my family . . . but it's too late for me. It's not for you. I loved you in my way. You have to love you more.

Kevin? So everyone I know from the spirit world is here? I am surrounded by ghosts! I felt a giggle bubbling. Then a remnant of my common sense warned me that hysteria leads to madness and then to—

I'd shake my head if I could. That ridiculous thought made me laugh as well. At least, I think I did. Realistically, I couldn't make much sound; so I must have been hysterical after all.

Again, I reached deep inside for that calm and determination I'd used so many times. If the end approached, then I would meet it with the best I could muster. The voices of encouragement during the last panicked moments reminded me of how precious life is to me.

No sooner had I made my latest resolve than the car began to slow and then turn off the pavement. I heard the tires crunch onto gravel and felt the car bump a couple of times before it came to a stop. A door opened and someone got out and then slammed it shut.

I waited, counting in my brain. I heard a door farther away opening and closing. Had he gone inside a building? When I hoped I'd waited long enough, I started rocking myself. I could feel the car moving a bit. Would anyone notice? I prayed someone would. I heard a door slam and stopped moving.

"That car moved," I heard a small voice say. "Did you see it?"

"Nope. You're always making up stories." It was another child, maybe a bit older.

"But—look!" The voice had grown shrill.

I started rocking myself again, tears once more running at the pain. Was it moving even enough to keep them interested?

"Hey, mister! Did you know your car moves?"

I stopped. Oh, no, please!

"That's because I have a special surprise inside."

"What?"

"Rattlesnakes."

Squeals then giggles followed. "You're a joker, mister," the first voice crowed.

He bade them goodbye, unlocked the door, and slid inside. But the car didn't start. Was I hallucinating?

Then somewhere off far away I heard music.

"Yeah?" The man had answered a cellphone. "Nah. Going as planned. You?" A pause. "See you there."

The realization of who my abductor was struck with the force of a lightning bolt! It was the imposter—the ranger we'd seen who told us his predecessor had gone home. I'd finally heard his normal speaking voice, not the hoarse whisper he'd used while I was driving. I had no clue why he'd done this, but I was determined to fight this monster to the end, even though my heart ached. Those I loved deserved that!

I heard the engine start and felt the car backing up. We were leaving Portal. I took as deep a breath as I could, knowing I needed to relax during the last part of the drive. The climb up to that cave would be a challenge, one made so much harder by my current condition. But I was certain of one thing at this point: This fight was far from over!

Chapter 51

I awoke with a jolt. Where was I? I couldn't see and when I tried to move, all of my joints screamed. My hands and feet were cold, and the burning in my leg urged me to grit my teeth, but I couldn't. My throat was parched. *If I could just have a drink of water*, I thought, as full reality slowly returned. Despite my resolve, the motion of the car had lulled me to sleep, and I now realized this nightmare hadn't been a nightmare at all. It was my current reality.

The motor shut off. Doors opened and slammed. I heard a scratching noise close by; then my prison door opened. Hands yanked me out of my cramped position. I screamed soundlessly into the soggy gag as my feet hit the ground, stinging in protest. Hands grabbed my shoulders and pushed me forward, pulling me up when I stumbled, guiding me through doorways, and forcing me forward. I tried to count steps. I must be walking down an indoor hallway.

A door opened and the hands pushed me forward. A jerking motion released my hands, and the hood was yanked off my head. "You have four minutes!" he growled behind me and slammed the door.

I blinked at the bright light and reached to my mouth to pull out the gag. It muffled my scream as my fingers and shoulder joints protested. But I quickly sent a mental thank you. I was in a bathroom. With stiff fingers and aching joints, I managed to avail myself of the facilities and washed my hands. I splashed water on my face and scooped some into my dry mouth. A sheet of stainless steel used in place of a true mirror crudely reflected my image, one I barely recognized as being me. Then I noticed something sparkling in the light: the crane necklace Reed had given me. I yanked the chain to break it and dropped it in between the toilet and the wall behind. Chances were whoever found it wouldn't pass it on to the authorities, but I didn't want this guy—or whoever else he'd teamed up with—to have it.

I finished just in time. The door behind me opened, and a hand grabbed my elbow and dragged me out through the door. My hands were pulled behind me and cuffed once more. Then the hand once more grabbed my elbow.

Wincing, I squinted up into a vaguely familiar face. It was the ranger! No, not the ranger, the imposter. I quickly averted my eyes, but his laugh told me he'd seen my recognition.

"Where's your cohort?" he murmured, shoving me down the narrow aisle.

I heard a bumping noise and glanced to the left. We were passing the snake enclosure. I shivered, and he snickered.

Since I'd seen my captor—and recognized him—my life had become more precarious. He didn't plan for me to live to identify him, else he'd never have removed the hood. I had to keep my wits about me and steeled myself against revealing any more emotions.

I felt weak and shaky, but I couldn't give in. Instead, I concentrated on lifting the foot on my injured leg, which needed a clean dressing, and setting it down without wincing.

We stepped through the outer door of the ranger station. Then he grabbed the back of my shoulders and marched me toward a dark sedan parked under some trees. He shoved me inside the back seat, fastened the seatbelt around me, covered my mouth with duct tape, slammed the door, and clicked the automatic door locks.

I watched him jog back to the ranger station, close the door, and lock it. A "closed" sign had been placed in the window. The real ranger must still be on vacation. Locals would know that and not stop by.

My heart sank. My chance of being seen any time soon had grown more unlikely.

The imposter didn't look at me or speak when he returned. But I heard him texting someone before he started the car. As we turned onto the narrow, winding road, I remembered remarking to Will that most of the mobile homes and cabins looked like they'd been closed for the winter. Seeing anyone—or receiving help from anyone—wasn't likely.

My captor glanced at me in the rearview mirror and grinned. I stared back into his eyes until he broke contact. I hoped I'd angered him by not cringing or crying. Anger might make him more careless.

When Will and I had met him earlier, I remembered that he'd focused more on Will. When we'd left, I'd remarked on that and Will had laughed. "And he doesn't seem to be very knowledgeable either," he'd said. "I'm surprised he chose the Forest Service for a career. He's more the city type, more interested in heavy metal music than wildlife and hiking."

So, I wondered, who was his partner in this enterprise . . . and why were they doing this? As a reporter, I'd learned that people usually kidnapped and murdered for one of three reasons: money, revenge, or sexual depravity, with the exception of serial killers. Although he seemed to be enjoying my discomfort, he didn't strike me as a sadist. Then again, how many of those had I spent time with? Still, he'd made no attempt to grope me and hadn't said anything sexual. And I could think of no reason for anyone to exact revenge from me. So that left money.

Did he think I had money left from my career in television? I'd made a decent salary, but I'd spent a large portion of my savings on a house when Kevin and I married. I hadn't replaced the savings in the short time we were married, and Kevin hadn't changed his life insurance policy, leaving his parents as the beneficiaries. In fact, he'd left me little more than the house and our mutual bank accounts. So money couldn't be the motive.

Motive aside, one thought took precedence: My only chance to survive would be that trip up to the cave. And in my weakened state—no food or water for hours and an injured leg—I wasn't betting on my success.

The car lurched to the left and slowed. I glanced in the mirror and met his eyes. He winked. He knew I'd been racking my brain and coming up with nothing. I stared until he looked away, letting my eyes reveal my disgust and defiance. Provoking him could be dangerous. But maybe anger would cause him to make mistakes. At this point, I didn't have many other options. Once his partner—and I felt sure he had one—joined him, I'd have two of them to outmaneuver.

We continued to drive slowly on the narrow road but had to stop when a loaded pick-up truck flashed its lights to indicate a wide load. We waited as it drove past. I stared at the driver, and he stared back at me. Hope flared until I remembered the darkened windows. I heard a chuckle from the front seat.

A short time later, he slowed the car once more. We had reached our destination, I felt sure, when I recognized the area. Will and I had parked on the opposite side of the road; the cave where the murdered man with my photo had been found high above.

He turned off the motor. I fought to maintain a stoic attitude and stared straight ahead. He punched the door locks but didn't exit. When my door opened, I fought hard not to flinch or look anywhere but straight ahead.

"Well, well, well," a deep voice said, "if it isn't the princess herself!" I didn't recognize the voice, but I'd never forget that phrase.

A hand reached out and grabbed my chin, forcing me to turn toward him. He'd gained a lot of weight and gone bald, but I'd recognize those eyes and that smirk anywhere. He reached down and ripped the duct tape from my mouth. I willed myself not to cry out, but he laughed at the pain reflected in my eyes. "What's the matter, Princess? Cat got your tongue? Or don't you have anything to say now that your daddy isn't here to defend you?" Anger and bitterness roughened his voice.

"Shane."

"So you do remember me!"

"Why, Shane?"

"Why? You remember my name, but that's all?"

"Why are you so angry?"

"Really? Should I be happy? After your lies made your daddy throw me off the ranch?"

"He was your daddy too, Shane. And I didn't tell him lies. You stole—"

"You stole, Princess! You stole my dad from me. He married your mama. And after you were born, he was never mine. I was only taking what I deserved. How could a few bucks ever pay for what you'd taken? He made a deal with my mom. I could never return, but he'd visit me at her place. Do you know how that turned out? Do you?" He was screaming by this time, spitting his words at me, his face red.

"He died."

"Yes, he died. And you sold the ranch."

I whispered. "Only to pay for his bills. Mom had to sell it."

"You took him and my ranch."

"We both lost him, Shane."

"Now, you'll pay me back," he said, his voice steely cold.

"How could I ever do that? He left us both, Shane. How can I bring him back?"

"I don't want him back, Princess. But I'll have the satisfaction of seeing you die." He laughed and I heard the insanity my mother had often claimed he had. "I spent money having you tracked down. You tried to hide from me, but I found you anyway. You cost me, but I'll enjoy every minute of seeing you suffer. They called you my sister. You were half a sister, they said. You were never a sister at all. You were just a thief. You stole my dad!" he screamed.

I knew nothing I could say would calm him. He had lost his mind, and revenge ruled his thoughts. "You never guessed it was me, did you?" He laughed.

"Shane?" The ranger impersonator had gotten out of the car. "Shouldn't we move to the other spot?"

Shane looked at him, confusion in his face at first. Then he seemed to pull himself back to the present. "I . . . yeah, we need to stay there . . . until dark." He stepped back and closed my door. His partner got back in the driver's seat and looked at me briefly in the mirror. For a moment, I glimpsed pity. Then he started the motor, and we pulled back onto the road.

Chapter 52

Pity? Pity! From a man who had attempted to terrorize me, who had abducted me, who had spoken to me with demeaning terms! I glared at him. His eyes dropped first!

I had no time for pity. Dealing with Shane was going to be a challenge. I needed to focus on getting out of this situation and returning to my life.

Shane had not even entered my mind until now. When my dad died, Mom told me that he was overseas with the military and married. I had never been privy to the full details of Shane's early years, but the version I'd been given was that Shane lived with his mama and that she and my dad were his parents. Nothing more was told to me until after Dad's death when I was in middle school. But Shane had stopped visiting long before then.

Shane had been a difficult kid. When my dad brought him to the ranch for the summer, Shane complained about the food, about having to help with chores, about me, about being on the ranch—about everything. He screamed sometimes and pouted others when things weren't going the way he wanted. My parents told me to try to be nice because he was missing his mother and that he'd only be here for a few weeks.

Then the summer came when he stole my birthday money and threatened to kill the baby kittens and then cut my throat if I told my parents. He terrified me. I started having nightmares and became clingy. I had stomach aches, stopped laughing, and stayed in the house more with my mama.

But when I came upon him hurting my horse in the barn, I launched into him with my small fists flying. He was much larger and stronger. After all, I was nine and he was thirteen. He laughed and reminded me that he'd mentioned hurting the kitties if I told. The horse wasn't part of the deal. But since I'd started the fight, he'd treat me like a big girl. When my dad returned from the feed store, he found me naked and tied up in the barn.

Shane never returned to our home, and he was seldom mentioned. Mama didn't say anything, but I doubted she'd notified him of my dad's death.

Before she died, I asked Mama about Shane. She told me that he had joined the military and was in Europe. I asked about his mother, and she said they had never met. She only knew that Shane's mother had identified my dad as Shane's father when he was a baby. My dad had met her when he visited a military base with a friend. Even though he'd accepted the responsibility, my dad had never believed it was true. She'd been dating many others at the time.

"Why didn't he have a paternity test?" I'd asked. Mama reminded me that those tests weren't common at that time and might not have been easily available.

Shane had obviously not changed at all. I still didn't know for certain what had motivated him to kidnap me—or to torture the person he'd hired to find me—but it fit the Shane I'd known years ago.

We had traveled only a short distance when we pulled into a narrow driveway and drove behind a dilapidated mobile home. The driver turned off the motor and opened the door; but before he left, he told me, "Resisting anything with this guy isn't a good choice." Then he walked around to the front door of the trailer.

I thought I could turn around and open the door, even with my hands bound together behind my back, except for the added problem of the seatbelt. Still, it was an old car and the seatbelt had been stretched out. I twisted as far as I could to the right and could almost reach the buckle. I turned my body as far as I could and wiggled my fingers. They brushed against the buckle but didn't reach quite far enough to pull the flap that released the catch. I gritted my teeth against the pain in my shoulder sockets and stretched toward that flap.

I could hear my captor talking to someone on his cell. I pushed and stretched until I thought I'd have to give up, tears of pain running down my cheeks. Then I touched it! I pulled with strength I didn't even have left. When the latch released, the belt whipped away with a clank.

Had he heard? I froze. Then I heard him laugh.

As quickly as possible, I leaned my back against the door and pushed the handle with both hands. It opened and I fell out onto the damp vegetation. I heard another laugh on the other side of the mobile home. With my feet, I eased the door closed so he wouldn't hear. Then I began rolling away from the car toward a ditch of some sort. The bushy grass and vegetation scratched my face, bringing blood, but once I'd rolled over them, they sprang back up without any evidence of my having crossed them.

I rolled over to a small grove of trees clustered near the ditch and flattened myself. I held my breath and focused on the sounds. I could hear nothing except the wind blowing through the trees. I heard no steps. Maybe he'd not discovered my escape yet, but I knew my time was quickly running out.

I struggled into a sitting position, my back against one of the trees, and wriggled my way up to a standing position. I edged around to the back side of the tree and squinted up at the hill across the road. Then I looked back at the ditch. It wasn't more than three feet deep. At some spots, I could see shrubs and underbrush peeking out.

Shadows had already gathered across the road. It would be dark in an hour or so, I suspected. But I dared not wait until then to make my move. The only choice was to jump the ditch. Dropping down into the ditch would be easy, but getting out without the use of my hands might or might not be possible. I hadn't jumped in years, but I'd won scholarship money in the hurdles when I was eighteen. Still, I'd not done it with my hands behind my back—and I'd not been this old . . . or tired.

I listened a moment but didn't hear any vehicles approaching, which wasn't unusual at this time of day or during this time of year. Of course, at least two would be coming in search of me. In a perfect world, one would be Reed; but at this moment, my world had never been more imperfect.

I stepped as far away from the tree and backed as far as I could into the clear space between it and those around it. I flexed my legs, focused on my goal, and whispered a prayer. Then I bent down into my favorite position.

It felt awkward to run without my arms bent at my chest. I slowed and stopped short of the first ditch. Then I walked back to my starting spot.

I took several deep breaths, returned to my position, and looked up to the skies. I remembered how Coach would stand close at the competitions and lean over to whisper, "May the wind push your back, and your heart push your feet!" If I ever needed a wind at my back, it was now.

"I can do this!" I breathed

My body flew with a mind of its own. I soared over the first ditch, across the narrow paved road, and across the second ditch on the opposite side. I'd made it! But however much I wanted to cheer, now wasn't the time to celebrate. I had to use my momentum and adrenalin to head up the hill and cover.

I had no idea how long I pushed up the hill. The muscles in my thighs burned and each breath forced its way through my tortured lungs. Orange light spread across the sky. Finally, the trees thinned and I sighted my goal—one of the hoodoos. I churned on toward it with the last of my energy and hope. There, I could crouch behind its high rocky face and rest.

As much as I longed to flop down, I knew I had one last chore. I used my tired legs to kick branches that had fallen during the winter winds into a pile against the bottom of the pointed rock. When I could not make another step, I fell into the pile and wiggled beneath it.

A peace fell over me. Even if I died here, it would be better than in some foul mobile home or hotel room. I had loved ones over on that other side. I had loved ones here. Either way, I couldn't lose.

Chapter 53

The branches and leaves covering my body offered scant protection against the cold, but the hoodoo served as a windbreak. Exhaustion overrode fear of the critters and varmints and I dozed off.

The moon was shining high overhead when I jerked awake at sounds foreign to those I'd fallen asleep hearing. Night birds whooshed high above. Was that an owl? I heard coyotes. Their frenzied barking suggested they'd killed a rabbit or some other small critter. I pitied those small critters. I heard leaves rustling and imagined field mice or skunks. I imagined a skunk spraying me. Would the stench protect me from my captors? The urge to giggle overpowered me until I remembered I might alert critters of my hiding place.

My leg throbbed and burned. Jumping and scrambling up the hill earlier had exacerbated the injury from the fire. I hoped it would ease or go numb when I continued moving at daybreak.

To settle myself, I thought about childhood camping trips with Mama and Dad. They'd zipped the sleeping bags together until I was about nine when I protested that I was "a big girl." We had sung around the campfire, and I'd fallen asleep to the soft hum of their voices. Even though I was a big girl now, I closed my eyes and dozed again with those memories snuggled around me for comfort. In my dreams, Reed and Sgt. Pearce found the necklace and continued looking for me.

I'm not sure what woke me: the bone-chilling cold that caused my whole body to first shiver and then throb, the faint pink and orange streaks above, or the crunch of steps. I held my breath, listening. The footsteps seemed to vary in distance from close to far. My throat was stuffed with cotton, and I needed to go to the bathroom, which had to wait for now. I had to relax, to calm myself so I could figure out what was going on and how to handle it.

Relax, I commanded myself, and tried to remember what a doctor had said on a talk show I'd watched about ways to divert yourself in times of stress. He'd encouraged us to listen to our own breathing and to count each breath until it slowed. Then we were to disassociate ourselves by pretending we were high above and looking down on the situation. He'd encouraged us to close our eyes and listen to our inner voice talking to us.

I hadn't tried the technique then, but now seemed the perfect time to try. I remembered the soothing voice of the doctor telling the women who'd volunteered on the show to let their bodies "float" above their minds. I could do that. I closed my eyes and soon my body floated up and my mind glanced up. Instead of lying among branches on cold ground, I saw myself in my soft, warm bed. I shivered and crazy thoughts began whirling above me as if chasing each other: Did animals eat people before they died or after? Would my friends wait to hold my funeral until after the sale? With that silly thought, I opened my eyes and fought the urge to giggle by biting my lips.

I peeked through the branches down the hill and saw streaks of light glancing off the trees. Flashlights? Reed? No, I was just hallucinating. No one would be searching for me until dawn. I squinted up at the sky. Dawn wouldn't be long.

What if those steps weren't human predators but animals? *Right, Sorrel. Animals with flashlights!* I pressed my lips together tightly as giggles started to erupt and threatened to never stop. Finally, I sobered and lay as still as possible, breathing shallow breaths, and squinting out into the predawn half-light. As if they too sensed me, the steps stopped. I counted in my head between breaths, spacing them out so I wouldn't alert anyone. Finally, as everything remained quiet, I began to relax. My imagination had been teasing me.

It was so cold my teeth wanted to chatter. That struck me as hilarious, but I couldn't laugh. I wondered if that doctor had ever truly used any of his techniques. I doubted it. How much of life did we waste anyway? Who said that? Some writer in one of my college classes talked about our returning to the simple life.

I shivered beneath the branches and crawly things, my eyes squeezed shut. Forget that crazy television doctor and his relaxation techniques. What did he really know? I knew what I wanted: a warm, soft bed shared with someone who loved me and the kitties at my feet. The kitties! My eyes teared. Would Reed take care of them? What about the little dog? I wondered about the little ones I'd thought I'd have someday.

Snapping—nearby—pulled me back. Had I been talking aloud? Was I delirious?

The sky had lightened more. I squinted toward the snapping noise. A large shape shuffled near me. "Reed?" I whispered.

"Sorry, Sorrel." Then he laughed at his own joke. Shane. I couldn't see his face, but maybe it was better this way. I just hoped he would be quick. Even though I wanted to squeeze my eyes shut, I wouldn't do that. He'd have to look into them when he killed me.

He approached until he stood only a few steps away. "I've dreamed of this moment for a long time," he said.

"Why?" I asked. "Why do you want to kill me?"

He snickered. "Because I can," he said. "I'd have killed him too. Should have. He wasn't really my dad, you know. They'd only married because she told him she was pregnant. It wasn't true, but he believed her and he was the honorable sort. She told me that before she died."

"You didn't—"

"Kill her?" He laughed as if I'd told a funny joke, but he sounded deranged. "She was heading there anyway," he said. "Just stepped out in front of my truck without even looking."

I'd been edging away while he talked, hoping to make it harder for him to reach me. But he put his foot on my arm and aimed the gun at me. In spite of my resolve to be brave, I shut my eyes.

Surprisingly, when he fired, I felt no pain. Shouldn't I feel different? Floaty or something? Instead, I heard something heavy fall beside me. I opened my eyes a slit. Eyes filled with pain and astonishment stared back at me.

Then I heard a voice coming from somewhere nearby.

"Sorrel? Honey?"

"Reed!"

Hands dug at the branches like a wild animal and pulled me up from the ground. Then Reed shrugged out of his coat and wrapped it around me before pulling me into his arms. "We're going to have to stop meeting like this," he whispered.

"I'm going to have to work on your lines," I laughed— croaked, actually—my voice shaky from the tears falling from my eyes. "But, if you don't mind, I'd like to wait until I get warm."

In the shout of laughter that vibrated against my ears, I reminded myself that it was that sound I'd waited for all night.

Epilogue

Reed insisted on carrying me into my little house.

"You're just out of the hospital," he argued. "I promised to make you stay off your feet as much as possible for a couple of days."

"But it's so dark. You should at least go in first and turn on a li—" Lights flooded us as we reached the steps and the door opened wide.

"Welcome home, Sorrel!"

"Will? How did you get inside? Whatever—"

Will stepped back, holding the screen, and Reed carried me through to my couch. The cats swarmed, leaping on my lap and purring. I peeked over their fuzzy bodies just in time to see Jose and the twins. "Where's Teri?" I asked.

"She's a little busy just now feeding Miss Sofia Sorrel. She'll be home tomorrow."

"Wait—did you say—"

"A little girl. Born early yesterday morning."

"And her name?"

Jose smiled. "Named for a dear friend we're relieved to welcome home."

Josef squeezed close to me and held his hands about six inches apart. "She's only about this big, so it's okay that she's a girl. She won't get into my stuff."

Javier squeezed in shyly on my other side. "And she won't make us play dolls and stuff like that." He wrinkled his nose in disgust.

Reed laughed. "You don't have a clue!"

I hugged each of the boys close. Then I spotted Will holding a spray of pink carnations. "Will? Are those from you?"

"And the staff at the paper," he said. "I appreciate you giving me the interview even while you were exhausted. After reading it, Mr. Byrd said I'll be a great reporter someday. So I guess I'll consider forgiving you for leaving me out of this."

Thank me would be a better choice, I thought. Instead, I accepted the flowers and sniffed them. "They're gorgeous! I'll put them out for the sale! Could you put them in a vase? I should have one in the cupboard."

When he brought one, I asked, "Are you upset with me Will?"

He flushed. "Not really." Then he said, "Yeah, I am kinda. You should have trusted me more."

"About?"

"The stuff you knew about our scene that I didn't. I thought we were working as equals."

I put the flowers in the vase. "Sit down, Will."

When he sat, I took a deep breath. "I was trying to protect those who might be hurt by things long in my past. You weren't in my 'need to know' list. That's no slur against you."

"When I received that message, you didn't think I had moved into that list?" He couldn't quite stifle his outrage.

"Yes, I guess you did," I conceded. "I apologize."

He wasn't accepting friendship yet. "Do you know who sent it?"

"Yes, it was the hacker—my half-brother, Shane. Apparently, he'd become quite proficient in computer skills while in the military. I don't know what he did there, but one doesn't get dishonorably discharged for a minor offense."

Then I looked at Reed. "Vicente!"

He nodded. "Cell phones aren't as private as we all think if the person is skilled. The same goes for answering machines."

"I'm so glad," I whispered. He smiled.

Will rose, but he had one more point. "Who was shooting at us?"

Reed shrugged. "He wanted to make Sorrel suffer like he imagined she had made him suffer. He didn't want to kill you, just scare you. In fact, maybe he was even trying to make you back out and leave Sorrel on her own. That's why we figured you weren't his target, and that helped point to it being a personal grudge for Sorrel. And since you didn't have a rattlesnake delivered to you, the snake solidified our theory."

Will shivered. Then he rose. "I'll have some wild stories to tell when I get back to the frat house," he said. He reached for my hand. "I won't say it was fun, but it certainly wasn't boring! Makes all of those sisters and their pranks look like 'child's play'."

Mercifully, everyone but Reed left shortly, teasing me about my not seeing their cars beside the pavilion. "She only had eyes for me," Reed drawled, as he walked them out amid the male laughter and teasing comments.

I let my eyes roam around the room, my eyes touching on familiar clutter. "I'm not sure I ever want to leave home again," I whispered.

"Oh, yes, you will." I jumped and paled. Reed hurried over, sat beside me, and cuddled me close. "I didn't mean to startle you," he whispered.

"I think I just startle easier right now. I'll return to my normal, sassy self soon enough."

Reed gave a delighted shout of laughter. "I couldn't have said it better myself."

"Chris Reed, you promised to tell me."

"Let's get you in bed. I'll make you a cup of tea, and I'll tell you all you want to you."

"I don't need tea, Reed. I just need my bed, the kitties at the foot, and you there filling me in on what I missed when you guys rushed me off to the hospital."

Once settled in my bed, Chris propped up beside me and cuddled me close. "Are you sure this can't wait?"

"I've waited already. I need to start putting it to rest."

We talked until the horror of the events settled into the less horrible category. Reed described how he, the sheriff, and Sgt. Pearce had received a frantic call from Celia. No one had seen me after I'd left the veterinarian's office. The search had turned up nothing until a state patrolman reported my Jeep parked behind the abandoned building. Later, they gathered volunteers and drove to Portal, going door to door. When they discovered the house where a lady remembered her kids saying they had seen a car shaking, Pearce dismissed the volunteers and called in the task force. "It's too dangerous to use volunteers with this killer—or killers," he'd said.

At this stage, Reed reached in his pocket. "I almost forgot," he said, and he fastened my crane necklace around my neck.

I fingered it. "I love this necklace. It was so hard to yank it off, but I hoped it might give you a clue."

"It did. Pearce and the rest of the guys didn't think he'd take you to the cave. They said it would be too predictable. They had decided we would return to Portal and stay in cabins until morning when we'd have better light. Then I found the necklace and I knew. I've never seen it off your neck since I gave it to you last Christmas."

My eyes filled. "It reminds me of John and you and how we so narrowly escaped other times."

"And we escaped again."

"Reed, what has happened with Shane?"

"He's in the prison ward in a hospital in Phoenix. After he recovers from the gunshot wound, they will return him to a Nevada prison. He had escaped from there earlier when he was on laundry detail and had been the focus of a whole different man hunt. Sometime in the future, they'll return him to Arizona for trial."

"Did he kill the private eye?"

"He hired the private eye to find you. We think this private eye gambled his money away and got mixed up with the Mexican cartel in the process. His execution is a classic example of their style. Pearce and I suspect they implemented the death, but we still don't know if there was any connection between

Shane and the Cartel. If it was, it was a lucky break for Shane. But we'll probably never know for sure, unless Shane decides to accuse them when he goes on trial. That would be death to him, because he'll be going back to prison anyway. But he certainly used the Cartel execution style to divert the attention from his connection to this guy and focus it on them. We suspect he hung around the casino after he'd paid off this guy— maybe hoping to steal some of his money back or to do away with him. This guy was addicted to gambling. He would have taken this job happily to get his hands on a little cash. His getting in trouble with the Cartel actually was a bonus for Shane."

"Had the PI discovered where I lived before he died?"

"We doubt it. Shane would know where you grew up. That clipping is from your hometown newspaper when you started at the television station. Your new name wasn't on it, but the station's name was. Shane contacted the station. The new girl must have heard about you from someone, and when Vicente questioned her, she pretended to send the information out because of a request that had come to the station. She had no clue it would cause him to fire her."

"But it didn't give a current address, did it?"

"Shane has been tangled up with the law often enough so that he would know how they operate. He figured law enforcement would find you through that clipping—and they did. The PI's death brought it to their attention, so he set the guy up. Then he followed us."

"Was killing the poor guy with rattlesnakes his idea?" I almost stifled the shiver that it caused.

"I doubt it. But Shane is deranged. My theory is that when he saw what had killed this PI, he delivered that box with the snake to you to terrorize you. That manner of death, the clipping with your photo, and the snake in your office—he only made one huge mistake."

I shivered. "What was that?"

"He underestimated a feisty redhead."

He cuddled me close for a bit. One last question nudged me. "Reed, why did they put you on the task force? Will you be leaving to continue with them?"

"No. Pearce included me after my connection with you surfaced."

"So you won't be leaving?" I needed to have that clarified.

"I have too much to do. Besides rebuilding a barn, keeping law and order here, seeing after a horde of dogs, and chasing after a feisty redhead—"

"Wait! Reed, did you say dogs?"

He sighed and frowned, but I could see the corners of his mouth twitching. "It's the only way to even up the playing field against you and these felines."

Tears sprang up in my eyes. "Reed—"

"Sorrel! Are you hurting? I—"

"Course not, silly! Surely you know we females cry when we're happy!"

Reed threw back his head and laughed. When he stopped, he wiped tears from his eyes, grew solemn, and reached for my hand. "Sorrel Janes, you continue to fascinate, frustrate, delight, and amaze me! Would you consider our entering into an old-fashioned courtship? I figure I need the time to get my ranch in order—and I need help with that horde of pups. If we still like each other after that, then maybe—"

"I've never heard anything so ridiculous in my whole life! If my leg didn't hurt so much, I'd stomp my foot!"

Reed plastered a phony hurt look on his face. "I just don't have the time to sweep you off your feet," he began, "and I know you—"

"One more word, Chris Reed, and I'm going to—"

"Kiss me?

Teri's Green Chili Stew

Ingredients:

leftover pork or beef roast (cut in chunks)

roasted and peeled green chilis (chopped or whole)

potatoes cut in "fourths"

a finely chopped onion

water

salt and garlic to taste

Cook atop the stove in a pot about an hour or until potatoes are done. Note: If chili flavor is too strong, add a tsp of lemon juice to neutralize. Green chili may be fresh or frozen.

Chris Reed's Bachelor Green Chili Stew

Brown ground beef in a skillet and drain. Season with salt and garlic salt. Add roasted, peeled green chilis (chopped or whole), water, onion, thick sliced potatoes, and cook for 30 to 40 minutes.

Author Biography

Lonna Enox is the award winning author of two previous mystery novels in the Sorrel Janes series. Her first book, *The Last Dance,* was selected Best First Novel by Chanticleer Book Reviews. Her second book, *Blood Relations,* won First Place for Mystery Thriller and First Place and Grand Prize for the Clue Awards from Chanticleer Book Reviews. Her books have been likened by *Readers Favorites* to Marcia Muller, longtime cozy mystery author. Visit her website at: lonnaenox.org and facebook at: www.facebook.com/lonnaenoxauthor.

STRIKING BLIND